Books by Cheyenne Meadows

Wind Warriors

Tiger's Lily
Loco
Summer's Night
Sky's Lark
Silver Spoon
Blue Blood's Trifecta
Ghost's Treasure

Sexy Snax

Triad
Broken Bridges

Single Titles

Turbulent Rain
Worth Fighting For
Cowgirl Up
Cowgirl Strong
Crashing The Net

Cowgirl Strong

ISBN # 978-1-78686-087-3

©Copyright Cheyenne Meadows 2016

Cover Art by Posh Gosh ©Copyright 2016

Interior text design by Claire Siemaszkiewicz

Totally Bound Publishing

Published in 2016 by Totally Bound Publishing, Newland House, The Point, Weaver Road, Lincoln, LN6 3QN, United Kingdom.

COWGIRL STRONG

CHEYENNE MEADOWS

Dedication

For those who have a dream and pursue it, no matter how difficult the journey.

Also for all those who work with the Humane Society. Employees, volunteers and donors are all so special, and without each of you, needy and deserving animals wouldn't have a chance at a forever home. Thank you.

And a special thank you to the Longmeadow Rescue Ranch in Union, Missouri. Not only do they receive abused and neglected farm animals, heal them and find them loving homes, but they also dedicate themselves to working with the public in an effort to continue saving every animal they can. Their remarkable response to a downed trailer of horses on their way to slaughter in 2006 showed their large hearts and caring nature in a particularly horrific crisis. I do believe this became one of their shining moments. I read about the accident and cried for the loss but also for the victories and successes that came out of such a tragedy. I wanted to tell a bit of their story in this book and share their amazing tale with my readers. I only hope that I did them justice enough for all that they do each and every day.

Chapter One

"Welcome home."

Lacey smiled at her mother as she set her suitcase on the kitchen floor. She'd driven most of the night, stayed a few hours at another barrel racer's house to sleep and let Candy, her mare, stretch her legs, before driving the rest of the way. After ten days in Vegas at the Finals Rodeo, she was worn out and extremely glad to be home. "Thanks, Mom." She went to the fridge, pulled out the pitcher of sweet tea her mother always kept and filled the glass she'd plucked from the cabinet along the way.

"I'm sorry we couldn't attend. But we watched it on TV. You did such a great job. We're proud of you." Her mother gave her a hug.

"Thanks. It's okay. I know things are tough right now."

Right now. Lacey wanted to snort at her own response. First had come the droughts. Then the floods. The family farm struggled as never before in her lifetime. Her mother, Helen, clung to her teaching job in order to provide some income along with all-important health insurance. Lacey's father, Dan, worked the land full-time, running beef cattle, cutting hay and alternating corn and soybeans as a side venture. Tate, Lacey's brother, helped in his free time from his job as an assistant football coach for the small local college. They all worked. Hard. Even she worked her ass off around the farm while picking up part-time hours at one of the large animal vet's offices. Anything to make it one more week. One more month. One more year.

"Your father and brother are building fence over at Chester McLeary's today. They should be back for supper."

"Okay." Lacey took a large drink and smiled at her mother. "I missed you."

A momentary grin took away the lines of worry on her mother's face. "No more than we missed you." She pushed a lock of auburn hair out of her eyes and behind her ear. "I wish there was some way we could have been there for you." Regret carried in Helen's voice and her eyes.

"Really, it's okay." Lacey gave her a quick hug. "We do the best we can, remember? As long as we have one another, we're doing mighty fine." The words came out automatically. The same ones she'd recited for years. Lately, they had begun to fall flat.

"Always such a cheery soul."

On the outside, maybe. Lacey kept her pasted-on smile. She'd spent a lifetime trying to earn her father's love, to no avail. Worse, since she'd started barrel racing, he'd given her guff right and left. Happiness with her family had slipped away lately, leaving bare bones, and prodding her to consider some big-time changes. None of those thoughts had she aired to her parents. *Yet.*

Helen sighed. "I wish we could give you more."

We? She knew her mother loved her. Never even questioned it. The other half of the parental unit, though, she couldn't really say.

Lacey waved her hand. "I'd rather have you than the pot at the end of the rainbow." She spoke the truth. Although, right now, that elusive pot looked damn good.

"I'm going to go pick up walnuts in the back pastures. Figured at fourteen dollars per hundredweight, it's worth it."

"Wait and I'll help." Lacey finished her drink then placed the empty glass in the sink. She'd attended to her mare before coming inside, so nothing pressing existed on her schedule for the rest of the day.

As they headed toward the old farm truck with the bed already filled with empty feed sacks and buckets, Lacey slowed her steps. Ransom Mathews pulled into the driveway in his shiny black truck. It wasn't new but he kept it in as close to that condition as possible.

"Hey, Lacey. Helen," he called out of the window as he eased up next to Lacey. "I promised to help Tate and Dan out today but can't remember where they were working."

"Chester McLeary's farm. North pasture, I think," Helen answered.

Ransom smiled. "Thanks. You don't mind one more showing up for dinner, do you?"

Helen beamed. "Of course not. You know that! Lord, no matter that the college has put up a fancy apartment for you to use, you still have a bedroom here and always a place at the table," Helen answered with loving enthusiasm.

Tate had dragged Ransom home in grade school. The rough-and-tumble little boy had worn clothes on their last leg, his unruly hair had needed a cut and the flatness of his eyes had told the family all they needed to know. The stray had needed a better home. They'd opened up their arms and taken him in. After some finagling with court system, they'd obtained legal guardianship as well. His mother, an alcoholic, hadn't even fought. To hear Helen tell the story, the woman had appeared relieved to be rid of her burden.

Lacey could barely remember a time without Ransom around. A whole three months separated them in age, putting him in her class at school. Tate, being a year older, had resided in the one above them. As she'd grown up, she'd idolized Ransom, teased him, and had fallen deeply in love by the time she'd hit the ripe old age of fifteen. Not much had changed since then. She still possessed deep feelings for him but kept them to herself as she'd watched a few women parade through his life, praying none of them stuck.

She noticed his grin, the dimple in his cheek, and sighed to herself. Big, strong and too handsome for his own good, Ransom caught the eye of just about every woman in the county. His broad shoulders, flat abs and flirty nature didn't hurt either. Neither did his full-time job at the same college as Tate, as a conditioning coach for the football team. He shared the apartment with Tate as well, though they tended to spend more time on the farm than in town. Pulling their own weight. Just the way they always had.

His short black hair looked freshly cut. Stylish and easy. Just shampoo, rinse and go. Quick, sexy and it fit him perfectly.

His blue eyes met hers. "Nice run at the finals, Lacey. Great job."

She smiled slightly at his praise. "Thanks, Ransom. I didn't win, though."

He shook his head. "I don't think anyone was going to beat that gray stallion."

She recalled Trinity and Legacy's final run. "It was their time. They deserved it."

"So do you."

Lacey shrugged. "Maybe next year."

He flashed another smile. "I better get out there or Tate will kick my ass for being lazy." He waved, circling the truck around, and left.

Lacey watched him go with a sense of excitement and loss. He'd be back for dinner, yes. But, more importantly, he'd treated her like a sister.

Just like he always has.

Her heart cracked a bit more.

'Pretend he's a goat and you're participating in the goat-tying event.' Trinity's advice replayed through her mind. She pictured herself doing just that, roping Ransom, tying him up and sitting on him. More of Trinity's advice replayed in her head. All along the lines of how keeping her feelings to herself wouldn't grab Ransom's attention, or getting him to see her as something more than family. Perhaps the time had come to spill the beans. The sooner she did, the less time she'd spend wishing and hoping for her dream to come true. Better to find out now than pine for him over the next few years. Just like she'd done for nearly a decade.

And look where that got me.

The time had come. Make or break. *I'll tell him. Tonight.*
With that decision made, she crossed her fingers for good luck.

"Lacey? You coming or not?" her mother hollered.

With a wicked grin to herself, Lacey hurried to catch up. Work waited for no one, but at least she knew the evening meal promised to provide some entertainment. Afterward, she'd corner her cowboy and get some answers.

* * * *

Five hours later, stiff and sore, Lacey forced her feet to keep moving. She set the roast on the large kitchen table along with the potatoes. Her mother followed with a couple more pans of vegetables and warmed homemade bread. The men stared at the fare with hungry expressions and wide grins.

"Looks like a feast." Her father winked at her mother.

Lacey rescued the apple pie from the oven. The afternoon had been a testament to stubborn determination. Fatigued from the rodeo and a long drive, all Lacey had wanted to do was find her bed and sleep. Instead she'd found herself spending much of the time bent over, picking up walnuts in order to sell them for a few extra bucks—a sign of their financial woes and the belief that nothing should go to waste.

Resisting the urge to rub her back, Lacey placed the pie on the counter to cool and took her seat beside her brother and opposite Ransom.

Ransom snagged the basket filled with bread and teased Tate by holding it just out of reach for a couple of beats before giving in. As soon as he handed over the goodies, he plucked the butter dish off the table, cut a generous piece and slathered it over the still-hot slice of bread.

Lacey watched the way he wrapped his fingers around his fork, and manipulated the knife with precision, before taking a large bite of meat.

"Lacey? Earth to Lacey." Tate nudged her. "Potatoes?"

She blinked at Tate, accepted the dish, and placed it next to her plate. In all honesty, she didn't really feel like eating. Butterflies danced in her stomach as she planned how to broach the subject with Ransom. The words she'd use to convince him that her love was true and that they'd make a wonderful couple. She'd had years to imagine that very moment when she confessed her love, heard Ransom echo her, promise undying commitment, wrap her into his strong arms and swing her around in a moment of joy.

Tonight she'd finally spill her heart and innermost secrets, and she prayed Ransom would find the same feelings inside himself.

"Tate tells me that you're dating a lovely young lady," Helen said.

Lacey added some food to her plate and dug in, knowing she had to eat or face concern from her mother. She cut the potato into bite-sized pieces, forked a piece and dropped it into her mouth. Her attention locked on Ransom while she eagerly waited to hear his response.

"Lizzie's great. We've been seeing one another for the last month, but got exclusive a couple of weeks ago."

Lacey stilled. Worry crept to the fore, especially as Ransom's face and eyes lit up at the mention of the girl's name.

"She's as sweet as she is beautiful," Ransom continued. He took a drink of tea. "I've been doing some thinking lately."

Lacey held her breath. A sense of foreboding flooded her. She steeled herself.

"About?" Dan asked.

"About asking her to marry me."

"That's wonderful." Helen beamed.

Tate fist-bumped Ransom.

"Bring her around. I want to meet this girl. Sounds like she's going to be a big part of this family." Dan smiled like a proud father.

"Congratulations." Lacey forced an expression of happiness on her face, one she certainly didn't feel. Her hopes and dreams for the past several years came crashing down at those words.

Ransom found a girl to marry. It isn't me.

Her heart broke completely open. In the back of her mind, Lacey knew that Ransom would never be hers. *Hope lives eternal. Until now.*

She resumed eating, going through the motions, not really tasting the food. The others chatted about Ransom's glorious news while she tried to tune them out and spare her tender feelings from another assault. She focused on biding her time until she could escape to wallow in self-pity alone.

"Lacey?"

The sound of her name grabbed her attention. "What?"

"I asked when you'll be going back on the rodeo circuit." Tate took a drink before forking another bite of food.

She glanced over at her father. *Not soon enough.* Her father never asked about her racing career. Hell, the only compliments he ever gave revolved around her cooking. The rest of the time she came up short when it came to attention from the head of the family. The two guys beat her out each and every time.

Water under the bridge. Let it go.

Her attention centered on Tate. "In a couple of weeks. I plan on hitting it hard this fall before the winter break."

Her mother frowned. "But you just got home."

"I know." Lacey pushed a pea around her plate. "I need the points if I'm going to get back to the finals. I hope to do better next time." She took a quick drink. "Speaking of, I need to check on Candy before I work on sending in those entry forms." She slid her chair back, replaced it, and strode out of the kitchen.

Fifteen minutes later, she was grooming Candy like she'd done every evening since she'd purchased the mare five years ago. She'd used up all her savings at the time, but hadn't been able to turn down the opportunity to buy such a top-of-the-line paint. Her pedigree shone, as did her athletic talent. Candy was her ticket to the future, she was sure of it.

"You didn't eat." Her mother's quiet voice carried easily in the barn.

"Not really hungry," Lacey answered automatically. It was the truth. Ransom's words had killed her appetite as much as they'd slashed through her very soul.

Helen approached, pulling her sweater around her shoulders.

The chill didn't bother Lacey. Numbness had set in before she ever left the house.

"I'm sorry."

"For what?" Lacey spared her mother a glance over Candy's back.

"I've known how you've felt about Ransom for a while now. He's never thought of you as anything but a sister. That's always been the case and always will be. I should have said something sooner."

"It's fine, Mom." Lacey traded out a curry comb for a softer dandy brush. "I'm glad for him. He deserves to find someone to make him happy."

"So do you."

Lacey barely contained her snort. "I've got all I need. My horse and my family." *That's more than some people have, supportive or not.* She didn't bother to take a detour about the way her father treated her like a non-person. That old argument never got anywhere, anyway. "A man isn't in the picture. No biggie." Those were the same words she'd told herself over and over again since collecting Candy and taking her inside for grooming. They sounded reasonable, almost flippant, but were only a cover. She hoped they carried sincerity. Judging by the regret and sadness in Helen's eyes, Lacey knew she'd failed. "Don't worry. I'm not going to say anything. Message received loud and clear." She sighed. "I care enough for him to leave well enough alone."

"You've never been interested in attending the fall circuit before." Helen leaned against a stall door.

"We need the money." Lacey spouted off one of the truths. Her parents never asked, but Lacey always gave them part of her winnings. Rent, she called it. Mostly it was to help them keep their heads above water and in the black. If Tate did the same, she didn't know about it.

"And you need time away," Helen finished for her.

"That too." No sense in lying. Her mother could pick out a fib in a second.

"I'm not sure the road can cure a broken heart." Helen pinned Lacey with her gaze.

Lacey shrugged. "No time like the present to find out."

Chapter Two

Two weeks later

Lacey sat at the front desk at Dr. Moore's vet clinic, tapped a pencil eraser against the appointment book and stared at the wall. Time was passing slowly that morning, with an empty office. Since Dr. Moore specialized in big animals, he didn't spend much time in the office, as evidenced by the two small exam rooms and lack of steel cages in the back. Some people brought him their smaller animals, but most opted to visit the regular vet just down the street. She didn't mind. Easy work and easy pay for holding down the fort.

He'd been out on a call all morning, leaving her to answer the phones. His regular receptionist had a doctor's appointment as well, allowing Lacey a few hours of time to fill in. She'd taken it. Not just for the needed paycheck, but for the convenient excuse to be away from home and her mother's worried looks.

The last thing she needed was for the rest of the family to pick up on the situation. No way would she ruin this for Ransom. Telling him how she felt would only be awkward, embarrassing and risky. He'd become an integral part of the family and she refused to cause a rift. Everyone loved him like he'd been born there. Considering the negligence and hunger he'd faced as a young child from an unconcerned and inattentive mother, Ransom didn't need her to make him feel uncomfortable at the farmhouse. No. Bottling everything up and putting on a fake smile would just have to do. She loved him enough to cowgirl up and forge ahead.

"Lacey. Let's go." Dr. Moore swept through the front

office.

Startled, she blinked at him. "Go? Go where?"

"The Humane Society farm. We've got to check on a couple of animals there and I'll need your help to contain them. Especially those damn pigs."

Lacey sighed as she stood up. She both loved and hated going to the rescue. Adored all the critters but grew sick at the sight of abused and starving animals. Anger coursed free as she added a new chapter of hate toward cruel mankind. The images of horses nearly transparent with skin pulled taut over their ribs never left her mind. She shuddered at the memory of the horrid conditions some of them arrived in. Thankfully, most survived and thrived. Some were too ill to continue. Those, especially, broke her heart.

She followed the middle-aged, salt-and-pepper-haired man to his truck complete with compartments full of veterinary items, from tools to medicine. "What about the clinic?"

"Sally will be in soon. It'll be okay." He shooed her to the passenger's seat.

By the time she clicked her seat belt, he'd climbed in, slipped the key into the ignition and cranked the engine. "I know you only planned on working a half day, but I expect I'll need all the help I can get."

"No problem. The extra money will be nice." She settled in for the thirty-minute drive to the farm.

He studied her for a long moment before pulling out onto the street. "Figured since you placed well in the finals, you'd received a decent payday."

Yeah, it had been. The biggest check of her life. Though not enough to live on, to quit her job, or to move out on her own. First of all, she needed a backup mount. The situation Trinity had experienced this past season had taught her that. Too bad high-end barrel horses cost upward of five digits. "It was good. Just not enough to allow me to become lazy."

He nodded slightly. "Ever thought about using your

degree?"

She propped her elbow on the door. "Animal science. I'm pretty sure I'm using it now. Not really getting rich from it." For as long as she could remember, she'd wanted to spend her life around animals in some capacity. Vet school gave her heart palpitations—the thought of all the difficult classes on top of the cost. She'd compromised with an animal science degree. Which had done little to enrich her life.

Barrel racing called her, drove her and promised success if she could just reach a little higher in the standings. Tough competition and Candy's increasing age had held her back thus far. She prayed for a breakthrough year.

"You're quiet today," he noted.

She spared him a quick glance. "Jet lag. The finals wore me out."

Dr. Moore pursed his lips. "Good enough explanation as any, though that was a couple weeks ago."

His speculative tone led her to believe he considered other reasons. She didn't elaborate further, preferring the silence over dredging up personal failures.

"You're working too hard. Even I can see that."

"Not much choice. Chores are always there." *Ain't that the truth?* If she didn't spend time at the vet clinic, she helped with the cattle, the fall harvest of hay, apples and a kitchen garden. The past week had been filled with apple butter, cows giving birth and a pile of laundry compliments of a household of busy people. Downtime didn't exist in her world, no matter how much she longed for a day to do nothing but laze around. At least walnut season had pretty much finished. Her back cheered that fact.

She watched the land pass by for a short while then opted to change the subject before he pried further. "What are we supposed to do today?"

"Look at a pig with a rash, a couple of horses and one llama they say bites," he grumbled.

She smiled faintly. "An animal that bites. How unusual."

Sarcasm she could do and well.

He snorted. "That's your job. Keep my hide intact and I might give you a raise."

"Really?"

"Yep. You've earned it." He pulled off the highway and onto a side road. "Truth be told, I've been thinking of taking on a vet tech. Someone to go with me on calls now and again. Sally is fine in the office but comes up short when dealing with irate stock."

Growing up on a farm had taught Lacey to deal with all kinds of situations, including barnyard animals with attitude. Nothing fazed her in that department. Sally, on the other hand, lacked a farm life and tended to gravitate more toward dogs and cats. Anything bigger than a Great Dane made her nervous.

"I'd appreciate that, Dr. Moore." Lacey soaked up the compliment. Any other time she'd have been smiling from ear to ear. Today she could barely muster a half-grin. "Every little bit helps."

He found an empty spot next to the main barn, parked, and shut off the engine before peering at her. "For you or your parents?"

She met his gaze steadily. "For both."

He shook his head. "It's not your responsibility to keep that place going. You work your rear off around there when you should be out enjoying your own life." His words hit home without coming across as sour.

Lacey had said the same thing dozens of times. The taproot of that land ran deep, though. Not to mention she couldn't let the dreams of her parents perish when she could lend a helping hand. It was all she'd ever known. All of them worked to keep the farm producing. No exceptions. Without a jackpot win, she couldn't fathom how they could retire, keep all of their possessions and start a new journey. They lived off the land more than anyone else she knew, even with outside jobs.

Which told her the state of their finances. Pretty damn

depressing.

"I do what I can." She offered up the truth.

He studied her for another second before opening his door. "Come on. The sooner we get this done, the sooner we call it a day."

She hopped out, took a second to inspect the surrounding pastures, and smiled at the dozens of animals grazing in the fields. Such a beautiful sight, though most of their individual stories proved downright tragic. At least they had a chance at a happy ending. More so than others.

"Dr. Moore. Good to see you again." Nila Cochran hurried out to meet him. She'd worked the rescue as long as Lacey could remember, climbing the ladder to manager a handful of years ago. Deservedly so. She turned to Lacey. "Congratulations on the finals. You did excellent. We were all cheering for you."

Lacey smiled softly. "Thanks."

"Where do we start?" Dr. Moore asked.

Nila chuckled. "Pigs, horses or one mean-tempered llama?"

"Decisions, decisions." He followed her into the side door of the barn.

Lacey brought up the rear.

The scream of a horse drew her immediate attention. Lacey turned to locate the animal, found him in a stall, rearing and kicking as a couple of staff members tried to latch onto his halter without success. White showed around his eyes and a coating of sweat shone on his neck and shoulders despite the black hide.

Lacey hurried over, reading the body language of the big horse quickly. The volunteers were anxiously trying to jump out of the way and wrangle the horse with grabbing arms. Their frantic actions only added to the issue. "Get out. Both of you. You're only making it worse."

The two girls didn't waste a second in following her orders.

Lacey slipped in behind them, speaking softly to the

frightened animal. The stallion flattened his ears, lifted them marginally and trembled as she stood in front of him. He didn't make to bite or kick, just rustled restlessly in the thick straw. Catching a glimpse of Nila out of the corner of her eye, Lacey asked her question in the same soothing tone. "What's his story?"

"Came in yesterday. Stallion with his own little harem of mares. The owner moved out and left them behind. No one realized they'd been abandoned until several months later." Sarcasm dripped from her words. "Who knows how much human interaction he's had or if that was good or bad. It was all we could do to get a halter on him and drag him into this stall."

Lacey thought about that for a second, ignoring the rise of anger at the audacity and cruelty of some people. "Was he wound in the trailer or when you led him to the barn?"

Nila's eyebrows furrowed. "Come to think of it, no. He loaded pretty well considering he'd probably been on his own for a bit."

"Didn't try to run when unloaded?" Lacey kept her voice soft and soothing and never took her eyes off the stallion as she pondered the reasons for his behavior.

"Not that I noticed." Nila looked over at her workers.

"He was fine until we came in the barn. Then he started getting all nervous. Took everything we had to get him in the stall. That's when he started going berserk," one of the girls who had been with the stallion chimed in.

"His mares?"

"Were in the trailer with him. We unloaded them first and put them in the smaller barn next door."

The puzzle pieces clicked into place. "So you separated him from his harem and brought him inside alone, then confined him to his stall?"

"Yes." The girl chewed her bottom lip. "I didn't realize—"

Nila gave the girl a quick hug. "It's okay. You didn't do anything wrong. God knows you're an angel with horses, Savannah."

If the horse had always been outside and with his harem, the abrupt change would sure not only piss him off but scare him to death. She re-evaluated the tremors quaking his body with new insight. A light bulb clicked on. "Bring one of his mares over. One of them that's quiet and laid-back."

"None of them are. All are pretty high-strung and skittish," Savannah answered.

"It's okay, big boy. We'll find you someone." She thought for a second. "Any other female horse will do. Just one that's calm and reassuring."

Lacey kept talking to the stud, watching as his ears flicked back and forth. She noted the swath of white that covered most of his face. That along with the deep blue eyes and bold splashes of white on either side declared him a paint. The wide chest and powerful hindquarters she'd seen as she entered the stall told her a carefully bred paint at that. A shame they had to geld him as the Humane Society rules said. He'd have made a great herd stallion in the right hands.

"Such a pretty boy." He seemed to settle marginally with her close by. Instead of approaching, she remained still, allowing him ample opportunity to get used to the idea of her presence. "Lead rope."

A tall, dark-haired man passed one through the bars to her, slowly and carefully.

"Thanks." She didn't have time to study the guy but made a mental note to do so later. He smelled like horse, leather and pure country. The perfect combination.

"You should let me in there. He's too dangerous," the man whispered in a deep voice that stroked Lacey's nerves in a calming caress.

"We're doing just fine. Aren't we, boy?" She edged closer, taking her own sweet time.

The sound of hoof beats came soon after. The stallion lifted his head and pricked his ears as he sensed the newcomer.

"That's it, sweetheart. Want to meet your new friend? We

can, but you have to let me put this on you." Gradually, she stepped closer, her entire attention focused on the big black stallion occupying most of the space. If he got nasty, she had nowhere to go and knew it. Her gut told her that wouldn't be an issue. She prayed she wasn't wrong. "It's okay. Just let me get this attached." Lacey held out her hand and the lead.

He snuffled it for a second, then stepped closer to the door, as if eager to see the mare.

"Here we go." She clipped on the lead rope, making sure to do so quietly and without jarring his halter in the least. Task done, she took hold of the rope right under his halter and turned to face the exit. "Open the door. We need to take him to a corral or round pen close by. It needs to be outside or at least have an open wall."

Nila nodded as she held the other equine steady. "We have a pole barn enclosure with two sides closed and the other two open in the next barn over. We can take him there."

Lacey walked the horse out of the stall, both feeling and watching every step he made. He shouldered her aside to get to the mare.

The man started to step in. Lacey shook her head. "Stay back. We're fine. Just don't get in the way." She blew out a breath and praised the stallion.

They left the barn without incident. The moment the horse emerged into the sunshine he seemed to relax. Tension left his body, easily detected on his lead as he followed the dun mare through one fenced-in area and through the gate of another. He didn't try to break free, to escape, or bite. Instead, he lifted his head, scented his surroundings, and whinnied to the other horses nearby.

"Social butterfly, huh?" Lacey grinned happily.

She led him into the paddock, then waited for Nila to release the mare and walk well out of the way. Taking a moment, she rubbed the stallion's neck and up around his halter. He trembled a bit but didn't make a fuss. "Such a good boy. You just needed to be outside, didn't you?"

He ignored her in favor of watching the mare.

After unsnapping the lead, Lacey backed away, keeping her eyes on him just in case. He did nothing more than go snuffle the new horse and walk the perimeter with obvious interest.

"Damnedest thing I've ever seen."

Lacey left the paddock, turned around, and stared up at the man who had tried to assist earlier.

Chocolate-brown eyes matched his hair, which appeared a bit unkempt, as if needing a cut two weeks past. High cheekbones told of his heritage while a square chin promised stubbornness. A button-down Western shirt was molded over wide shoulders full of thick muscles, as evidenced when the material tightened with movement. Dark blue denim flowed down to scuffed brown cowboy boots. She could only see the front of him, but judging by his prime physique, his ass would be just as perfect as the rest. She was a sucker for a great ass.

He raked her with one glance, an expression of awe covering his chiseled features.

"Seabiscuit."

He blinked at her. "What?"

"Seabiscuit. He had the same separation anxiety issue." She glanced over as the stallion lowered his head, flicked his tail at a fly and snorted. For all intents and purposes, he appeared more like an old plow pony than a high-strung beast. "Add in the fact that he's probably not been inside a barn in forever and, *viola*, panic attack."

The man shook his head and smiled. "You've got some talent. Impressive. Damn impressive. Not many women can handle a stud like that."

She shrugged and ignored the double innuendo screaming in her head. The guy might be fine, and she'd definitely look. But that was it. Nothing more. She'd had her fill of lousy men.

"If you're not working with horses, you're wasting your

life." He wiped his forehead and stared down at her.

Her stomach flipped at the intensity in his eyes. She tried not to enjoy the sparkly sensation. Men weren't on the docket. Now or later.

Still, she couldn't help answering, "I barrel race when not assisting Dr. Moore."

"Lacey. Lacey Bright."

Surprised he knew her name, she tilted her head. "Yes. And you are?"

"Jonas. I'm the head trainer here at the farm." He held out a hand.

She shook it with a firm grip. "Nice to meet you. Seems my reputation preceded me."

Nila came closer and laughed. "I'm afraid so. We all watched your runs on the computer. Every night."

"Nice paint mare you have." Jonas hooked one hand on his belt.

"Thanks." Lacey glanced over his shoulder to find a grinning Dr. Moore contentedly leaning against a fence rail as if he had all the time in the world. Tempted to roll her eyes, she resisted. Barely. The good vet might be around the same age as her father and he had a penchant for giving advice just like one as well. Or, in this case, encouraging her to take a moment to get to know a man. She'd worked for him long enough to read him like a proverbial book. His wish to hurry up had obviously evaporated under the influence of his matchmaker gene.

Yeah, he had one of those. She'd seen it rear its nosy head now and again. Namely in Sally's life and now hers.

Not happening.

"Did you say we were starting with the biting llama?" She shot him a haughty look.

He stood up straight and nodded. "I think that's as good a place as any." His lips twitched.

Lacey sighed. She gave a quick nod to Jonas before walking away, already regretting the loss of those sexy eyes peering down into hers. He made her feel unique, interesting and pretty.

Qualities she'd longed to read in Ransom's eyes for the past few years. To no avail. "Where's the llama, Nila?" Lacey stiffened her spine and followed the director, refusing to dwell on the past.

* * * *

Jonas watched Lacey from afar as he worked with a pretty little mare called Bridget who'd been at the rescue for a few months. Healthy, up to weight and full of life, the horse offered him a chance to use his advanced skills. Normally he stuck to the basics, breaking horses or simply getting them to load into a trailer or stand quietly for the farrier. Bridget had proved smart and loved to try new things. He'd already taken her out on trails and now focused on prepping her for cutting or reining classes.

He tightened the cinch, automatically checking the snugness as his gaze returned to the lithe brunette with the amazing touch. The sight of her entering the stallion's stall earlier had caused his heart to skip a beat. He'd raced to the area as soon as he'd heard the stallion's frantic whinnies, only to be too late to stop Lacey from going in. Though he'd feared the worse, he'd ended up witnessing a small miracle as she'd not only calmed the upset stud, but figured out his issue and solved it on the spot. Never in his years of working with horses had he seen such a thing. Probably wouldn't ever again.

She sidestepped, bent over, and held one of the hogs against a fence for the vet to check the animal's hoof. Jonas noted the curve of her backside and almost grinned. She had sass, guts and sense. Add in a tough package in a mighty fine body and he couldn't help but be amazed. Lacey carried her own beauty, and not the type skinny runway models did, either. Cowgirl strong. He didn't doubt she could rope a calf, throw it down and tie it in record time with a smile on her face and maintain the freshness as if she'd just stepped out of the shower. He'd pay to see just that.

Holy hell. When did I turn into a mushy fool?

He shook his head to dislodge the sappy thoughts. No sense in thinking, wishing, or fantasizing. Those days were gone.

Since the surgery several months back, he hadn't dated. Testicular cancer had left him with one nut and a complicated decision. He could get a prosthesis to look more normal, but those weren't without their risks. No matter how many times he told himself that women didn't care about a man's balls, his ego disagreed. Odd, he'd never been that vain before. Luck had been with him in that the cancer had been detected in time, right after he'd taken a hard fall from his horse and ended up with a broken leg. The MRI had showed the small tumor before it could hardly be felt. All good as the doctors had concluded that surgery should be enough. He'd opted for radiation therapy as a precaution, though, needing to hedge his chances for the future as much as possible. Routine checkups and scans every six months for the next few years were a given. He'd even suffered the embarrassment of freezing up sperm in case he needed it for children one day, since his sperm count would dive with only half the equipment as before. It could have been worse. A hell of a lot worse.

Still, his confidence had taken a major hit. When it came to women, his courage had flown the coop. To put all his worries in a single basket and offer that up to a date made a lump form in his throat and his stomach clench with dread. Worries flooded his system along with the increased fear of performance.

No, I can't take that chance. Not yet.

He glanced over his shoulder once again. *No matter how good she might look.*

As he watched, Lacey released the hog, stood up straight and rubbed at her back. Probably stiff from trying to hold the slippery animal in place. At one point in life he might have approached her and offered to rub the soreness out after a dinner date. Now he only watched from afar and cursed his rotten luck.

"You okay?" Nila eyed him with concern.

He turned his attention back to the mare. "Yeah."

He'd heard Nila and the other girls mention Lacey's name now and again. Even the men who worked at the farm spoke of her with fondness and a hint of wishing. They all seemed to follow her career, obviously proud of the local girl making it to the big leagues of the rodeo. He'd watched a few of her runs himself, but hadn't given the events much thought until he saw the woman in person.

She didn't seem to recognize him, either. Not surprising since he'd only been pro for a bit over a year, gradually making his way up the leader board in the Midwest Region of the Rodeo Association, when the accident had happened. The break had sidelined him for three months. The cancer twice that time.

He caught a flash of brunette hair and saw Lacey leave the pen, dutifully closing the gate behind her. Her trim body and sure steps spoke of fitness, stamina and natural grace.

Not much inspired or impressed him these days. She made for an unexpected exception.

"Are you angry about something?" Nila asked.

He shook his head. Nila had proved to be a godsend both as a boss and as a friend, but that didn't mean he shared everything with her. Some secrets he refused to utter to another soul.

Nila turned around, paused, then faced him once more. "Are you worried about Lacey? I can vouch for her. She's an old hand at this. Never seen the likes of her way with animals. She can get a pissed-off stud eating out of her hand in minutes."

Jonas didn't doubt that for an instant. Not after what he'd witnessed earlier.

"I wouldn't have let just anyone else near that black stallion. But Lacey... She's special."

The sentiment clicked with Jonas. "I've never seen her

around here before." Curiosity got the better of him.

"She's born and raised over in Goodman. Spends much of her time on the road going from one rodeo to the next. Works with Dr. Moore and helps around the family farm in her spare time."

What spare time? To him that sounded like more than a plateful. "She's spreading herself too thin." He bit back the concern before it could slip into his voice.

Nila shrugged. "That's Lacey. Never known anyone to work harder or be as sweet as the day is long. Always polite, offering a smile, or a helping hand if you need that as well."

He sensed that in the lady. A selfish or hard person couldn't have bonded with that stallion at all, let alone so quickly. He started to ask more, but stopped. Nila would probably pick up on his interest in a heartbeat—the last thing he wanted.

Besides, Lacey's life story really didn't matter to him. Or so he told himself. He had a full life with a job he loved, was surrounded by friends, and had plenty of horses to fill his days. *What more do I need?*

He dared not answer that question.

Climbing up on Bridget, he found his natural balance, gathered the reins and clicked to her. She responded eagerly, trotting around the outdoor corral with enthusiasm.

Breathing deeply, he savored the moment as he nudged her for a ground-eating lope. Nothing like the excitement of the mad dash of calf roping, but enough. For now. Horses were his life and no place was he happier than in the saddle.

He peered over at Lacey as she climbed into the truck and shut the door. The doctor did the same before quickly driving away.

A tiny prick of regret flickered.

Ignoring it, he focused on his mount and the lesson at hand.

Chapter Three

"He's a great mover. Powerful hindquarters. Low-centered and fluid. Deep chest, too. He'd make one hell of a barrel horse."

Jonas turned to find Lacey leaning on the paddock fence, one boot resting on the lowest rail. Her shoulder-length straight brown hair was pulled back into a ponytail, showing off her round face and big green eyes.

His breath caught at the pretty sight of her in a long-sleeved T-shirt and jeans. Definitely his favorite outfit on a girl. Beat prom dresses hands down every time.

Absently, he wondered what had brought her back. When she and the vet had left before, he'd not really expected to see her again so soon, especially since the farm only used Dr. Moore once in a great while, when their regular vet couldn't squeeze them in. "I didn't see Dr. Moore drive up."

"He didn't. I came by myself. Couldn't forget this guy. Thought I'd swing by and check on him."

He glanced at the black-spotted horse. "He's got a lot to learn, but seems willing if a bit hesitant." A few carrots had established a tentative friendship between him and the horse as he groomed the animal and assessed his knowledge of basic ground manners.

She nodded. "Too bad he had to be gelded. With that conformation, he'd have made some pretty babies."

Jonas agreed. Yet there was already an overabundance of horses in the country. By not castrating one, the Humane Society allowed the potential for even more to be produced. A vicious circle indeed. Stallions were gelded. Period. Adopters of mares and fillies were forced to sign a no-breeding contract. Hopefully all followed through. "Yeah. Rules are rules for a reason." He stroked the horse's neck and whispered quiet praise.

He had a couple of dozen horses to work with each day, all demanding segments of his time. Yet something drew him back to Knight, as he called this one, day in and day out. Maybe because he understood the horse needed hours of training before he could be considered for adoption. Maybe because he saw huge potential in the mount and needed to do his part in allowing that to blossom. Maybe he looked at Knight and thought of Lacey, recalling her patience, her confidence, her gentle way of settling the big guy down.

"Think he'll ever be ridable?"

"With time." Jonas rubbed his hand lightly along Knight's cheek. "He's been worked with, doesn't really fear people. Just leery of them. I'd bet in that time he was out in the field he's forgotten some lessons. Those take a while to catch up on."

"But he's sound?"

"Yeah." Their regular vet had performed the gelding surgery the day after Lacey had shown up. "Vet said he's one tough son of a bitch. Hooves are great despite the fact he's been barefoot probably most if not all his life. Strong legs, no injuries noted. Even though he's likely four or five and been on his own a lot, he's in great shape." Jonas had been both relieved and thrilled with the news. He'd conceived some beginning plans for the animal and hoped they wouldn't be railroaded by health concerns. So far, so good.

She flashed a smile. "Not surprising. He's a survivor. Now he just needs a gentle hand to lead him the rest of the way."

Jonas' heart skipped a beat at her words. The sentiment hit home. Hard. And stuck.

Get off it, dumbass. Time to move on. He chastised himself while softly stroking Knight's nose.

He spared her a glance, finding her in the same position,

only her gaze raked him along with the magnificent horse. Interest flared in her eyes. Whether for him or Knight, he couldn't say.

Silence reigned as he walked Knight in a slow circle, wishing Lacey would both stay and leave at the same time. He didn't need the complications or the possibilities she presented. Yet, as she continued to stare, he found himself absorbing her approving looks, soaking them in like a thirsty man downed a glass of ice-cold water after a long day driving cattle in the heat and dust.

"Where did you learn to work with horses? You have a way about you. Not all big men can pull off soothing and calmness with them." Her tone carried truth and respect along with a healthy dose of curiosity.

He debated answering. As much as he wanted to keep his mouth shut, he found himself rattling off. Something he never did. "I've been around horses all my life."

Lacey drew him out. Her innocent questions, her refreshing spirit, the way she watched him like an art enthusiast stared at a Picasso. Without trying, she'd busted through his outer shell.

The realization would have rattled him if it didn't also fan the flame of hope at the same time.

Jonas couldn't decide whether to be angry with his loose tongue or upset with Lacey's interest. Hell, he could kick his own ass for encouraging her with a bit of conversation and sharing. If he'd just ignored her...

Yeah, right.

"Did you rodeo?"

"Some," he answered vaguely.

"Why did you quit?"

And there's the million-dollar question.

Jonas stopped mid-circle. He petted Knight before unsnapping the lead rope from the halter. Task done, he made a beeline for the gate, stepped through, and fastened it behind him.

Lacey approached, a scent of vanilla preceding her.

He tightened his grip on the rope. "I'm busy. Don't you have someone else to follow around?" He bit off the words, needing to send a message. Personal questions were off limits and he needed space. Comfortable, Lacey-free space.

Her face fell for a split second before she recovered. "As a matter of fact, I do. Sorry I even bothered." She spun on her heel and strode off.

Not before he caught the flash of pain in her eyes, mixed with deep-down fury.

That telltale sign bothered him more than it should have.

For a second, he reconsidered his curt rejection. Either she wore her feelings on her sleeve or he'd struck a nerve. He'd bet on the latter. A girl as strong and confident as Lacey appeared to be would have told him to go fuck himself, not stormed off with tears threatening.

Regret came fast. He should have been more tactful. Guilt settled on his shoulders as he recalled what Nila had said.

When did I become such an unfeeling bastard?

The moment he'd laid eyes on a courageous woman trying to calm a frightened horse that could have easily trampled her to death.

Because, at that moment, he'd seen something in her that he appreciated. That he craved. That he knew would soothe him if only given a chance.

Too bad he didn't have the gumption to try.

As he started off, Nila stepped into his path. She crossed her arms over her chest and glared at him. "Since when did you develop a mean streak?"

He narrowed his eyes. "Since she started getting personal."

Nila snorted and waved her hand. "We can't have that. Oh, the horrors. Becoming friends with Lacey would end the whole damn world."

He would have laughed at her vastly overdramatic view, but his raw emotions found little humor in the situation. Instead, he rolled his eyes. "I don't like to be bothered. Is that so hard to understand?"

She pursed her lips. "It is when a pretty, sweet girl like

Lacey comes around."

He pushed past her into the tack room, hung the lead rope up, and slung a bridle over his shoulder.

Nila stopped at the entrance and leaned on the doorjamb. "Jonas. She won't care."

He stiffened, not bothering to glance in her direction. "You don't know that." Nila was the only person on the farm who knew of his surgery. He'd pretty much had to let the cat out of the bag when he'd needed time off for all the doctor's visits and follow-up scans. She'd deserved to know the truth and he'd given it to her. To give her credit, she never gaped or even blinked, just thanked him for his courage and openness, told him he could have as much time as he needed, and promised to be there for him if he needed anything at all. He'd never tested her vow, but knew she'd hold to her words.

"Yeah, I do."

"Nila." He released a long sigh and turned to face her. "I might have been interested in her beforehand. Now I need time to cross those bridges again."

She studied him for a long moment. "I saw the way she looked at you. She sees a man worth having."

He snorted. "Don't be too sure of that."

Nila *tsked*. "Let me tell you something. That girl isn't like all the rest. She's got a heart of gold, even if it's broken at the moment." She stepped back and walked away, leaving him with that gem of a hint.

What in the hell did she mean by that?

He blew out a deep breath and scrubbed his face. That little morsel would drive him mad. He just knew it.

Well, shit.

* * * *

I need a damn vacation. Even as she considered the words, she knew the possibility hovered right around absolute zero. Her job and the farm wouldn't take care of themselves for a long period of time. *Hell, I just got back from two weeks off.* So it happened to be a working vacation. It still counted.

She rolled her shoulders, feeling the stiffness and a pinch of pain. Stress ate at her. Day and night. Tension had become her constant companion, sapping her energy and turning her mood disinterested and sour.

How long can I keep this up? As long as I have to. What choice do I have?

The abbreviated fall rodeo season would begin next week, providing an excuse to get away. Away from Ransom and his perfect girlfriend. Away from the endless chores and reminders that the next day would only be a repeat of the present one. Away from a family that made her want to scream due to their stubborn determination to make farming pay no matter what it cost them. Away from a father who saw her as a failure to the whole female population.

She saw her parents' rapidly graying hair, the lines of fatigue and worry on their faces. The fewer smiles and laughter.

Was it worth it just to hang onto all that land? Not in my book.

Their dream, though. As long as they were willing to sacrifice for that, she couldn't say anything. Just plow ahead and plod along.

Lacey pulled into the parking lot of the grocery store. Her conversation with Jonas flashed through her mind, stirring her ire once again. She had a list to fill, but anger and frustration existed too much on the surface for her to be halfway civil in case she ran into anyone she knew. "Damn men. Absolutely useless. Just wanted to get to know the guy. Is that so bad?" She sighed heavily. "Why do I even bother? And why am I letting one grouch ass get to me?" Self-disgust reared its head.

She recalled how quickly Jonas had transitioned from amicable to icy and shook her head. Obviously she'd hit a nerve, but what the hell? No reason to snap. *Men are overrated.* No matter how nice he looked in those jeans, he wasn't worth the effort of trying to tame. She'd be a hell of a lot happier — and saner — if she gave up on the opposite sex completely. At least she didn't have to worry about seeing Jonas again. As long as Dr. Moore didn't have to fill in for their regular vet again, she'd be sitting pretty.

Disappointment cascaded over her with that realization.

Since she'd arrived home from the finals, her life had sucked more than usual. Ransom was talking engagement. The whole family, minus her, was giddy with excitement. She worked harder than ever and seemed to be overlooked in the whole process. Not for the first time she wanted to dash off, do something fun, just for herself, and find some happiness in the process. What that happened to be, she didn't have an earthly clue.

Drawing in a breath, she realized how much she missed the rodeo circuit. Seeing Trinity and the other girls every weekend. While she and Trinity weren't as close as sisters, they still shared a few secrets, chats and worries. Trinity never judged and always made her see a brighter side of life. Just what she craved right now.

Lacey dug out her phone, found Trinity's number and called.

"Lacey?"

"Hey, Trin." Lacey forced cheeriness into her voice. "How's it going?"

"Great, actually."

"How's Cody? Did you two get together after the finals?" They were a hot item when the season ended. Lacey hoped it had worked out. Trinity'd had one hell of a time and deserved all the happiness she could find.

"You could say that." Trinity giggled. "We're engaged. Haven't set a date yet, but probably by spring, maybe a bit earlier if the weather is still good."

"Wow. Congratulations." Lacey meant the words. The thrill for Trinity didn't seep into her own mood, though. In fact, she felt that much worse.

"You're definitely invited. I'll send you an invitation."

"Okay. I'll watch for it."

"Would you be my maid of honor?"

"Sure. Just don't dress me in some frilly mess that I'll never wear again." Lacey crossed her eyes at the thought.

Trinity laughed. "No worries. We're wearing jeans and Western outfits. Casual."

"Thank goodness."

Always the bridesmaid and never the bride. The wind knocked out of her sails, Lacey slumped in her seat.

"What's wrong, Lacey? I can hear it in your voice."

"Nothing. I'm fine."

"Lacey. Don't lie to me."

Knowing Trinity read between the lines, Lacey opened up. "Remember that guy that didn't know I existed? The one I was going to goat tie?"

"Yeah."

"He's next best thing to engaged."

"Oh." Trinity went quiet. "I'm so sorry, Lacey."

She pulled on her waning bravery. "It's okay. Some things just aren't meant to be."

"Don't you dare give up. There's a man out there for you. I know it." Her strong encouragement bolstered Lacey only marginally.

"I don't think I'm up to the fight. Maybe life is better without a man. Who needs to pick up socks and dirty underwear off the floor anyway?" Sarcasm came easily to her.

Trinity chuckled. "Oh, Lacey. Find the right guy and you'll be the one tossing the underwear on the floor."

"Uh-huh."

"Tell you what. Why don't you come to visit me at the farm? I'd love to have you. We both would."

As gracious as the offer was, Lacey couldn't accept. Trinity and Cody were freshly engaged, madly in love and still discovering each other. No way would she show up and become the third leg in the middle of their happiness. "Thanks, but I can't. I'm working more hours with the vet. Not to mention helping out on the ranch. I'll be gone enough hitting the fall circuit." Normally the riders started in the spring, when the major rodeos were scheduled. Late in the year, only a few regional events graced the calendar. Lots of miles, little payoff and not many points to be gathered. By the time the end of the year rolled around and winter took hold of the Oklahoma countryside, the short fall season would grind to a halt.

"You're beginning earlier this year." Trinity's tone carried concern.

"Yeah. I want to make it back to the finals. See if I can move up a few notches." She spoke the truth, even if those reasons were only part of the complete picture. "The practice won't hurt me any, either."

"I wish you'd come stay with us for a while. Bring Candy. Legacy misses her."

Lacey grinned at that. "I hear he's had plenty of pretty ladies to play with lately."

"Some, but I think Candy is his favorite." A pause followed. "I was going to tell you. I've decided what your birthday present will be."

Surprised, Lacey blinked. "It's not for four more months."

"So?"

Lacey shook her head, her spirit lifted somewhat. "Okay. I'll bite. What is it?"

"A free breeding to Legacy."

"What?"

"You heard me. You've earned it. Besides, I'm just as eager to see what kind of baby those two make as you are."

"Trin, that's too much." His breeding fee wasn't cheap. Not to mention Lacey didn't have a backup barrel horse to ride when Candy grew big. As much as she'd like to get a baby out of Legacy, she couldn't see how it would all play out. Regardless, she wouldn't forget Trinity's more than generous offer.

"Nope. I've already made up my mind. So now you have to come visit. Just load up Candy and bring her with you. She can stay in Carmen's pasture. Carmen already offered it."

Lacey wiped at the single tear that trickled down her cheek. "I don't know what to say."

"Say yes, silly."

"Yes."

"Great. Just let us know when you plan on bringing her. I'll get all the arrangements made."

"Thanks. Trinity?"

"Hmm?"

"You're the best."

She laughed. "Only because you showed me what was right in front of my eyes and didn't let me give up. Turnabout is fair play, you know."

Legacy groaned dramatically. "That's what I'm afraid of."

"Fear? You?" Trinity snorted. "You're the gutsiest woman I know."

"Not really." Lacey glanced at her watch. "I need to get going. Thank you again. For everything."

"No problem. Don't be a stranger and don't worry. A good man is bound to come along soon. If not, there's a few vets on the circuit I'm sure Cody can set you up with."

"No matchmaking services needed. Thanks anyway." She rolled her eyes but a grin snuck out anyway. "I'm going now. Bye." She disconnected the call, tossed her cell phone into her purse and blew out a breath.

The groceries won't buy themselves.

Just another task to mark off the to-do list.

Before she could climb out of the car, her phone rang. Not recognizing the number, she answered hesitantly. "Hello?"

"Lacey. It's Nila. From the Humane Society farm."

"Oh, hi." Perplexed as to why Nila would call her, Lacey waited for an explanation.

"We're needing a part-time horse trainer. With all the new rescues coming in almost daily, one trainer isn't nearly enough."

Lacey's breath hitched. She could well understand their predicament after seeing all the horses grazing in the fields.

They were full. The greatest majority of horses adopted had at least some training. For those that could be ridden, under saddle. For others, just the basics to allow them to be a pasture pet that anyone would love to spoil. That took time and energy from trainers and volunteers to get them all to that point.

"You're the first one I thought of. After the way you settled Knight right down and realized his issues, I couldn't think of another person I'd like working for us."

Lacey bit her lip. She could use the money. But another job? She couldn't keep up with what she had already. "I'm going on the rodeo circuit again. My weekends will be mostly filled."

"That's not a problem. Like I said, it's part-time. You make your own schedule. I'm willing to work with you on that."

Working with horses. Her dream job. Lacey cautioned herself not to get too excited. "How many hours are you thinking?"

"Whatever you can give us. A couple of days, maybe? I know you've got your hands full, but we really need a person like you."

"Will I be under Jonas' thumb?" Lacey chewed her lip, needing to know ahead of time.

"He's the head trainer, so you'd fall under his jurisdiction. However, you'd have your own horses and free rein to work with them in whatever manner you choose. He might oversee and give direction, but you'll essentially be two different trainers working with separate groups of horses."

She did quick calculations in her head. Dr. Moore only used her now and again. Nothing set or routine. If he called, she could always work around his needs with the flexibility Nila offered.

Indecision flared for a second before something clicked. Excitement blossomed. "When do you want me to stop by so we can iron out details?"

"Wonderful!" A pause followed. Lacey could hear a page turn in the background. "Tomorrow morning?"

"I can come over after caring for Candy. Say around eight?"

"I've got you down. And, Lacey?"

"Yes?"

"Don't worry about anything. This will pan out just fine. I know it."

"Okay." Not quite sure what Nila meant, Lacey shrugged it off. "See ya tomorrow then."

"Definitely."

Lacey punched a button and ended the call. She sat back and considered this latest development. A job. As a horse trainer. Something she'd always wanted but never had the opportunity to try.

Maybe, just maybe, my luck is changing.

About time.

Chapter Four

"Jonas. Hold up a second."

Jonas paused on his way to his truck, watched Nila approach and wondered what in the world she had on her mind. Judging by the spark in her eyes, most likely something that would needle him.

She stopped in front of him, her red hair once again escaping the bun she tried so hard to pull off. "I wanted to ask how your doctor's visit went this morning."

"Just fine. No signs of trouble." He appreciated her asking, but didn't care to go into details of his quarterly visits checking for any signs of the cancer returning. Always nerve-wracking, especially waiting on the CAT scan results. Thankfully, each time had been good news. Nine months out and still clear. It boded well for the future.

"Great. You're as healthy as a horse and a good guy to boot. I'd like to keep you around for decades to come."

He offered up a small smile. "I plan on it."

"Good. Then I should tell you the latest news. With this new crop of horses coming in, I know you're overworked. There's only so many hours in a day and you can't spend quality time with all the horses on the list needing work. So I've found some money in the budget to hire a part-time trainer."

Oh, no. She didn't. He read her face easily, already knowing the answer. "Who?"

"Lacey."

Well, hell. "Why her?"

Nila frowned at him. "You saw her with Knight. With that kind of touch and insight, why wouldn't you want her here?"

He blew out a long breath, scanned the fields and pasted on his business expression. He had to give credit where credit was due. "She's good. I'll give her that."

"Exactly. We're lucky to have her. She's juggling the rodeo circuit on weekends, working for Dr. Moore here and there, and gonna give us a couple of days per week. One thing about that girl. She's a damn hard worker."

The sound of her schedule tired him out. How she stood up to the pressure, he didn't know. Burnout would certainly hit at some point. "I have to supervise her?" He sure as hell hoped not. The girl called to him on a very masculine level. Spending more time with her would only make that attraction worse.

"No. I told her she would answer to you, but would be pretty much on her own. I gave her the short list of horses started under saddle. She can work the kinks out and get them ready for adoption fast while you're still dealing with the more difficult ones."

He truly needed the help. The sheer numbers of equines at the rescue told the story. Had for a while now. Lacey could take some of the pressure off, move things along, and hopefully ease the congestion on his endless list. If they could adopt out even a few of the horses, the overcrowding would ease and they'd free up hands and space for more needy animals.

Just what the doctor ordered.

Except it had to be Lacey.

He shoved his personal concerns aside and nodded. "She's a good pick." He still marveled at the memory of her stepping into Knight's stall and taking charge of the situation. She had guts, brains and a talent he hadn't seen in a long, long time.

Nila studied him for a long moment. "I know I should have asked you first, but it all sort of happened while you were away this morning. If you're not happy with the situation, say so."

"No. It's fine. She'll work out and the potential adopters will love meeting a locally famous cowgirl when they come check out the horses." *Damn, it's true.* The rescue needed Lacey.

Almost as much as I do.

The thought came out of nowhere.

Well, shit.

He rubbed the sleeve of his shirt across his face. They'd just met and he'd already set his sights on her. Not good. Not good at all.

"Okay. She starts next week, after her rodeo this weekend in Grain Valley." Nila eyed him for a second longer before turning away and returning to her office.

Grain Valley. Just a hop, skip and a jump from here.

He climbed into his truck and set a course straight for home.

Ten minutes later, he entered the house and froze. Jason, his brother, sat on the couch, his feet propped up on the coffee table, remote in hand. Loose sweats covered his body. Unusual in that Jason preferred jeans to just about anything else. The only time he traded in his Levi's was when he had a trip to the gym on the agenda.

Jason owned a house across town but seemed to spend more time hanging out with Jonas than chilling in his own home. More times than not, Jonas actually enjoyed the companionship.

Jonas would have grumbled about the lack of notice, but he never truly minded Jason's visits. They had been close as kids, roping buddies growing up, and were now business partners in the oil industry. Still, he couldn't let the lack of manners slide by. "Mom would smack those shoes off the table if she were here."

"Yep. Good thing she's at home with Dad." Jason clicked the television off. "I thought we could work out together."

"Okay, but you're buying dinner afterward." Jonas had made a habit this last year to make exercise a priority. Anything to keep him in shape and stave off the chances of a recurrence of the dreaded disease. The doctors weren't quite willing to declare him cured, but they grew more optimistic with each passing appointment.

"Sure." Jason stood and followed as Jonas went to his room in the small, two-bedroom house in order to change clothes. "Oil prices are down some, but the analysts aren't too concerned. Seasonal switch-over stuff. Dad blew me off when I talked to him about it today."

Their father had started his own oil business way back when, grooming both of them to step into the industry as they came of age. While Jonas happily remained pretty much a silent partner and held his stocks, Jason took a more active role. He watched the markets and kept abreast of all the financial reports. Too many numbers and headaches for Jonas to begin to tackle. "Okay."

"I need you to come into the office this week and sign some papers. Since the branch is in our name, the powers that be insist on it."

"Whatever." Jonas gritted his teeth. He'd much rather spend his days in the sunshine surrounded by horses and the scent of the great outdoors than occupying an office chair.

He needed away from the desk covered with piles of paper all concerning the oil business and back to nature. One of the reasons he'd immediately applied when he'd spotted the Humane Society ad for a horse trainer. His diagnosis had given him a new perspective on life. Time was too short to spend behind a desk. Money might be necessary but it didn't rank in the top three anymore. Other things had grown in precedence. Namely living on his own terms and spending his days at a job he loved. Priorities had changed. He'd changed.

The refreshing newfound insight and resulting adjustments had breathed life back into him. Mostly.

He traded out jeans for shorts. Boots for tennis shoes. Nothing tight in the least. He didn't want to take a chance on someone noticing his lopsided sac. Tighty whities helped as well.

"How did your appointment go? Everything okay?"

The concern in Jason's voice touched Jonas. They'd always been there for each other and Jason had been a pillar through everything. "Yep. Got a thumbs up."

"That's great." He smiled readily before his lips thinned. "Then care to tell me why you're pensive?"

Too perceptive for his own good. Jonas pulled on a T-shirt and returned to the living room. He collected his keys. "Not really. You driving or me?"

Jason jangled his keys. "I've got it."

Jonas climbed into the passenger seat, clicked his seat belt and stared out of the side window.

"Come on, bro. You're distracted. What's up?"

Jonas sighed. "Nila hired an assistant trainer for the farm."

"You've been clamoring for that very thing for weeks now."

"Yeah. It's not the fact that she finally did, but who she hired."

"Some idiot that doesn't know a hoof pick from a halter?" Jason pulled out onto the highway and hit the gas.

"That's not it. She's qualified. There's no question about that."

Jason spared him a glance. "I know you're not sexist or biased against women. So what's the problem?"

Jonas rubbed his palm on his shorts. "It's Lacey."

"The girl you told me about who took on that panicked stud and had him eating out of her hand in two minutes?"

"Yeah."

Jason swung the truck into the parking lot. He cut the engine and turned to Jonas. "She sounds perfect for the job."

"She is."

Jason narrowed his eyes as if trying to read Jonas' face. "You have the hots for her."

"No."

Jason snorted.

"Well, sort of." Jonas ran a hand through his hair. "I barely know the girl."

"Sounds like you'll have plenty of time to know her better."

Jonas met his brother's gaze. "I'm afraid to give her a try." The soft confession came straight from the heart. Cancer had stolen more than his left nut. It had stripped his formerly abundant self-confidence down to a bare stalk.

Sympathy and compassion replaced the previous tautness of Jason's features. "Jonas…"

"What if I'm wrong about her? What if she can't see past the disfiguration?" He rarely let his deepest fears out. Every now and again he needed someone to listen, to understand, to prop him up and nudge him to keep going. Jason had always been there.

"You're a good judge of character. Always have been. One-night stands notwithstanding."

Jonas rolled his eyes. They'd both had their fair share of crazy women during their glory days. Still would, except for the broken leg eighteen months ago followed immediately by his diagnosis of testicular cancer. He'd missed one and a half rodeo seasons and quite a bit of life in that period of time. Making up for it was proving harder than he'd ever imagined.

"This is the first I've heard about interest in a woman since you broke your leg. Honestly, I'm thrilled for you. That tells me you're ready to get back in the game. If Lacey is the one who can make that happen, then I'll forever be in her debt."

Jonas turned his head to the side.

"Just give her a chance, Jonas. Don't slam the door shut before you know what you're turning away."

The advice carried truth and reason. For the first time Jonas smiled slightly, returning his focus back to Jason. "How did you get to be so smart?"

"I learned from my big brother." Jason grinned, patted Jonas on the shoulder and pocketed his keys. "Let's go see if I can kick your ass on the treadmill."

"Wishful thinking."

Never know until you try. The phrase resonated with him.

"Before I forget to ask, want to go to the rodeo with me Saturday evening?"

"Sure."

No time like the present. Or in this case, Saturday night, to take the first steps in getting to know Lacey a bit better and determining if, indeed, she was the one who could see past his scars and to the true man within.

A weight off his shoulders, Jonas followed his brother into the small gym.

Chapter Five

"Lacey."

She stopped and turned to the sound of her name. Candy paused behind her, not hurried in the least.

Spying Jonas, Lacey gaped, recovered, then reminded herself to be nice. Irate bitch in public never boded well. "Jonas." Automatically, she checked him out, finding him as sexy as ever in those blue jeans. Too bad his bark proved disagreeable. She couldn't speak for his bite.

He stopped a couple of paces away and gestured to the man beside him. "This is Jason, my brother."

Jason's smile reached his dark eyes. "My pleasure." He took her offered hand and brushed his lips over her knuckles.

Lacey laughed even as she rolled her eyes. "Not sure that was wise. I was just cleaning up horse shit."

Jason shrugged. "Been there, done that. Hasn't done me any harm yet."

As flattering and fun as Jason proved to be, she found herself sneaking glances at Jonas and comparing the two men. They were built alike—big, tall and filled out. Both had brown hair and matching eyes, although Jason's ran a shade lighter. His facial features seemed not as chiseled and a bit rounder, giving him a less intense appearance. Still, there was no denying they were brothers.

"Lacey is our new part-time trainer. When she's not barrel racing, that is." Jonas spoke with a hint of affection in his voice. Odd considering their run-in a couple of days earlier.

"Heard all about you. You're the local hero in these parts." Jason flirted outrageously with a well-timed wink.

She smiled. "I'm sure all the rumors are exaggerated."

"I don't think so."

Jonas elbowed his brother. "If you'll quit throwing yourself at her feet, I can get a word in." His features turned serious. "I realize I came across pretty snappy the other day. It was rude and uncalled for. Can you accept my apology?"

Lacey blinked. Just when she'd written Jonas in on the 'not worth the time of day' list, he threw her for a loop. She rarely held grudges, so didn't bother arguing over one tense moment. Life was tough enough without carrying around the weight of negativity. "No worries. We all have bad days."

His eyes dulled a shade.

She received the impression that he knew all about bad days. Experienced more than his fair share. Her heart ached for him.

Recalling his prickly temperament from before, she refrained from asking. Instead, she offered up a friendly smile. "Having a good time?"

"Yeah. I miss the rodeo," Jason answered. "We used to rope together. Been a while, though."

Ropers. Made sense. Their size and build alone put them in the roping category, or even steer wrestling. Big men as a rule didn't do well riding broncs or bulls, but there was no denying they were cowboys through and through. "Maybe you two can get together one day just for fun? Although what you'll rope might be an issue."

Candy snorted and stamped her foot, reminding Lacey of her presence. They had been on their way to the warm-up zone when Jonas had hollered.

The chirping of a bird cut through the conversation.

"Excuse me." Lacey dug out her cell phone, glanced at the caller ID and frowned. "Hi, Mom. What's up?"

"Tate's football game is in overtime. I wanted to let you know because I don't think we'll be able to get there in time to see your run."

Lacey deflated. Once again, her brother had won out over

her. Nothing new, though still hurtful. "You sure? The rodeo grounds aren't far from the college."

"I'm sure, dear. I'm sorry. We'll make it next time. I promise."

"Yeah, sure." Lacey drew in a resigned breath. "I've got to go warm up. I'll see you later."

"Have a safe trip."

"Thanks." Lacey disconnected the call with a weary sigh. Seemingly all her life she'd tried to earn her family's approval, especially her father's. Rarely did it come. Most of the time they were so fixated on the two boys that Lacey felt invisible.

"Everything okay?"

She peered up to find Jonas staring at her with concern in his eyes. She'd almost forgotten he'd been standing there when her phone rang. Forcing a small smile, she waved her hand. "Yeah. The parents are at my brother's football game and won't make it. No biggie."

He studied her for a long moment, his cheek clenching for a brief second before relaxing again. "Need a leg up?"

The abrupt change of topic made her blink. "Umm. I can do it."

Jonas grinned. "Come on. Think about this as payback for me being such a hateful bastard."

Lacey smiled warmly. "Since you put it like that..." She gathered the reins, lifted her left leg and felt his strong grip. He shoved with power and ease, which left her impressed and a bit breathless as she settled gently into the saddle. "Thanks."

"My pleasure." He met her gaze steadily. "You're one of the best horsewomen I've ever seen. Go out and show the rest of these folks what you can do."

With those words of encouragement, Lacey pointed Candy to the warm-up area.

* * * *

Jonas led the way back to their seats. As soon as they settled, a shiny pickup truck drove into the arena. Men jumped out and started placing the three barrels in preparation for the next event.

"She's a beauty." Jason caught Jonas' eye. "I'd never poach, but if you decide to keep looking elsewhere, I might take a chance on her."

The thought of his brother moving in on Lacey sent a stab of annoyance through Jonas. He'd always been a bit possessive and protective when it came to his dates. He didn't share and maintained a strict code of commitment while dating. He expected the same from the lady.

"I'm not ready to throw in the towel just yet." Presumably she'd forgiven him for his lashing out at her. His luck had held and he refused to waste the golden opportunity.

"Poor girl. Did you see how upset that phone call made her? Got to be hard when her family canceled at the last moment."

Jonas frowned as he recalled how Lacey's face had fallen. He could have sworn she'd bobbled between crying and raging at the news. The pain in her expressive green eyes had hit him square in the chest. His gut told him this wasn't the first time they'd skipped out on her. Probably not the last.

Sure, shit happened. If only this had been an uncommon occurrence. He'd bet his part of the oil company she'd heard the same excuses over and over again. "I have a feeling this has happened more times than we know."

Jason turned to him with furrowed eyebrows. "Why would her family do that to her? She's damn sweet. Talented, too, from what I've heard."

"Got me." Jonas shrugged but vowed to watch his manners around Lacey. Obviously she had more going on than he'd imagined. The last thing she needed was one testy bastard to chew her ass for trying to be friendly. *Never again.* He could promise her that much.

"Ladies and gentlemen, if you'll take your seats. We're

ready to begin the barrel racing competition."

One girl after another dashed in, circled the barrels and darted back out.

"Next up is Lacey Bright on her paint mare, Candy. That's right, the local girl who made it all the way to the finals in Vegas just a few weeks ago."

Candy surged into the arena. Lacey hauled on the reins, grabbed the saddle horn and guided the sturdy horse around the first barrel. She repeated the same motions twice more before making the final turn for home.

Jonas scooted forward in his seat, quietly cheering her on. The amazing sight of her moving in perfect rhythm and balance with the horse stole his breath.

She zipped down the middle of the stadium and out through the door.

"Thirteen-forty. She's taken the lead," the announcer said.

"Wow." Jason shook his head. "She's got one hell of a horse under her."

"Horse? What horse?" Jonas chuckled, feeling better than he had in a while. "All I saw was a damn pretty lady with her hair flying behind her."

Jason's eyes twinkled. "That's the brother I remember. Welcome back to the big leagues."

Jonas held up his hands. "Whoa. I haven't even asked her out, let alone had her jump on my offer. Hell, I'm not even sure she cares to be around me."

"She accepted your apology pretty well. If she was still pissed, she would've thrown it back in your face. Trust me. Been on the receiving end of a woman's fury before. Not a good place to be."

Jonas empathized. "Yeah." She hadn't appeared angry still, just surprised. All had seemed on the up and up until her mother called.

He opted to see the bright side of their quick meeting. "Maybe I'll catch her at the farm in a couple of days. See if she wants to grab some lunch with me then."

"That's the spirit."

"If she shoots me down, I'll just wallow in self-pity and hang out at your bachelor pad." Jonas rubbed his nose and shot his brother a teasing grin.

Jason snorted. "Hang out all you want. The day you make me watch some chick flicks is the day I'll boot your ass out." Jason's eyes twinkled.

"Yeah, well. We can't have *that* happen." Jonas shook his head at his brother's antics. In truth, he loved his brother. They'd grown closer over the past year, becoming best friends as well. He never had a doubt Jason would step up to the plate and do anything for him. The fact added much-needed stability to his life and emotional health.

"That's the final run, folks. Lacey Bright is your winner."

Jonas watched the arena, saw Lacey re-enter, riding Candy in a slow gallop around the ring. She waved now and again at the crowd, earning enthusiastic applause.

He couldn't take his eyes off her. Damn beautiful.

The way she rode, as one with the horse. Her trim body with curves in all the right places. Her gentle hand on the reins. All the details registered, snapped into place, and brought the picture into focus.

Lacey was one special woman. A lady after his own heart. *If only she could accept me.*

He craned his neck to catch one more glimpse of her as she exited the building.

I'm not giving up on her until I find out.

With a plan in mind, he blew out a breath and caught his brother's eye.

Jason grinned at him like a Cheshire cat. For once, Jonas couldn't take offense. Not when he shared in the lighthearted moment and hope flared brightly.

Chapter Six

Tuesday arrived crisp and cool. Jonas dismounted from one of the green broke geldings he'd been working with the last couple of weeks and led the horse to the far end of the corral.

Hearing hoof beats, he glanced up to find Lacey loping a pretty palomino mare in large circles around the biggest training paddock. He watched as she shortened the reins, used her heels to encourage the mare to flex more and cut the area in half. A few strides later she nudged her again, getting the horse to change leads after a couple of tries.

He stood at the fence, reins in hand, and simply watched her in action.

He'd started the mare a while back. She had proved headstrong and stubborn, but her flashy hide and nice build would make her popular and get her adopted if they could work the kinks out. He'd butted heads with the mare over and over, finally getting her to accept a saddle and rider without too much of a fuss. Despite his best attempts, he hadn't been able to get her to move like she did for Lacey. After only a couple of hours, no less.

He shook his head in sheer amazement. That girl had a touch and a talent. No denying the truth before his eyes. A natural in the saddle and definitely born to ride.

She navigated a few more rounds, keeping up the brisk pace, before slowing the mare to a trot, riding out of the paddock and heading for the saddling barn.

Jonas watched her a moment longer before leading his mount that same direction.

He entered the saddling area to find Lacey already

stripping the tack from the pretty mare. "How did you get her to change leads? Every time I tried to teach her that trick she chewed the bit and absolutely refused."

She peered over the horse's back with a small smile. "I sweet-talked her."

His heart thumped at her words combined with the pretty grin. He found himself mimicking her expression. "If I buy your lunch, will you tell me the secret?"

She blinked at him before schooling her expression once more. "You don't have to do that. I'll tell you for free."

"I want to take you out to lunch. Today. Right now." He coaxed her with his quiet tone, needing her to say yes.

She studied him for a long moment. "Okay. If you're sure."

"I am." He breathed a sigh of relief and unhooked the cinch on his horse. "Let's go to Mama Jean's. They're close and always good." Quiet and laid-back too. A place they could sit down and have a conversation while eating.

"Sounds good to me." She carried her saddle, complete with blanket, over to a nearby wooden fence and set it on top. Task done, she exchanged the bridle for the halter and hung the tack on the wall hook. With the lead rope in hand, she took a moment to clean the bit before gathering up the horse once more.

He watched her perform the chores with familiar ease, full of grace, without excess movement. "As quickly as you're getting that mare advanced, she'll be ready for adoption really soon."

Lacey nodded. "That's the plan. Find her a good home and make room for more. I hate the thought of Nila having to turn away any horse due to lack of room."

"Yeah. The situation is pretty dire. All the work we do helps out a lot."

"That's what I'm counting on." She clicked at the mare, tugged on the rope, and led her back out and toward one of the pastures.

He frowned at her odd words and shook his head. No

sense in trying to figure out that particular riddle. Besides, he had bigger items on his plate. Namely lunch with Lacey.

Swiftly, he stripped his horse of the tack, slipped on a halter, and led him in the opposite direction. The sooner he released the gelding back into his pasture, the sooner he could meet up with Lacey and drive them to their first lunch together.

Thirty minutes later, he took a bite out of his turkey sandwich, his attention centered on Lacey as she sipped her soup.

On the ride over, he'd caught her peering over at him as if trying to figure out a complex puzzle. Or wondering when Mr. Hyde would make another appearance and bite her head off.

The lack of conversation thus far hadn't been uncomfortable. Just a little awkward. *Time to change that.*

"That paint mare of yours is remarkable. You trained her yourself, right?"

"For the most part. I purchased her five years ago when she was seven. She'd been a trail horse, but I thought she had more potential than that. I knew I wanted to barrel race professionally. The prices of finished barrel horses blew me away. So I changed gears and opted for a well-put-together animal that I could train." She glanced up at him. "It worked out pretty good."

"I'd say so." He took a sip of his tea. "Thinking about retiring her soon? She's getting up there a bit."

Worry clouded Lacey's eyes. "I don't have a backup mount. Don't have the money to buy one, either. Yeah, I made a decent paycheck at finals, but it's expensive to haul a trailer all over the country. Dr. Moore is a great man, but can't pay a huge salary, especially when I only work for him when he needs me." She blew out a breath. "I keep saving up my money. For another horse. For a place of my own. For another chance at the finals."

He read the fatigue and worry in her features and heard sadness in her voice. His heart broke for her dilemma. Not too long ago, he'd been in similar boots. Banking on one roping horse to get him to the championship level of the sport. His medical issues had frozen that dream and fast. He still had Noggin, his bay gelding, who'd retired his roping saddle for babysitting duties for the Humane Society farm's weanlings and yearlings last year.

The same for money. He and his brother hadn't been born with a silver spoon in their mouths, they'd worked hard. Still did. However, finances weren't nearly as much of a concern. Their father had gotten into the oil business at the right time, stepped up to CEO of a company, and passed his good fortune down to his sons in the form of a branch of their own.

"Candy is doing great, but I have no illusion that she can keep going another five years. The sport is too hard on horses."

He nodded. "True. Maybe this training job will help get you enough money to buy another horse. Nila has connections all over the horse world. Maybe she can make some inquiries."

Lacey's chin lifted as interest covered her face. "I hadn't thought of that."

"When you're ready, talk to her. She won't mind at all. Hell, she sang your praises to me."

"She did?" Lacey glanced down at her bowl and spooned another mouthful.

"Oh, yeah. Said she's lucky to have you. I agreed."

Her green eyes met his. "I'm surprised you said that. I got the feeling you didn't care for me the other day."

His gut ached with her truthful words. "It wasn't you. It was me in a shitty mood."

She tilted her head. "You didn't seem that way until I started asking questions."

"You just caught me at a bad moment is all. No worries." He kept his tone level and sincere. The last thing he wanted to do was make her feel guilty. Lacey had enough to deal with without his adding more.

"Too personal. Too fast."

She read him like a book.

He took another bite and chewed. *Honesty is always the best policy.* He considered her observation and maintained eye contact. "Maybe."

"I'm sorry," she whispered.

"Don't worry about it. Really." He reached across the table and brushed his fingers over the back of her hand. "I'm a bit protective about details of my life. That's just me. You didn't do anything wrong. I'm the one that got too gruff. My fault."

She glanced down at his hand, but didn't pull away. A second later, she looked up. "Maybe we can call this one a draw and start over?" Her beguiling smile tugged at his heartstrings.

"I'd like that." Relief washed over him.

"Me, too."

Reluctantly, he removed his touch and crunched on a potato chip. "Lots of miles driving all over the country by yourself. Don't you get tired of always being on the move?" He recalled the years he'd done just that. By the end of the season, home looked damn good.

Her earlier brightness faded. "I don't mind. Seeing the countryside makes for a nice change."

The vagueness and hesitancy reminded him of her brief conversation with her mother the night of the rodeo. He guessed that she preferred time away rather than months being a homebody. "Nila says you live on your parents' farm and help out there, too."

"Yeah. My mother works as a teacher. My father runs the farm. Tate, my brother, and his friend Ransom help out around their full-time jobs. I fill in the gaps."

He noted the way her lips tightened as she mentioned her brother and his friend. Something flashed in her eyes. *Hurt? Regret?* The emotion passed too quickly for him to really grasp.

Needing to lighten the mood and put a sparkle back into

her face, he offered up a crooked smile. "A girl that can ride like the wind, drive a tractor and wrestle hogs. Pretty damn impressive."

A coy grin appeared on her lips. "You're easily amazed."

"That's me. A simple guy."

"Simple guy? I've never met one of those." She peered up at him through her eyelashes. Not quite flirting. Not quite, but close.

"Oh, men are really simple. We have basic needs. Take care of those and we're pretty content."

She tapped her chin. "Sex, beer and a television remote?"

He chuckled. "That's a nice start."

Lacey rolled her eyes. "Start?" She pursed her lips and counted off on her fingers. "Sex. Beer. Television. There's more?"

Jonas caught her playfulness and healthy amount of mischief. "Of course there's more. If we let women think that in three steps they could have us roped and tied, we'd never hear the end of it."

"Aha. So it boils down to three categories, but men want women to think there's more to it?"

"Bingo."

She took a drink and smiled over at him. "Why do I think you're the exception to that rule?"

He shrugged. "I don't know."

"Hmm." She finished her soup and placed her spoon against the rim. "A mysterious man."

"Nah. Just a man." He soaked up her interest, the casual glances she sent his way as she tried to figure him out. The appreciative expression bolstered his self-confidence all the more.

"A good man," she answered softly.

Warmth spread through him.

The waitress dropped off the check at the table. "Whenever you're ready."

Lacey reached for it. Jonas beat her to it. "My treat."

"At least let me pay for my part."

"Nope." He smiled at her as he dug his wallet out and placed money in the small folder, including a decent tip.

"You're going to spoil me." She sighed.

Yeah, I am. Because you deserve it.

The sentiment hit home.

He refrained from sharing the thought with her, preferring to go slow, one steady step at a time.

"Which horse are you going to work with this afternoon?" she asked.

"Knight."

Her eyes widened as she sat up straight in her seat. "How's he coming along?" Her fondness for the former stallion came through loud and clear.

"Good since you diagnosed his issues. I keep a mare around when I'm working with him, and always outside. He's smart and quick. He's had some training in the past. Didn't fuss with the saddle too much. I think his trust was broken at some point. Repair that and we'll have it made. Give him a few weeks and he'll keep me on my toes."

"That's wonderful. I was worried about him ever settling down." She finished her water. "He's a great horse. I hope someone who will treat him right winds up with him."

"If I have anything to do with it," he assured her. The moment he spoke, a plan began to form. Goals lined up and shone brightly in his mind. He didn't dare utter a hint about his idea. Let it be a surprise if everything worked out the way he expected. He's sure as hell do his damnedest to make it happen.

Energy and motivation flooded him. For the first time in a while, he found something exciting to look forward to. Well, two things. Knight and Lacey.

He checked his watch, a bit eager to get back to the farm and start the ball rolling. "You ready?"

"Yeah." She wiped her hands and mouth with the napkin. "I've got to tackle Crackers this afternoon. Nila warned me she's sneaky."

"She's figured out every trick in the book to get a rider off her back. Be careful, she's not above scraping you off on a fence or in tree branches."

Lacey grinned. "She might *try*."

He noted the determination and challenge in her eyes, adding to her prettiness. Women with boldness and confidence always snared his interest and stoked his male hunger.

His pulse kicked up a notch.

"I have a feeling Crackers just met her match."

Lacey laughed, the sound a symphony to his ears.

He vowed to make it happen more often.

* * * *

Jonas stepped out of the shower and started towel-drying himself. He quickly ran the cloth over his body and lightly scrubbed it over his head before dropping it to the floor. Standing nude, he glimpsed himself in the mirror.

For a long moment, he stared, automatically seeking the many small scars from years of living. Then he dropped his gaze farther.

His sac hung lopsided to the right, as that was the only remaining testicle. He cringed at the sight and once again wondered if he should go for the prosthesis. "At least I'd look normal."

But I wouldn't feel normal. How could I?

He took in the sight in the mirror and cringed at how unnatural his sac looked. The single ball, the healed line where they'd made the cut. All a gross reminder of his cancer, his continuing battle with the disease and the resulting disfigurement that stole his confidence and put him on the defensive at the very thought of stripping down in front of anyone. Especially a woman.

How could a woman look at me, see this, and believe they're with a real man?

Simple. She couldn't.

Women wanted perfect men with perfect bodies. Sure, a

few minor marks on a man's skin might increase the rugged factor in the handsomeness category. But this... This was over the line.

His libido had crashed after the surgery and hadn't returned. While he'd jacked off a few times, he hadn't really put much effort into jumping back into the dating game. He still liked women. There was no doubt. But he feared that a woman's reaction — disgust or laughter at his expense — would kill off what self-esteem he'd managed to rekindle over time.

"Quit being such a damn, whiny fool." He purposely spoke the words in order to jolt himself out of the pitiful mood. It only helped marginally.

One thing cancer had taught him was that time could be short and fleeting. No putting off until tomorrow what could be done today, because there were no guarantees another day would come.

He reached down and cupped himself, tracing his thumb over the old incision.

Oh, how he wanted a woman to take his sac in hand and do the very same thing. To idly stroke him, to show appreciation and caring. To prove his doubts wrong. To show him that he was still worthwhile and deserving, sexy and desirable, ball or no ball.

In order for that to happen, he had to be willing to take a chance. A big one.

He needed someone special. Someone who could see past his scars. Someone who valued a man for who he was, not the package he presented.

The image of Lacey popped into his mind.

A long sigh escaped his lips.

Stop putting the cart before the horse, buddy, and take things as they fall.

With that advice, he quickly combed his hair and headed to the bedroom to get dressed.

Chapter Seven

"Lacey. Hang on a minute."

Lacey paused by the door to her truck. Sunset offered waning light to see by, enough to clearly identify Nila approaching her.

"I'm glad I caught you."

"What's up?"

"The farm is having their annual fall open house a week from Saturday. Can you be there? Not only to help with the questions about the horses, but to maybe sign autographs for your fans?"

Lacey couldn't refuse Nila anything. Not after she'd kindly given her the best job in the world out of the blue. "Sure. Want me to bring Candy along as well?"

"If you want. I'm sure the kids will love petting her."

"Okay." Lacey climbed into the seat of her truck. "I'll see you tomorrow."

"Thanks." Nila waved before turning around and heading back to the house stationed on the land for the manager to use.

As she drove, Lacey reflected on the day. Working with the horses had been grand, but not the epitome. Lunch with Jonas held that position. Unexpected and insightful, the time they spent together had flown by. She'd enjoyed watching the dimple pop in his cheek when he smiled. The lazy relaxation on his face. Even the way he'd watched her as if she magnetized him. He made her feel like something special.

Don't get your hopes up.

She recalled how long she'd pined away for Ransom only

to have her bubble burst. The scalding burn had receded into an ache with the weeks that had gone by. Her heart still bore the jagged scar.

The last piece of sunset held on to the horizon as she pulled into the driveway and parked her truck in the usual spot. She climbed out, locked the door and followed the delicious scents inside. Her stomach growled hungrily. She opted to go and eat the hot meal before tending to her horse.

The smell hit her more strongly as she stepped through the back door, making her mouth water.

"Dinner's on the table," her mother said.

"Thanks, Mom." Lacey pulled off her boots in the mudroom and made her way into the dining area. Tate and Ransom sat on one side of the table. Her mother was at one end, her father at the other. She took the remaining seat.

"You're late. Where have you been?" her father asked.

She bit back a smart-ass retort and answered civilly, "My job at the Humane Society. I thought I mentioned it to you last week." *I know I sure as hell did.* When he stared at her, she continued on. "I'm helping train some of their horses so they can be more easily adopted. It's part-time, but I love it already."

Her father chewed and swallowed.

"That's great, Lacey." Tate handed her a bowl to ladle chili into. "Right up your alley, too."

She offered up a smile to her brother. Many times he'd taken the role her father should have filled, showing her support and tossing in praise. She didn't begrudge him all the attention from their father. She couldn't. It wasn't Tate's fault their father favored him and basically ignored her.

"The farm manager even asked me this evening to be a guest at their fall open house a week from Saturday. She wants me to bring Candy along and sign autographs." She spooned up a bite of chili and blew on the steaming food.

"A week from Saturday? That's Tate's next home game," her mother pointed out.

Lacey put the spoon in her mouth and took her time

before answering. "This is a big event for the Humane Society. Their meet and greet time with the public to help get some horses adopted. I need to be there for them." She glanced from her mother over to Tate. "I'm sorry."

"No problem. I'm sure you've seen plenty of football games over the years." Ransom's voice contained acceptance instead of condemnation. Thank goodness.

She had. For almost as long as she could remember, Tate had started in the youth programs. Once Ransom had joined the family, it seemed every Friday night she'd found herself at a game, no matter the distance or the temperature.

"Looks like you could actually attend a game now and again and show support for your brother." Her father's voice carried over like a weighted drone about to crash.

"Dad." Tate turned to his father with a stormy expression.

"Dan," Helen gasped.

Lacey glared at him. *Support for Tate? What about support for me?* He hadn't attended a rodeo since she was sixteen and able to drive herself.

She bit her tongue but not hard enough. "This is important for more than just me. Since I seem to be the black sheep of the family, I suppose you can't understand."

Tate, Ransom and her mother glanced from her, to her father, and back to her again.

"I think it's a great cause, dear. You'll be a hit." Helen smiled tightly.

"Exactly," Tate seconded.

"The farm is lucky to have you as a spokeswoman. You'll do great." Ransom's praise and support caused a dull pain in the region of her heart.

She read a variety of emotions in their expressions. Concern. Encouragement. Cheer. And a hint of fear from her mother.

"Do whatever you want. It's not like you have much to do with this family anymore, anyway," her father snapped out, ire showing in his clenched jaws.

She narrowed her eyes. "I'm pulling my own weight.

Thank you very much."

"Bullshit. The day you pull your own weight is the day your mother doesn't have to come home from a long day at work and slave away to put dinner on the table all by herself."

It wouldn't kill you to help her.

"That's enough, Dan," Helen scolded. "She works as hard as or harder than the rest of us. Leave her alone."

Tate opened his mouth but Helen shook her head. "That's enough on that topic. Let's just have a family meal in peace."

Annoyance and anger flashed in her father's eyes. At least he kept his mouth shut. For now. No telling how long that might last.

Lacey pulled on all her restraint to hold back those words. She slowly stood up, lifted her chin, and raked the others with her eyes. "Excuse me. I have a horse to see to." As regally as she could, she walked out of the room, slipped her boots back on and strode out of the door.

Several minutes later, she stood brushing Candy, using the methodical strokes to release her tension and ebb her temper.

"You didn't eat," Tate pointed out. "Mom fixed your meal to go." He held up a plastic bag filled with a couple of containers.

Lacey spared him a glance. "Not hungry."

He sighed and stepped closer. "He's a jerk at times, Lacey. You know that."

She tossed the brush into a bucket and picked up a finishing cloth. "I'm sick of his outdated attitude toward women."

"I know."

She ran her hands over Candy's shiny hide. "I don't get it, Tate. I've tried everything to make that man happy and earn his attention and respect. Nothing works. The only time he gave me a compliment was when I baked a pie for his birthday years ago."

"You know he's old-fashioned in his beliefs. Hell, if he

could afford it, he would have Mom staying at home, too. He was raised that way. Look at our grandparents, what he learned from them."

She sighed. Her paternal grandmother had always embodied the idea of women's work. Her grandmother never took a job outside the home, moved straight from her parents' house to live with her husband. She baked, raised kids and did all the good things a homemaker was supposed to do. To her dying day her grandmother still worked hard to take care of her husband and the house while he tended to spend more time in front of the television than anywhere else. Lacey couldn't recall a time when her grandfather offered once to help his wife do a single thing he deemed as women's work. He'd passed soon after.

All the things Lacey rebuffed.

She didn't mind housework. It was the domineering attitude of a man ruling the roost with an iron fist that didn't sit well. She had a fine mind and intended to use it. In whatever career she chose. *Well away from this place.*

Tate's comment replayed through her mind. "He's never forgiven me for following the rodeo circuit?"

"That's what Ransom and I think. We've never asked, but, if you look at the evidence, it makes sense. He expects women to do one thing, and that's to stay home and take care of a family."

She snorted as a fresh wave of irritation shot through her. "Nice to know that I'm a failure because I'm a modern woman with dreams of my own."

Tate's lips thinned. "That's not true and you know it. The rest of us don't feel the same as him. We're proud of you."

His soft voice encased her in a calm embrace — something she'd craved from her father since she was a young child and had never received.

"Thanks." She met his gaze. "Are you upset that I've not been to your football games this year? It's not because I don't want to be there for you."

He leaned against the wall of the stall and stared at her.

"Hell, Lacey. I know that. You can't help it if your races fall on the weekends as well."

She nodded once, reassured. "I can't do both, Tate. And barrel racing is the key to my future. My freedom." She whispered the final phrase.

Tate regained his feet and walked over. "I know that, sis. You have a right to your own life and happiness. No matter what anyone else might think." He handed her the bag and pulled her into a hug.

She squeezed him tight and battled back tears. "Thanks." Pulling away, she wiped at the moisture. "I don't know what I'd do without you."

He grinned down at her. "You'd figure out something. You've always been pretty damn resourceful."

She snorted. "Let's not find out, okay?"

"Yeah, I agree." He ruffled her hair. "If things get too tough, let me know. I'll help you out all I can."

Her heart buoyed at his words. As much as she needed to do this on her own, she appreciated his offer and knew it to be true. "*If* I need help, I'll keep you in mind. Thanks, Tate."

"That's what big brothers are for. Now, sit down and eat before your dinner gets cold."

"Yes, sir." She plopped down on a nearby bale of straw, smiling when Tate sat beside her.

Chapter Eight

Lacey went through the motions of grooming a tall, leggy, bay thoroughbred gelding with practiced ease. The methodical strokes lured her mind to wander. It didn't go far, stopping at the night before.

Could Tate and Ransom be right? The reason I don't stack up in Dad's eyes is because I'm a modern woman who refuses to sit around waiting for a man to order me around?

She considered her mother and shook her head. Her mother worked outside the home. Granted, as a teacher, a traditionally female-dominated field. Busy, determined and seemingly happy, her mother came home, fixed dinner and doted on her family before spending the evening grading papers. Nowhere could Lacey recall her father laying into her mother like he did her. They rarely fought, at least not in front of Lacey.

If the problem stemmed from the way her father had been raised, she was doomed. Attitudes didn't change without tons of motivation and attention. Her father wouldn't come close. Most likely he'd carry the very same sentiment toward her to his grave.

The realization slumped her shoulders all the more as she changed sides on the horse.

Tate had cited their grandfather being the same way. She barely remembered the couple. The only true memory she carried revolved around Christmas years ago. Her grandmother had held court in the kitchen, baking, cooking and cleaning. No men had ventured into the room for long, or offered to do more than place their dirty plates in the sink. Lacey pulled on what she recalled about that particular generation and found the separation of men's and women's tasks to be common at that time. Women stayed home, raised the kids, kept the house. The men held jobs.

Boy, have times changed. Back then, obviously, a family could live on one income. Not so anymore.

The writing on the wall only emphasized how badly she needed to get her feet solidly under her and find a way to fly the coop.

Which brought her back to her current situation. She longed for a place of her own, to spread her wings and live life on her own terms. Barrel racing fired up her blood. The joy of speeding around the arena in an attempt to beat the clock got her heart pumping each and every time. The long miles between rodeos grew monotonous at times, though they provided her the opportunity to see the country and get away from the stress of living at home.

If she wanted to pursue the career for the long haul, she needed another mount. Candy possessed the will and talent. Unfortunately, age crept up and would, at some point, become an issue. Before that happened, she needed to have another horse, a home with some acreage to keep them and enough money to care for them and herself without having to resort to a soup line.

Lacey sighed at the obstacles between her and her dream. Mountainous barriers that refused to budge.

How am I supposed to save enough money to buy a place of my own when I'm basically holding down three part-time jobs and still struggling?

The million-dollar question.

The work kept her busy, too busy at times, but didn't fill her bank account near fast enough.

Lately, she'd tossed around the idea of applying for normal jobs in town. Nine to five stuff with the flexibility to allow her to take extra time off when the rodeos lasted longer than a weekend. Great in idea. If only the small town offered open positions with decent pay, nice benefits and a bit of understanding on time worked. Those jobs simply didn't exist in a town of less than three hundred. Farming ruled. Kids wanting more than working their butts off for a lifetime on the hard land attended the local college a couple of towns over, then migrated to another location, one that could fulfill their potential and dreams. Rarely did those people return.

Farm life had fallen out of style years ago. Too hard. Too little money. No vacation or down days or sick time. The endless struggle turned most people off and sent them searching elsewhere. Elderly farms, falling into disrepair, were eventually sold off when the owners passed as the children wanted no part of the back-breaking work they'd tasted as a youngster.

Lacey guessed she was an exception to the general rule. She didn't mind the long hours or labor-intensive work. She loved being outside, watching things grow and spending every day as part of nature.

If she could just find a happy medium or catch a break, she could make something of herself. *I just know it.*

She tossed the brush into a bucket, grabbed a saddle blanket off the rack and placed it on the gelding's back. The saddle followed, as did the bridle. Ready to go, she hauled herself onto the tall animal, gathered the reins and turned him toward the exit and sunshine on the crisp fall day. Immediately, she tightened her grip and checked him as he tried to bound away. He danced for a few paces before settling down enough to listen to her cues. Gradually, she eased the pressure on his mouth, allowing him to stretch his neck. "Let's try this again. Slowly."

She released a breath when he complied without any more difficulties. "Much better."

As she walked by a corral, she found Knight playing. He shook his head, sending his mane all which directions, and trotted over, sporting his newly acquired unkempt hairdo.

She smiled. "Well, hello, Knight. You're looking good today."

He whinnied, half turned, then shot off like a rabbit,

galloping around the pen.

Damn, he's beautiful.

The black hide shone in the light, emphasizing the contrast of sparkling white on his face and the large, uneven spot extending from his chest and down his stomach. Deep, gorgeous blue eyes full of intelligence added to the picture, setting him heads and tails apart from most horses in her opinion. Not only had his coloring snared her attention, the strong build, powerful hindquarters and perfect conformation drew her focus from a cowgirl's point of view. He'd been put together just right for any Western sport, including barrel racing.

She looked at him with longing. *He could be my future.*

Reality checked her idealistic thoughts.

The amount of time Jonas needed to spend with Knight would result in a jacked-up price. Definitely worth the cost, yes, but it would put the grand horse out of her range. That was just to get him consistently ridable. Hours of practice would have to follow in order to turn him into a barrel horse. They weren't made in a day, after all. Time, patience and attention to fine details made the best barrel horses. Considering where Knight had started, half a calendar year might fly by before he could potentially step into an arena. If ever.

If only she had the money to buy him, the place to board him and the time to teach him the pattern. If only she could catch that pesky leprechaun and make him show her the gold at the end of the rainbow.

Since neither were in the cards, she refused to get her hopes up. Miracles were created rather than just appearing spontaneously. Too bad she wasn't lucky enough to have either.

Life happened. She reacted and kept plodding along. Not much else to do but cowgirl up.

Moping around doesn't fix a damn thing and will only give me a headache in the process.

She clicked her tongue and nudged the gelding to the far

paddock for a workout.

* * * *

Jonas tightened the cinch on Bridget, tied the ends, and pulled himself into the saddle. He scanned the area and found Lacey riding a pretty, gray Arabian mare with a lovely dished face and a flowing trot. He appreciated the sight as they came together in a natural grace few riders reached, especially in less than a week.

He nudged Bridget with his heels, lifted the reins and pointed her toward the entrance to the fence line near where Lacey worked.

She made another circle, glanced up and headed his direction at a slow lope. As she approached, she slowed the mare and finally pulled her to a halt a couple of feet from where Jonas waited. "What's up?"

He studied her face, noting lines of fatigue and circles under her eyes. Yesterday she'd been bright. Today she appeared worn out and sleep-deprived. *What in the hell happened after we parted ways yesterday?* Worry ate at him. "I was going to ride along the dirt road for a bit, get her used to any traffic that might pass by. Want to come along?"

The fresh scent of vanilla wafted in the breeze. He'd forgotten the fragrance from when he'd seen her at the rodeo. Whether her shampoo, soap, or perfume, the aroma complemented her and tickled his hunger.

Her gaze lowered to the mare before meeting his eyes again. "Sure. I imagine she's ready to go when someone wants her. Might as well do something a bit different today. Meet you at the gate." She clicked her tongue and made a beeline for the only gate in the field.

He considered trying to get to the root of the frown on her face, then opted to keep to the basics. Light and easy. Delving too deep too fast made a recipe for disaster. Maybe she'd relax around him and open up. *Only one way to find out.*

A couple of minutes later, she caught up with him as he crossed from the gravel drive onto the old dirt road that bordered the back section of the immense farm.

He nodded at the mare. "She's doing great."

Lacey petted the horse's neck. "Angel is just that. An angel. Calm. Elegant. Refined. I could easily see her in an Arabian costume class."

The image of Lacey dressed in silky layers while riding the pretty gray horse lodged in his mind and promised to stay. "Definitely." The word came out a bit gruff. He cleared his throat. "She's too small to carry a big rider, though. You're perfect for her."

A sad smile hovered over Lacey's lips. "If trail riding or showing was it, yeah, she'd be perfect. She lacks the pep to be a barrel horse."

He hadn't missed the way she'd stared at Knight earlier, as if picturing herself in the saddle. Obvious interest radiated from her every time she neared the former stallion. Hell, he'd caught her sneaking him carrots before getting to work this morning. The horse had stolen her heart that first day.

Just as she'd made a big indentation on Jonas' as she'd smoothly stepped into a boxed-in death trap in order to soothe a frightened stud that probably hadn't felt human hands for a couple of years.

Through working with Knight, Jonas knew the animal had had a good amount of training at some point in his life. Thus far, he'd tried Knight on a rope hackamore and found the fit acceptable to both him and Knight. Most riders preferred a bit when it came to speed events, though. Jonas didn't think one outdid the other. It all boiled down to the horse and the rider. He'd try a snaffle bit next and see what that gained. The gelding already responded to the basic cues, though he tended to want to run at the least touch of a heel.

"That thoroughbred gelding I rode earlier had pep. Plenty of it. Probably too much to stop on a dime and swing around a barrel."

"Those retired thoroughbreds off the track tend to have that issue. They have one speed — run like the hounds of hell are on their heels."

Lacey chuckled. "They come pre-programmed, huh?"

"Oh yeah. Takes a while to get them to understand we don't have to get everywhere in less than five seconds. They tend to do great once they figure that part out."

"You've worked with many of those?"

He settled into their conversation, pleased with her curiosity and the topic at hand. "A few. There are rescues that specialize in them. We just take whatever comes our way. Now and again we'll get one. Most are pretty high-strung and rarely adopt out very easy without tons of re-training."

Lacey nodded. "Makes sense." She glanced ahead. "It's sad. I always both loved and hated coming here with Dr. Moore. So many animals in such need. The horses arriving with extreme neglect and abuse turn my stomach. I don't think I could work with that every day and still give a fig about the human population in general."

"I agree." He'd seen his fair share helping out when the new ones arrived. Anger became an understatement when he glimpsed the condition of some of those poor animals. None of them deserved such. He could only imagine the horrors they'd suffered along the way. "At least once they make it here, they'll have a home for life. Either here or through adoption."

She turned toward him. "How do you know their new home is always on the up and up?"

"Simple. Nila. She keeps track of every single horse like they're her babies. I'm sure she feels that way. She makes home visits unannounced. She makes the owners keep updated contact information. If they move, she gets another rescue to check up on them. Owners are told about this ahead of time and consent with signing the adoption papers. If they're responsible, they have nothing to hide."

"Has she ever found them not to be?" Lacey rested her

right hand on her thigh, rolling with the motion of the horse under her.

"A time or two. She contacted the authorities, hauled in a horse trailer and confiscated the animal on the spot. In both cases, the owners weren't happy and tried to get ugly, but a copy of the contract, the cops, a vet and the Humane Society lawyer changed their minds real quick."

"Wow. Nila is special lady. Those horses need a champion and she's a great one." She rode in silence for a few paces. "My best friend on the circuit works at a thoroughbred farm in Kentucky. She talks about how pampered those horses are. I can't imagine how so many hopes and dreams ends up abandoned in a field and left to starve."

"Industry-wide problem. Hell, it's an issue with all animals." He neck-reined the mare to the right in order to take another side road.

Lacey kept abreast.

"Which one is your friend?" He didn't keep up with barrel racing much, but he'd watched a few runs courtesy of Nila and the other farm workers, who always cheered Lacey on.

"Trinity." Lacey grinned. "You'd probably recognize the horse instead of her. Tall, gray, thoroughbred-quarter horse cross that goes by the name of Legacy."

"No kidding?" He blinked over at her. "The son of Another Victory Gallop?"

"That's him." Lacey perked up. "He's a handful. Gorgeous. Big. Strong. In love with Candy." She giggled.

He shook his head in amazement. "Now that's some horseflesh."

"Yep." Lacey adjusted the reins in her hand. "Trinity offered to let me breed Candy to Legacy for free."

"Are you going to do it?"

"Yeah. That's one expensive stud fee that I couldn't pay. I'm not about to shun an offer like that."

He smiled. "Makes you wonder what that baby would look like."

She peered over at him with a grin that brightened her

features. "Probably like its mother, but carry his father's nasty attitude."

"Now that's a combination." Jonas chuckled. "I can just see you trying to coax him into doing what you want. Carrots and all."

She shrugged. "Hey, they work."

"True."

They came to another junction. Jonas turned his horse around, maintaining the lazy pace. He watched Lacey in the saddle and knew she'd been born to ride. She added something to the short trail ride. Spunk. Fun. Entertainment. He knew he'd think of her every time he took this particular route and wish she rode at his side.

She'd seemed to enjoy lunch before. No kiss, no cuddling, but the smile on her face had proved payment enough. He craved that breath of fresh air once again. Replace the sadness and worry with happiness.

I'll just have to make it happen. Starting with today.

"Want to do lunch with me?" He held his breath as he waited for her answer.

She turned to look at him while seeming to carefully consider the request, judging by her tightening lips and lowered gaze.

As the silence dragged on, his hopes plummeted. He wanted to kick his own ass for being so impulsive and making a fool of himself. Just as he opened his mouth to fluff off the suggestion, he caught a glimpse of her face.

A soft smile appeared on her lips as she met his eyes. "Yeah. I'd like that."

His heart buoyed. "I'm not the world's greatest cook, but I can throw together a mean grilled cheese sandwich."

"I happen to like those."

* * * *

Lacey bit down into her hot sandwich, chewed, and closed her eyes. "You're right. You do make a mean grilled cheese."

Jonas grinned. "Not much of a great talent, but I claim it."

She noticed the small dimple in his left cheek that popped out when he smiled. Boyish, cute and added to his appeal.

When he'd asked her to lunch, she hadn't been sure. Having learned that Ransom had found the girl for him and thought of marriage still unsettled her. She'd initially thought to turn Jonas down, but one glimpse of his hopeful face and she'd reconsidered. *After all, it's not like I'm getting any younger or Ransom will suddenly change his mind.* Besides, she'd had a great time with him at the café. Relaxed. Friendly. She'd thought about a kiss at the end then balked at the last minute. The timing hadn't been quite right. Today? Only time would tell. Certainly, things were looking good so far.

As she sat in his small kitchen, she found herself having a pleasant afternoon. Surprising, refreshing and just what the doctor ordered. Delicious food. Nice company. *Things just might be looking up.*

She took another bite and chewed. "I should make you some of my special chicken and vegetable soup. It goes perfectly with hot ham and cheese. Add in a homemade pie and you have a fall meal that'll leave you stuffed and satisfied."

His eyes flashed. Whether in reference to the meal or his mind slipping into the gutter, she didn't know. Nor did she care. Either one worked for the moment.

"You name the time. I'll fix the sandwiches. We'll make it happen." He crunched a potato chip. "I'll do just about anything for homemade pie." He waggled his eyebrows.

She grinned mischievously and lowered her voice to a sultry tone. "Be careful. Giving a girl that kind of ammo can be dangerous."

He met her gaze steadily with a hint of amusement and challenge. "I like to live dangerously."

She cocked an eyebrow. "Oh, really?"

"Yeah." Jonas rested his elbows on the table. "I'll take my chances."

Her stomach somersaulted. The intensity in his expression stole her breath. The way he stared at her roused her self-confidence and made her feel beautiful. As if she had the power to hang the sun in the sky each morning. A rarity and something she vowed to treasure as she memorized the moment.

He scooted his chair closer and cupped her cheek with one hand.

She stared into his deep, smoky eyes as he leaned in. Instinctively, she met him halfway, let her eyelids drop closed, and received the first brush of his lips with sweet delight.

His first contact, light as butterfly wings, whetted her desire for more. She didn't have long to wait. The second pass lasted longer than the first. A clinging kiss that asked for nothing more than a moment in time to share. So gentle. So sensitive. Her heart skipped a beat.

Jonas rubbed her cheek with his thumb, catching her attention. She opened her eyes and found him peering directly into her soul. The smile on his face softened the intensity in his gaze, making for a spicy combination which tugged on Lacey's heartstrings.

"Nice. Very nice," she whispered.

"That's just a sample." He kissed her again, this time with tender passion. Their lips adjusted and clung, molded and fit. He broke off long enough to suck her bottom lip and lick the seam before sitting back once more.

"Wow." She blinked at him in amazement.

Having had her heart set on Ransom for so long, she'd never considered another man could move her like Jonas just had. His laid-back demeanor, the care he showed the horses, even his easygoing nature added to the allure of his ripped body. Yet she'd never expected the zing of electricity in such a gentle kiss. Filled with pleasure, curiosity and want, Lacey savored the moment while smiling coyly at Jonas.

He grinned. "Nice to know I haven't lost my touch."

His reply prodded her to delve further. "I'd say not, though I might not be the best judge of kissing in the land." She ran her fingers over his forearm. "Been out of the kissing game long?"

He drew in a deep breath and blew it out. Tension flashed across his features before ebbing slightly. Pain radiated with those apparent memories.

Lacey needed to soothe it all away and replace the frown with another addictive, teasing grin. She rubbed her nose against his. "Maybe we can get back up to speed. Together."

He stared at her for a long moment. "I'd like that."

"Me too." She watched him from under her lashes as she picked up her sandwich and took another bite.

He did the same, eating until he'd finished the meal entirely and emptied his glass. "You've got a rodeo this weekend?"

"Yes. Oklahoma City. Friday and Saturday night."

"Then come home and crash on Sunday?"

I wish. Lacey shook her head. "I'll have to catch up on work at home. Thought about putting in some hours at the Humane Society farm too."

He nodded. "Think you can get away Monday afternoon?"

She stilled. "Probably. Why?"

"I'd like to take you out to eat somewhere nice, then maybe we can catch a matinee or do something fun after that. Whatever you'd like."

Lacey's troubles fell away. "That would be great."

He rewarded her with a nice smile, complete with dimples.

Oddly enough, Ransom paled in comparison. *Definitely an improvement and step in the right direction.*

Chapter Nine

Monday afternoon came around fairly quickly. After a half-day's work, Jonas had cleaned up, picked up Lacey from the farm and taken her to one of the small cafeterias for lunch. They'd eaten in relative silence, both too hungry to say much. Now, with their stomachs full, he ushered her along in order to catch the latest movie at the theater.

Jonas opened the door of the cafeteria, letting Lacey out in front of him. "I'm stuffed."

"So am I." She smiled up at him, then twisted as if she'd caught a glimpse of someone she knew.

Two men sauntered over. One resembled Lacey enough to clue him in. The other, while of the same build, had slightly different facial features.

The first one greeted them. "Now this is a surprise."

The second followed. "Hey, Lacey. Who's the new guy?"

Lacey smiled. "Jonas. He's the head horse trainer at the Humane Society farm." She turned her gaze on Jonas then back to the other two men. "Jonas. This is my brother Tate and my next best thing to a brother Ransom." She gestured to each in turn.

Jonas held out his hand. "Nice to meet you." After shaking, he dropped his hand back to his side, still appraising them. "You've got one hell of a sister."

Tate arched his eyebrow. "You better be talking about her talent with horses."

"That too." Jonas read Tate's protective stance as well as the curiosity that flashed through his eyes. Unless he missed his guess, Lacey hadn't mentioned him in the least. Not surprising, considering they were more coworkers than boyfriend-girlfriend. For right now.

Lacey smacked him lightly on the arm. "Quit trying to yank their chains. We've just started dating. Nothing serious yet."

Jonas smirked at the other guys. "As you can see, she can take care of herself. No use in debating whether to fight her battles. Trust me, I'm on the winning side. Beating the shit out of me won't change my mind, either."

Ransom rubbed his forehead, the earlier tension ebbing from his face.

The corners of Tate's lips curled up. "Spoken like you've been there."

Jonas shrugged. "Maybe a time or two." He preferred to lighten the conversation instead of getting into a pissing contest with her brothers. The last thing he wanted was to put Lacey on the defensive because her family didn't approve. She had enough on her plate already. "Those girls hit damn hard, too," he added with a rueful grin.

The guys chuckled.

"You're smart. I'll give you that." Tate gave a quick nod. "Someone needs to lasso her in. Maybe you're the guy to do so." He stared at Jonas as if measuring him for the task.

Jonas shrugged. "I'd rather let her run free and be happy," he answered truthfully, catching a glimpse of Lacey's grin at his comment.

"See why I like this guy?" Lacey asked.

Ransom nodded. "Yeah."

Tate ruffled her hair before turning back to Jonas. "Good to meet you. Since she hadn't said a word about dating, this is a surprise. A good one."

Jonas gave a small nod in acknowledgment. "Sorry to rush, but we've got tickets to the show. If we don't get moving, we'll be late."

"I want to get good seats," Lacey added.

She didn't seem too tense about the situation, but Jonas knew they both wanted to avoid any embarrassing questions about a relationship that was in its infancy.

"Bring him around sometime, Lacey," Tate said.

"Yeah. Definitely. I'm sure the whole family would like to know more about him." Ransom eyed Lacey with a steely gaze.

Jonas bristled, stepping forward enough to place himself between Ransom and Lacey.

Lacey grasped his hand in hers, took a stride farther down the street and tugged at him. "We've got to get going or we'll miss the start of the show. Bye, guys. Catch you later."

Jonas studied them for a second longer before walking abreast of Lacey. Protectiveness washed over him as he recalled the somewhat stiff reception from the men.

"Don't let them get to you. We just took them unawares is all."

"I'd say they would like nothing more than to wrap you in a carpet and haul you off to the nearest convent." Jonas heard his grumbly tone and blew out a breath. "Sorry."

She squeezed his hand. "No worries. If they didn't like you, they would have said so. As it was, I think you gained their respect by standing up to them and answering the way you did."

"The only person's respect I'm interested in earning is yours."

"You already have it." She glanced up at him with a soft grin. "I mean it. There's no other man I would consider walking down the street with like this. In a small town, people talk."

Concern eked into his happy jaunt with her. "Are you worried about the gossip?"

She stopped and spun to face him. "Not at all. Let the tongues wag. If people have nothing better to do than to spread rumors about me, then they live a pretty pitiful life."

He grinned down at her sassiness. "Unlike us, huh?"

"Exactly." She started moving again, her chin high in the air. A royal queen couldn't have done it any better.

He found her view refreshing and delightful. In the past, women had wanted to show him off, thinking others would become jealous of their catch. He hated that. Being put on display like a prize stud never sat well. Instead, he preferred to go about his way like a normal person. Out of the spotlight and down to earth. Nothing extravagant. No big scenes. Just a couple out for a stroll on a decent fall day.

Just like right now with Lacey. He hadn't even considered what other people would do or say. It simply didn't matter.

"Have you thought about what you wanted to do in the future? Move away? Join the ranks of the nine-to-fivers?"

She seemed to ponder his question for a long moment. "All I've ever wanted to do is barrel race and work with animals. Barrel race, especially. If I can just make it to the top levels and stay there, I can focus on it full time."

He heard the longing in her voice, the determination, along with a hint of exasperation. "Following the rodeo circuit is a hard life." He'd been there, done that. Endless miles of travel just to compete where a hundredth of a second could mean the difference between a paycheck or none.

"I don't mind. Since I've been chained to the farm all my life, getting out and seeing the country is almost a vacation for me." She shrugged. "It's all in what you want out of life, I guess." A few more steps passed before she turned back to him. "You weren't always a horse trainer. So, what's the path that brought you here and where do you want to go?"

"Like you, I was raised on a ranch. As you already know, my brother and I used to rope at rodeos. It was more of a hobby than a career." He knew that now, anyway. Back then, he'd truly thought he could make it to the top of the leader board and stay there. His injury and illness had cleared up that line of thought. "My father groomed us both to follow him in the oil business. Jason is more into the business than I am. He's happier dealing with companies, stocks and contracts. I drifted back toward my roots. Horses." He looked both ways before leading Lacey across a small intersection. "That's where my future lies. I'm pretty damn happy where I'm at."

"Wow." She shook her head. "An oil tycoon. I would have never guessed."

He snorted. "Not even close to being a tycoon. More like a middleman. There's a bit of meat left on the bone by the time we get involved. Not as much as you'd think, though." He spoke the truth, but didn't bother to mention that when you took that margin and multiplied it by the numbers of barrels that they sold in a year, that sum grew exponentially. Never would he consider himself filthy rich. More like comfortable. Really comfortable. He could easily subsist on the salary from the Humane Society and not worry about any large purchases that might come down the pike. Enough existed in savings and kept coming in to support him for probably the rest of his life if he was careful.

He glanced down at Lacey, trying to read her face. Some women had, in the past, latched onto him because of his money. Long ago, he'd learned to keep his mouth shut in that department. With Lacey, he found himself warring between telling her the truth and withholding certain details that might make her uncomfortable. He couldn't see her as a gold digger. She worked too long and hard to just throw up her hands, plop down on the couch and let others wait on her hand and foot. However, he could see her becoming a bit self-conscious at the difference in wealth between them. Her clothes were clean but worn, her truck more than a decade old and probably had more miles than it should have. Though she carried herself proudly, he understood she had learned to make do with what she had from an early age. He respected her all the more for that.

"It must be interesting to see all the different trails that you've been down. From businessman to cowboy to horse trainer. Worlds apart." Her voice carried interest and fascination.

"You could say that." He grinned reluctantly. "They have one thing in common."

"What's that?"

"Make that two things. Hard work and a willingness to get dirty."

The corners of her mouth curled up. "The story of my life, too."

"Yep." He stopped at the entrance to the theater, held the door open for Lacey, and they presented their tickets to the hostess. "Did you want anything to snack on or drink?"

"No thanks." She rubbed her stomach. "I'm way too full from lunch."

"Okay then. Let's see if we can find some good seats."

"Yeah. I want to be close enough to see the hero's butt in a bird's eye view."

He chuckled. "You have a thing for a guy's ass."

She blinked innocently up at him. "True. Just another reason I like you."

He shook his head, absorbed the compliment and led her into the theater. She found seats toward the front and sat down. He checked his watch and settled in. "Since we're on the topic, do you want to farm on the side, or just barrel race?"

She turned to peer at him. "I'd love to raise horses. Well, a handful of barrel racing horses. With all the overpopulation issues, I refuse to add to the problem."

"So you'd train full-time and race full-time?" He didn't think her dream was that far out of reach. She had her mare, who could easily be bred, then Lacey could start raising the next generation of athletic equines. She'd mentioned that her barrel racing friend had offered a free breeding to the crossbred son of Another Victory Gallop. That would be a damn fine start indeed.

"I'm not sure." She pursed her lips as if in thought. "I'd have to have someone at home to care for the horses while I'm on the road. So unless I can find a helper, I'll just have to do one or the other." She sighed. "That's getting way ahead of myself, though. First I have to find a place to buy, one that I can actually afford and is suited for horses. Not to mention get a backup mount. That's near the top of the to-do list. There's the price of hay. Feed. Vet care. The list goes on and on."

Jonas bit his tongue. He'd approached Nila and put the money down for Knight already. The gelding would be a gift for Lacey, if Jonas could get the horse calmed down enough to accept a rider under some pretty stressful conditions—such as an arena filled with loud fans, lights and a booming voice behind the mic. "You've been looking around, right?"

She nodded almost sadly. "Nothing really suits that I can afford."

He opened his mouth then shut it. This wasn't the time to say anything about his plans. Let him spend some time with Knight and make sure it would be a fit before getting her hopes up.

"Don't give up. Things have a way of working themselves out." He patted her hand on the armrest between them.

"An optimist, huh?" Her teasing grin nearly stole his breath.

"Not always. But, on this, I have a good feeling." He smiled then said no more as the lights went out in the theater.

Chapter Ten

Jonas checked the trailer gate once more, then knocked on the metal. The truck engine roared and pulled ahead. Bridget was on her way to a new home and a pampered life where she would be loved and cared for well. He'd interviewed the couple himself and found them to be sincere and devoted. They'd connected with the mare right away and couldn't wait to get her and the other gelding they'd adopted home so they could start enjoying trail rides.

Happy at the outcome and seeing his work paying off, Jonas smiled and waved before starting back toward the main barn, only to pause as he caught a glimpse of Lacey.

She stood next to Candy, holding the mare while patiently letting the kids pet her barrel horse. Most sporting equines would be too high-strung for such treatment, but not Candy. She just swished her tail at flies as if this regal attention occurred every day.

Lacey smiled at one of the little girls before leaning closer and laughing. She radiated beauty, grace and happiness. Even dressed in old jeans, scuffed cowboy boots and an oversized flannel shirt, she took his breath away.

All morning, she'd been on exhibit and in demand. Not only had she signed autographs and spoken with her fans, but she'd found time to direct potential adopters to horses suited to their individual needs. The respect she garnered showed in how the adults listened and even changed their minds, looking at another horse in new light.

He'd taken his fair share of questions, certainly. Most people listened. Those who didn't he'd directed to Nila or Lacey, figuring another opinion might do the trick.

The endless lines of interested parties surprised him. He'd never expected so many to attend, let alone seriously inquire about adopting. A welcome relief, as the farm remained at capacity until some of the animals found new homes.

Nila hurried by, waving as she passed. She'd been hard-pressed to keep up with all the adoption contracts and questions. Judging by the wide smile on her face, she didn't mind at all.

He checked his watch. After two. None of them had taken lunch and he highly doubted Lacey had sat down long enough even to take a drink of water or a short break. Thirsty, and knowing Lacey had to be as well, he raked the grounds with his gaze, found a vendor, and made a beeline that direction.

A few minutes later, he juggled two ice cream cones and a plastic sack with three bottles of soda. Lacey still stood next to Candy, though the crowd had dissipated for the moment.

She turned, her gaze landed on him, and a slow smile appeared on her face. "What do you have?"

He closed the gap between them, handed her a cone and lifted the bag higher in the air. "I figured you'd be thirsty. Probably hungry."

She licked the treat. "So you brought dessert?"

Jonas shrugged. "Sounded pretty good to me." He took a bite out of his own and delighted in the taste. "Definitely hits the spot."

"Yep." She tugged at the bag, peeked in and drew out one of the bottles. "You're a godsend." Her eyebrows furrowed as she stared at the lid in frustration.

He chuckled. "I'll take the cap if you just hold onto the bottle."

"Okay." A second later, she tipped it up and took a long drink. "Much better." She delved into the bag once more, pulled another out, and held it as he unscrewed the top.

"Thanks." He drank thirstily and glanced around the

large area. "Pretty damn busy today."

"Oh, yeah. I couldn't believe it. But it's good for the animals. The more people see them, the more likely they are to find homes." She worked more on her ice cream.

He did as well, trying to eat fast enough to prevent it from melting under the afternoon sun. Though the temperature hovered in the comfortable range, lines of white liquid dripped down the sides of the cone.

By the time he'd finished, Lacey crunched on her final portion and sighed happily. "I think I'll live now."

"Was there a question otherwise?" He grinned at the spark of mischief on her pretty face.

"Maybe. It was getting close." She took another long drink and wiped at her forehead.

Jonas noticed Nila approaching. "I saved a soda for you." He handed her the container.

Nila opened it and took a swig. "Thanks. I needed that." She raked the area and shook her head. "Talk about a circus. Never seen this many people at an open house. It's got to be because of you, Lacey."

"I doubt it. I just think the word got around better. That or people are in the market for horses," Lacey replied.

"We've adopted out six so far today. Add in a small herd of ducks, a couple of geese, all the chickens and a couple of the donkeys, and I'd say this is the best adoption day ever."

"Excuse me. I was wondering about one of your horses." A tall man wearing typical Western gear, including a cowboy hat, sauntered up. He fit the bill for a working cowboy. Jonas had been one long enough—and been around plenty more—to recognize the breed.

"Which one?" Nila asked.

"That black paint gelding in the round pen next to the pole barn. He's a beauty."

Nila smiled. "Yes, he is. I'm sorry, but he's already spoken for."

Jonas noticed the widening of Lacey's eyes along with the flash of regret. She quickly masked her reaction, but not before he read her clearly.

"Well, damn. He'd make one hell of a roping horse." The guy bumped his hat back on his head.

"Possibly, but he's got a long ways to go," Jonas broke in. "He just came off the range. He's prone to panic attacks when left alone or when stalled."

The man sighed. "Waste of good horseflesh."

"Maybe you'd be interested in another horse? We have Trusty, this buckskin gelding that might work..." Nila led the man toward the southern paddock.

Lacey turned to him. "Did you know Knight had been spoken for?"

He considered how to answer for a couple of beats while sipping his soda. "Yeah. Nila mentioned that to me a couple of days ago. Said he'd stay here and remain in the training program until I had a chance to get him much more rider friendly."

"Oh." Lacey glanced over at Knight, who lounged in the sun, one hoof cocked and head down, as if he didn't have a care in the world. Since his area was roped off, he could enjoy the day without people approaching his corral all the time. Safer for everyone involved that way.

Jonas caught the regret and longing in her tired expression. He almost blurted out the surprise, but managed to bite his tongue. There would be a better time than now to tell her of his plans. "Are you still looking for a backup barrel horse?" He knew the answer before he even asked.

She focused back on him. "Kind of. I need one. Unfortunately, good barrel horses cost a pretty penny. Much more than I have."

"Checked out all the horses at the farm? Their adoption fees are quite reasonable."

"I've thought about them. But nothing I've been on thus far has come close."

He patted her shoulder. "Don't worry. Something will come along."

She pasted on a lukewarm grin. "True." After taking

another sip, she stole the cap from his hand and screwed it back on. "Thanks for this and the ice cream. You don't know how much I appreciate it."

"You're very welcome. Anything to put a smile on your face." Leaning in, he brushed his lips over hers. Once. Twice. The third time he lingered, molded and absorbed her response with relish.

She edged closer, opened her mouth and flicked her tongue over the seam of his lips.

Fire shot through his blood, making a straight line for his groin.

Reluctantly, he eased back with a rueful grin. "No more of that."

She blinked up at him.

"You go straight to my head like whiskey. To other parts as well."

A pretty blush brightened her face. "Oh."

"Yeah. As much as I'd like more of that, we should probably save that for another time. When we're alone."

Lacey sighed and kissed him once more. "Count on it." She turned on her heel and headed back to Candy.

I'll definitely do that.

He watched her saunter off with a sassy sway to her hips. The sight added to his already snug jeans.

She made him feel like the Jonas of old. More carefree, flirty, and appraising the opposite sex with an eye of appreciation. He'd missed being that person. Only, he'd changed along the way. His intentions and plans were definitely different. Less playboy and more sincere.

Something about Lacey told him he could trust her. She'd see him as whole. A marvel, in his opinion.

The mixture of innocence, tartness, intelligence and vulnerability made him want to protect her, take the burdens off her shoulders, take her to bed and show her erotic delights she'd never dreamed of. The absence of one nut didn't matter in that regard. Only Lacey's acceptance did.

I'll find out soon enough. Just give it more time.

Chapter Eleven

Please, please. Don't let this be anything bad, Lacey begged a higher power as she braced herself for the answer. Her luck didn't run along the lines of good news. Not lately, anyway.

Lacey watched Dr. Moore's face carefully as he studied the X-ray, searching for any indication of what the matter might be.

The week had proven uneventful leading up to the weekend. She'd loaded up Candy and driven the couple of hours to the next rodeo, raced both nights and won. At what cost she didn't know yet.

She'd noticed Candy favoring her right front foot on the way back to the barn. Extremely concerned, she'd carefully loaded Candy into the trailer and headed straight for home, praying along the way. She'd also called Dr. Moore and pleaded for him to meet her at the farm and examine Candy. Though it was Sunday evening, he'd readily agreed.

"What's going on?" Her father's voice echoed across the barn.

Lacey flinched and turned to see her parents and Tate walking toward her. They appeared to have just finished Sunday dinner, noticed the lights at the barn and come to investigate. "Candy's favoring her right front. I called Dr. Moore on the way home and asked him to meet me here to check it out."

Her father glanced at Dr. Moore with a scowl that Lacey didn't understand.

"How bad is it?" She petted Candy's cheek and sent up another prayer.

Dr. Moore sighed, lowered the X-ray and met her eyes. "The fetlock is hot and there's new bone proliferation on the film. The spells out sesamoiditis." He delivered the bad news quietly.

Lacey's hopes plummeted. The injury, fairly common among barrel horses, meant down time at the best. Retirement at the worst.

"I'd call it mild. Six to nine months off with a daily anti-inflammatory drug for at least the first couple of weeks should do the trick. We have to consider her age though." He ran his hand over Candy's back. "She *could* make it back, but I'd start looking at a replacement horse if I were you. It might be in her best interest to retire her from the sport for good." His expression told Lacey how much he hated to impart that last bit.

"Well, that settles it. Now you can stay home and help your mother around the house like you should have been doing all along," her father added in a commanding tone.

Lacey swung around in fury. "I'm not giving up on my dream. Just because Candy is out doesn't mean I'm throwing in the towel."

"You have no business driving all over the country like you do. It's not right. Especially when your mother and I are footing the bills while you gallivant around."

"The hell you do. I pay my own way." Incensed with anger, Lacey bit each word out as if gnawing on a particularly hard corn cob. "I'm not quitting."

"You belong at home, cleaning the house and helping around the farm. Until you marry and have a family of your own, that's where a girl is supposed to be. Home and kids. That's what you're good for, not rodeoing. About time you faced the facts and toed the line."

Lacey's mouth dropped open at his overly harsh, critical words.

Just as she started to form a comeback, Dr. Moore beat her to the punch. "You judgmental jackass." He glared at her father with a rage Lacey hadn't ever seen before. "She's worked her butt off around this place only for you to belittle her at every turn. Not because of anything she's done but because you can't get past that little burr in your hat."

Her father's lips thinned.

Her mother paled. "Randy…"

"You're still not sure that she's your daughter, are you?" Dr. Moore snarled.

"Holy shit." Tate's mouth fell open.

Lacey blinked, struggling to keep up, let alone make sense of this turbulently opened can of worms.

"We checked when Lacey was a baby. She's not mine, as much as I would have wished it to be different," Dr. Moore said.

Lacey looked at her mother, seeing the stress and truth written all over her face.

"You fucking bastard. If you had any decency you wouldn't have touched her anyway," her father bit out.

Dr. Moore fired back. "You two were separated at the time. If you had been a caring and attentive husband instead of making your wife the low rung on the totem pole, she wouldn't have ever wanted another man."

"It's not like you didn't play around during that time either," Helen added with a bit of hot sauce. "At least those other girls didn't get pregnant and their children have to pay the price that you've forced on Lacey."

"Are you absolutely sure of that, Mom?" Tate pinned his father with a hard gaze and fired his loaded question at him. "Is that the reason you accepted Ransom so readily? Because he might be your child?" Tate asked, his voiced filled with suspicion.

Whoa. Lacey quickly did the math in her head. Tate was a year older than her. Ransom three months younger. *Ransom is my stepbrother?*

Her father's jaw ticked. He spared Tate a quick look before turning his focus back on Helen. "Why the hell didn't you tell me you had a paternity test done?" her father bellowed.

Mom faced him and lifted her chin with determination.

"It shouldn't have mattered." Her voice carried strength and conviction. "Besides, you wouldn't have believed me anyway."

Dad's flickering gaze and lowered chin told the story. He'd made up his mind years ago and nothing anyone else said would have mattered.

"Why didn't you tell me you suspected Ransom was your son?" Mom fired back.

Dad cut his gaze to his wife, his nostrils flaring and his fists clenching.

Lacey's blood boiled as she faced off with her father. "Let me get this straight. You hate me for being outspoken and wanting to get out and see the world. Strike one. You hate me for possibly belonging to another man. Strike two. And you hate me because I don't sit at home and jump when you command. I have dreams and a career outside this damn farm. That's strike three. I guess in your book that means I'm out." She clenched her fists.

"Lacey…" Mom said.

"No. Just no." Lacey turned her anger on her mother. "You've done nothing but stick up for him. It would have been nice if you two could have worked this out before I wasted all that time trying to please a man who will never appreciate me just because I don't ask how high when he tells me to jump. Hell, you had years to tell me the reason, to stand behind me and support me, but all I heard were excuses and lies. Since you knew the reason all along and kept that little gem to yourself, I blame you for this as much as him." She couldn't bring herself to call him her father. Not after this latest blow. "Neither of you cared that I suffered just as long as your dirty little secret didn't get out. Well, that doesn't fly with me. Not anymore." She blew out a breath and fought to keep some sort of composure. "Leave. All of you. Just leave."

Dr. Moore rested his hand on her shoulder. "I've always wished you were mine, Lacey. No matter what, my door is always open."

"Thank you," she whispered, too rattled to do more than that.

"She doesn't need your kind of help, you bastard." Her father stepped toward Dr. Moore with intensity and aggression.

Tate moved between them. "Stop it, both of you. This isn't the time or the place."

Dr. Moore nodded briefly and stepped around Tate.

Her father narrowed his eyes. "Don't ever step foot on this property again, Moore. You'll regret it."

"Threats? How predictable." Dr. Moore peered back at Lacey. "Remember what I said. If you need anything, a place to stay, a stable to board Candy, anything, just let me know."

Lacey bobbed her head, the large lump in her throat preventing her from speaking.

Tate patted her arm before pulling up the rear.

As soon as they left, Lacey hugged her horse's neck and let the dam burst. Tears rolled as heart-wrenching sobs shook her body.

Her entire world had splintered in one night, leaving her lost and alone. She cried for her loss — her family. Her barrel racing career. Her bleak future.

How long she sat in the chilly barn alone with Candy, having a pity party, she didn't know. All she knew was that life had just thrown her the worst pie in the face ever. Reeling from the unbelievable confessions and occurrences, she blew out a breath and lifted her chin.

Time to cowgirl up, Lacey.

Great in theory. Not so good in real life. For she lacked direction, even a place to go for the night. Sure, she could march back into the house, slam her bedroom door and try to keep the world at bay. All for naught. Her family, while meaning well, would be pounding on her door until she gave in just to get some peace and quiet. Nothing would be gained, including sleep.

Instead, she eyed her truck. Wouldn't be the first time

she'd curled up on the seat for the night. Probably wouldn't be the last.

She released Candy into her paddock, fed her and gave her fresh water. After a quick grooming, she bid her horse goodnight, hopped into her truck, snuggled in as best she could and stared at the stars, knowing sleep would be long in coming.

Chapter Twelve

Lacey entered Dr. Moore's clinic first thing the next morning. She expected to find Sally at the desk. Instead, Dr. Moore met her as she stepped inside.

"Lacey."

She pasted on a wan smile. "Dr. Moore. I stopped by to pay my bill and pick up Candy's medicine."

His eyebrows furrowed. "I'll get you the medicine, no problem. But you don't owe me anything."

Her mouth fell open. "The farm call, the X-ray, the exam. I definitely owe you."

He glanced around before speaking. "No. It's the least I can do. I won't accept your money. Besides, you know workers receive free vet care."

She tilted her head and wracked her memory. *Nope. Nothing on file concerning that.* "Since when?"

"Since now." He gestured her inside. "I'm really sorry, Lacey. You shouldn't have had to learn about those things like that. It's my fault for even bringing it up. My only excuse is I lost my temper after the way he spouted off about you staying home and helping your mother. That was a jackass thing to say and it burned me to hear it, especially directed toward you." He sat down on the corner of the desk.

"Thank you for sticking up for me." She held no anger toward him. He'd not only always been supportive, but had become a fatherly figure somewhere in the couple of years she'd worked for him.

"I'll always stick up for you." He blew out a breath. "I meant what I said. I wish you were my daughter. You're smart. Kind. Brave. Everything that any parent would be proud to see."

The compliment stung. "Except mine."

He reached out and pulled her into a gentle hug. "I would change it if I could."

She bit her lip and shoved back the tears. Falling apart now wouldn't solve anything. Compassion worked. Pity, she refused. As good as it felt to be held like a treasured child, she forced herself to step back, breaking the contact. "Thanks."

"If you need a place to stay, my door is always open. I spoke with Charlotte last night. She agreed and would love to have you."

"I'll think about it. It's just... I don't want there to be more problems between you and my...Dan. It's not worth it."

"You're worth it." Truth and sincerity carried in his voice.

She nodded. "I don't want any rumors or scandal to start because of me either. Those could hurt your business and I won't have it."

He snorted. "All my clients know me. If they're wishy-washy enough to believe ridiculous gossip from the local café and fire me over it, then I don't want their business to begin with."

She smiled at his firm stance and uncaring attitude toward mud-slingers. "Still..."

"No pressure. Just know you have a place to go that will welcome you." Dr. Moore stood up, went to the medication room and came back with a large bag. "Tell me you'll still work for me."

A sense of relief nudged her self-confidence. "Of course. Although, I need a few days off."

"Understood. Just call me when you're ready to go back on the schedule. You'll always have a job here, Lacey. Always."

She turned to leave then paused and looked back. "For the record, I wish you were my father, too."

His jaw slackened and his eyes grew misty.

Impulsively, she hurried over, gave him another hug, and

started to leave. "I'm going to Kentucky to get Candy bred. She should come into season in the next few days. If you think she'll be sound enough?"

"Yes. She should be in good enough shape for that."

Lacey nodded. "I thought so." She paused for a couple of seconds. "I'll check in when I get back."

He nodded.

She left, a large lump in her throat and tears streaming down her cheeks.

* * * *

Jonas watched Lacey push a pea around her plate for over a minute. Silence reigned as he ate and she played with her food. She'd taken maybe three bites of her meal before staring off into space, obviously in her own world.

"If you don't like the stew, you don't have to eat it. I can fix you something else." He spooned another chunk of beef and ate it.

She glanced up. "The food is good. Really."

"Then why are you so quiet and distracted? I'd say my sexy presence has you all tongue-tied but I don't think that's quite it."

A small smile played across her lips. "You are a nice, sexy distraction."

"Uh-huh. Tell me another story."

"It's nothing." She waved one hand dismissively before gathering her glass and taking a drink.

"If you tell me 'it's nothing' one more time, I'm going to start gnawing on my hat in frustration."

The amusement almost reached her pretty green eyes.

She sighed wearily. "If you must know, my life sucks."

"Ah. That makes perfect sense. Now can you be a bit more specific?" He studied her and waited patiently for her response.

"Let's see. After Sunday's race, Candy came up lame. Sesamoiditis. She's out for a minimum of six months.

Maybe longer. Dr. Moore recommended getting a backup horse and probably retiring her."

"Damn." Jonas blew out a breath. He'd been afraid of just that happening. All the rodeo events, including barrel racing, took their toll on animals. Injuries were fairly common, especially with time, repetition, speed and hard starts and stops during an endless rodeo season. "What are you going to do?"

She shrugged and scooped up a piece of carrot on her spoon. "I haven't gotten that far yet. Been too busy dealing with my family going down the drain with a truckload of bullshit drama."

He blinked at her. "Meaning?"

"Oh, just that my parents unloaded a bombshell last night. Seems my father hates me for a number of reasons. Namely because I'm a girl, don't stay at home knitting like he thinks I should, while he dotes on the boys. Oh, yeah. And he also thought I might actually be Dr. Moore's love child conceived when my parents were separated for a few months."

"Holy shit." Jonas couldn't fathom what to say. Never in a million years would he have expected that kind of convoluted mess to exist. Let alone involving Lacey. No wonder her parents never showed up at her events. She came in as a second-rate child behind their son. "That's..." He struggled for words. *Pretty chickenshit* came to mind, though he didn't expect her to appreciate his candor.

"Yeah." She rested her spoon on the side of her bowl. "As if that wasn't enough, seems like dear old Dad screwed a few women on the side during that time, too. There's a possibility that Ransom might actually be his son." She swallowed. "I suppose it's a good thing that he never saw me as more than a sister and he's on the verge of being engaged. Having a crush on your own brother for the past eight years borders on damn pitiful."

"Fucking hell." Jonas shook his head, trying to absorb all the twists and turns. Difficulties abounded.

Shock hit him hard as he replayed her confession through his mind.

She'd been in love with Ransom for eight years until just recently, when she'd learned the truth of Ransom's parentage and his impending engagement. Eight damn long years. Where did that leave him? How could he compare or stack up against a man who would forever be in her life? Sure, Ransom was most likely her blood relative, but still...

How would he know that she wanted him for him, not just as a rebound for a broken heart? Would she even want him, considering his scars?

The heavy weight of worries pushed his shoulders down.

Like he needed another uphill battle and obstacle on the road back into the dating game.

Shit.

One glance at Lacey told the story. Pain creased her face and her eyes welled up. He'd never seen her as upset as this.

He could only imagine what Lacey felt.

He drew in a deep breath and shoved the concerns aside for the moment. Lacey needed help and he had to step up to the plate. His personal concerns would wait. "What a hot mess."

"Tell me about it." She took another sip. "Nice to know that it wasn't me, per se, that he couldn't stand. Just my DNA and the fact that he raised me but blamed that big blunder on another guy." Sarcasm dripped from her words.

He suspected she hid behind sarcasm rather than let herself break down in tears. Most women would have lost it at the first hurdle, let alone the rest of the night's revelations. His heart bled for what she'd learned and the rotten luck fate had tossed her way. His pride soared as he witnessed the feminine strength she possessed in the face of major adversity.

She's strong. Cowgirl strong.

Respect for her grew. "What did your mother have to say?"

Lacey's face tightened. "That it shouldn't have mattered who my father was. She'd known my father wouldn't believe her when she told him of the paternity test, so she never bothered to do so."

"Hell of a time for all that to be put out in the open."

"Yeah. Especially as Dr. Moore let the cat out of the bag after my father cheered Candy's injury. My father said I should be at home helping my mother anyway. It's where I belong, in his eyes."

"Patronizing bastard." Fury raced through Jonas. The thought that any father could be so cruel to his daughter clawed at him. That man didn't deserve Lacey and her goodness. He deserved a horsewhipping instead.

He bit back his anger and focused on Lacey. The circles under her eyes told of little sleep last night. Now he understood why. "You need to move out of there, Lacey. Get away from all that mad mess. Be free for once in your life."

She met his eyes briefly before lowering her gaze back to her plate. "Dr. Moore offered to stable Candy and let me move in with him. He and his wife never were able to have kids. They would have made great parents."

Jonas cheered the man for stepping up when he didn't have to. "Are you going to?"

Lacey's shoulders dropped as she slumped. "I don't know. He's a kind man. Even said he wished I really was his daughter. But I don't want to get in the way or cause more problems between him and my parents. He doesn't need my irate father tossing out threats and throwing temper tantrums."

Jonas clasped his hands and rested his elbows on the table. "Move in with me."

Lacey's gaze flew to his face. Her lips parted on a gasp.

He offered up a small smile of encouragement. "I have plenty of room. Two spare bedrooms just waiting to be used. There's a barn and several acres of fields that could use a horse to mow them down a bit. Noggin needs a pasture mate. He's ready to be rid of the youngsters, I'm sure, and return to a lifestyle more fitting for a mature older gentleman."

"Are you sure?"

"Absolutely. You'll be doing me a favor."

Her eyebrows furrowed. "I will?"

"Yep. We can have date night every night and I won't have to chase you down very far in order to ask." He offered up his best persuasive smile.

She seemed to ponder the situation while taking a couple more bites of food. "I'll think about it."

Indecision covered her face.

Too much, too fast.

He tried again. "Or, if you prefer, I'm sure Nila will be happy to have you stay with her. She's alone in that house, and think about the short commute to work."

"I'll consider it. Right now, I'm thinking about going to Kentucky and spending a week or so. I've already spoken to Nila and she gave me the time off."

His heart skipped a beat. He wouldn't blame her for leaving the state, but damn. "What's in Kentucky?"

"Trinity. I think I mentioned her before. Since she's offered to breed Candy to Legacy for free, I'm going to take her up on that offer. Now."

He blew out a breath in relief. "Since you can't ride her you might as well try to get a baby out of her for the next generation of barrel horses."

"Exactly." She took another drink. "I was planning on going back...to the farm, packing, loading up Candy and leaving tonight."

He frowned. "That will put you in Kentucky in the wee hours of the morning. No one will be up or expecting you then." Worry gnawed at his gut. "Why don't you wait and leave at dawn tomorrow morning? That way you wouldn't have to drive in the dark and would arrive in the afternoon."

Her eyes dulled. "Because I don't want to stay another night with my parents. That's one of the reasons I want to gather up everything right after lunch. Mom is at work. Father is building fence. Even if he comes in to eat, he'll be back out right after."

The pain written on her face touched his very soul. He reached across the table and took her hand in his. "I'll help you get packed and loaded. Come back here and stay the night. You'll be away from them, get some rest, and can take off first thing in the morning."

She glanced down at his hand then met his eyes. "I don't want to be a bother."

"There's no way on earth you can be such a thing. You're a sweet, caring, pretty lady going through a tough time. I'm here for you. In whatever capacity you need. For as long as you want."

Lacey studied him for a long moment before slowly nodding. "I'd like that."

"Good." He squeezed her hand. "Let's finish eating and get this cleaned up so we can go to your folks' place and get you moved." He released her and started to get up, only for her to catch his sleeve. After sitting back down, he looked at her.

"I..." She sighed. "Thank you. I can never repay you."

He smiled. "Just being around you is payment enough." Standing, he gathered up his dirty dishes and placed them in the sink. As soon as he turned back for more, he found Lacey standing right in his way. She smiled, lifted up on tiptoe, and brushed her lips over his. "You're one hell of a man, Jonas."

With a sweet grin, she started clearing the table.

He couldn't move for a few beats, the kiss and her words soaking into his very core. Surprised and amazed, he counted his blessings.

Maybe Jason is right. Lacey could be the one.
Hope surged.

* * * *

"You don't have to pack everything and the kitchen sink to go with you. Your stuff isn't going anywhere without you." Jonas leaned on the frame of the bedroom door and grinned as Lacey shoved, grumbled and finally sat on her suitcase in order to zip it closed.

She blew out a breath, which ruffled her bangs, and smiled over at him. "Whew. Got it."

"I see that. I've got some duct tape if that'll help."

"Nah. It'll hold." She climbed off the overstuffed container and slid off the bed. "Well, I guess that's it. Just have to get up, get cleaned up, dressed, load this and Candy, and I'll be off."

He applauded her rekindled spirit and the lightness he heard in her voice. Presumably she couldn't wait to head out. More to get away from the crap surrounding her than anything else, he knew. Still, he hated to see her go. Even for a few days. "When you come back, my offer still stands. You can stay with me as long as you like."

She tensed. "I don't really know what I'm going to do yet."

He held up his hands. "No pressure. Really. I just want you to think about it and realize you do have friends here. There's some of us who will gladly open our doors for you as long as you need."

"Thanks." The smile she gave him didn't quite meet her eyes.

Dumbass. Slow down. She's still reeling. Back off and be a friend.

He latched onto the fat bag. "I'll put this in your truck if you want." He lifted and grunted. "Damn heavy, too."

"Sorry. I can get it."

"Nope. I've got it. I'll just put it in the passenger seat, or would you prefer it in the gooseneck portion of the trailer with your tack?" He stood at the doorway and waited.

"Passenger side is fine." Her phone rang. She checked the caller ID and punched the ringtone off.

Not the first call she'd ignored since he'd been around

today. Probably far from the last. "Okay. I'll be right back." He headed out, deposited the bag and shut the door soundly.

As much as he hated her leaving right now carrying such a broken heart, she needed the time away. He knew her friend Trinity would help, if what little Lacey had told him was true. The girls shared a bond forged in the tough rigors of the rodeo circuit. That would hopefully prove strong enough to assist Lacey through this time and get her moving steadily down a new path.

Back to me.

Jonas re-entered the house and heard Lacey's voice. He walked a bit closer before halting, not about to invade her privacy and make her uncomfortable. She deserved his respect, after all.

A couple of minutes later she stepped out of the bedroom and into the living area. "Sorry about that. I talked to my brother, Tate. Told him where I was going."

"Good idea. Let him deal with the others."

Lacey strode over to the couch and plopped down. "I think that's for the best right now."

Jonas sat down beside her. "You need a break. It's okay. Take some time for yourself." He watched the emotions flow across her face. Sadness. Anger. Regret. Her eyes met his and he noticed something else. Interest. Curiosity. Want.

"You've been nothing but kind and strong for me," she whispered before reaching out to rest her hand on his knee.

He placed his hand on top of hers and rubbed with his thumb. "I'll always be there for you."

Her breath hitched. Slowly, she leaned forward until her lips brushed over his as softly as butterfly wings.

The slight touch sent his level of arousal skyrocketing.

She tried again, this time lingering and applying a bit more pressure. Her lips molded, adjusted and sealed once more, opening just wide enough for her to tickle his mouth with her tongue.

Jonas took the receiving role, letting her lead the way. He

licked her bottom lip then sucked, keeping the caress light and teasing. Steeling himself, he tightened the reins of his control and focused on Lacey. Her wants. Her wishes. Just her.

Lacey inched closer and swiveled until she sat on his lap. She wrapped her arms around his neck and added fiery demand to her kiss.

The flames of passion prodded him to do more. He stayed the course, rested his hands on her hips, and lightly stroked her back. When she sought a deeper taste, he opened, sneaking a bit for himself.

Before she could get carried away, he placed his hand on the top of her head then let it slide down. Petting, he waited for her to ease up.

She did so with a long sigh.

His groin tightened even more. "I want you, don't get me wrong. But not like this." He whispered the words as he nuzzled her ear. "You're hurting right now. I don't want that to be the reason you're turning to me."

Lacey leaned back enough to peer down at him. She grinned at him crookedly. "A chivalrous cowboy. Those are indeed rare."

He smiled at her teasing, glad to see her softer side line up with reason. "That's me. Ladies come first in my world. And this is too good to take a chance on. Take some time to yourself. Figure things out. I'll be here when and if you're ready."

"No other cowgirl will snatch you away in the meantime?"

"No way."

"Good." Lacey kissed his chin then snuggled into him. "You're the phoenix that has arisen from the fiery collapse of my life."

"Poetic." He felt her smile against his shoulder.

"Truthful." She breathed out and relaxed in his arms.

A long time later he carried her to bed, tucked her in and watched her drift back to sleep.

He hoped before long he'd be climbing in with her,

enfolding her into his embrace and going to sleep with her breath tickling his arm.

A dream waiting to come true.

Chapter Thirteen

"Whoa." Lacey stared at the rolling hills, the gorgeous barns, paddocks filled with prime horseflesh and the perfectly manicured grounds with awe and amazement. *Absolutely beautiful.* No wonder Trinity insisted on staying here.

In order to make sure Lacey came in from the correct direction and made it to the right barn, Trinity had met her just off the highway and provided an escort the rest of the way.

Lacey pulled in next to Trinity's truck on a gravel parking area and stepped out to meet her friend. "I can't believe this place. It's heaven."

Trinity beamed. "I agree. Wait until you meet some of the stallions. You'll be catching flies when you see the royalty waiting inside."

If she didn't have such strong ties to Oklahoma, she'd beg for a job here. Serenity surrounded her. Much different from home, for sure.

A glimmer caught her attention. She stared at Trinity's left hand and grinned. "Let me see that rock."

Trinity laughed. "It's perfect. Not too big or gaudy. Just right. I can even wear it doing my chores without worrying about losing diamonds."

Lacey nodded and inspected the beautiful but simple ring. Most women wanted huge diamonds, but that wasn't her friend. This fit Trinity perfectly in personality and attitude. "Cody did a great job. It's gorgeous."

"His father helped him."

Lacey blinked. "Really?"

"Yep. They went ring shopping while his mother kidnapped me for some girl time."

Lacey liked Cody all that much more. "It's gorgeous. And so are you."

"Thank you."

Dropping Trinity's hand, Lacey glanced back to the trailer. "I need to unload Candy."

"Carmen has an empty paddock reserved for her." Trinity walked to the back of the trailer and unlatched the hitch.

Lacey stepped inside, gathered up Candy's halter rope and guided her back onto solid ground. "Lead the way."

Together they walked the short distance to a moderate-sized brick home on the south side of the property.

"I'm so glad you called and came out. I've missed you." Trinity smiled over at Lacey as they ambled along. "So much has happened and I wanted to share it with you."

Lacey heard the excitement in Trinity's voice and found the enthusiasm contagious. "I knew you and Cody were a hit."

"He's the best man I could ever have wanted. I don't know what I'd do without him."

Ignoring the tendril of jealousy, Lacey tapped into Trinity's happiness. "Speaking of, where is the man of your dreams?"

"He's at the equine clinic. Applied for a job there. Today is his interview."

"I was going to ask, but that answers my question. Staying here." Lacey glanced around. "I don't blame you one bit. This is definitely a slice of horse heaven, even if it's not reminiscent of barrel racing."

"It's home. I don't know how else to explain it." Trinity glanced at the woodchip trail they were taking toward the house. "I hate making Cody move when his family is all back in Oklahoma. He's already decided that this is his new home and says as long as we're together, the where doesn't really matter."

"You're damn lucky, Trin. He's a fine catch." Lacey

offered up a smile. "You two are made for each other."

Trinity's face lit up. "I think you're right. He fills all the empty voids in my life and makes me feel like the sun rises just for me. I never thought that feeling existed. Now I don't want to live without it."

Lacey nodded. She wasn't sure she'd ever experience such an intense love. Right now, her life had turned bleak and love sat on the back burner. Jonas popped into her mind. He had a good heart, a gentle hand. He'd also make a fine catch. If only she had more to offer than herself and one endless struggle after another. Until she got her head screwed on straight and figured out a new path, it wasn't fair to give him hope and lead him on. Except for one important detail. She wanted him. They might have gotten off on the wrong foot, but he'd redeemed himself tenfold. His support meant the world. His kisses were divine. Hope flared with him near. No way could or would she turn her back on the potential for a relationship with the sexy ex-roper.

He'd kindly offered up his spare bedroom. Definitely tempted, Lacey hadn't quite jumped. She'd considered the pros and cons all the way to Kentucky, finally deciding that their relationship, in its infancy, wasn't prepared for living together. Skipping the necessary steps in between would make for one gigantic blunder. Too much, too soon. She needed to stand on her own before even thinking about moving in with him.

And thinking about such an event was putting the cart way in front of the horse. *First things first. I just have to get my ducks in a row before I go back. Then I can move forward with a brighter future.*

"Lacey? Earth to Lacey."

Lacey blinked over at Trinity. "Yeah?"

Trinity shook her head. "You were lost in daydreamland."

"Sorry." Lacey smiled sheepishly. "What were you saying?"

"That Cody can look over Candy when he gets home. See

what he thinks about her injury and breeding her. Never hurts to get a second opinion."

"Okay."

Trinity's eyebrows furrowed. "You've got something on your mind."

Lacey sighed and opted for redirection. No way would she dump her problems on Trinity, especially after only arriving five minutes ago. Besides, Trinity radiated joy. Lacey wouldn't take that away for anything. "I'll be glad to get a hotel room for the stay. I really don't want to be a third wheel when it comes to you and Cody."

Trinity opened her mouth, closed it again, then shook her head. "No way. My apartment in the stallion barn is only one room. Probably a bit awkward for you with Cody there too. So I spoke to Carmen. She's more than happy to have you for as long as you like. She's a doll, like a second mother, and pointed out that you'll be close to Candy that way. I'm just a hop, skip and a jump away, too."

"I don't want to be a bother."

Trinity snorted. "You're not, nor would you ever be. We're glad to have you. Heck, Carmen is eager to meet you. Says she can't wait to see the girl who kept me on track all season long."

Lacey grinned. "Like that was hard to do."

"Oh, I don't know. I think I was pretty hardheaded at times."

"Aren't we all?"

Trinity laughed. "*Touché.*" Trinity reached over and gave Lacey a quick hug. "I'm so glad you made the trip. I have the feeling you need a vacation and this is just what the doctor ordered."

Talk about hitting the nail on the head...

* * * *

"I don't have the X-ray in front of me, but I don't see anything that doesn't line up directly with your vet's diagnosis." Cody stood up and patted Candy on the shoulder. "Rest and anti-inflammatories should help." He pinned Lacey with his gaze. "She's not a spring chicken. Arthritis probably isn't far behind. If I were you, I'd find me a replacement horse now and retire her to the breeding shed."

Lacey sighed. "Thanks for looking at her. I knew the answer would be the same, but hope springs eternal."

"Corrective shoeing will help, but not enough to get her up to speed for the spring rodeos," Cody added.

"The farrier is coming in a couple of days. We'll add her to the schedule." Trinity scratched Candy's neck.

"I'll pay you…"

Trinity waved her hand. "My treat."

When Lacey started to protest, Cody shook his head. "I've learned not to argue with her. She can out-stubborn a mule."

"Yep." Trinity grinned proudly before sobering once more. "Do you have another horse in mind?"

"Well, I sort of did. That fell through." She ran her hand over Candy's rump as Cody led the way out of the lean-to shelter in the paddock and through the nearby gate.

"What happened?" Cody shut the barrier behind them and clicked the chain, ensuring Candy didn't get out during the night and wander.

"I don't know if Trinity told you. I took a part-time job as a horse trainer at the local Humane Society farm. Figured I'd be around enough horses, that maybe I'd find one to take Candy's place." She pictured Knight as she'd first met him, in a full-blown panic. "There's a beautiful paint gelding, formerly a stud, that had just come in. He'd been ruling over a harem of mares for a few months unattended. Gorgeous. Definitely has some breeding behind him because he's put together perfectly."

"Too wild to consider training as a barrel horse?" Trinity held open the door to Carmen's house, ushering Cody and Lacey inside.

"Actually, no. Jonas, the head trainer, has been working with him. He's been ridden in the past. Just forgot some things. Jonas believes with lots of work Knight will come around and end up a great mount. Unfortunately, I learned not too long ago that he's already been spoken for. He's staying in the training program until he's settled in and would make a good horse for a fairly experienced rider. After that, he goes to his new home."

"None of the other horses will do?" Cody pulled off his boots right at the door before moving ahead to make way for the girls to do the same.

Lacey considered the others and shook her head. "They have some wonderful horses, don't get me wrong. Just nothing else that has potential as a barrel racer. A top-level one at that." Even Knight would be a wild card. The chances that he'd be ready for competition in just a few months hovered around slim to none.

"Well, shoot." Trinity, standing in her socks, led the way through the mud room and into the kitchen.

Delicious aromas filled the air, transporting Lacey back to a typical Sunday lunch with her family. On the heels came bitterness. *Not like I'll be doing that any time soon.*

"Carmen. This is Lacey. Lacey. Carmen."

Lacey pulled herself back to the present and smiled up at the dark-haired middle-aged woman. With such a wide smile and eyes snapping with happiness, Lacey found herself liking the stallion farm manager already. "Nice to meet you. Trinity's told me about you."

Carmen laughed. "Same for me. She credits you for getting her and Cody together."

Lacey shook her head. "I didn't do anything." She cut a rueful glance toward the couple who stood in each other's arms as if they couldn't help but touch. "With or without me, they would have found their way."

"I'm not so sure. Trinity can be stubborn," Carmen said.

"Oh yeah, definitely," Cody added.

Trinity lightly slapped at his flat stomach. "Takes one to

know one."

He peered down at her with such an expression of stark love Lacey felt as if she were invading their space. Or soaking in the brightness emanating from them. One of the two. Lacey couldn't decide which.

Cody leaned down and kissed Trinity.

Carmen cleared her throat. "If you guys don't get a move on, the food will be cold and the cook unhappy."

"Yes, ma'am." Cody guided Trinity to the sink, where they washed their hands before finding seats at the table.

Lacey looked around the room. "What do you need me to do? I can bring stuff over to the table if you'd like."

Carmen smiled with appreciation. "If you'll grab the casserole, I'll get the bread and baked apples."

Dutifully, Lacey did as bid, noting that Trinity poured tea into each of the glasses while Carmen set the rest of the meal on the table.

"There we go. Dig in." Carmen took a seat next to Lacey and started dishing out food.

When they started eating, Carmen glanced over at Lacey. "Trinity told me you brought your mare to be bred."

"Yes, ma'am."

Carman rolled her eyes. "Ma'am was my grandmother. Please, just call me Carmen."

Lacey smiled. "Okay, Carmen." The casual atmosphere and sweet chef lightened Lacey's load and eased her worries. For the moment.

"Not going to wait to breed her after the year ends and plan for a spring foal?" Carmen asked.

"I figured there was no reason to wait since she won't be racing and that magical birthday for thoroughbreds doesn't apply to quarter horses and paints." Lacey sipped her drink. *Besides, what else am I going to do right now? Twiddle my thumbs, search for buried treasure and hope my screwed-up family finds a way to forgive and forget?*

"Makes sense. Maybe the other racers can help you find another horse." Cody blew on a fork filled with casserole before placing it in his mouth.

Lacey flinched. "Great in theory. Only problem is I don't have the kind of money needed to purchase a finished barrel racer. I'm going to have to find one and start from the ground up."

"Are you sure the person that wants Knight won't reconsider?" Trinity asked.

Lacey took a bite of her food, chewed and swallowed. "I didn't ask Nila, the manager of the farm, but Jonas sounded pretty certain."

"Jonas?" Cody turned his attention to her.

"Jonas. He's the farm's head horse trainer. Former rodeo roper. His horse's name is Noggin." Lacey tilted her head. "I don't even know his last name. How pitiful is that?"

"Where's he from?" Cody pursued.

"Same area as me. Southeast Oklahoma."

"Tall. Dark hair and eyes. Built like a steer wrestler?"

Lacey blinked at Cody. "Yeah. Do you know him?"

"If he's the same guy I'm thinking of, yeah. Jonas Marshall. He used to hit the rodeos through college as a roper. He and his brother both. They were moving up in the ranks. Heard he had a bad fall and broke his leg a year or so ago."

Lacey processed that information. While the facts seemed to click, a broken leg shouldn't have made Jonas anywhere near as defensive about the end of his career. Injuries happened. They were no reason to get your dander up and snap when someone asked why a person quit participating in a sport.

A necessary piece to the puzzle remained missing. "He's not been back to rodeo. Says he's not going back. I'm not sure why." She sighed, hoping she wasn't breaking a confidence with her statements.

Cody shrugged. "Maybe he lost his edge or his guts. A bad enough accident will leave scars on a man's soul as well as his body. Those don't go away and climbing back into the saddle doesn't cure them." His eyes dulled.

Trinity reached over and slid her fingers between Cody's

and kissed his biceps. "Badges of courage. Every last one of them."

He turned his head and nuzzled her cheek. "You're one special lady."

Trinity blushed.

Carmen chuckled and nudged Lacey with her elbow. "Don't pay them any attention. Since Trinity returned from the finals, those two have been making goo-goo eyes at one another from dawn until dusk."

Lacey watched them in fascination. Obviously Cody carried some major wounds of his own. Wounds that only Trinity could heal. Pride and happiness for her two friends bolstered her spirit. "You should have seen them at the rodeos. Each time they'd look at each other, I swear fireworks would go off."

"You think that was fireworks? You should see Trinity when I—"

"Cody!" Trinity placed her hand over his mouth as her face pinkened all the more.

Lacey laughed. "He was always incorrigible."

"Uh-huh." Carmen ate a few more bites. "Before I totally forget my manners, how did the interview go?"

Cody waggled his eyebrows at Trinity, kissed her palm and lowered her hand back to his lap. "Very well, actually. The only big sticking point might be that I told them I've already verbally committed to the Midwest rodeo circuit again next year. I'll be gone almost every weekend, which might be an issue as the clinic is staffed twenty-four-seven for emergency calls."

"You'll get it. Those vets know quality when they see it," Carmen replied.

Lacey finished eating, her energy levels draining in the process.

"You look ready to drop. How about I bring your suitcase down here so you can hit the sack early?" Trinity offered.

"I can get it." Lacey hated for Trinity to go out of her way.

"Nah. I'll get it. No sense having you run all over creation the first day you're here." Cody stood up and placed his empty plate in the sink.

Lacey gathered her own dirty dishes and walked them over. "You guys don't need to treat me like a pampered princess."

Trinity chuckled. "Sure we do. It's in the friend code."

"The friend code?" Lacey arched an eyebrow.

"Yep." Trinity added her china to the growing pile. "You steered me and Cody together. That means you have great benefits for life."

Lacey groaned dramatically. "I'm not so sure that's a plus."

Cody grinned. "Just wait until we start lining up a man for you. Now that'll be fun."

"Not." Lacey shook her head. "Thanks, but no thanks. Carrying my luggage is one thing. Finding a man worth having is another."

"Well, shucks." Cody headed out of the room and started pulling on his boots, Trinity right on his heels.

"We'll be right back."

"Thanks again." Lacey watched them go then returned to the sink. "Wash by hand or dishwasher?"

Carmen gestured with her head. "Dishwasher please. And you don't have to do that."

"I want to. Being lazy and waited on isn't me." She went about loading up the dirty dishes.

"Your turn will come soon enough."

Lacey twisted to peer at Carmen. "My turn for what?"

"To be happily in love." Carmen smiled knowingly.

"I'm not so sure." Lacey returned to the task.

"Give it a chance, dear."

Lacey spared her one more glance.

No wonder had Trinity set down roots here. Surrounded by horses, fields and beauty. Add in a motherly figure like Carmen. No girl in their right mind would leave.

Except me.

Lacey shoved the thought aside and focused on the chore.

An hour later, freshly showered, she plopped down on the bed and stared out of the window into the night sky. No time like the present.

She dug out her cell phone, turned it on, and grimaced at the number of messages left. With a heavy heart, she scrolled through them, replying to a couple from Tate, and finally to her mother. She didn't have the energy to argue or get into a discussion, but understood Helen's worry. A quick text that she was fine and in Kentucky to get Candy bred would just have to suffice.

Just as she started to lay the phone on the nightstand, it rang. She checked out the caller ID, then answered. "Hello?"

"Lacey? It's Jonas."

The sound of his voice gave her strength. "Hi."

"I take it you made it there okay."

"Yep. You should see this place. It's better than a postcard. The horses are amazing. All of them big names. Pampered pets now." She rambled on, eager to share with Jonas.

"You sound more chipper. I think getting away is agreeing with you." His voice held a tinge of hesitancy mixed with relief.

"It is and it isn't." She bit her lip and offered up the truth. "This place is wonderful. I'd consider staying except for you and Nila."

Silence followed. "I miss you too, Lacey. I meant what I said about always being here for you."

His words coated her heart in comforting warmth. "Thank you."

"Enjoy your break. When you get back will be soon enough to get back into your relentless work schedule."

She smiled softly. "Gonna make me another grilled cheese when I return?"

"Absolutely."

She could hear the grin in his voice. "Good. Because I miss those too."

He chuckled. "I'll feed you as many sandwiches as you want. Just come home when you're ready."

"I will. I promise. Kentucky is tempting and beautiful, but it's not home." She glanced at the clock. "I better get going. The farrier comes tomorrow and I need to figure out a way to earn my keep while here."

"Just don't work too hard," he cautioned.

"I won't. Thanks for checking on me, Jonas. It means a lot."

"Welcome."

"Bye."

"Bye."

She hung up and lay back on the bed with a long sigh. A handful of kisses and she couldn't get Jonas off her mind. After the ordeal with Ransom, she would have expected no man would catch her interest or compare with the guy she'd had a crush on for years. Fickle Fates. They'd taken Ransom away and immediately presented her with Jonas. She made a mental note to thank them.

Curling up under the covers, she kept her phone close by while replaying the conversation with Jonas. His thoughtfulness touched her and provided shelter from her present storm.

A man like that didn't come along often.

One thing was for certain. She might not be ready to move in with him, but come hell or high water, she'd stand by his side and fight whatever battles they both faced. After all, he called to her on a level she couldn't ignore. Didn't want to, either.

Life had given her lemons. She'd find a way to squeeze out the juice into lemonade. Jonas added the sugar.

With a smile at the analogy, she drifted off to sleep.

Chapter Fourteen

"What's wrong, Lacey? You've got a lot on your mind, I can see it," Trinity said as she plopped down on a bale of straw beside Lacey.

They'd just returned Candy to Carmen's private paddock after breeding her to Legacy. The stud had been damn happy to see his old girlfriend again and even flirted sweetly before covering her and hopefully creating a foal.

"It's been a pretty lousy week."

"Why do I have a feeling there's more than Candy's injury that's bugging you?"

Lacey met Trinity's gaze. "Because there is." She drew in a deep breath. "I've never told you this, but my father doesn't understand my love of rodeo or even believe women should be more than housewives. He always wanted me leashed to the farm, the house and kitchen in particular, and made no bones about it."

"Ouch." Trinity flinched.

"Yeah, well, that came to a head. When Dr. Moore declared Candy lame and out for a few months, my father spouted off about how I could now be at home, helping my mother, where I belonged and should have been all along."

Trinity gaped.

Lacey snorted. "It gets better. Dr. Moore was there. He fired back, accusing my father of treating me like shit because my father still thinks Dr. Moore is my father. Seems my parents separated for a while and each found new lovers until they worked things out and got back together again."

"What a mess." Trinity shook her head in astonishment.

"Oh, there's more."

"More?" Her eyes widened.

"Seems they had a paternity test done. I'm really my father's daughter. My mother didn't think he'd believe her so she never told him. Dr. Moore wanted me, but the paternity results didn't go his way. Oh, and one more gem."

Trinity groaned. "I'm afraid to ask."

"Remember that guy that I wanted? The one who never saw me as more than a sister and is pretty much engaged?"

"Yeah."

"Turns out, there's a great possibility that he's my father's son, conceived during that separation time. Most likely Ransom is my stepbrother."

"Holy crap."

Lacey shrugged. "I'm waiting for Jerry Springer to call any day now and invite us on the show."

A ghost of a smile hovered on Trinity's lips. "Look at the bright side. At least you learned of your blood relation to Ransom before you married him. That would have been a bit awkward."

"There is that." Lacey slouched.

Trinity wrapped an arm around Lacey's shoulders and squeezed. "This too shall pass. We'll make it right."

"I don't know how." She waved her hand. "Hell, I don't even know where I want to live or who with."

"You know you can always stay here. We'd be more than happy to have you."

Lacey smiled sadly at Trinity. She appreciated the offer more than she could say. "I wish it was that easy. I'd love to be here, to walk away from the rest, settle down in Kentucky. I'd even beg for a job from Carmen."

"You wouldn't have to beg. She'd gladly give you one."

The support and friendship helped take the pain out of the past few days. "If my ties in Oklahoma weren't so strong, I'd snap up a job in the blink of an eye."

"What's keeping you in Oklahoma?"

"I love my job at the Humane Society farm. For once I really feel like I'm doing something worthwhile—helping the animals in a way that will earn them a new forever home. There's no better feeling in the world."

Trinity grinned. "I bet. What else?"

Lacey rubbed her hands on her jeans. "Jonas."

"Jonas?" Trinity arched an eyebrow. "The one you mentioned last night?"

"Yep. The head trainer at the Humane Society farm. Former roper. Big. Strong. All cowboy." Lacey smiled at the memory of the kiss he'd bestowed on her as she left.

"I saw your face light up. He means something more to you than just a coworker."

"I guess he does." Lacey lifted her gaze to meet Trinity's knowing expression. "He's kind. Gentle. But mysterious too. He doesn't talk about his rodeo past. Something bad must have happened because he shuts me down when I get too nosy."

"Mysterious isn't bad."

"True. I just feel it's a hurdle I have to overcome before we can get serious." Lacey paused for a couple of seconds. "He asked me to move in with him."

"Wow. For a girl that believes she has no family worth mentioning, you've got people offering up homes right and left." Trinity nudged her with her elbow. "Gonna do it?"

"I'm not sure," Lacey answered truthfully.

"What does your gut tell you?"

"That Jonas has the best rear in Oklahoma?"

Trinity chuckled. "That's a good start, although I think that idea is coming from parts a bit lower than your stomach."

Lacey laughed. Her troubles dwindled with Trinity's view on her messed-up life. She felt better and, for the first time in a few days, optimistic about what the future might bring. "True." She tapped her lip. "I think that moving in with Jonas might be a big temptation."

"Too big to ignore?"

"Possibly, but it's too soon. We're moving along at the speed of a racing turtle." Lacey chuckled. "If I hang my unmentionables in his shower, he might reconsider his offer."

"Somehow I doubt that."

"I'll probably move in with my boss at the Humane Society farm. She's nice and the drive to work will be just a hop, skip and a jump."

"That's a big plus. Trust me." Trinity smiled with understanding.

"I haven't figured out the rest yet. I'll have to speak to my parents at some point. Sooner rather than later."

"Decided what to tell them yet?"

"Not a clue. I want to lay into them, but that won't help. One thing I do know is that I'm making my own journey right now. They can run the farm themselves. That part of my life is finished."

"Good for you. You've given more than enough of yourself there. Time to find a new horse and get back in the saddle on the way to fulfilling your dream." Trinity glanced around before locking gazes with Lacey once more. "Cody and I will help all we can. Surely we can track down a horse that might work. Or perhaps give that man of yours a big nudge in the right direction." Trinity grinned wickedly. "Don't throw away his ropes quite yet. You might need them."

Lacey shook her head in amusement before giving Trinity a hug. "You're just what I need right now."

Trinity beamed. "That's what friends are for. You know that."

"Yeah, I do."

* * * *

Jonas took Knight around the first barrel, using the heel of his boot to make the gelding bend. "That's it. Nice and close." Though only at a walk, Jonas was pleased. Knight had taken to the saddle without too much fuss, accepting Jonas on his back with a brief pin of his ears and two whole bucks. After that, he'd focused on the man and tried hard to please. Jonas couldn't have been happier or more proud.

"Look at him. A few weeks ago he ran nearly wild. Now you've got him calm, attentive and eager to work. Amazing. Downright amazing."

Jonas grinned over at Nila. "He's really smart. Remembering his earlier training more each day. Someone worked with him extensively in the past. When he realized the rewards for his efforts, he jumped in with all four hooves."

She crossed her arms and rested them on the top rail of the corral. "Learning barrels, huh? This wouldn't be for someone else I know?"

"You already know the answer or you wouldn't be asking." He chuckled. "If you must hear the words, then yes, he's for Lacey."

"Thought so. At first I thought you asked for him to train as a roping horse. Now I see that idea was wrong."

His gut clenched at the mention. Sure, the idea had floated through his head for a brief moment before he'd discarded it. He'd hung up his spurs. For good. "I'm retired from roping, Nila. It no longer appeals."

She studied him for a moment with pursed lips. "Too bad. From what I heard, you were good. Put you and your brother together and you guys could have made it to the top."

"That's water under the bridge. I've taken another path in life." He finished the cloverleaf pattern and rode around the rail at a slow trot.

"Does this new path include Lacey?"

And here we go.

He spared her a glance and opted to spill the beans. "I'm not sure yet, but I'd like to try. *If* she'll have me." *And if I stack up in her eyes compared to the man she loved and set her sights on until just recently.*

A slow grin appeared on Nila's face. "You're good for each other." She sobered. "Poor girl is going through a tough time right now. She needs friends. She needs you."

He blew out a breath, wondering how the word had spread so quickly. *Damn small towns and their lack of privacy.* After drawing Knight to a halt, Jonas sighed. "Don't tell me the gossipmongers have their tongues flapping already."

"Not that I know of. Helen called me yesterday to check on Lacey. Seems Helen is worried about Lacey, who's not saying a whole lot and seems to be putting a big gap between her and her parents."

Jonas snorted in disgust. "Those people don't deserve her. Taking their frustrations out on her to cover up their own bad decisions, screw-ups and tempers. Lacey took time away from them to chart her future. I highly doubt she'll go back."

"She can stay with me. I'd be more than happy to have her."

"I told her that." Jonas nodded. "I offered my house as well. Told her I'd bring Noggin home to keep Candy company."

Nila's lips parted. "Is she going to take you up on it?"

Jonas shrugged. "I don't know yet. She spent one night before hurrying off to Kentucky. If I had my way, she'd stay permanently."

Nila tilted her head. "Permanently means commitment. I had no idea you two were that close."

He opened his mouth and shut it again while considering his words. "We're not to that level. *Yet.*"

"Your goal is to reach that?"

"I think so. Maybe." Knight shifted his weight restlessly. Jonas soothed him with a pat to his neck. "I'm taking it slow. Not about to push her with her life crumbling around her. When the dust settles, I hope she can still love a man after all she's been through. I have some hurdles of my own to conquer." Those words slipped out before he could bite them back. The truth was never far from the surface with him.

"That girl is full of love, if you haven't noticed. She might be rattled and shaken-up right now, but her spirit is still intact. Just show her the way a real man treats a lady. That's what she's been longing for."

"*If* she even comes back." He vocalized his fear.

"Think she'll grow roots in Kentucky?"

"Her best friend is there. Lives on a thoroughbred farm and owns the stallion Lacey intends to breed Candy to. She's two states away from this shitload of drama. What's here that she can't live without?"

"What indeed." Nila rested her boot on the bottom rung.

"You're not helping." He frowned over at her.

"Let me tell you something I noticed on open house day. You took the time and energy to bring her a drink and an ice cream cone."

"Yeah, so?"

"Maybe you didn't see her face light up as you approached. Hell, if was as if you carried a diamond ring and keys to a flashy new truck. She lit up. Not just because of the gifts, either. I saw how she feels written all over her face. You could have brought her a ratty halter rope and a bag of horseshit and she would've been thrilled. Lacey likes you. Cares for you. Has her sights set on you."

He adjusted the reins in his fingers and shifted in the saddle.

"It's true." She reached out and patted his knee. "She'll be back because her heart is here."

Jonas read the truth on Nila's face. "I hope you're right." He clicked to Knight and returned to the front of the corral in order to start the barrel sequence all over again.

Jonas prayed Nila knew and understood the workings of Lacey's mind. He had plenty of patience and lots to offer Lacey, if she could just bring herself to give him a try.

A hint of worry pinged in his mind.

He shook it off. No sense worrying about her acceptance of his deformity now. Too many baby steps existed before they'd close in on the issue.

One day at a time.

With a strengthening sigh, he nudged Knight into a trot

and headed for the first barrel.

* * * *

A rap at the door caught his attention. Jonas glanced up, found Jason at the front door, and waved him in.

"Developing a fondness for thoroughbreds, huh?" Jonas teased Lacey, who had called to update him on the day's activities in Kentucky. The fact she'd taken the initiative and called him said something. Namely that she'd been thinking about him and wanted to share part of herself with him, even from a few hundred miles away.

It's a damn good start.

"They are pretty, I'll say that. But, Trinity's stallion aside, they probably aren't made for running barrels as well as some of the other breeds."

"Maybe you should consider a Clydesdale instead?"

She snorted. "Yeah, I can see me now. Clunking around the barrels. You must have gotten tossed on your head for thinking such a thing."

He grinned at her lighthearted teasing. He heard the difference in her voice, the peppiness. The responses gave him both happiness and concern. First, thrill that she could shed some of her stress boosted his hope. On the other hand, although she promised she'd be coming home, he couldn't help but worry she'd fall in love with what Kentucky had to offer and never come back. "It would take a pretty rank bronc to buck me off. Have no worries on that."

"So I don't need to Super Glue your butt to your saddle?"

He shook his head. "You do that and I *will* paddle your rear."

"Threats. Threats."

"Oh, no. That's a promise."

Jason grinned at him before wandering down the hall, presumably to use the bathroom.

Lacey sighed, the small sound reaching out to brush Jonas with sweetness and want. "I need to get going. Feeding time doesn't wait for anyone."

"True."

"I'll talk to you tomorrow?"

"Definitely. Call me or I'll call you. Either way, I'll be catching up with you tomorrow."

"I look forward to it." She paused a second. "Thank you, Jonas."

"For what?"

"For being you."

He absorbed the compliment. "Any time. I'll talk to you tomorrow."

"Okay. Bye-bye."

"Bye." He hung up, lowered the phone to his lap and drew in a deep breath. He had to give her credit. She seemed to be bouncing back from a hard blow with the help of her friends. He wanted to count himself in that number — as well as something more.

She was strong. He could be too. For her.

Regardless of the past, he wasn't about to throw this exceptional opportunity out the window because he got cold feet. Lacey was more than worth the effort in order to gain the reward of her love. A battle worth fighting.

"What's with the clothes strewn across the bed? Unless you've been hiding one hell of a secret, I don't think those pastel blouses belong to you."

Jonas rolled his eyes but couldn't hold back the wicked grin. "Well, now that you mention it..."

"You've taken up cross-dressing?" Jason snorted. "Nice try."

"Don't believe that?"

"Not when those shirts are about three sizes too small. No."

"Well, hell." Jonas loved having his brother around. Whenever he needed a pick-me-up or someone to just hang out with, Jason fit the bill. Steady and true, Jason took what Jonas offered — anger, brotherly affection, even smart-ass comments — and went with the flow. Just another reason

Jonas counted him as his best friend.

"Come on, already. Spill. Why are there women's clothes in the spare bedroom?" Jason grabbed a beer from the fridge, plopped down and rested his boots on the coffee table.

Jonas arched an eyebrow and glared at the offending footwear.

Reluctantly, Jason removed them, making a point to do so at a caterpillar pace.

"Lacey spent the night."

"Hot damn." Jason raised his hand up in a high five.

Jonas shook his head. "Not like that. She needed a place to stay. I suggested one of the spare bedrooms. She took me up on the offer."

Jason dropped his arm and peered at Jonas with confusion apparent on his face. "I don't get it."

For a second Jonas debated how much to tell Jason. The story belonged to Lacey, but impacted more than her. His trust in Jason sealed the deal. "Lacey's had a rough go lately. Her barrel horse came up lame."

"Well, hell. She has a spare?"

"No."

"How long is she out?" Jason took another sip.

"Up to nine months. The vet recommended retiring her horse. So she took her to Kentucky to be bred, thinking that if her horse won't be able to run anymore, she can produce the next great barrel horse."

"That sucks, but doesn't explain why she's camping out with you." Jason pinned Jonas with his gaze.

"Seems her parents have some issues, especially her father. He sounds like a real prick, always criticizing and demeaning her. If that isn't bad enough, on the same night she learned her barrel season bit the dust, her vet spilled the beans that he'd been with Lacey's mother during a time she was separated from her husband. There was a question of who her real father is."

"Fucking hell." Jason's eyes widened.

"Seems the mother had a paternity test. Lacey belongs to the prick, but her mother didn't tell her father and the father has always known the possibility that Lacey came from another man. I guess every time he sees her, he's reminded of his wife's affair."

"That's one fucked-up mess."

"Oh, it gets better. The father had his own flings while separated. Now there's a big question whether the son's best friend that they took in might also be the father's offspring, too."

Jason's mouth fell open. "So, her father hates her because he's always wondered if she isn't his. He took in his son from an affair and didn't tell anyone his suspicions. The boys are wanted, but poor Lacey gets the brunt of his attitude?"

"That's the way I take it."

"What does her mother say?"

Jonas rubbed his hand on his leg. "I really don't know. Supposedly, not too much. Seems they were all in shock and pretty pissed off that night. As far as I know, Lacey is only communicating with her brother, the one she's always had, and avoiding her parents for the time being."

Jason bobbed his head. "She doesn't want to stay in the middle of the war zone called home. Understandable."

"Her vet offered to take her in. She refused, not wanting to cause any rumors or trouble for doing so. I told her she could stay here. Or with Nila, if she'd be more comfortable there."

"Good for you." Jason paused for a second. "So when is she coming back and is she moving in?"

"I don't know. On both counts."

Jason stared at him for a long moment. "Afraid she'll end up staying?"

"She says not, but…"

"But she's hundreds of miles from her troubles, with a friend, and finding the bit of freedom to her liking," Jason finished for him.

"Yeah."

Jason took another drink and glanced at the coffee table. "Seems to me that girl needs a horse."

"Working on it." Jonas shrugged at Jason's apparent surprise. "She bonded with that black paint stud the first day. He's built for barrels. Smart, too. I've been training him already. He's getting the idea. If only he can handle the crowds, the noise and the craziness of the rodeo arena."

"Does Lacey know you're doing this?"

"No. I've been waiting for the perfect time to tell her."

Jason pursed his lips. "If a girl is down and out, that little gem should put a smile back on her face."

Jonas grinned at his brother. "How do you remain single?"

Jason snorted. "Too many women, too little time, bro."

"Uh-huh."

Jason smiled like the Cheshire cat.

Jonas saluted him and his tomcat prowess. He'd been there once. Now he thought of himself as a tamed house cat. *Just waiting for Lacey to come home and pet me.*

He grinned at the sensual image.

Soon. Very soon. I'll show her how much I care.

Chapter Fifteen

Lacey ran the brush over Candy's sleek hide as the mare greedily ate her supper. The routine provided comfort and ample time to consider her options. Namely, her upcoming future.

A week away had provided rest, pressure relief and much-needed insight. Carmen, Trinity and Cody had taken her in with open arms, providing just about everything she'd missed back in Oklahoma. The most notable exception being Jonas.

They'd talked every day. She'd grown to crave his calls, to touch base with him every day, to hear his baritone voice. *Absence makes the heart grow fonder.* In her case, the phrase resounded solidly. She missed him. Big time.

She saw her feelings on Ransom for what they were—a crush. Sure, those emotions were deep and true, but they'd faded quickly enough once she'd realized the truth. Ransom and she were destined to be siblings instead of lovers. Good thing, considering the great possibility that they shared plenty of DNA. She'd been trailing behind Ransom forever, trying to get noticed. Her efforts had proved futile and clouded her judgment of other men.

Then Jonas had come along. Tough on the outside with a softer center, he reminded her of a truffle. Handsome, alluring and delicious when tasted.

She snorted at her own naughty thought. "Candy, I've lost my mind."

The mare swished her tail in answer as she continued to eat.

"Jonas has been everything I could ask for and then some.

So why aren't we hot under the sheets yet?"

"That's a logical question."

Startled, Lacey swung around to find Trinity walking toward her.

Trinity offered up a small smile. "Unless that was rhetorical?"

Lacey shook her head. "Not necessarily." How many times had she and Trinity talked at rodeos, especially about Cody and the slow progression of their relationship? Several. If anyone could have insight, Trinity would be the one.

Trinity patted Candy's shoulder. "Let me feed the words you told me back to you. You're a romantic. Nothing wrong with that. Love is your goal and anything less leaves you disinterested." She blew out a breath. "I can vouch that love is worth waiting for. I also know that you've had so many distractions lately that you can't focus on Jonas and what's happening between you two."

The observation sounded reasonable. "So what do I do?"

Trinity walked around to lean against a stall door before peering over at Lacey. "I think you already know what to do. You just have to find the courage and jump in with both feet."

Lacey blinked. "How did you know?"

"We're peas from the same pod, I do believe. I've been in your shoes and your nudges helped me buck up and take a chance. Now I'm returning the favor."

"I'm not sure if I should run for my life or thank you." Lacey chuckled as she dropped the brush into a container loaded with grooming tools.

"You'll thank me. Eventually." Trinity laughed then sobered. "I've seen your face when you talk to Jonas. Hell, even when you speak of him, you light up like a Christmas tree. That tells me all I need to know."

Lacey sighed and voiced her fears. "How do I know he's the right one? I thought I was in love with Ransom for years. The last thing I want to do is fall into that same hole again."

"No guarantees in life, Lacey. You know that." She pursed her lips. "I'll say this. If I didn't take a chance with Cody, I would have missed the best part of my life. We all have to put our hearts on our sleeves now and again. If Jonas is half the man I think he is, he's worth it."

Lacey nodded. "He's been right there with me through thick and thin. It's only been a few weeks, though."

"Seems like if he was going to split, he'd have done it by now. Cut his losses while they were marginal."

"True." Lacey nodded.

"How does he make you feel?"

"Like I'm pretty. Smart. Worthwhile."

Trinity grinned. "I really like that man."

Lacey chuckled. "As long as you only look and don't poach."

"As if..." Trinity rolled her eyes. "Made up your mind yet?"

"Actually, I have." Hope and optimism flared back to life. "I'll make a couple of phone calls tonight then pack. I'll be pulling out of here early tomorrow."

"I hate to see you go, but this time it's for the best. After all, you have a man to rope."

"Yeah. I do." Lacey rubbed Candy's forehead and smiled at Trinity.

"Tomorrow is the first day of the rest of my life."

"Yep. So you better make the best of it," Trinity replied.

Lacey'd had no idea she'd spouted the phrase out loud. She placed a kiss to Candy's nose and lifted her chin. "I intend to."

* * * *

Just when Lacey stepped inside the house, her phone rang. She checked the caller ID, took a deep breath, and answered. "Hi, Mom." She'd texted once to update and reassure her mother, but hadn't felt motivated to do more than that. Now, it seemed, her mother had decided to keep calling until she got more than a quick text.

"Lacey! Are you okay?"

Hearing the worry in her mother's voice, Lacey flinched in regret before immediately toughening once more. Her mother bore responsibility for this mess, though not as much as her father. "I'm fine. Like I told Tate, I brought Candy to Kentucky to breed her."

"He told us. He also said you were taking some time away from the rest of the family…" Her voice trailed off.

Lacey headed for the spare bedroom and plopped down on the bed. As much as she'd dreaded this conversation, she had to tackle it head-on at some point. *No time like the present.* "I needed some space to clear my head, yes. That doesn't mean I'm going to come home and be the same person as I was before. I'm not a whipping post for Dad and I refuse to let him continue to belittle me. The way I see it, he shouldn't throw rocks at glass houses."

"You're right, dear. We have some issues. We're working on them now."

"I hope you figure something out," Lacey replied truthfully. Her decisions weren't her mother's, after all.

"We're trying." She paused for a second. "You're coming home, though, right?"

"I'm returning to Oklahoma, yes. As far as where to stay, I'm going to call up Nila this evening and see if she'll offer room and board."

Helen remained silent.

"I don't think I'll be moving back in with you and Dad again." Lacey braced herself for her mother's reaction.

"I understand. Honestly, I don't blame you a bit. You were right. I should have stepped in and done something about the way he treated you. I just never expected the reason to be that he still thought you were Randy's child. That was so long ago, I thought he'd come to terms with all that and simply came by his stereotypes because of the way he was raised. I'm sorry. I should have said something. Done something. It's not right that you had to bear the brunt of our mistakes."

For a second, Lacey considered forgiving her mother. It would only be a lie, anyway, if she said so. "True. I've paid the price of distrust and I refuse to pay any more. I'll be staying elsewhere until I can get a place of my own." Lacey lifted her chin and patted herself on the back for her firm stand.

"Will you at least come have Sunday lunch with us? Ransom is bringing his fiancée over, too. It would be nice to have the whole family together for that, at least."

As much as Lacey wanted to refuse, she couldn't turn her back on Ransom and his future bride. They were as innocent as Lacey in this fiasco. "Okay if I bring someone?"

"You want to bring a friend?" Helen's voice rose in surprise.

"Yes."

"Sure. There'll be plenty of food to go around."

"I'll bring a dessert." Lacey rubbed her forehead and hoped her appearance didn't cause a grenade to go off in the room, especially if she could lure Jonas to come along.

"You don't have to, but thanks."

"I'll see you Sunday."

"Lacey?"

"Yes?"

"I still love you."

"Love you too, Mom." Lacey hung up the phone and blew out air.

Either I just made the first step in civility toward my family or set myself up to enter the snake pit. The chances of one or the other appeared just about equal.

The ringing of her phone caused her to jump. She quickly checked the number and answered. "Hello?"

"Lacey?"

"Hey, Jonas."

"What's wrong? I can hear it in your voice."

Obviously, after nightly phone calls he'd learned to read her pretty well. "Just spoke to my mother. She's invited us over for Sunday lunch."

"Us?"

She picked at her jeans. "I'm sorry. I should have asked first. If you don't have plans on Sunday, will you go with me to my parents' house for lunch?"

"Of course, but maybe a better question is, do you really want to go?"

She sighed. "Not really. I need to start patching things up somewhere, though."

"By entering the lion's den?"

She chuckled. "Oddly enough, I just called it a snake pit. I guess great minds do think alike."

"Absolutely," he said in a voice laced with amusement. He paused before speaking again. "That means you're coming home?"

"Yeah. Tomorrow."

"Great. Decided where you want to stay yet?"

Of course he'd throw out the hard questions first. "I'm going to ask Nila. Before you jump to conclusions, you need to know that I would love to stay with you, but I was afraid that would be too much, too soon. We've been rolling so smoothly, I just don't want to blow it by having you see me first thing in the morning with bed head and bad breath."

He laughed softly. "Lacey, it's going to take a hell of a lot more than that to send me scurrying away."

"I don't know. I can be pretty scary."

"Never."

"Uh-huh." She bit her lip. "You sure you're not upset with me?"

"Honey, like I told you before, no pressure. You're holding the reins on this whole thing. Just tap me with your spurs when you want to go a bit faster."

His analogy made her smile. Her stomach took the opportunity to flip-flop at the not-so-subtle sexual innuendo. "Spurs? Does that mean you're kinky?"

Jonas laughed.

The sexy sound wrapped her in warmth as well as turned

140

up the fire on her libido.

"Baby, you just wear those spurs to bed one night when you want to find out."

"Oh, my." The image racing through her mind dried up her mouth and sent tingling sensations straight to the delta between her legs.

"Oh, yes. Maybe I should tell you that I'm a force to be reckoned with in the sack."

She heard the truth combined with a healthy dose of teasing. Unable to resist, she tossed it back. "Think you're up to the challenge of me, huh?"

"Bring it on."

Those words replayed through her mind. A new goal formed. Soon, very soon, she'd get Jonas alone and see if he'd ante up. She couldn't wait for that day.

Chapter Sixteen

Sunday came around too quickly. Lacey had no more gotten settled in Nila's spare room, turned Candy out in the paddock with Noggin, and made a work schedule with Dr. Moore before the day sprang up. She hadn't even had time to do more than share a couple of kisses with Jonas as he welcomed her home. Unfortunately.

She slid out of the truck still holding a fresh apple pie. Jonas climbed out of the driver's seat, hurried to her side, and escorted her up the front porch steps.

"You ready for this?" he whispered in her ear.

She lifted her chin and drew in a steadying breath. "As ready as I'll ever be."

He knocked on the door.

Her mother opened it, greeting them with a warm smile. "Lacey." She glanced to Jonas with furrowed eyebrows and a perplexed expression.

"Mom. This is Jonas. Jonas. This is my mother, Helen."

"Mrs. Bright." He dipped his head for a second.

"Please, call me Helen." She stepped back and gestured with her hand. "Come on in. We're just about ready to eat." After snagging the pie from Lacey, she shut the door behind them.

Lacey entered the familiar living room, noting the normality despite the recent happenings. Tate and Ransom sat on the sofa, bracketing a pretty brunette wearing an ankle-length sapphire-colored dress. Nothing fancy, but nice and appealing all the same.

They stood as she came closer. "Lacey, this is Lizzie. Lizzie, Lacey."

Lacey smiled. "It's so nice to meet you. Ransom has been singing your praises."

Lizzie glanced up at Ransom. "All good, I hope."

"Of course." Lacey sized them out and decided they made an excellent couple. Lizzie appeared besotted with Ransom while he watched her with a smile on his face. Happiness radiated from them. For once, Lacey mentally thanked Ransom for his inattention through the years. He'd never looked at her that way and never could – something she now knew to be a hard fact. "Oh, where are my manners? You guys remember Jonas?"

"Yep." Tate held out his hand. Jonas shook it followed by Ransom's.

"Good to see you again." Ransom tugged Lizzie against his side. "And this is Lizzie, my fiancée."

"Congratulations. She's a prize." Jonas grinned at the couple.

"Thanks." Lizzie laughed. "Not sure I'm quite that, but I'll take it."

Ransom brushed his lips across her forehead. The tender expression of affection made Lacey smile. *That's what love is all about.*

Jonas caught her hand in his, giving a light squeeze.

She stepped back in order to lean against his side. *We'll get there if I have my way.*

"Everyone come eat." Helen's voice rang through the front room.

Lacey hung back, allowing the brothers and Lizzie to go first. Her father came down the steps and spared her a glance before checking out Jonas.

Lacey bristled as she read the haughty expression on his face. "Dad, this is Jonas. Jonas, my father, Dan."

"Nice to meet you." Jonas held out a hand.

Dad stared at it for a long moment before shaking almost reluctantly. "What do you do?"

"I'm the head horse trainer at the Humane Society farm." Jonas kept his head high and didn't look away.

Lacey squeezed Jonas' arm in appreciation.

"Huh." Dan cut him one more glimpse before heading into the kitchen, where he warmly greeted the boys and smiled sweetly at Lizzie.

Jonas tugged Lacey tightly against his side.

"I'm sorry," she whispered.

Jonas shrugged. "No biggie. I'm here for you. Not to impress anyone."

"Thanks," Lacey answered, happy to have Jonas' support right now. After the last disaster, she'd hesitated to step back into the house. Too much had been said, and more than likely, not enough forgiveness found.

Lacey took a seat. Jonas chose the one opposite her, leaving the end one for Lacey's mother.

Helen promptly placed one final dish on the table then sat down. "Dig in already." She nudged Lacey and smiled encouragingly.

Automatically taking the containers of food as they were passed around, Lacey added only small portions to her plate. Her stomach had started clenching as soon as she'd stepped into the house and didn't appear to be settling any time soon. When the final dish made the rounds, she picked up her fork, speared a green bean, and dropped it into her mouth.

Quiet chitchat followed as Helen asked Lizzie a few questions, engaging the younger lady in conversation.

Lacey listened in, but didn't contribute. Instead, she tried not to squirm on her chair when her father's focus turned to her. His baleful gaze warned her of his censure and displeasure — all aimed at her.

"When are you coming back home? Your mother needs help." Sternness laced Dan's tone.

And here we go. She'd known he wouldn't be able to play nice, even with the whole family in attendance, and Lizzie.

"Dan. We discussed this." Helen's chastising voice carried softly across the room, a frown accompanying the words.

Lacey blotted her lips with her napkin while strengthening

her courage. "I'm not."

Dan's eyes narrowed as his gaze flicked from her to Jonas and back again. "Shacking up with him instead?"

Lacey straightened. Before she could do more than open her mouth, Jonas beat her to the punch.

"I offered to let her stay with me. She declined. She's working her ass off to make it on her own first. Until then she's staying with the farm manager and juggling two jobs." Jonas stared at Dan with an intensity Lacey had never seen before.

Lacey saw Lizzie's eyes widen at the question and response. Ransom wrapped his arm around her chair in a protective gesture as he glared at Dan.

Tate's jaw ticked.

"I'm moving forward with my dreams, Dad. That includes leaving home and making my own way in the world."

Dan chewed for a moment. "How? By driving all over the country every weekend? Doesn't sound like much of a career choice to me."

"Dad. That's enough," Tate snapped.

Dan glanced at him before focusing back on Lacey.

Rage flashed through Lacey. The condescending words along with the fresh hurt of losing Candy for the season boiled in her blood. Reining in her emotions, she glared at her father and forced her voice to remain calm and cool. "That's because it's not your career choice. It's mine. I'm not throwing in the towel just because you don't approve."

"What do you think of a single woman spending her life on the road chasing rodeos?" Dan asked Jonas.

Jonas grinned at Lacey. "Sounds like a perfect job for anyone motivated enough to give it a try."

"What in the hell do you know about it?" Dan asked in a near bellow.

"I used to rope professionally. Participated in more rodeos than I can count." Jonas drew in air. "The rodeo isn't for the faint of heart. It takes hard work, guts and sacrifice to make it. Lacey has paid her dues and just happens to be one of the world's best. As long as it makes her happy, I say go for it. That's what anyone who cares for her will say. Follow those dreams as long as they still matter." Jonas bumped Lacey's foot with his own.

She smiled softly at him. "Thank you."

"It's true. You're one special lady. Anyone who says different is dense and blind." He didn't drop eye contact in order to deliver the retort obviously directed at Dan.

"Lacey has done nothing but sacrifice and work hard all her life. If she's ready to spread her wings and fly, then more power to her," Helen added.

"It's about time. She's getting long in the tooth hanging around here," Tate tossed out.

Lacey rolled her eyes at her brother.

"She's a feisty one, that's for sure." Ransom winked at her. "I have a feeling Jonas is the man who can lasso her in if need be."

Lizzie elbowed Ransom in the side. "If anyone needs lassoing, it's you."

Ransom's eyes lit up.

Smitten. He's definitely smitten. Lacey grinned at the byplay between Lizzie and Ransom.

"If I try to rope her, I have no illusions that Lacey would kick my ass." Jonas' eyes twinkled with mischief.

"You bet right." She smiled at him before checking on her father.

Dan snorted, but shut his mouth and resumed eating.

Thank goodness.

* * * *

"That was interesting." Jonas ambled toward Lacey, two steaming mugs in hand. He figured the chilly, rainy afternoon called for a hot treat, especially considering the awkward and tension-filled meal they'd just endured.

After leaving her parents' house, he'd driven them back to his place, not quite ready to part ways for the day.

Lacey took the offered mug of hot chocolate from his hands, immediately taking a sip. "Mmm. Marshmallows. My favorite."

He grinned and sat down beside her. "You look like a girl who appreciates marshmallows."

She arched an eyebrow. "I'm not sure what that means."

He chuckled. "Neither do I."

Lacey smiled widely before slowly sobering as if she'd just recalled his comment. "I'm sorry that lunch ended up ruined because of me." She slouched her shoulders.

"You don't bear responsibility for that. Your father does." Irritation zinged through him when he remembered the stabbing comments her father had aimed at her. Instead of being a father, he'd acted like an ass. Probably no differently than he'd behaved her entire life. *The bastard.* Jonas didn't care for the man one bit and had worked hard to walk a fine line between supporting Lacey and resisting the nearly overwhelming urge to march to the other end of the table and punch Dan in the mouth.

He stroked Lacey's hair with his free hand. "I'm sorry for the way he treats you. I don't understand men like that. Never have and never will." She made her own choices, but Jonas vowed she'd never be forced to live under that man's roof and endure his verbal garage and abuse any longer. "The rest of your family stood up to him as well. They have your back, even if they're trying to keep a precarious peace."

"Poor Lizzie. She must be having second thoughts about entering this family." Lacey sighed. "I hope Ransom straightens her out and makes her understand that it's nothing to do with her. My father actually likes her and will treat her accordingly."

Jonas' heart tugged at that last phrase. To be a child fighting endlessly to earn a father's approval that would never come. Lacey had turned out damn well considering the environment in which she'd been raised. "I'm sorry, but your father is an ass. At least your brothers and mother stuck up for you. I have a feeling that's not always been the case."

Lacey sighed. "Mom always apologized for him, made excuses, in private. I guess since their secret is out in the open, she's found her tongue and a bit of a spine as well. The boys have tried to keep the peace. I guess Ransom sees clearly now that he has Lizzie. Dad's harshness will make her leery, too, even if it's not aimed her direction. Ransom won't like that. I have a feeling he'll be ducking out of more dinners from now on."

"Smart man. His woman comes first."

"Thank you for supporting me." Lacey turned and met his eyes. "I think what you said might have gotten through to him a little bit. Enough to shut his mouth when he decided he couldn't sway you."

"I wouldn't do anything less. You don't deserve such treatment. No woman does." His gut clenched at the thought of how many years she'd suffered the verbal abuse laid down by her father. *Never again. Not if I have anything to do with it.*

He dropped his hand and sipped his drink. Lacey stared at him with open curiosity.

"What?"

She tilted her head. "Just thinking. When we first met, I thought you were so gruff, off-putting. Now that I've been around you more, the opposite is true."

"Meaning?"

She grinned mischievously. "You're not the ogre I thought you were."

He snorted, but amusement danced between them.

"Something tells me you'd had a bad day. That's why you were so snappish."

Jonas considered her statement and how to respond. He took another sip to fortify his courage and looked her in the eye. "It wasn't so much a bad day but a bad couple of years."

She watched him closely, but remained mute.

"I think I mentioned that I broke my leg, which ended the roping season."

Lacey nodded.

"Well, there's more to it than that." He released her gaze and stared at the coffee table in front of him, recalling the doctor breaking the awful news. "One of the follow-up visits found something unexpected."

"What was it?" she whispered.

He made himself turn back to her, study her face and await her reaction to the news. "Testicular cancer."

Lacey's eyes widened, concern swamped the depths. "Oh, I'm so sorry."

"They surgically removed it." He blew out a breath as Lacey's features conveyed support and worry. No red flags. "I was lucky. They got it all, though it left scars. Ugly scars."

Lacey reached out and cupped his cheek. "Scars are marks left from living life. Everyone has them. I'd say if a person didn't have any, they haven't done much."

Her sentiment touched him. Still, he needed her to understand the whole picture. When and if they reached the point of getting naked, he had to be assured she could deal with his disfigurement. "Lacey, this isn't just a small surgical cut. I'm missing a nut."

She trailed her fingers along his jawline as if trying to ease the tension. "Would you think differently of me if I were missing an ovary?"

He shook his head, careful not to disturb her caress. "That's different. It's inside. No one can see the difference."

"The value of a man isn't in his testicles. It's in his heart and his head." She scooted closer, settling on his lap.

Jonas automatically wrapped his arms around her, holding her in place.

"You're a damn fine man, Jonas. Balls or no balls, I'm not about to trade you in."

"You say that now—"

She silenced him with a finger over his lips. "I'll say that again when the time comes. No scar is going to change my opinion of you. Ever."

Almost afraid to believe, Jonas pulled Lacey against his chest instead. If only she kept her word, he'd be the happiest man alive.

For a long time he did nothing more than hold her, sharing the evening in the comforts of another's arms.

He wouldn't have had it any other way.

Chapter Seventeen

Lacey removed the saddle from a young gelding she'd spent the whole morning with, placed it on a stand along with the blanket, picked up a brush and went to work. Her mind, as usual, followed a bunny path in a quick slideshow of memories of her less-than-prestigious life.

Several days had passed since Lacey had last seen her family. She'd settled into a routine, working at the Humane Society farm every day unless Dr. Moore needed her. Her mother and brothers kept in touch fairly often, though the conversations tended to avoid the whole complex situation surrounding her father. Much to Lacey's relief.

In her free time she checked around for another possible barrel horse. Each potential mount had fallen to the wayside for one reason or another, namely price, location and abilities. Five figures might be the going rate for quality barrel horses these days, but that ended up putting every animal out of her reach.

What am I going to do? The only alternative she'd come up with was to give up barrel racing for a few years, until the foal Candy hopefully carried right now would be old enough to enter the circuit. The thought of postponing her dreams tasted like sour mothballs. Fear rose with the idea that being away from the sport that long would end her chances completely. The freedom to spend her weekends away existed right now. If forced to get a nine to five, she maybe could make it work. The odds were against it, though. Cowgirls tended to leave the rodeo and never return. They found full-time jobs or became mothers or both. *Hooray for them.* Unfortunately, Lacey couldn't see herself in those roles. Not right now, anyway.

"Lacey? Oh, Lacey?"

She blinked up at the sound of her name to find Jonas staring at her with an amused smile.

"You might want to change sides before you brush all the hair off the poor guy. I think he's plenty clean over here." Jonas gestured to the glistening coat left behind after her brushing.

Lacey nodded and walked around the horse to start over again.

His eyebrows furrowed as he frowned. "What's wrong?"

"Nothing." Lacey made long strokes with the soft brush. After a quick go-over, she plucked the hoof pick out of the bucket and cleaned the horse's hooves.

Jonas stepped closer. "I thought we were past the silent treatment."

Lacey blew out a breath. "We are. I just tire of dumping my shit on you. You probably think I'm pretty damn incapable of taking care of myself." She finished the last hoof and stood up.

Jonas edged closer, lifted his hand, and ran his knuckles down her cheek. "First of all, I don't think any such thing. You're one of the strongest women I've ever met. Hell, most everyone, man or woman, would have crumpled under the load you're carrying a long time ago. You, on the other hand, cowgirl up and press on." He brushed her lips with his thumb. "As for the other, I ask because I care about you. Nothing you can do or say will change that."

Lacey met his gaze and pulled on her big girl panties. His words bolstered her. The least she could do was stand up and earn his praise. "I've been searching everywhere for a new barrel horse. Nothing. Anywhere. I've tried other rescues. Even online. Every horse that might possibly work is either way too expensive or on the coast."

For a long moment, Jonas simply looked down at her, as if trying to figure out a puzzle. Gradually, a ghost of a smile covered his lips. "Go put your gelding up. I'll meet you in the arena in a few minutes."

She blinked at him. "What?"

He dropped his hand to her hip and gave her a nudge. "Put your gelding up. I have a surprise for you when you're done."

"Umm. Okay." Perplexed, Lacey untied the rope and led the horse out of the barn. After releasing him back into his paddock, she made a beeline for the large indoor arena.

She stepped inside, took a second for her eyes to adjust, then cocked her head in curiosity.

Jonas stood near the entrance, holding a saddled Knight by the reins.

He smiled as she walked toward them. "Come on. Up you go."

She peered at the horse then back at Jonas. "You want me to ride Knight?"

"Yep." He gave her a boost into the saddle before gesturing across the large space. "Time for you to give him a try."

Lacey followed his line to find three barrels placed strategically toward the far end. A gasp escaped as she turned her focus back to him. Her mind whirled at the possible meaning.

"He's yours, Lacey."

The words both stunned and amazed her. "But... Nila said he was spoken for."

Jonas grinned coyly. "I knew you wanted him from day one. I bought him for you. Wanted to work with him enough before springing this surprise on you."

"Oh, Jonas." Her eyes grew misty. She wiped them as a single tear rolled down her cheek. "I've never been given a gift so sweet."

He patted her on the thigh, a true smile covering his face. "You deserve it, sweetheart. That and so much more." Taking a pace backward, he motioned toward the barrels. "Going to give him a try?"

Lacey's heart leaped. "I can't wait." She whirled the gelding around, dried her eyes again, then took a deep breath. Knight danced under her for a second before she touched him with her heels. He took off.

Holding on to the saddle horn, Lacey guided him around the first barrel, surged for the second, turned the corner, and aimed for the final one. He slid into a wide turn, straightened up, then dashed for home.

Lacey pulled him up and jogged him around the outskirts of the arena, making her way back to Jonas. She couldn't suppress the smile on her face and didn't want to.

"Looked damn good to me."

Lacey patted Knight's neck. "I still can't believe you. Buying him. You've been spending so much time working with him." Happiness replaced previous worry and melancholy. "I don't know what to say, Jonas."

"How about thank you?" He rested his hands on his hips.

"Thank you." She leaned over and brushed her lips over his. "Dinner tonight is on me."

She saw the spark of joy and knew the same feeling.

"I'd like that."

Hope returned with gusto. All thanks to Jonas.

Previous hesitation and indecision dissipated like a mud puddle in the Sahara. In all the darkness, she'd found a shining star — Jonas.

* * * *

"You sure can cook, I'll give you that." Jonas took another bite of the cheese-stuffed shells and closed his eyes in dining pleasure. He reopened them to find Lacey smiling proudly.

"Thanks. I'm glad you like them."

She'd run to the store quickly after hanging her saddle up for the day. Less than an hour later, she'd placed piping hot food on the small kitchen table. The aroma alone had made Jonas' mouth water. The taste kept him coming back for more.

"Can I ask a question?"

"Go for it." Jonas shoveled in another bite of the steaming

meal.

"I understand why you took time off the rodeo circuit. Yet you're fine now. Why aren't you going back to roping?"

He took a long drink of soda. "By the time I'd regained my strength from everything, the drive and enjoyment of calf roping had disappeared. I tried to get back in the saddle, I did. The fun was gone. So, I retired Noggin, told my brother I wanted to cut back in the oil business we ran, and turned my life in a different direction."

"Wow." She blinked at him. "You did some major changes."

"When you're told you have cancer, priorities change. I no longer wanted to go through the motions of life, waiting for retirement in order to finally take control. I didn't know if I had that much time. Still don't."

Lacey frowned. "But, you're cured, right?"

He shrugged. "Cured isn't applied to cancer cases until years down the road without a relapse. I go in every three months for a check-up and scans to make sure it's not returning."

"Oh." Sympathy flashed through her eyes.

He stiffened. "Don't pity me. That's the one thing I can't stand."

Her eyebrows furrowed. "I don't pity you. Not in the least." She drew in a breath. "I feel many things for you. Pity isn't on the list."

Jonas relaxed by margins.

She stole a piece of broccoli off his plate, stuck it in her mouth, chewed then swallowed. "I like you. A lot. You're caring, sweet and unselfish. Brave and kind. You treat horses like favored pets. Even-tempered, quiet-spoken and sexy as hell. Not to mention you've got the best ass this side of the Mississippi."

Jonas perked up as the list continued, reluctantly smiling as she finished. "You've been checking out my ass?"

"Uh-huh." She peered up at him from under her eyelashes.

He shook his head in amusement. Leave it to Lacey to

throw him for a loop now and again.

"One of these days I'll get you to strip down so I can bounce a quarter off it."

He burst out laughing, unable to contain the humor at her silliness. "Think it will bounce far?"

She smiled ruefully. "I bet it will."

The sultry teasing and the heated expression on her face sent a fire zipping through his blood and straight to his cock. "Do I get to return the favor?"

Lacey arched an eyebrow. "We'll see." She offered up a wicked grin before forking another bite of pasta.

Damn. A bit of sensual banter and a couple of shy glances had cranked his libido and hardened his dick. The thought of what would happen once he stripped her down nearly made him groan.

One thing was for certain—Lacey would rock his world.

If she can handle my scars. Saying she could was one thing. Seeing and doing was another.

Only time would tell.

Chapter Eighteen

The next week flew by as Lacey fell into a routine. She worked at Dr. Moore's office on Mondays. The rest of the days she spent training Humane Society horses and spending her free time with Knight.

He'd gotten the hang of running barrels, but had more bridges to cross before he could be a contender—namely his anxiety when away from his new best friend, a female mule called Mabel. As long as she was in the arena, he held himself together like a pro. Without her nearby, he clomped down on the bit, danced in circles and whinnied for her. Listening and responding dropped to the wayside.

She'd resigned herself that Mabel would just have to accompany them to the starting line and meet them as soon as he finished. Great in theory. A bit more difficult considering she'd have no one free at that time to handle one slow-moving mule. Not to mention the concern with huge crowds, the booming announcer's voice and the cheers that could be loud enough to shake the building. How she was going to get him used to that issue, she didn't have a clue. Not yet, anyway.

In the meantime, she taught him lead changes, how to get close up to the barrels and how to wait patiently at the starting line until ready. The last part became a consistent struggle. Knight had pep and loved to run. As soon as he saw the barrels, he preferred to get down to business, no matter what Lacey wanted.

At least they had a month or so to work some kinks out before attending their first barrel race. Thank goodness. She'd taken a chance with submitting her entry fee on the first rodeo, with the hopes that she could work the kinks out of Knight in time.

Lacey finished grooming Knight, collected her tools and shut the gate to his paddock behind her. The moment she left his side, he trotted over to Mabel and started nibbling on her neck. Love-speak for horses. Except Knight had been gelded and Mabel had proved sterile, like virtually every other mule with very few exceptions. Those facts didn't put a dent into their romance, though.

Lacey rolled her eyes. "You're such a goose."

She checked the time, plucked out her phone, and made a quick call.

"Hello?"

"Trinity."

"Lacey. I was just thinking about you. How's it going?"

Lacey watched the two equines with fondness. "Much better. You'll never believe this. Jonas bought Knight for me. He even started him on barrels."

"That's wonderful." Excitement came through in Trinity's voice. "Will he be ready by spring?"

"Hopefully. He's running great. It's the noise, distractions and his separation anxiety that are issues."

"You'll get him there. You're a great trainer, Lacey." Trinity paused. "How is Jonas, by the way?"

Lacey rolled her eyes at Trinity's nosiness. "He's wonderful. I still can't believe that he bought Knight for me."

"Sounds like you two are getting along."

"Uh-huh. You could say that." Lacey watched as Knight stopped fussing over Mabel and went back to nibbling at what was left of the late fall grass in the paddock.

"Have you roped him yet?"

Lacey grinned. "Not yet. But I'm getting closer."

"Just don't spur him too hard." Trinity giggled.

Lacey joined in. "No worries about that." She drew in a breath. "Thanks, Trinity. For everything. I'm flying by the seat of my pants and having you as a cheerleader keeps me going."

"No problem. That's what friends are for."

"Well, I need to get going."

"Keep in touch. I want to hear all the latest news," Trinity ordered.

"Yeah, yeah. Mother hen."

"Yep, that's me." Trinity chuckled. "Really. If you need anything just holler. I'm here for you."

"Thanks." Lacey knew the offer for the truth. "I'll talk to you later. Bye."

"Bye."

Lacey clicked off the call, tucked the phone into her back pocket and watched Knight move across the paddock as if he didn't have a care in the world. His strides were long and easy. Gliding and gorgeous. *If only I can get him to the professional barrel racing level in quick fashion.*

"How's he coming along?"

Lacey glanced up to find Jonas leaning against the doorjamb of the barn. Dressed in his typical jeans, a Western shirt and a thick jacket, he looked like a real-life cowboy. A sexy one at that.

"Getting there. The racing isn't the issue. Prying him away from his girlfriend is."

Jonas flashed a lopsided grin. "Typical male."

She read the mischief in his expression and opted to play along. "Every six seconds, huh?"

He regained his feet, took the bucket from her hands and followed her into the barn. A couple of steps later, he dropped off the supplies in the grooming area and returned to her side in the aisle bracketed by presently empty stalls. Though still chilly, the horses went out nearly every single day to the fields.

Jonas stopped in front of her, grabbed her hips, and lowered his head. "Sometimes more than that." He brushed his lips over hers. Gently. Teasingly. Coaxingly.

She wrapped her arms around his neck and met him on the next pass. He swooped down, sealed their lips, then licked at the seam until she opened. The moment she did so he delved in, swirling his tongue all around as if tasting her then returning for more.

Lacey took advantage of the closeness, ran her hands down back, and lower. Planting her hands on his rear, she squeezed.

Jonas moaned, jerked and pulled back just enough to allow them to breathe. "You're playing with fire."

She peered up at him with a grin. "Think so?" Boldly, she pinched again. "Funny, I wouldn't call this fire. I'd call it…" She didn't finish. He grabbed for her. She squealed and darted down the empty aisle.

He snagged her in three strides, locking his arms around her so her only escape remained to back up. Which she did. Right into an unoccupied stall.

Her boot hung, sending her tumbling to the ground.

Jonas caught her, lowered her the rest of the way down, then covered her with his powerful body.

Lacey took inventory, enjoying his weight pressing into her. With the cushion of the thick, fluffy straw under her back, she could stay there for a long time to come. Especially if Jonas kept kissing her the way he was.

She rested her hands on his shoulders and nipped his chin until he lifted his head to stare down at her. "This better be a clean stall. If it's filled with horseshit, I really *will* kick your ass."

He grinned wickedly down at her. "I might be a bit rough around the edges, but I have more manners than that." He peppered kisses across her neck before finally covering her lips. His hand tunneled under her shirt, skimmed over soft flesh until he covered a breast, gently molding and strumming through her bra. The novel sensation set loose a burst of pleasure.

She arched under his touch. The few kisses she'd shared with other men paled in comparison to Jonas'. Thorough, attentive to detail and downright delicious. She opened her mouth and invited him to explore again.

He didn't disappoint. Soft lips caressed before he changed the angle, adjusted his position and got down to the serious business of cranking on the heat with one lip-lock after another.

Lacey mimicked his actions, letting her hands roam as he slid his hand around back, unsnap her bra with his fingers then push it aside. She gasped as he touched her bare flesh for the first time, weighing, before rubbing his thumb over her sensitive nipple.

Reason returned by increments amidst the ocean of pleasurable sensations coursing through her body. "Are you...we...?"

He pulled back just enough to meet her gaze.

She noted the hooded eyes, the sultry expression filled with hunger. *For me.* Her stomach flipped over as arousal flooded her system.

"This is just fooling around, darlin'. When I get serious, you won't have to ask those questions." He flicked his tongue over her earlobe. "Besides, I'm not going to take you in some cold barn, on a bed of itchy straw."

"Good to know." His words pleased her as they presented a picture for the future. "Because I'd hate for you to frostbite something important out here."

He chuckled. "That would be pretty damn horrible. Guess that means we better consider my toasty, comfortable bed for the big stuff."

"Might be safer," she replied, tongue in cheek. The silly bantering, oddly enough, eased her concerns as well as whetted her desire. Wrapping her arms around his neck, she lifted her legs, bent them, and anchored them on his hips. His bulge rasped the junction of her thighs, through both their jeans. She could only imagine how good it would be when no garments stood in their way. Her stomach somersaulted in decadent agreement.

He kissed her like there was no tomorrow, thrusting his tongue past her lips to plunder every corner. She met him with enthusiasm, needing to give back as much as receive.

He tapped her tongue on the first pass. She reciprocated and pushed back in order to get a deeper taste of him. Springtime. That was what she found. A delicious combination of sunshine and spring. Instantly, she developed a craving for more.

Jonas pulled back in order to rain kisses down her neck and to her upper chest. At the same time, he released her breast in order to lightly caress her stomach before moving back upward to explore her bare breasts once again.

Bright pleasure speared through her as he molded the area then worried the nipple. Lacey arched into his touch.

"So responsive. I knew you'd be." He whispered the words against her ear then sucked on her lobe.

Her breath hitched as she tried to process the novel sensations. She trailed her fingers down his chest, noting the hard muscles under the material. "So, when do you expect to get 'serious'?"

His low groan proved to be music to her ears. He raised his head and stared down at her. "Is that an invitation?"

Lacey bit her lip. Decision time. Good thing she didn't have to think too hard about it. She'd wanted Jonas since the moment she saw him. They'd had a rocky patch or two, but things had straightened out. He made her days eventful and fun. Steadfastly, he supported her and didn't shy away from all her troubles. On the contrary, he stood strong with her, like a true champion of old. A knight ready to fight for his queen. She'd never found a man like that and probably wouldn't ever again.

So what do I do?

Trinity's words came back to her. *'I think you already know what to do. You just have to find the courage and jump in with both feet'.*

"Lacey?" Jonas' voice drew her back to the present.

"Yes."

He stilled. "Yes, what?"

"Yes, I want you. Yes, I need you. Yes, I can't wait any longer to be with you in every sense of the word."

A smile crossed his face then grew. "Are you sure?"

"Positive." She linked her fingers with his. *Because I love you.* She didn't have the courage to speak the words aloud, but had every intention of showing him with her body. In his bed. Where it was warmer.

He stood up, held out a hand and pulled her to her feet. "Then I guess we should finish up here and head back to my house."

"I like that idea." She brushed her lips over his chin. "Maybe you can fix your special grilled cheese sandwiches, too?"

His grin turned wolfish. "I suspect I can."

"Great." Lacey paused, not wanting to leave him, but knowing she had equipment to put away before she could depart for the day. "I guess…"

He gave her a nudge. "Go. Finish what you need. I'll be here when you're ready. Even if you change your mind and only want the food."

His understanding and compassion touched her. "I won't change my mind. No way. But I do believe a shower is called for." Reality clicked. "I'll have to stop by Nila's and gather some overnight stuff."

"Okay." He pulled her close for a quick kiss. "Call me or find me when you're ready. I'll be around."

"Will do." Lacey sighed, stepped back, looked at Jonas one more time then hurried off. *The sooner I get started, the sooner I'll be done.*

Nearly twenty minutes later, she shed her boots in the mud room of Nila's house. Lacey quickly washed her hands, then headed for the guest bathroom, intent on a fast shower before packing some items to get her through the night.

She'd just stepped from the bathroom and into her temporary bedroom when Nila called her name.

"I'm in here."

Nila peered through the open doorway. "There you are." She checked her watch. "Quitting early?"

A smidgen of guilt landed on Lacey's shoulders. She brushed it aside. "I have a date with Jonas." She couldn't contain the grin, though she vowed to keep the details to herself.

"Well...that's certainly good news." Nila smiled. "I've been watching the way you two look at each other. There's some major sparks there." She stepped into the room and sat down on the bed.

Lacey adjusted her towel, not outgoing enough to drop it and start dressing with Nila in the room. "He's a good man. Kind. Caring."

"Not to mention handsome as sin." Nila's eyes lit up.

Lacey chuckled. "That too." She sobered. "I thought I loved another man. Now I can see it was just infatuation."

"Do you love Jonas?"

"I think so." Lacey blew out a breath. "So much has happened so quickly that I'm still trying to figure some things out. But I know a bit already and Jonas is...special."

"He's strong. A true cowboy in the sense that he'll fight by your side, pamper you to all his abilities and love you to his dying day." Nila smoothed a wrinkle on the comforter. "They don't make men like that anymore."

Lacey thought of Cody. "Not many."

Standing, Nila appraised Lacey for a couple of beats. "Why do I get the feeling that I'll be losing my roommate soon?"

"Now who's putting the cart before the horse?" Lacey smiled.

Nila shrugged. "Just calling it like I see it." She patted Lacey's hand. "I'm happy for you. If anyone ever deserved anything good in their life, it's you."

"Thank you," Lacey whispered. She met Nila's gaze. "Just so you know, I might not be home tonight..."

Nila waved her hand. "Girl, I'm not too old to remember those days. If you find yourself in bed with a great man wrapped around you, then that's the place where you belong."

"You're a godsend, Nila."

"Nah."

Lacey hugged her warmly. "Yes, you are. Like a fairy godmother."

"Ugh." Nila rolled her eyes then tapped her lips with a finger. "Although one of those magic wands would be nifty. All the dishes I wouldn't have to wash. The stalls I wouldn't have to clean..." She left the room still muttering to herself.

Lacey shook her head in amusement. She had the green light from Nila, which meant a lot. Now she just had to get ready and go in search of her prince charming.

Chapter Nineteen

"Hey there, cowboy."

Jonas turned to spy Lacey ambling toward him with a carry bag in hand, the straps resting on her shoulder. The scent of vanilla wafted to him, sending a jolt of pleasure through him as well as making his stomach growl with hunger. He smiled. "There you are. Ready to go?"

"Yep."

He raked her with his gaze, finding every curve and flare of her hip in the process. Beautiful. But there was so much more to Lacey than just the outside. Many more layers he'd just begun to discover.

She stopped in front of him and toed the dirt of the barn floor. "I told Nila not to expect me home tonight."

He parted his lips, a bit surprised at her candidness with Nila, although it made sense. She wouldn't want her boss to worry if she didn't show back up. "What did she say?"

Lacey's eyes met his. "She cheered me on. Told me that I'd found a true man. One of the very few good ones left."

The expression on her face told the story. Lacey not only believed Nila's words, she found them solid as an old oak herself. The realization struck a chord with him. "I want to be that man for you."

Her face softened as she stepped close enough to place her palm against his cheek. "You already are."

He nuzzled her hand then blew out a breath, his emotions welling up just from her presence and sweet words.

She grinned ruefully. "Change your mind about using one of the stalls?"

He snorted. "No way."

"Then perhaps we should get a move on?"

He chuckled. "Eager to taste my sandwiches again?"

She arched an eyebrow then dropped her gaze to his groin. "That too."

He bit back a groan, took her by the hand and led her toward his truck. If they stood there much longer with the sultry longing so apparent in her pretty eyes, he'd be hard pressed to drive. *Hard pressed, indeed.* Her light teasing had set a fire in his blood, zipped straight to his cock and hardened it in less than three seconds. He didn't think that particular ache would go away any time soon. Not until he slid balls-deep inside her and watched her shatter under him.

I can do this. After all this time, I can bare my body to a woman. To Lacey.

They'd no more than gotten out of the driveway when his phone rang. He pulled to the side of the road, checked the caller ID then immediately answered. "What's wrong, Nila?"

Lacey glanced over in concern.

"I'm sorry to bother you. I just got a call from the police. There's been an accident. A double-decker trailer full of horses on the way to slaughter has turned over on its side on the interstate."

Jonas' gut clenched. "Where?"

"One mile east of Riley Junction. East bound lane."

"On our way." He clicked the call off and placed the phone on the console.

"What's the matter?"

"A trailer full of horses turned over on the interstate. Nila's been called in." He sped toward the nearest intersecting road to cut the time in half.

"Oh my God." Lacey paled. "How bad?"

He shook his head. "I have no idea. It can't be good."

She yanked out her phone. "Dr. Moore? Have you heard about the wreck? Okay. Yeah, we're on our way." She placed it back in her pocket. "He's nearly there."

"Good. I have a feeling we're going to need all the help we can get."

Fifteen minutes later, he pulled up behind the wreck and sucked in a breath. A few horses stood outside but it appeared many more were still inside the wreck. Most down. Others with trailers had stopped as well as all kinds of first responders. While they might not have experience with horses, they could at least be useful in getting the animals out by cutting through steel.

Lacey jumped out of the passenger seat and dashed to the front. He followed right on her heels. When he spied inside the back of the trailer, his stomach sank. How many horses were trapped or dead, he couldn't count. All he could see was a sea of colored hides.

A horse's scream of panic rang through the air.

Lacey climbed into the right side of the trailer and started making her way back.

"Lacey. Wait!" He hurried after her, bracing himself for what he might find.

She tiptoed over one horse, touched its open eye, and shook her head before moving on. Another rescuer was near the back, trying to speak to an animal standing up against the far wall.

"He's frightened. Stay away from him." Lacey's calm voice carried despite the quietness. "Let me take him. Can you find a way to move the dead horse near the front so we can get the others out?"

The man, dressed in a police uniform, Jonas could now see, nodded briefly. "We've got a tractor outside with a sling they use for downed cows." He stepped back, allowing Lacey to take his place. "I was trying to keep him calm so he didn't injure the other horses right under him."

Jonas' eyes adjusted to the darkness just in time for him to glimpse a foal standing next to a downed mare, presumably its mother. "Son of a bitch," he muttered.

Lacey neared the baby, Jonas right on her heels.

The foal whinnied and pawed at his mother, getting no

response.

Jonas' heart broke at the sight. He took off his belt and carefully wrapped it around the baby's neck before buckling it snug enough to use as an improvised collar. Task done, he bent down, picked up the probably three-month-old baby, and carried it outside. Nila met him.

"Oh, mother of God." She clamped her hand over her mouth at the realization that the baby had been on his way to the slaughterhouse along with his mother.

"Bastards." Jonas bit off the word.

"His mother?"

"Down and most likely dead."

Nila's face fell. She ran a hand over the foal's face and tried to soothe him. The colt struggled all the more, still calling for his momma. "Let's put him in the trailer. I'll have someone stay with him until we can ascertain the status of his mother."

Jonas nodded, walked to the trailer and deposited the foal gently inside. A volunteer met him there, immediately taking hold of the belt and petting the little one. Jonas left him with the girl and hurried back to help Lacey.

He was prevented from re-entering by a group of people moving the dead horse onto the sling in order to move him out of the way. For several minutes they fussed with getting the tough fabric under him, then hooking it up to the tractor prongs. Finally, in what seemed like forever, they had him out of the way.

Jonas stepped inside and peered into the darkness. "Lacey?"

"I've got the stud calmed for now. We have to either get him out or these couple of horses up and out of the way." She pointed to a bay and a sorrel near her feet.

"Are they alive?" He hated to ask, but knew that many of the occupants were already dead before help arrived.

"One is. She can't stand because of the metal over her head. The other one, I'm not so sure."

Jonas glanced around, finding a firefighter behind him.

"Can you use the Jaws of Life to remove that metal piece so that mare can stand up?"

The guy studied the area for a minute. "It doesn't seem to be supporting anything right now so, yeah, I think so." He strode back out, presumably to gather the troops and get the device.

"Lacey? Can you keep him quiet while they cut the metal near him?" He held his breath, noting the wild white eyes of the stallion. Flashbacks of Lacey and Knight flew through his mind.

"I can try." She spoke softly, encouragingly, to the horse, keeping a solid grip on the halter he wore. "The foal's mother..."

He glanced to the side, finding no sign of movement, including breathing. "Gone."

"Just. Please. Just check to be sure." Her voice broke.

The sound nearly tore his heart open. He stepped between the mare's outstretched legs and ran his hand down her side, searching for breathing. No flinch or tremble followed. He blew out a breath and had opened his mouth when the slightest flutter of her eyelid caught his attention. Jonas moved closer. "Come on, Momma. Do it again."

Sure enough, she blinked.

"She's alive. Barely." He stood up and hollered to the group of people outside. "We need a vet in here, stat!"

Dr. Moore appeared. "What do you have?"

Jonas led him to the mare. "She's blinking, but no other movement."

Dr. Moore kneeled at her side, ran his hands over her entire body, then started moving her legs. She flinched, but didn't jerk away.

Jonas waited with bated breath, knowing her chances were slim unless they could get her on her feet.

"I need an IV kit. Fluids. We need to find a way to get her out of here and onto the grass, too," Dr. Moore ordered.

People filed in quickly. Firefighters, rescuers, other vets. They set up an IV in less than a minute while others worked with the sling to get her out of the way. Several minutes later, they moved her out of the trailer and placed her on some nearby grass well away from the highway in order to work on her.

In the meantime, another set of firefighters passed by Jonas carrying the Jaws of Life. He moved ahead, pulled off his shirt and used it to cover the face of the mare trapped under the bar. Glancing up, he found Lacey had done the same thing for the stud, despite the chilly afternoon temperatures. He commended her silently, trying to soothe the frightened mare as the rescuers went to work. She struggled. He lay across her, keeping her down.

As soon as they removed the bar, the men stepped back. Jonas spoke softly to the mare, removed his weight and rallied her to try to stand. She did so, shakily. He breathed a sigh of relief and encouraged her to follow him out of the trailer and back onto solid land. Once she did, he removed his shirt and handed her over. Nila took hold of the halter and led the traumatized mare toward her trailer. Jonas noticed the size of the mare's stomach and cussed some more. Obviously heavily pregnant, the mare had been on her way to the slaughterhouse. He'd never understand people.

With that sour thought, he returned to the same spot, hoping they'd made enough headway to get the stud out before he went berserk and hurt Lacey in the process. As it was, he heard the stallion's screams, his hooves banging on the metal floor in a display of fear and displeasure.

"You okay, Lacey?"

She pulled the horse back down using all her body weight and a sure hold on his halter as he tried to rear. "Yeah." His hoof scraped down the side of her leg. She flinched but didn't otherwise let on.

Shit. At this rate she'll be black and blue at the best, trampled to death at the worst. "Let me have him." Jonas stepped toward him.

Immediately the horse erupted in another fit, kicking at

the wall and lashing out with sharp teeth toward him.

He stopped.

"Back off, Jonas. He's not going to let anyone else close." Lacey crooned to the horse though she spoke to him. "Work on clearing the way."

Jonas grumbled in frustration but put some distance between himself and the spooked stallion anyway. The sooner they could get him out, the sooner Lacey would be free of her ward and safe.

However long they worked, he couldn't say. Slowly but surely, they managed to extract the horses. Someone said there were thirty-nine total. Maybe twenty that had survived. A couple were on the fence, including the mother of the foal. He sent up a prayer for all of them, especially that one. While he and Lacey, along with several others, including first responders and vets, worked on the right side, a duplicate team worked on the left. Each managed to make progress without jeopardizing or getting in the way of the other.

For a ragtag group of people called to this atypical and heart-wrenching situation, we've done pretty damn good. He took a second to glance across the area, finding several horses being tended to. A few had been taken away in a horse ambulance brought in from the equine hospital less than an hour away. Others had been loaded into trailers and taken to the Humane Society farm under Nila's direction. They'd have several new animals to board and work with. While they didn't have much room, he knew Nila would never turn these animals away. She'd transform her own house into a barn first.

All the while, he kept an eye on Lacey. No one could do anything for her until the path had been cleared. Unfortunately, that took time. Dr. Moore didn't want to try to get close enough to sedate the stallion, not knowing what injuries he might have. So they all relied on Lacey to keep the horse as relaxed as possible until they had a way to get him out without further injuring other horses.

As soon as the tractor picked up the last remaining dead horse on their side of the trailer, Jonas guided it out, then eased closer to Lacey. "It looks like we're there, sweetheart. Think you can handle getting him out? We can put a rope on him if needed."

"I think we're good."

He heard the weariness in her voice and saw the slight tremble to her arm—fatigue setting in from holding him still for over two hours. Jonas didn't know how banged up Lacey was but knew she'd carry some marks. "I'm right here if you need help."

She took a step backward, lightly tugging on the stallion's halter. "Come on, big guy. It's finally our turn."

Jonas held his breath as the stallion followed her at an excruciatingly slow pace. One step after another. Even with the cover over his eyes, the horse still jerked, screamed and reared up once again.

Lacey hung on, tugging him back to his feet. "You're going to hit your head doing that. Now, come on." She pulled at his halter while steadying him with one hand on his shoulder. "Just like that. You can do this. We're almost free."

Jonas jumped out of the trailer and cleared the way, fearing the crowd of people would set the stallion off. He watched as Lacey nudged the horse to take the final step from the smashed trailer to the solid ground. The stud seemed to relax marginally once he scented the fresh air and felt stability under his feet.

"Let's go to an empty trailer with him." Jonas glanced around.

A man dressed in jeans, a Western shirt and a cowboy hat stepped forward. "You're welcome to use mine. I heard the news, hooked up my trailer and came on the double in order to help."

Jonas smiled at the man. "Thank you. Do you know where the Humane Society farm is?"

He nodded. "Yes, sir. I was there looking for a roping

horse on that open house day."

Jonas' light clicked on. "Now I remember. You took Trusty home."

"That I did. He's learning fast. Going to be one great horse." The man led the way to the back of his trailer.

"Great." Jonas followed.

Lacey pulled up the rear with the still-agitated stallion. It took three attempts and plenty of coaxing along with a hefty shove to get the stallion into the trailer. "I'll ride with him. Just in case."

Jonas turned on her with a stern stare. "You'll do no such thing. That stud will likely rough you up if not squash you like a bug in that trailer."

She lifted her chin and glared right back. "He could have done that already. He's scared, is all. Leaving him alone right now won't help that matter."

Jonas shook his head. "Just leave that shirt over his eyes and he'll be fine. We'll worry about the rest when he gets to the farm." He tried not to notice Lacey standing in only her bra, but wasn't quite successful. Unfortunately, his shirt was long gone, used on several horses, or he would have offered it in a second.

"Here." One of the firemen slipped off his T-shirt and handed it to Lacey.

She beamed up at him and slipped it on. "Thank you."

The fireman dipped his head. "Welcome." He slipped his yellow coat back on and started back the way he came.

"I'll return it."

The man didn't pause while he waved. "Keep it."

She looked down as if reading the name of the department on the front. "Timber Valley. Do you know where that is?"

Jonas nodded. "Yeah, why?"

"Because I'm going to wash this guy's shirt and return it to him at work."

He smiled for the first time since Nila's urgent phone call. "How's your leg?" He'd not seen her limp on it despite the mark surely left by that stallion's hooves.

"Fine. Probably just a scratch. Nothing to worry about."

He shook his head but didn't bother to argue. It would take more than that to sideline Lacey. Her tenacity amazed him. "Are you ready to go? I'm sure Nila is getting flooded with horses and could use the help."

"Yeah." Lacey paused and scanned the wreck, now empty of horses.

Some of the horses had been pronounced dead, and were lying on the side of the road, waiting for the rendering truck to pick them up. Too many. Jonas couldn't help but see the irony. They had been on their way to die. While some had met the same fate, others had been saved because of the wreck.

He could only hope nothing like this happened ever again. The tragedy was too hard to bear.

"Come on." He wrapped an arm around Lacey and escorted her back to his truck.

He drove them back to the farm in silence, still trying to absorb how a day with so much potential had turned to shit. He'd never regret saving the horses they could. It was the fact the situation happened in the first place that turned his stomach. He'd seem some goodness in people today. Too bad the brightness dulled under the heavy fog of sadness and anger at the cruelty and uncaringness of humans when it came to animals in general.

Horses deserved nice homes with owners who loved them. There just weren't enough homes. Horses were cast aside and ended up either forgotten, neglected, abused, or left to wander on their own. Others were packed into trailers and sent to slaughterhouses. Neither option sat well with him.

All he could do was bust his butt in getting the farm's horses ready for a new start in life. A small cog in the wheel of homeless animals.

He sighed heavily.

Lacey took his hand in hers and twined her fingers through his. The action didn't need words. He knew she felt his pain as much as he did. Maybe more. No one could respond to such a tragedy and not be on an emotional rollercoaster.

He peered over at her and offered a sad smile. "We'll do the best we can for them."

"Yes, we will," Lacey answered.

Chapter Twenty

"Did you hear? The foal's momma, she's up and moving. Back to taking care of her little one, too." Lacey hurried over to Jonas as she stood on the other side of the largest barn, checking out the horses in a line of stalls. She hadn't been able to wait to tell him the good news.

They'd been working nearly all night long with Nila and other volunteers in order to get the new horses settled into stalls. Dr. Moore and their regular vet had visited, checked each animal out and written orders for each one that needed treatment or medication. They'd promised to return the next day to look them over once again, but recommended food, water and rest after their harrowing day.

Jonas' mouth fell open. "Really?"

"Yep. Nila just heard from the equine hospital. They had the mare on her feet at the site, though she was really shaky. They think she was down for a while with another horse on top of her at some point. That caused a pinched nerve and some decreased circulation. By the time they got a couple of liters of fluid into her, she was trying to stand and looking for her baby. They were reunited at the hospital and seem to be doing well."

"That's wonderful." He smiled wide. "I was afraid she was dead and the poor orphan foal would have a hard time adjusting."

"Me too." Lacey's face fell as she pushed away a stray lock of hair that had escaped her ponytail eons ago. "So much sadness, yet a glimmer of hope now and again."

"True." He peeked through the wooden planks at the stallion inside. "What do you think about him?"

Lacey approached slowly, knowing the stallion had yet to chill completely from his experience. The solid black hide helped conceal him in the shadows. "He's beautiful." She'd spent nearly two hours trying to keep him calm until they could get him free. He'd settled down just enough to allow that to happen. Barely. She'd lost count of the times he'd tried to beat his way out of the wreckage.

Now, free in his stall, the stallion caught her eye. Big. Built. A quarter horse, if she didn't miss her guess. While not nearly as tall as some of the thoroughbreds, he wasn't small, either. His long tail dragged across the thick layer of straw while his tousled mane spoke of many days without seeing a comb. Edgy and nervous, he moved restlessly in his stall.

He reminded her of Knight. The apprehension seemed all too familiar, although in a totally different way. Knight had been obviously panicked and had settled down once he'd found a friend and an outside place to stay. This horse still seemed rattled by his ordeal and confused by all the changes. Understandable considering all he'd been through. A concussion had been mentioned as a possibility, which would only add to his pacing and antsy behavior. The vets weren't sure, but reassured them that food and rest would be the treatment regardless of whether he'd banged his head or not.

Images of the wreck paraded through her mind. Her eyes welled up at the memory of those that couldn't be saved. Those that were on the fence with a long road ahead of them. Tears overflowed and trickled down her cheeks. Exhaustion overtook her, leaving her bereft and lackluster. Add in the emotional outpouring and her remaining energy fled in a heartbeat.

"What's this?" Jonas brushed the drops away.

She drew in a breath and tried to put words to her feelings. "I'm sorry that I couldn't have done more. Saved more. They didn't deserve such a fate."

He pulled her into his chest and held her tight. She felt his lips press against her crown. "Shhh. We did all we could. The rest was, and still is, in God's hands." He rocked her slowly as she cried her heart out, her abundant problems colliding with this recent tragedy to make a perfect storm of emotions.

Exhausted and wrung out, she could only soak up Jonas' strength and grapple with her composure, failing the first couple of times before finally managing to stem the flood of tears. She sniffed and rested her cheek against his wide chest, letting the *lub-dub* of his heart soothe her.

"It's almost dawn," he whispered. "Do you want to go back to Nila's house or to mine?"

She didn't have to think hard. "Yours."

He rubbed his cheek against hers. "Let's clean up, get some food and hit the sack. We're both beat."

She nodded, then stepped back in order to meet his eyes. "I guess we can skip a day of training."

He wiped a final tear away with his thumb. "I'd say we earned a day off. At least half of one." His eyes scanned her face.

"I could use a hot shower," she admitted.

"That makes two of us." He wrapped an arm around her waist. "We'll go to my house and take it from there. We're not doing anyone any good hanging around here, and working until we drop won't help, either."

"You're right." She drew in a deep breath and forced her heavy feet to carry her to his truck. In recent memory, she'd never been this worn out. Even after driving hundreds of miles to and from a competition, she hadn't been ready to fall on her face. Not like this. Fatigue had set in and refused to lessen its hold. Her entire body ached and the thought of having to walk to his truck nearly sucked the last bit of life from her. Stubbornness kept her upright and going. No way would she crumple in front of Jonas. Crying had been bad enough.

Her shoulders slumped in defeat as she climbed into his truck and fastened the seat belt. She needed a distraction and a sunny beam to brighten the day. Too bad darkness blanketed the area and would do so for a while longer.

"I'm thrilled about that mare and her foal. That one just about broke my heart." Jonas drove with his focus on the road, the headlights illuminating the path in front of them.

"Mine too. There was so much sadness already. I'm glad she's going to be okay." Lacey recalled the moment she'd seen the baby trying desperately to rouse his mother. The image would be imprinted on her forever. Along with the rest of the harrowing scene. She recalled the stud and how Jonas had seemed enamored with the big guy. "You like that black stallion." She made the words a statement of fact.

"Yeah." He turned onto the side road. "He's built like a champion. Powerful. Probably speedy too."

For a split second, she considered him for a backup barrel horse. "Think he'd do well in the rodeo circuit?"

Jonas shrugged. "Too early to tell. With that conformation, he might have a chance."

She studied him for a long moment, noticing a thoughtful concentration on his face. "Thinking of keeping him? Turning him into a roping horse?"

Jonas stilled, his only movements related to turning into his driveway, hitting the automatic garage door button and pulling the vehicle inside. He cut the engine and shut the door behind them before turning to her. "I don't know, Lacey. For a second there, the idea crossed my mind."

She smiled softly. Rodeo tended to stick in a person's blood. Jonas might have been out for a bit, but some of the inner fire had seemed to flare to life when he'd sighted the big horse. "That's not such a bad thing, you know. Hobbies are good for a person."

"Uh-huh." He climbed out of the driver's seat and headed to the door leading into the house.

She followed. "Just don't throw the idea out the window yet. Okay?"

He turned back to her, paused, then gave a quick nod. "Okay."

Hope resurfaced briefly as Lacey saw the truth in his tired eyes. "Since that's settled, why don't you take a shower first? I'll fix us something hot to eat and expedite things."

"I don't mind waiting." He opened the door, stepped into the mud room and closed the door behind him. After removing his boots, he walked carefully into the kitchen.

Lacey shook her head and gave him a light shove. "Shower. Now. Go."

He grinned at her. "I kind of like this bossy side of you. What does that say about me?"

Lacey opened her mouth but no snappy comebacks emerged. She thought another second. "I'm not sure."

"Guess we'll figure it out later. Together."

"Yep. After your shower."

"Going. Going." He flashed a smile and headed off toward the far bathroom.

Lacey watched him go, appreciating the flex and snap of the muscles of his back and rear until he disappeared from sight. Only then did she start rummaging through the pantry and fridge for ideas for a quick, light meal, her mind never far from the man presently stripping down in the other room.

He'd been a hero today. Stepping up and lending a hand. All that and then some.

Nila was right. *Jonas is a true man.* A cowboy of old filled with chivalry, caring and a protective streak Lacey had never known.

She could easily envision a future with him. Jonas and their horses.

The thought put a smile back on her face.

Chapter Twenty-One

Sun streaming in through the window roused Lacey from her sleep. She opened her eyes, blinked at the glare, then took inventory. Warmth surrounded her while a rock-hard wall supported her back in a comfortable softness despite the lack of give.

Momentary confusion hit then lapsed. She'd crashed on the couch, too tired to do much more than gather a blanket and pull it over herself.

She realized Jonas had her wrapped up like a cocoon. Obviously Jonas had carried her to his bed sometime later, which explained her present circumstance. His left arm was crooked over her waist, holding her snug against his chest. Her bottom fit in the angle created by their molding into a spoon position complete with bent knees. She wiggled a smidgen, noticing how well they fit together. *Like two peas in a pod.* Even his lack of a shirt didn't put a snag in her serenity. Instead, it added to the specialness and feeling of rightness. Natural and perfect.

She sighed and soaked in the moment, thoroughly content to rest in his embrace. *I can get used to this.*

He sighed and tugged her closer.

Lacey grinned, taking advantage of the position to run her fingers along his forearm while checking out the clock. Eight a.m. Past time to be up and about on a normal day. Considering they'd just gone to bed a bit over three hours ago, she didn't harbor much guilt for not climbing out of their nest sooner.

Still, she knew the luxury would end quite soon. Real life didn't stop just because she'd found a comfortable spot in

Jonas' bed. Unfortunately.

The Humane Society farm had a full docket with vet visits entailing everything from basic checkups and immunizations to wound treatments. Evaluations on the animals had to be made, along with pictures and documentation of each one. All this in addition to the usual hefty workload each worker carried on a daily basis.

"You're thinking too hard."

Lacey heard as much as felt Jonas' words with their skin-to-skin contact and the puff of air against her nape. She grinned at his observation. "Making a mental list of all the things that need to be done at the farm today."

He scooted back and used his arm to roll her until she could peer up at him. She read his face, saw the lopsided smile, and her heart melted. "I take it you're thinking of something else?"

"Uh-huh." His eyes darkened and turned smoky as he lightly caressed her stomach through her shirt.

Her stomach flip-flopped in response, sending a delicious tendril of need zipping through her body.

The ringing of a phone interrupted the moment. Lacey sighed as Jonas rolled over, grabbed his cell phone from the bedside table, and answered. "Hello, Nila. Okay. Okay. Yeah. We'll be there soon." He clicked off, sat up, and peered down at Lacey. "The vets are back in force today. Nila needs help with that black stallion and a couple more horses too spooked to play nice."

Guilt rushed through Lacey. She sat up, glad she still wore her old ragged pajamas, and slid off the bed. "Of course. I should have thought of that." Hurrying out of his room, she strode next door to the spare bedroom, found the few clothes she'd left there before heading to Kentucky, and quickly changed.

By the time she'd dressed and brushed her teeth and hair, she'd woken up enough to carry on for the day. Lacey headed toward the kitchen, finding Jonas standing in front of the open fridge. "I'm not really hungry and Nila wouldn't have called if she didn't need us soon."

Jonas nodded, grabbed a couple of small bottles of milk, and shut the door. "Here." He tossed one to her.

She caught it, then set it down in order to pull her coat on. "I'm sorry." The moment had come and gone, leaving her regretful.

He studied her for a couple of seconds with furrowed eyebrows and a tilt of his head. "For what?"

"That we couldn't finish what we started." The admission came out much more easily than she'd imagined.

The corner of his lips crooked upward. "Me too. But I have no doubt we'll get back there soon enough." He grabbed his coat and walked over to her before pecking her on the cheek. "When the time is right, Lacey, it'll happen."

She read the truth in his face. "I sure hope so. Because I've fallen for you."

His smile widened. "As have I for you."

Her heart fluttered at his admission.

He swooped in for another kiss, pulled back before it could turn serious, and nudged her toward the door. "Duty calls. We better get to it before I carry you back to that bed."

"Raincheck on the lovemaking then. For today." While it wasn't quite the three little words she longed to hear, it was pretty much the same thing in her book. A declaration. One that told her that they were on the same page in the emotional department.

We'll get there soon enough. First things first. The horses need our help.

Fifteen minutes later, Lacey entered the main barn, finding people running around like a colony of busy ants. Staff, volunteers and veterinary personnel filled the area, caring for several of the horses in different capacities.

She spied Dr. Moore and headed his direction. "Need a hand?"

Dr. Moore glanced up from checking a horse's hock and grinned. "There you are. I was wondering when you'd show up."

She entered the stall, automatically running her hand over the gelding's side to keep him calm and aware of her presence. "A girl has to get her beauty sleep now and again, you know."

He shook his head and stared at the animal's leg once more. "Could have been an issue beforehand, but I'd lean more toward the fact that it was probably strained from the wreck. No wounds that I can see. At his advanced age, it wouldn't take too much for the ligaments to have issues." Dr. Moore stood up and patted the gelding on the rump. "Stall rest for him. We'll see if that works. If not, we might try an injection." He brushed his sleeve across his forehead as if to scratch an itch.

Lacey nodded. "I'll pass that on to Nila." She rubbed the horse's hip. "He's too old to ride anyway." The slightly swayed back and abundance of gray hairs around the muzzle told the story. She was sure his teeth would back up her findings if she checked them out. Since Dr. Moore probably had already in his typical thorough exam, she didn't bother.

"Retirement for him, definitely." Dr. Moore studied her for a bit. "I saw you coming in with the other trainer. Couldn't help but notice the way he looked at you."

Lacey couldn't hold back the grin. "I hope it was like I was a glass of sweet tea and he had a mighty thirst."

Dr. Moore chuckled. "Yeah, that was pretty much it." He stepped toward her. "I see you don't mind at all."

"Not in the least."

"I'm happy for you. It's time you had something good in life."

Lacey nodded slowly. Dr. Moore had been a rock through this mess, as had Jonas. She'd often wished things had been different and he'd been her biological father. While those dreams had fallen short, she still saw him as the surrogate father she really needed. "Jonas is a good man."

"I've heard that about him. Nila praises him all the time." Dr. Moore patted her shoulder. "If he makes you happy then hang onto him."

"I intend to."

"Good." He brushed his hand over the horse once more and exited the stall, holding the door for Lacey, then shutting it behind her. "You haven't said anything lately, but how are things with your family?"

Lacey shrugged. "I talk to Tate often. Mom sometimes. Haven't spoken to my…Dan for a while and that's fine with me." She sighed. "I've moved on. It's my turn to have a life."

"That's my girl. You've worked your rear off for them. It's time to follow your heart and dreams. Wherever they take you." He glanced across the room before meeting her eyes again. "If Jonas is part of that, then all the better." A small, rueful grin appeared. "Let me know if there's an upcoming wedding."

She rolled her eyes but smiled back. "You're putting the cart before the horse, Doc."

"I don't think so." He collected his medical bag, pulled out a notebook and jotted some notes. Finished, he returned the book. "Come on. You can tell me all about this man of yours while we examine the next horse."

Oh boy. Lacey didn't bother to argue. For once, she couldn't wait to spill the beans about her and Jonas. And who better to listen than the man who was almost her father?

* * * *

"Where have you been, bro? Sleeping away while the rest of us have been slaving all morning?" Jason arched an eyebrow at Jonas.

A little surprised to see Jason there, Jonas blinked at him.

"I heard of the wreck. Thought you guys could use a hand." Jason shrugged. "So where have you been hiding?"

Jonas snorted. "If you *must* know, Lacey and I were here until just before dawn. We went back to my place, caught a little sleep, then just got back."

Jason forked horse manure and dirty straw into a waiting wheelbarrow then paused to rest his arms on the top of the tool. A wicked grin creased his face. "You and Lacey, huh? Finally making some moves?"

Knowing Jason's curiosity and his well-meaning attitude, Jonas didn't get pushed out of shape by his questions. "We're dating, but you already knew that."

"Is she spending nights with you now?"

Jonas shook his head. "No. Not yet." *If life would slow down and give us a break, maybe.*

He recalled their promise and his spirits lifted. They'd get there. Her confession that she'd fallen for him told him quite a few things. Namely that she was in it for the long haul. He agreed perfectly.

If she can only see past my scars.

The single concern lingered. He grasped onto hope with a firm hold. Time would tell.

"It won't matter to her." Jason's voice broke through his thoughts.

Jonas wasn't surprised at his brother's words. After all, they were close. Jason could read him as well as Jonas read Jason. "I'm betting on that."

"Good man." Jason went back to mucking the stall.

Catching a glimpse of the black stallion, Jonas considered the possibilities. "Do you ever miss roping?"

Jason spared him a glance. "Now and again. Why?"

"I might have found a horse."

Jason stood back up and followed Jonas' gaze. "That black stud? I saw him when I came in to help this morning. He's a beaut, all right."

"He's giving me some ideas."

Jason grinned. "He'd give me ideas, too." His attention landed back on Jonas. "You decide to get back into the sport, let me know. I'll start practicing again." A frown appeared. "But I don't have a horse." He'd sold his right after Jonas had announced his retirement.

Jonas waved his hand. "I believe I can find just the right

one." The idea clicked into place. He and his brother competing once again in roping held potential and promise. Almost as much as him and Lacey as a couple.

Life is looking up.

"Are you coming in the office this week?" Jason asked.

"Yeah. After we get all these horses settled. It'll be a couple of days."

"That'll work. I'll drop off some papers for you to look over. Analysis and future prediction stuff. The market is due for a correction. We need to be prepared."

Jonas nodded. "Drop them by or email them to me. I'll look it over. We've weathered corrections well in the past. If it extends into another recession…" He blew out a breath. Oil had been a stable asset for a while. Now things were getting more complicated. The wars in the Middle East, the oil spill in the Gulf, the dangers inherent in drilling and acquiring the stuff… Thankfully, they centered their business around the oil drills in Texas and Oklahoma. But that didn't mean the local oil would be shielded from the global market's volatility.

"I know. Worries me too." Jason picked up his fork again. "When you get a chance, look over the papers, then we'll have a chat with Dad. He's really good at reading between the lines on these kinds of things."

Now that was the truth. Their father had started from the ground up, turning his small business into a rapidly growing one, filled with branches and assets worth millions. He had a head for the game and always managed to land on his feet. "I'll work on it as soon as I can."

"Good deal." Jason went back to his task.

"I'll catch you later." He waved at Jason and headed to the stallion in question. "Hi, buddy."

The stud's ears perked forward to listen. He snuffled Jonas' arm before returning to eating hay.

"Want to be a roping horse?"

The horse eyed him for a moment, pulled up another mouthful and chewed.

Jonas smiled at the lack of enthusiasm shown by the equine. "We'll see how it goes. Let you get over your concussion and have some time to remember you're a horse before getting started. What do you say?"

The horse snorted, shuffled in his stall and pulled another mouthful to eat.

"Good enough." Jonas appraised the animal for a bit longer before moving on.

A couple of familiar guys caught his eye. He walked over, stopped, and watched as one cleaned out a stall while the other added new straw to the one next to it. "Now this is a surprise."

They jerked their heads up, peered at him, then offered up welcoming smiles. "Hey, Jonas."

"Tate. Ransom." Jonas easily recognized them from the torturous family dinner Lacey had dragged him to, and from before. He hadn't seen or heard from them since despite all the time he'd spent with Lacey. The fact they were chipping in now said something, though.

"Heard about the wreck. Figured you guys could use some help with the new additions," Ransom said.

"Definitely. Thanks for doing this. All the extra hands are greatly appreciated. This will mean a lot to Lacey." Jonas glanced around, not finding her nearby. "Speaking of, does she know you're here?"

"Nope. Not yet. We figured we'd see her soon enough." Tate rested the pitchfork in the wheelbarrow before moving it forward a few feet.

"She's been pretty scarce lately, I hear." Ransom finished with his bale of straw and stepped back into the aisle.

Jonas eyed him. "Reasonably so. It's nothing but a war zone at your parents' house. She's away from that now and finding her own way. Happy too." He didn't really blame them for Lacey's troubles, but he couldn't help but think they should have stood up to their father and made a difference sooner.

"I'm glad to hear it. She's needed to find her wings and fly for a while now," Tate replied.

"Yeah. She's given up everything for that farm because she's just that kind of person. No matter how little appreciation she received for it." Ransom sighed heavily. "I didn't know how bad it was until recently. Lizzie was shocked by the way Dan treated Lacey. She's madder than a wet hen and refusing to have anything to do with him."

Good for her. A few more allies for Lacey never hurt. Jonas nodded. "Sounds like a woman with a head on her shoulders."

Ransom beamed. "Oh, she has that. And more."

By Ransom's reaction, Jonas didn't doubt for a second he loved his fiancée.

"Thanks for sticking by her, by the way. I'm not sure that we said that before." Tate lifted the fork and set the prongs on the ground.

"I'll always be there for her." Jonas scratched at his arm and turned to go.

"Make her happy, Jonas. She deserves that more than anything."

Tate's words drew Jonas back. He shared a look with Lacey's brother, inclined his head in acknowledgment and strode off.

Chapter Twenty-Two

Three days later, Jonas went in search of Lacey, finding her fussing over the three-month-old colt as he lipped at her hair. She giggled and rubbed his whiskery chin.

Jonas paused and watched her interact with the baby, a smile creeping up on his face at the scene before him. Ever since the mare and foal had arrived at the farm, he'd been Lacey's favorite horse. Right behind Knight, of course.

"You're spoiling him."

Lacey peeked over her shoulder at him. "If so, are you going to take me to task for it?"

Jonas grinned. "How could I when everyone else does the same thing?"

"Including you?"

He nodded. "Including me."

She smiled and rubbed the foal's cheek.

"Thinking of turning him into a barrel horse?"

Lacey turned her head this way and that, obviously sizing up the colt. "I don't know. He's got potential, but needs a lot of growing before then."

Jonas agreed. More than likely he'd be adopted as a weanling and move on to the rest of his life, hopefully in a wonderful forever home. The hope and dream of all of them for their charges. "You ready to go?"

"Yep." She petted the baby once more, stood up and spun to face him.

Her jeans were clean and form-fitting, outlining her curves perfectly, while her Western shirt added a splash of color with a combination of green and blue mixed in. For once, she'd left her hair down. The slight breeze teased the locks now and again. Shiny brown cowboy boots and a heavy plain tan jacket finished the ensemble. He couldn't take his eyes off her.

Though they'd been busting ass from dawn to well after dark, Lacey still appeared perky and playful. She'd pulled her own weight and then some. So had he. Together with all the volunteers and the rest of the staff, they'd managed to settle the new horses in, fall into a routine, and be able to focus part of their time back on the already established horses still in need of training in order to be adopted. Lots to do and only so many hours in a day to get it all done.

One reason he'd invited Lacey out for a date night. They both needed a bit of down time and to get out of the barns for a while. The wreck had put a raincheck on the next step in their relationship. He intended to get them back on track. Starting tonight.

He'd already spent last night and most of today in meetings with Jason and his father. They all agreed that whatever storm came in the stock market, they were as prepared as they could be. On the other hand, Jason had suggested diversifying their business, including investing in wind or solar power. Or both. Jonas had jumped in with both feet. He'd spent a few hours at the office making contacts, researching and lining up ways to get in on the ground floor of some wind turbine operations. For once, excitement surrounded him at the idea of meetings and business lunches. He'd found a new niche, one that could become his future.

Horse training owned his heart, but typically didn't pay well. He needed a backup plan and the family business supplied that.

Now, if I could only find more hours in the day…

Lacey had been working her tail off too, filling in for his absence. She needed the down time as much as he did.

He took her hand and led her to his truck, parked nearby. After settling inside and pulling out of the driveway, he took a second to peer over at her. "How's Knight coming along?"

"He's got the idea and, certainly, the talent. I just worry about the actual arena and event itself. Tons of noise, the bright lights, flashing cameras, people scurrying about. Not to mention the longer rodeos where we have to spend the night or more in a stall."

"I've got a buddy that runs the arena over in Pillar Gulch, not too far away. It's an indoor arena with lights and a PA system. I can ask if we can use it for a night or two. Try Knight out with the place and equipment to see how he handles it."

"That would be great." Enthusiasm carried in her tone. "I think if we can get him past those hurdles, he might be on his way to excelling in the sport."

Jonas nodded. "I'll call the guy tomorrow and ask. The sooner we expose Knight to those things, the better." His gut told him the horse wouldn't care for the venue change or the additional stimulation. Knight had run free for way too long to simply accept such big changes easily. They'd been lucky thus far that he'd had some saddle training and responded well to a rider. The barrels fit his personality and gave him a challenge to keep his mind busy. The rest... Jonas had some doubts. Not that he'd vocalize them. Lacey knew the score and she didn't need a reminder of the pitfalls looming ahead. Especially tonight.

He drove for a bit in silence, found his turnoff, and pulled into the parking lot.

"Oh, I love this place. Best buffet around," Lacey said.

Jonas grinned. "Yep. Tonight is seafood night, too."

"Just count me out for frog legs, ick." She laughed and stepped out of the truck.

He did the same, hitting the fob to lock it after they were both out, and the doors shut. "Be sure to try the hush puppies. They're delicious."

Her eyes lit up as he held the door open for her. "Thank you."

"You're welcome. I know this isn't a typical place for a

date, but I knew the food would be worth the stop."

Lacey paused to rest her hand on his forearm. "I'd gladly go anywhere with you. Even if it's just a picnic in the barn."

Her warm smile touched him as much as her statement.

"Where have you been all my life?"

She tilted her head and peered up at him. "I'm here now, does that count?"

"Oh, yeah." He led her to an empty spot in the corner and sat down.

Other women he'd dated would have scoffed at his choice of restaurants. Not Lacey. She appreciated anything and everything, from a minor gift to a major surprise. Just another reason she'd stolen his heart.

Love.

He stared into her eyes and knew the word rang true. From both of them. No, they hadn't talked about feelings really, not yet. Still, he wasn't wet behind the ears when it came to dating and women. Lacey's inexperience and innocence carried across easily. She'd probably had little time to date considering how hard she worked.

That had all changed with him. She was his to care for and he wasn't about to let her down.

With that revelation came another. His lingering apprehension and fear of intimacy had nearly subsided. Somewhere along the path of their time together, he'd lost focus on the 'can't' and moved forward with the 'can'. All because of her. She'd given him confidence and hope. A generous gift that he appreciated.

Now he couldn't wait to take Lacey home, strip her down, and show her how he felt.

Which meant one thing—he'd cowboy up, bare his body, and let Lacey make the call.

Because deep down, he knew she wouldn't disappoint him.

* * * *

"Want dessert? I've got some ice cream in the freezer if you're interested." He closed the door leading from the garage to the kitchen behind Lacey.

"No thanks. I'm still full from that buffet. You were right. Those hush puppies were to die for."

He grinned. "Uh-huh."

Lacey slipped off her shoes, stood up and appraised him from head to toe and back again. The fire in her gaze spoke of longing and hunger.

His body responded with a surge of blood to his groin, igniting a powerful hard-on. "Do you want me?"

She closed the distance between them.

He wrapped his arms around her and waited.

"Yes." She whispered the word before initiating a kiss that started out sweet but soon turned to molten lava.

He thrust his tongue between her lips, searched every nook and cranny and savored the taste of Lacey once again.

She rested her hands on his chest for a few seconds before unbuttoning his shirt and pushing at his coat. He discarded both, letting them fall to the floor. His hands free, he pulled the hem of her top out of her jeans and immediately slid underneath, roaming until he cupped her modest breasts. She gasped as he rubbed his thumbs over the pebbled tips.

Breaking off the lip-lock, he stepped back in order to tug off her blouse, adding it to the growing pile of clothes on the floor. He stared at her still bra-clad chest with admiration. "Beautiful. Just beautiful."

Color flooded Lacey's cheeks. He hoped to see that same flushing expand as she writhed under him on the bed, overcome by a powerful orgasm that rocked her world. "Maybe we should take this to the bedroom?" Although the kitchen table held great potential, he filed that idea away for later. Much later.

"I should brush my teeth…" Lacey hurried away to the bathroom.

He watched her disappear, removed his boots, then headed toward the other bathroom. She had a good idea.

The last thing he wanted to do was turn her off with fish-smelling breath.

As soon as he'd finished with that task he stopped near the bed, shucked his jeans, and waited.

Lacey appeared dressed in only her bra and panties. The sight turned his mouth dry and reaffirmed his earlier thought. She could put other women to shame with her fine figure. Flaring hips, a flat stomach and toned legs caught his eye. She carried muscle and strength from manual labor over her lifetime. The result stole his breath. "Wow."

She smiled. "I was about to say the same for you." She walked over, stopping directly in front of him only to trail her hands over his chest and down his stomach. She paused at the waistband of his boxers and dipped her fingers underneath.

He sucked in air as her fingertips brushed idly over his swollen tip. She licked her lips and met his gaze.

The undeniable arousal painted on her face jacked up his need all the more. He unsnapped the latch on her bra and pulled the unwanted garment off, giving it a toss across the room. Tempted to do the same with her panties, he held off. For the moment.

Slow and easy. No way would he rush this first time together.

Bending over, he took a breast into his mouth and lapped.

Lacey's hands latched onto the back of his head, holding him in place. She arched into his touch.

He took advantage of the closeness to trace a line up her inner thigh, nudge her panties aside and slide his fingers through her folds. Slick dampness met him, as did a strong tremble surging through her body.

He lifted his head. "You're so wet. Wet and hot." Turning to the other side, he licked over the nipple, earning a low moan for his efforts. At the same time, he slipped his finger inside.

She tensed at the invasion.

"It's okay. I'm not going to do anything you don't want

to do," he reassured her. Another lick to her breast and she eased her stance, although the snugness around his finger didn't abate. Jonas pressed for a deeper exploration, only to be barred by a flimsy barrier. The second he bumped it, Lacey jerked.

Reality hit him hard. "You're a virgin." The fact wasn't a huge shock. Still, he couldn't believe that many people made it to her age still innocent. Not in this day and time. Especially with rodeo folks, who seemed to go into heat at the events. He'd seen more than his fair share of escapades around fairgrounds and arenas. Hell, he'd participated more than once. A lifetime ago.

"Yes." Her hooded eyes and parted lips told him she liked his touch.

Heat radiated to his cock, starting a demanding ache. He leashed the reins of his control, vowing to take his time with Lacey. "Are you sure you want to do this?" He needed the words.

Lacey grinned wolfishly, cupped the bulge in his undershorts, and lightly squeezed. "Absolutely."

Instinctively, he jerked.

She frowned and withdrew her touch. "I didn't mean to hurt you."

He regretted his reaction instantly. Leaning in, he brushed his lips over hers and gathered her hand in his before placing it back on his crotch. "I haven't had a woman since my surgery. You caught me a bit unexpectedly is all."

"Are you sure?" She stared up at him while worrying her bottom lip.

"Yes. I hunger for you, Lacey. So explore to your heart's content. Your touch is magical."

A tiny smile appeared on her lips.

He breathed out a sigh of relief, steeled himself and let her check him out for another couple of minutes before he could take the incredible pleasure no more. He lifted her hand away. "Keep that up and I'll come in my pants. I'd rather do that inside you."

She bit her lip as another spark ignited in her eyes. She pressed her mouth against his, more enthusiastically this time. Almost frantic in hunger. He let his passion free in order to feed her need, running his hands over her bottom, hooking her panties and pulling them down and out of the way.

Lacey lifted first one foot then the other, escaping the shackles of the garment, as she busily pressed small kisses along his throat and jawline.

"Lay down, Lacey. For me." He nudged her with a pat to the rear, glimpsing pink folds as she crawled to the center of the bed and rested on her back.

A sudden thought sent him to the bedside table, where he opened the top drawer, pulled out a condom and tossed it onto the mattress. Ready, he approached the bed and climbed in. "Open your legs."

He guided her with one hand on her inner thigh. When she was splayed to his satisfaction, he scooted closer, then lay down on his stomach. Her dark, tight curls intrigued him nearly as much as the dampness inside. He inserted his first finger marginally once more then licked all along the slit.

"Ohh." Lacey tried to close her legs, but he blocked her.

"Shh. Relax. Enjoy." He went right to work, intent on bringing her such pleasure that his penetration would be seamless. He refused to hurt her in any way, especially if a bit of extended foreplay might prevent it.

After two more passes, she let her legs fall to the sides, opening herself to his attention.

He kept his touches light and teasing then turned his attention to her clit. The first nuzzle made her hips lurch. On the second, she cried out. With exquisite precision, he ran his tongue around the area before worrying the small nub.

Another quake racked her body. "Jonas. Oh, Jonas."

Glancing up, he found her eyes closed, her head tossing on the pillow.

She was close. So very close.

He didn't have the heart to deny her.

Edging closer, he feasted on her, leaving no area untouched while focusing most of his time on her tight clit. He added a second finger, rotated his wrist, and worked the muscles to prepare for his entry. At the same time he fixated on her nub. He licked. He laved. He sucked.

Lacey's body grew tense. She planted her feet on the bed and lifted into him. A tiny cry left her throat as she surged against his hand, forcing his fingers past the barrier and as deep into her body as he could go. Immediately a series of rhythmic contractions clamped down on his fingers.

He stayed the course until she wilted back into the bed and shivered. Only then did he remove his hand and back away from her sensitive folds. Pride rushed over him, knowing that he'd given her pleasure, although not quite in the way he'd imagined.

We'll get there. Next.

He lifted over her, pulled her snug into his body and pressed his lips to her forehead. "So responsive. So beautiful," he crooned to her, easing her down from the summit.

She blew out a breath and opened her eyes.

He saw the satisfaction then a spark of desire rekindle. "Okay?"

"Better than okay." She smiled wickedly. "Wonderful." She lowered her hand to rub his dick through the boxers. "Now is it your turn?"

He chuckled at her enthusiasm. "Whatever you want, Lacey. However you want it. I'm putty in your hands."

"Oh, I like that." Her eyes widened as she continued to lightly caress him through the material. "How about you take this off?"

He rolled to the side of the bed and stood up. The time of reckoning had arrived. After hooking his fingers in the waistband, he paused as his gut clenched.

What are you waiting for? He closed his eyes and grappled

with his failing courage.

Now that the time had come, uncertainty reared its ugly head. What if she couldn't accept his deformation? What if her face screwed up in distaste? What if—

When did I turn into a fucking wuss? Just get it over with.

He braced himself and slowly slid his boxers down, letting them puddle at his feet. The entire time his gaze never left her face, searching for the tiniest flicker of disgust.

She moved closer and sat on the side of the bed. Ever so gently, she reached out to delicately cup his sac. "Does this hurt?"

He shook his head, unable to speak around the lump in his throat at her unbelievable reaction. She lightly rolled his remaining ball, then lifted her eyes to meet his. Appreciation. Awe. Lust. All those things flashed across her face, warming his heart and rebuilding his confidence brick by brick.

"This isn't what makes you a man."

He arched an eyebrow, challenging her to explain.

She pursed her lips. "Okay. *Literally,* this is *one* of the parts that makes you a man. But it's not the part that I'm interested in." She brushed her hand over his chest and down past his abs, stopping just short of his throbbing dick. "There's more to a man than his looks, his build, his skin tone, or his backside painted in Wranglers. A man is truly a man when his heart is in the right place. When he knows his spot in the world and gives all his love and devotion to another and isn't afraid to show it. A man who takes out the trash is a hell of a lot sexier than one who can bench press three hundred pounds and run the one-hundred-yard dash in less than ten seconds. At least to me. Give me a man of substance, one of caring, one who isn't too proud to cuddle at night, or kiss his woman in front of his buddies, or play house with his little girl. That's the man I want." She brushed her lips over his stomach, still fondling him with a tender touch. "I want you. The man of my dreams."

His heart skipped a beat. Emotions rolled through him at

her actions and words. For the first time since his diagnosis, he felt like a real man. Able to do anything from fighting for what was his to pleasing his woman in bed. The way she looked at him gave him the strength to be bold, to stand up straight and to make love to the one lady who'd captured his very soul. "Lacey."

She grinned mischievously up at him. "I wondered what you'd taste like." Without warning, she licked the tip of his shaft, using her other hand to wrap around the base and hold him still for her inspection. She followed with a light squeeze, as if testing the resiliency.

Bright, hot pleasure shot straight to his ball, his cock, and up his spine. He sucked in air and focused on staying upright.

She trailed the tip of her tongue along the bottom of his shaft and back again before opening wide and taking the head into her mouth, where she treated him to a flurry of laving.

He saw stars. "Lacey, you don't have to."

She pulled back long enough to answer. "I want to." Boldly, she took him again, adding vacuum and a low moan that vibrated though his whole body.

Gritting his teeth, he savored the sensual torture. He pushed her hair aside to watch, noting the hollowed cheeks and the way she peered up at him. "Damn, baby." He groaned as she flicked her tongue over the sensitive spot just under the head.

Drawing in air, he pulled on his control and eased back a step. "Let me pleasure you." The words came out a near growl.

She grinned, sat back up, and moved to the center of the bed once again. "I was hoping you'd get around to this."

He smiled. He wasn't sure what he expected with a virgin, but Lacey took on the situation like everything else, with a sense of humor and optimism. All the more reason he wanted to make this first time perfect. "No way would I miss out on this." He pressed her into the mattress with a melting kiss and positioned himself between her legs.

Sitting up, he searched for the condom, located it, then opened the foil wrapper and rolled the rubber on. His gaze met Lacey's as she stared up at him with a look of anticipation and something deeper. More intense. Love.

Pleasing her took precedence. Nothing else mattered to him. Not the possibility of a rusty performance or his damn testicle. Only Lacey reaching climax held importance.

His heart skipped a beat as he lowered himself into position, nestling his cock between her folds while supporting his weight on his forearms, bracketing her shoulders. He nuzzled her cheek then lapped at her earlobe. "Bend your legs up. Open for me."

She complied, then ran her hands up and down his back. Lingering on his rear, she gave the area a squeeze.

His breath *whooshed* out.

"I don't think I need that quarter after all."

Jonas chuckled and started forward, languidly joining their bodies inch by slow inch.

Heat and tightness welcomed him after a brief moment of resistance. Slickness eased his entry, leaving no doubt of her readiness. Absently, he recalled he'd punched through her hymen with his fingers right before she'd come, leaving him with an obstruction-free penetration. Thankfully so.

He continued steadily forward, keeping his gaze locked on Lacey's face, constantly searching for signs of discomfort. None ever showed, even as he lodged his full length inside her. "That's it. You've got all of me."

Her eyes locked onto his. She opened her mouth on a gasp and wiggled her hips. "You're big, all right." Another shifting of her lower body followed.

Concerned, he remained completely still. "Hurt?"

She shook her head. "No. Just trying to find room to fit all of you."

He would have laughed if her body hadn't caressed his cock like a velvet glove with every tiny movement on her part. Instead he peppered kisses over her face and chest before finding her breast and sucking.

She raked her nails lightly along his flanks, sending a flash of pleasure surging through him.

Unable to remain motionless, he eased back a couple of inches then reversed course. "Still okay?"

She bowed her back and lifted to him. "Yes. Oh, yes. Do that again."

He did so, using a long, slow stroke this time. He was rewarded with a low moan. "Like that?"

"Uh-huh." She lifted enough to kiss his chin and nibble on his collarbone, while tweaking his nipples before skimming his chest with her soft lips.

He adjusted his angle, aiming a smidgen higher, then gritted his teeth when she bucked in response. Her breath hitched and another sharp cry echoed through the room. Picking up the pace, he focused on long, sure thrusts, guaranteed to hit all her hot spots. He ground against her, making sure to brush her clit along the way.

Her nails bit into his back, adding to the burning cauldron about to overtake him.

A need for oxygen caused him to pant. He noticed Lacey was suffering the same dilemma. She began to breathe faster even as she lifted to meet each of his motions, adding a frantic need to the mix.

Jonas' spine began to tingle in imminent warning. He pulled on all his control to stay the course and bring Lacey to another climax before finding his own. Nothing mattered more.

"That's it, sweetheart. Take from me. Whatever you need." He reached back to lift her upper leg until she clamped her thighs on his sides like a vise. The new position rolled her pelvis forward, giving him more traction and ability to plunge deep. He pressed forward, testing the waters.

Lacey's mouth opened but no sounds emerged. She dropped her hands to grasp the comforter with a grip so tight her knuckles whitened.

The leash on his control snapped. He surged into a rapid

rhythm, quick, short jabs that ended with him buried deep. "Let go. Just. Let. Go." He gritted out the words and grunted as she lurched under him.

Locking their bodies together, Jonas felt the first spasm of her core and rocketed off the cliff. Wave after wave of powerful crests cascaded over him as he hit fiery rapture at the speed of a runaway train. He shouted, rocked against her and rode out the mind-blowing climax as long as it lasted.

Warm puffs of breath next to his ear brought him back to reality. He realized he'd lowered his weight on top of Lacey at some point and hurriedly relieved her of it. Glancing down, he found her staring at him with a small grin on her lips.

She reached up and pushed a lock of hair out of his eyes. The action told him more than enough.

"You okay?"

Her smile widened. "Better than okay. Happy. Ecstatic. If you asked me to fly, I could do that as well."

He shook his head and chuckled. "That good, huh?" The sense of accomplishment bolstered his self-confidence tenfold. His deformity no longer mattered. Not right now. Not when Lacey looked at him like he alone hung the sun in the sky.

"Uh-huh." She caressed his cheek and met his gaze. "You're amazing."

He didn't hesitate to answer. "I'm just an old, weathered cowboy. You, though, are an angel sent to earth."

"Old? Weathered?" She shook her head. "You're no more those things than I'm an angel complete with halo."

"You are to me." Leaning in, he kissed her slightly swollen lips for good measure before rolling off her. It only took a second for him to remove and discard the used condom in a nearby trashcan. Task complete, he gathered her in his arms, tucked her against his body and pulled the cover over them.

Lacey sighed.

Not sure what the sound meant, he rubbed her stomach in lazy circles. "What is it?"

She rested her hand on top of his and scooched back so that her rear lodged against his cock. "I never thought I'd find a man who would want me for me. Let alone one who had the gumption to deal with all my baggage."

He pressed his lips to her nape. "We all have baggage. Besides, you outshine all the other women around. I'm damn lucky."

"I'm the lucky one." She brought his hand up and kissed his palm. "How long until we can do that again?"

He arched an eyebrow. "Why?"

"Because I want you again." She grinned saucily.

He groaned to himself. "Why do I have a feeling you're going to wear me out?"

Lacey sat up, rolled him to his back, then straddled his hips. Her hands rested on his chest as she stared down at him. "That's what happens when you please a girl. She begins to have these ideas and cravings."

Pleased, Jonas cupped her pretty rear, holding her in place. "Keep wiggling like that and you won't have to wait long at all."

She beamed.

He licked her chin. "First things first, baby. A visit to the bathroom. After that, I'm all yours."

The spark in her eye told him everything he needed to know. Namely that he'd just turned on her motor and she wasn't ready to shut it off quite yet.

"Up. Now. Before I get too distracted to think." He moved her off him, slid from the bed and headed to the bathroom. The sounds of footfalls told him she was taking the opportunity to escape to the other restroom down the hall.

Stepping inside, he glanced at the mirror. His image surprised him. Not the tousled hair or the five o'clock shadow. More the shit-eating grin and lack of tension. He felt like a huge weight had been lifted off his shoulders with her acceptance of him. More than that. She made him whole again. A true man. Whom she encased in her love.

She'd given him his masculinity back. He'd given her love in return. A very good deal indeed.

Chapter Twenty-Three

"You see something in him," Lacey commented as she approached Jonas.

He spared her a glance before turning his focus back to the big-boned black stallion that had snared his attention from day one. The horse's powerful hindquarters spoke of sprinting power. A wide chest and sturdy legs promised he could withstand the rigors of sporting while the unmistakable intelligence in his eyes spoke of the ability to learn. The stallion had plenty of potential, if only he was given a chance.

The question became, did Jonas want to take a leap of faith and enter the rodeo ring again?

"He's built. Great conformation."

Lacey stopped alongside him, rested one booted foot on the lower rail of the paddock, crossed her arms on the top bar and stared at the horse lazily dozing in the bright sunlight. "He's gorgeous. Strong, too. Add in a bit of training and I bet he could do just about anything."

"Yeah."

She turned to look at him. "Ready to pull your roping saddle out of storage?" Her eyes flashed with newfound insight.

"Maybe." He'd convinced himself that rodeo existed only in his past. Now, looking at the stallion, he wasn't nearly so sure.

"Give it a try. Only way to find out for sure."

He grinned at her basic logic. Leave it to Lacey to hit the nail on the head in a single sentence. "I just might." Reaching for Lacey, he tugged her flush against his body before brushing his lips over hers. "How are you feeling?"

Color stained her cheeks. A sweeter blush he'd never seen. After their first round of sex, she'd returned to bed for another, more leisurely, adventure ride on top. He'd enjoyed every moment. As had she, judging by the speed and intensity of her resulting climax. Thankfully, she'd been tired enough to simply snuggle afterward. He'd have stepped up to the plate if she'd insisted, but worried she'd be plenty sore as it was.

"Fine. Better after that kiss, though."

Jonas smiled at her sassiness and hint of teasing. He doubted she'd own up to any aches or pains consequent of their passion. Still, he needed to ask. The urge to take care of her was strong, especially after last night. He'd never been given a gift as rare or treasured as Lacey and intended to hang onto her for as long as she'd have him. "There's more where that came from." He grinned and teased her earlobe with a quick nibble.

She giggled and squirmed. "Are you always this hot and bothered?"

He paused and stared down at her seriously. "No. Only with you."

Her eyes sparked with the information. "Can we keep it that way?"

"That's the plan."

Her mouth softened into a warm smile.

"Hey, you two." Nila approached, dressed in her usual attire of jeans, boots and a heavy jacket for the brisk afternoon. "I see that you've become quite the item."

Jonas kept one hand on Lacey's back as she turned to face their boss. "You could say that."

"What can I say? I took your advice," Lacey added.

"Smart girl." Nila grinned. "Now, what I came out to tell you. Three of the semi wreck horses have perked up nicely. The vet clinic will be shipping them here today along with another mare someone found abandoned and neglected a couple of weeks ago that no longer needs as much care."

"Ohh, I can't wait. Bringing those poor horses here just seems like bringing them home. Well, at least for now."

Jonas heard the excitement in Lacey's voice, which matched his own. "I'm glad they're pulling through. After that tragedy, each one that survives is a blessing."

"Exactly," Nila replied, the dark circles under her eyes seeming to stand out all the more.

Despite the obvious fatigue, she'd kept on working in order to get the horses settled and cared for. Their needs above her own. Just another reason Jonas worked for her. Her dedication and commitment couldn't be any stronger.

"What about the pregnant mare?" Jonas asked. He'd glimpsed her in a stall earlier, but hadn't heard any updates.

"Dr. Moore thinks she'll foal within the next couple of weeks. Maybe sooner because of the stress from the wreck."

"So the foal is okay?" Lacey asked.

Nila nodded. "One of the equine clinic vets brought out his ultrasound machine to check her out. Baby seems to be fine despite her ordeal."

"Her?" Lacey sidestepped to lean against the fence.

"Yep. A little filly. Probably will be cute as a button, too. Her mother certainly is."

Jonas recalled the dappled bay mare with the rounded belly. She probably didn't quite reach fifteen hands tall. Small and compact, she'd been easy to work with. Placid, though she had to have been severely rattled from her ordeal.

Rarely did the farm have foals to work with. Whether good or bad, he didn't really know. However, that filly and the young colt would grow up knowing love and gentleness. They'd make sure of it. A stark difference from what the outcome would have been if the semi hadn't wrecked. An odd twist of fate to say the least.

"How's Knight coming along? I've seen him take those barrels in the arena like a pro." Nila wiped some dust off her jeans.

"Great. He's figured out the basics. Seems to like running.

It's just the noise and crowds that I have concerns with," Lacey answered.

Nila nodded. "Understandable. He'll come through, though. Jonas will make sure of it." She smiled then spun around. "I've got horses to see and volunteers to organize. See ya later."

"Bye." Lacey glanced up at him. "When will you tell Nila that you want that black stallion?"

Jonas blew out a breath. He'd only toyed with the idea. Nothing solid on the decision front yet. "Soon." He couldn't really say more than that.

Lacey's face pinched. "Better speak up before someone else puts their dibs in for him."

"I know." Jonas ran a hand through his hair. "Who are you working with today?"

"Lana first, I think. Crackers needs to work. I hope to do a few rounds with Knight before calling it a day."

He nodded. As much as he'd have loved to pick her up and take her back to his bed, they would have to wait until the nearly endless list of chores was finished. "Don't push yourself too hard."

She rolled her eyes then ruined the effect by grinning wickedly. "No worries. I might even save enough energy to climb into your saddle again tonight."

Jonas groaned as blood shunted down to his groin. "Why do I have the feeling that I'm not the only one 'hot and bothered'?" He borrowed her terminology and fed it back to her.

She pursed her lips. "Maybe because you're not?" She kissed him, patted his rear, and scurried off before he could catch her.

"Vixen."

"Randy hoss."

He laughed at her comeback, watching the decadent sway of her backside as she walked toward the equipment room, presumably to collect gear for her training lesson.

"Yeah, I've got it bad." With that comment, he went about

his way. The sooner he started, the sooner he finished. The promise of another blissful night with Lacey motivated him to get the lead out.

* * * *

Lacey ran the brush over Knight's back, enjoying the relaxation that came with the routine chore. They'd just finished a great training session, which had sealed her faith that Knight knew what was expected of him. With that hurdle out of the way, she had to focus on getting him used to noise, new arenas and the chaos of rodeos.

"Such a smart boy. I'm so proud of you."

Knight bobbed his head as if in agreement.

Lacey chuckled. "We'll make it to a race yet. I know you can win, too." She changed sides and continued her task. "Jonas was so thoughtful. He bought you, started training you, just for me. I still can't believe his generosity."

Knight swished his tail, his ears at half-mast. The sign of a contented horse or one about to fall asleep.

Her thoughts returned to the evening before, when Jonas had showed her how a real man treated a woman in bed. Her stomach flip-flopped in a delicious way as she recalled some of the sexier details of their lovemaking.

"Jump in with both feet, Trinity said." Lacey grinned ruefully. "Don't tell her this, but she was right."

Knight's ears flicked her direction, the only indication that he was paying her any attention.

"I think he's the one for me, Knight."

He turned and rubbed his face against her arm.

Lacey laughed and petted him. "You're quite the listener." She kissed his forehead. "And a definite keeper."

She tossed the brush into her bucket of grooming tools, untied the lead rope and unsnapped it from his halter. He stood still for a moment, then casually turned and walked over to Mabel and nickered at the old girl.

Mabel spared him a look before returning to her late

afternoon nap.

"Keep trying, buddy. She'll fall head over heels yet." Lacey watched Knight rest his chin on Mabel's back for a few precious seconds. The sweet picture put a smile back on Lacey's face.

With Candy left to groom and care for, Lacey picked up her bucket, turned around, exited through the gate and walked toward the home pasture nearest Nila's house.

By the time she'd poured out grain and hay for both Noggin and Candy, the sun had started toward the horizon, promising to leave her in darkness before much longer. With no lights in the front paddock area, Lacey hurried through grooming first Candy, then Noggin. They'd been rolling in the mud at some point, which had dried on their bodies. Thankfully, her curry comb worked well on ridding them of the mess.

"Why is it that I clean you guys up every night then you go back and roll in the mud again?" she asked both of the horses as they ate side by side. "I've heard it's good for the skin, but geez."

Noggin completely ignored her. Candy stamped her foot without pausing the slightest in gobbling down her dinner.

Lacey traded the curry comb for a soft brush, running the gentle bristles over Noggin's hide. "Maybe you can skip a day tomorrow. Stay out of the mud for once."

"The chances of Noggin overlooking a mud puddle is about zilch."

Startled, Lacey gasped and jerked around to find Jonas leaning against the wall of the lean-to, his hands hooked in the pockets of his jeans. "I didn't know anyone was around."

His lopsided smile made her heart skip a beat. "Too engrossed in lecturing them to notice. Not like it will do any good." He drew closer, ran his hands over Noggin's back and patted the horse's neck. "Thanks for caring for him."

"No problem. I have to do Candy anyway, so one more

is no big deal." She raked him from head to toe. Despite the smudges of dirt on his clothes, she found him as sexy as ever. Images from last night rushed back into her mind, heating up her cheeks and sending a healthy dose of arousal zinging through her.

One night and he's turned me into a sex addict.

She mentally shook her head and pondered Jonas and his magical touch. The way his hands rubbed over Noggin reminded her of the way he'd caressed her. Slow. Gentle. Reverent. Soothing. And oh, so right.

Jonas placed his hand over hers, stilling the practiced motions.

She blinked at him.

He smiled softly, leaned in and brushed his lips over hers. "I've been wanting to do that all day."

"You have?" She coyly peered up at him through her eyelashes.

"Uh-huh." He repeated the affectionate gesture, deepening the kiss after supping at her lips, leaving her breathless.

"Wow."

"What do you say we go back to my house and get cleaned up? Together?" His molten eyes promised a passionate ride, one she wouldn't regret in the least.

Her distracted mind kicked into gear. "You want to share your shower?" The thought sped her heart and sent another tendril of wicked pleasure through her stomach straight to parts a little lower.

His lips parted as he cupped her cheek, brushing his thumb over her mouth. "And then some."

Lacey read the question on his face and smiled. "Wild horses couldn't drag me away."

Jonas grinned wickedly. "Then let's finish up here and get to that shower."

Thirty minutes later, Lacey's courage faltered. It was one thing to strip down in a bedroom during a moment of lovemaking. And entirely different to shuck clothes in the bathroom and step into an occupied shower. With the lights and extreme closeness, there'd be no hiding flaws or imperfections. Sex in the dim light was one thing. This was another.

"Come on in. There's plenty of room and the water's hot."

Quit being a ninny and just do it. Lacey blew out a breath, removed her clothing and stepped inside.

Jonas moved to the back, giving her ample room.

She noticed the way his eyes lit up as they traveled from her face downward, lingering on certain areas, then back again.

"Nice."

She couldn't help but notice his nude body with rivulets of water trickling over the hills and valleys. The sight quelled her nervousness and turned it into desire. Wanton, wild desire. "You're quite the stud muffin yourself." Her gaze landed on his rapidly expanding erection. Her stomach somersaulted as he continued to harden right in front of her eyes. The sexy sight turned her on all the more.

His gaze clouded for a second. "Are you sure my missing ball doesn't turn you off?"

She read the tension in his face and knew he spoke from the heart. She'd meant every word before their first lovemaking session, but had no problem with telling him the truth each and every day of their lives. "Jonas, you're gorgeous. Drop-dead gorgeous. Inside and out." Gently, she found his sac and weighed it lightly in her palm before tenderly caressing the soft skin with her fingertips. She lifted her gaze to meet his. "This is part of you and you're the best man I've ever met." Lacey grinned saucily. "As far as turning me on, all you have to do is smile, walk by, or shovel manure. All that is plenty able to get my motor going."

Jonas chuckled, the happiness extending up to his expressive eyes. "Shoveling manure turns you on?"

Lacey shrugged. "What can I say? I'm hot to trot, but only for you."

A groan escaped Jonas' lips as she raised her hand enough to brush over the head of his big erection. "That's what you do to me. Make me hard. Exceptionally hard." He lathered up a washcloth and stroked it over her chest, paying particular attention to her breasts. "So fucking hard that all I can think of is having you."

Those words unleashed Lacey's passion, setting her desire free. She stole the cloth and began soaping him up. Chest. Torso. And lower. She couldn't resist the urge to run the sudsy material up and down his shaft while watching Jonas' face.

He closed his eyes and braced his arms against the walls of the shower. A fine shiver ran through him, telling Lacey how powerful her touch was on his body. She finished and dipped lower to his sac, carefully cleaning while exploring at the same time.

Jonas' breath hitched.

She knelt down, washed his legs, then motioned with her free hand. "Turn around."

As soon as he complied, she reversed course, caressing his legs, over his scrumptious rear, and northward until she could go no farther. "Time to rinse." She stood up and traded places with him.

He stepped under the showerhead, letting the water wash away all the soap.

Lacey knew she'd never forget that image. Nor would it fail to speed her heart or steal her breath. "That's the sexiest thing I've ever seen."

She didn't realize she'd uttered the words aloud until Jonas grinned. His eyes met hers as he held out his hand. "My turn to wash you."

Their fingers brushed as she gave him the cloth back. A small electrical shock rushed through her. That was nothing compared to when he began cleaning her. Every inch of her body. Slowly. Thoroughly. She turned to mush under his ministrations even as her libido hit record heights.

The moment he dipped the cloth between her folds, she

quaked with primed need. A small cry escaped her lips as the rough material found all her sensitive places begging for attention.

"Right there." Jonas' voice carried sultry hunger.

"Yes. Oh, yes." She spread her legs and held her breath as he made another pass.

"I want you so fucking bad, baby. Hang on a second so I can get this condom on."

She watched as he did so, unable to keep from exploring his body in the process.

"Turn around, Lacey. Turn around and brace your hands on the wall."

She didn't dare argue. Instead, she assumed the position, making sure to keep her head close enough to the front to allow the steamy water to hit her back and flow downward instead of smack her in the face.

Jonas pressed kisses down her spine while running his hands over her sides and around to her breasts. He plumped them, tweaked her nipples, and jacked up her arousal tenfold with the erotic play.

"Please, Jonas. I can't wait any longer."

She whimpered at the loss of his touch, but only had to wait a few seconds before feeling his cock slide into her slit. A delightful stretching followed as he slipped inside, not stopping until he lodged deep, filling her to capacity.

"Okay?"

"Yes." She grunted as he pulled back then surged back in.

"Still all right?"

"Yes. Please, Jonas."

"Please what?" He settled into a rocking motion that moved him only a couple of inches at a time.

She needed more. Anything more than this simple teasing. "Harder. Faster. I need…" Her words trailed off as he gave her exactly what she asked for — a moderate pace filled with long thrusts strong enough to nearly lift her each time.

He latched onto her hips, tugging her into his strokes while keeping her safely upright.

The combination of his cock darting in and out along with the hot water cascading down her back took Lacey to the very edge. She lifted, angled her pelvis, and gyrated in an attempt to find that exact spot to send her over. All to no avail.

Jonas wrapped an arm around her middle then used the other hand to burrow between her folds. He found her clit and ever so lightly pinched.

Lacey jerked and began to pant. Her world narrowed down to Jonas and his magical touch. "Again." Great tension overcame her body, stretching her on a rack of passion so tightly she feared she'd shatter. Yet nothing short of just that would be enough.

He slid his finger around her nub, then brazenly strummed it.

Stars danced in front of Lacey's eyes. She slammed against him, moaned, and rode the mighty crests of release.

Behind her, Jonas grunted, rubbed her clit once more, then shouted as he bucked against her. His vise-like grip held them joined so tightly not even the water could trickle between.

Her legs trembled.

Jonas pulled her upright until the water hit her chest. The additional stimulation on her nipples added another degree to the quickly fading climax. He breathed harshly against her ear then pressed his lips to the area. "Damn, vixen."

She didn't have the ability to answer. Not with him still locked inside her and the water peppering her breasts like small beads of pleasure.

"Lacey?"

She rested her head on Jonas' shoulder. "Hmmmm?"

"Are you all right?" Concern laced his tone.

"Perfect. Wonderful." She shivered despite the still hot water streaming down her middle.

Jonas chuckled. "You're a dream come true, lady." He nuzzled her cheek. "But we better get a move on before the hot water runs out and turns to ice."

That threat snapped her back to reality. She maneuvered forward as Jonas took a pace in the opposite direction, disengaging their bodies.

Lacey felt the loss immediately. *We'll do it again soon. First things first.* She grabbed the shampoo bottle and stuck her head under the water. Damp enough, she traded places with Jonas, who'd removed the condom and placed it on a nearby shelf in the shower, rubbed the liquid into her hair, then rinsed. Conditioner followed. Thankfully the hot water held out until the final rinse, where lukewarm temperatures encouraged her to finish in a hurry.

She stepped out of the shower, found Jonas holding a large, fluffy towel open for her, and accepted the small gesture with a sincere smile.

The more she hung around with Jonas, the more besotted she became.

And that's so bad why?

She had not a single answer.

Chapter Twenty-Four

The next couple of weeks flew by. Lacey worked full-time and then some at the farm, trying not only to keep up with the training demands, but to also help out with the daily chores. The trailer wreck horses especially needed attention and care. Most were able to be handled with little or no difficulty, yet their level of trust seemed to have been broken at some point. She didn't blame them. Not in the least. So she started from scratch with a few, in an effort to communicate that they'd never suffer at the hands of people again.

At least one benefit came of the wreck. Public donations poured in after the media frenzy that had followed the accident. Volunteers offered their services and people opened their hearts to help out with the substantial expenses of caring for the injured animals. The public eagerly asked for updates on the animals, adopted a few of the older horses, and several people put in applications to adopt the victims of the wreck when they became available. In addition, the vets treated wounds, wormed, vaccinated and tested the horses in preparation for getting them ready. The farrier saw each of them. Lacey and Jonas spent some time assessing their prior training and readiness for new homes. Life became a whirlwind for her. Between her job with Dr. Moore and the Humane Society farm, she decided she met herself coming and going way too often.

Jonas became the one stability in her life. She spent the day with him, for the most part. They teamed up when they could, ate lunch together often, and tried to work in some alone time now and again. Hard to do, especially when the winter cold arrived and the days shortened. Volunteers faded into the woodwork, leaving the handful of staff to take care of all the animals' needs. Training fell lower on the totem pole behind daily chores.

In her spare time she worked with Knight, pleased with how far he'd come in such a short period. Just yesterday, she'd filled out an entry form for the first large rodeo next month. A hope and a prayer that just might come to light. With luck, she could try him out at a couple of smaller places first.

The bell rang on the door to the vet's office. She glanced up then froze as her father entered the building. His steely gaze locked on her and refused to budge.

She swallowed hard and stood up, uncomfortable with him towering over her. She lifted her chin and stared back solemnly. "Is there something I can help you with?" She prided herself on the even, bored tone despite the nearly boiling cauldron in her stomach at his sudden appearance.

"Your mother is upset because you're not coming for the holiday." He spat out the words as if they were bitter.

Lacey shrugged. "I explained my reasons to her and the others. They understood."

He stepped closer. "Can't you get off your high horse for one damn day to make your mother happy?"

Fury erupted. "Can't you get off your high horse and treat me with respect?" She paused and let the sarcasm carry through. "Oh, that's right. You're the one that has a stick up his ass because of the past and can't seem to remove it long enough to care one iota about his only daughter." She tilted her head. "Or are there more that we just don't know about?"

His jaw ticked as his lips thinned. "How dare you talk to me like that?" He fisted his hands at his sides.

She blew out a breath and countered with reason. Clear, concise reason. "I know in your eyes I'm a waste of good semen. Too bad. I've spent all my life trying to gain your approval. I'm done. Nothing will change your view of me and nothing can mend the Grand Canyon-sized hole in your black heart where I'm concerned." She stepped from behind the counter. "I have my own life and I'm going to live it. *Without you.*"

Sally stepped into the room and froze, staring at them both with wide eyes.

Dan flicked his gaze toward her for a split second before focusing back on Lacey. His eyes darkened with obvious anger. "You always were a selfish brat."

Lacey crossed her arms over her chest. "Was there something else you wanted? Because if there's not, I have work to do and you have a farm to run," she quipped.

His glare increased as he narrowed his eyes at her.

For a second, she thought he'd explode or even resort to violence. Instead, he growled, spun around, and left the way he came.

She watched him go with a sense of finality. "Good riddance."

Sally stepped closer with her mouth hanging open. "Oh my God. Are you okay?"

Lacey nodded. "Yeah. Old news."

Sally shook her head. "You never mentioned any problems at home. Obviously you've been keeping it under your hat."

Lacey sighed and returned to her seat.

Sally perched on the corner of the desk next to her. "I have a feeling there's more to the story than what anyone knows."

"It's a huge, convoluted mess that no longer matters. I've moved on. Staying with Nila until I can afford a place of my own." *Well, more often than not sleeping over at Jonas' house, but I'm not about to open that can of worms with Sally.*

Sally's eyes conveyed pity and sadness. "I'm sorry."

"Not your fault." Lacey glanced down at the appointment book.

"You can always come spend Thanksgiving with Ryan and me," Sally offered.

Lacey looked up. "Thanks, but I'm going to be working at the Humane Society farm and having lunch with Nila."

"Well, if you change your mind..." Sally returned to her feet.

"Thanks, but I'm already set."

"Then you better get going. I'll close up for the day. The news is fussing about a big ice storm and I know you'll be needed at the farm."

Lacey nodded, gathered her purse and coat, then headed toward the door. She paused and turned back. "Thanks, Sally. You're a good person."

Sally grinned. "Go on. Get out of here before it starts getting nasty. And happy Thanksgiving."

"Have a wonderful Thanksgiving, too." Lacey called over her shoulder as she walked to her truck, eyeing the dark clouds looming. Gusty winds filled with frigid air foretold the events to come.

The news had been on the fence between sleet, freezing rain, or a cold rain. Obviously the weather people had made a decision, and it wasn't good.

She hurried back to the farm, preparing for the long night ahead.

As soon as she pulled her truck into Nila's spare garage space, she hopped out and made her way to the barn, knowing all the staff would be furiously working to prepare for the worst.

"Lacey."

She spun around to find Jonas closing the distance between them with long, ground-eating strides. "I heard the ice storm is on the way."

He nodded, worry conveyed in his eyes. "We've got every single stall assigned. Spreading tons of straw. Nila ordered feed, hay and straw yesterday. It arrived this morning. Just in time." He slowed his steps to allow her to keep up as they continued toward the main building. "We don't have enough stalls for them all."

The words chilled Lacey more than the dropping

temperature outside. "How many are we short?"

"Four at last count." He opened the side door and gestured her in ahead of him.

She blinked for a second to adjust to the dimmer light. A flurry of activity greeted her. Volunteers and staff worked in a frenzy, moving bales of straw to stalls, then spreading them into thick carpets of bedding. They worked in teams. Some dropped off the bales. Some went from stall to stall shaking them out. Others stacked more bales near the back wall, presumably for easy use in the upcoming days as well as an insulating force against the coming cold. "Wow. You guys have been busy."

"Yeah. The volunteers came out in droves once they heard of the upcoming weather. They probably won't make it back once the ice starts, but they were gung-ho about chipping in today."

She watched the commotion for a second longer. "We're four stalls short?"

"Yes." He rubbed his forehead. "Nila has wracked her brain about what to do about not only that but about Knight's claustrophobia."

Lacey cringed. She'd forgotten about his issues since he'd settled so nicely into the smaller paddock next to the barn. Certainly, he couldn't stay outside in the storm. Not only due to the frigid temperatures, but because he couldn't get any more traction on the ice than a person or a car. The chance of a fall was too great. One broken leg was one too many, especially since it normally spelled out the ultimate death of the animal.

Nila walked up to them. "We've got the pigs and llamas set. The geese are hanging out in the old chicken coop area. The horses are next. The weatherman said the wind chill will hit minus forty. Too cold for anything to be outside and exposed to the elements." She sighed wearily. "I just hope we don't lose power. I don't know how we're going to get water to the animals if the well isn't working."

Lacey patted Nila's arm. "We'll figure out a way." She

shared a look with Jonas and sudden inspiration hit. "Jonas, your barn is empty, right?"

He nodded, understanding lighting up his eyes. "I have three stalls, but an open area where another animal can be free to wander."

"We can put Noggin and Candy there. Maybe a couple of the older mares as well. That'll take care of housing for the horses." Nila nodded.

"Except Knight," Lacey reminded them.

"We've not tried him inside since that first day." Jonas glanced around and frowned. "Too close with all the stalls and other horses."

"The arena might work." Lacey faced the other two. "He and Mabel can have the whole arena to themselves. Plenty of room. High ceiling that should help with his fear of close quarters."

"That just might work." Nila tapped her chin. "Yes, I think it's more than worth a try."

"Great. Now we have a plan. So where do you want me to jump in?" Lacey asked.

"Start collecting the horses." Nila blew out a breath. "Start with the pregnant mare that will probably drop her baby during this storm. The mare and foal to follow. I don't want either of them stressed in the least."

Lacey nodded. "On it."

Jonas followed. Together, they headed to the equipment shed, grabbed a few lead ropes and hurried to the nearest pasture.

The wind beat at Lacey's coat, sending a decided chill through her body. She noted the darkening skies and knew they had limited time before things turned ugly.

"I'll get those mares and the foal. You go to the other pasture and start bringing in whomever you can catch." Jonas hooked a left, let himself through a gate, and strode toward a small group of horses.

Lacey did the same, only entering the next pasture, where a large group of horses stayed. She prayed they'd agree to being caught without much difficulty, as tended to be the case most of the time. Now and again, one or two would act up and play a game of 'catch me if you can'. Definitely the last thing she needed right now. "Come on, Ace. Brie. Nelly." She called the names of the closest horses, alerting them to her presence. "We need to go inside before it gets really nasty out."

The horses lifted their heads and let her approach without concern.

Lacey quickly snapped the lead ropes to their halters and tugged until they followed. She made her way back to the barn, placed them in stalls, then backtracked.

Over and over again, she repeated the same process. As soon as she dropped off a horse, one or two people jumped into action, supplying the animal with fresh water, hay and grain. Each time she noticed how the stalls were filling up, leaving fewer and fewer empty. She counted heads, kept track of the threatening clouds and hurried when she could, knowing they still had to load up Candy, Noggin and a couple of other horses to take to Jonas' barn before ice covered the land.

As she began her third trip, freezing rain pelted down. "Damn." She hastened her steps all the more, heading toward Jonas, who'd rounded up another handful from her field.

"Take them. I'll go after Trouble." Jonas handed over the leads of four more horses. At least his thick coat contained a waterproof outer shell, which allowed the moisture to trickle down the sides instead of soaking in. The fact comforted her a little in the face of the situation.

Lacey groaned as she scanned the area, finding Trouble trotting along the back fence. The filly lived up to her name most days. She'd had little socialization before coming to the farm and excelled at escaping. The size of a large pony or small horse, Trouble could duck and zip away before a person could barely have time to react.

She saw him clutch a rope in his left hand and a lead rope

in his right as he strode deeper into the field. "I can head her off..."

He shook his head. "Go. I'll get her. Take those in then get Knight and Mabel."

Lacey nodded, clucked to the horses, and got the whole group moving in the right direction.

The skies opened up so hard she could barely make out the main barn in the distance. Frigid water saturated her coat and seeped down to the clothing underneath, sending a shiver through her. She tried to ignore it, focusing on her task.

Immediately after she placed the horses in the stalls, she dashed over to Knight's paddock, finding him hunkering against Mabel as they cozied up against the barn wall in an effort to get out of the freezing rain. Lacey snapped the leads onto their halters and crooned to them. "Come on. Let's go inside." She would have crossed her fingers, but needed both hands to handle an antsy Knight as they left the paddock and entered the side door of the arena.

He balked at the door—planted his hooves and refused to budge.

"Knight. Move it." She pulled on his halter.

He remained steadfast.

She glanced over at Mabel, tossed the lead over her neck, then shooed her inside. The mule eagerly trotted to the middle of the arena before shaking some of the water off.

Lacey turned back to Knight. "See? There's nothing to be afraid of. Mabel is right here. It's warm and dry. Much better than standing out in that storm." She faced him and started backing up.

Knight took a single step.

"That's a boy. Come on. You've been in here before. A dozen times. Nothing to be afraid of." Normally they entered through the large sliding door at the end of the arena. Since it was closed, she didn't have much choice but to use the smaller entrance.

He whinnied to Mabel.

She ignored him and snuffled at the ground as if in search of grass.

"She's not going to come to you. You're going to have to step inside and go to her."

As if understanding, Knight shouldered past Lacey and into the building. She hurriedly shut the door then the gate, ensuring he didn't try to dash back out. "That's a good boy." Once inside, he didn't appear the least bit upset, especially with Mabel only a few paces away. Lacey patted his neck, collected the lead ropes and promised to return with food and water as soon as the other animals were settled.

She started back to the field only to have Nila pull up in Jonas' truck, complete with the farm's trailer attached.

Nila cut the engine and jumped out. "I've got the last two mares loaded. Everyone else is already in and accounted for. There's hay, straw and grain, plenty for a few days in the front section. Buckets, too. Take everything and get Noggin and Candy, then follow Jonas home."

"Knight and Mabel." Lacey pointed toward the arena.

"We'll take care of them. Promise."

"But you'll need help tomorrow."

Nila shook her head and hollered over the roar of sleet now hitting the ground. "A handful of the college kids are staying with me. They weren't planning on going home for the holidays anyway. Decided to hang out here, help out, and have our own holiday."

Relief rushed through Lacey. "Thank God for them." She knew Nila needed the assistance, especially with nearly fifty stalls to clean and more than that many animals to care for. Not horrible unless the power went out. "I don't mind to stay. You'll need everyone if the electricity goes."

"Nope. We've got it. You and Jonas head to his house and take care of those horses. That'll be enough."

"But…"

Nila's lips firmed as she pinned Lacey with a stare. "Listen up, young lady. You've done more than enough. Hell, I should be paying you overtime." She wiped the water from her face. "Just get those horses to Jonas' barn, care for them, then spend some time with that man of yours."

Lacey's mouth fell open.

Nila grinned. "What? You think I didn't know what I interrupted when I called?"

"Well…" Lacey swallowed, having no words.

"Get going. Once you're in and safe, stay there. Spend time with Jonas. Tell him you love him."

Lacey marveled at Nila's perception. Sure, she'd almost admitted it to Nila before, but she hadn't been able to quite commit. Obviously Nila didn't need to hear the actual words to see the truth. "You know that too?"

"Yep. I ain't blind." Nila gave her a quick hug. "Now go."

Lacey didn't argue. Instead, she took the keys from Nila and drove the truck over to the house before backing up next to the gate.

She hopped out, checked the front section divider to make sure it wouldn't open and let the first two horses out, then opened the gate. Still holding a couple of lead ropes, she entered the paddock, making a beeline for the lean-to where the horses presently stood out of the weather.

"Candy. Noggin. Let's go home." She attached the ropes and led them easily across the area and into the trailer. Once inside, she tied the ropes loosely to keep them in place, shut the gate, and checked the latch. Satisfied, she drove back to the barn area, spied Jonas stepping out of the door, and drew up near him. "I've got the horses for your barn loaded up. Nila filled it with everything you'd need."

Jonas stepped closer, allowing her to catch a glimpse of muddy streaks coating his shirt, arms and the front of his jeans.

Lacey cringed. "Let me guess. Trouble decided to be a pain in the ass?"

"You could say that." His clipped tone told her he'd just about lost all patience with the filly.

She placed the truck in park, jumped out and gestured toward the seat. "Here you go. Nila says several of the volunteers are staying with her so we're not needed tomorrow."

His eyebrow shot up. "Are you staying here, too?"

"No. She told me to follow you home and stay there." *She also said to tell you that I love you.* Those words didn't quite make it past her lips.

"Remind me to thank that woman." The corners of his lips curled up. "Grab your truck and let's get out of here before the roads get bad."

Lacey didn't have to be told twice.

* * * *

Jonas handed her a cup of hot chocolate.

"Thank you." She blew on it then took a hesitant sip, thrilled with the taste and heat. Wrapping her hands around the ceramic, she soaked up the warmth.

By the time they'd settled the horses into his stable she'd began to shiver. Her coat had become soaked earlier, allowing the frigid gusts to chill her to the very bone. Shivers had shaken her body enough that Jonas had sent her back to the house with orders to go straight to the shower and not come out until she could claim to be pert near toasty. She'd done just that, even donning one of his sweatshirts and a pair of soft boxers to snuggle in afterward since her clothes were in the washer.

He sat down on the couch next to her and took a drink before placing his mug down on the coffee table. His damp hair had been recently combed. Sweatpants had replaced jeans and a heavy shirt had taken the place of his typical one. Along with a pair of white socks, they completed his present attire. Casual and comfortable.

Twisting, he studied her for a few seconds. "You're pensive. What's on your mind?"

She blew out a breath, not really wanting to relive the confrontation from earlier, but knowing Jonas wouldn't stop pestering her until she did. "My father came by the

229

office today."

Jonas' eyebrows shot up. "For?"

"To lecture me about declining the invitation to Thanksgiving. He claims it upset my mother." She snorted. Lacey had already spoken with the rest of the family, including her mother. They'd all accepted her reasons without the least bit of malice. In fact, her mother had promised to meet her for lunch one day in order to make up for the missed occasion.

"And?"

Lacey peeked up at Jonas and clutched her mug as if trying to dispel the negative vibes with her grasp alone. "I went off on him. Told him that I'd tried for years to please him, all to no avail. That I was a waste of good semen in his eyes and always would be. So I was done."

Jonas blinked. "You told him that?"

"Yeah." Lacey lowered her head for a moment then lifted her chin. "Everyone is right. I've spent way too much time worrying about him. Things have changed. *I've* changed."

Jonas borrowed her cup and placed it on the table next to his. Task complete, he tugged her against him and pressed his lips to her temple. "I know that wasn't an easy thing to do. Hard but necessary."

Lacey nodded, unsure she could speak around the sudden lump in her throat. Emotions welled up. Frustration and liberation from the encounter. Humble adoration for Jonas and his unbudging support.

"I'm proud of you."

The softly spoken words eased the burden immensely. She turned to meet Jonas' gaze. "Make love to me."

His breath caught.

She trailed her fingers over his cheek, smiling when he kissed the tips. "I want you, Jonas. Right now."

The fire of arousal lit in his eyes. "All you have to do is ask." He cupped the back of her head and held her steady for his kiss. A kiss filled with spice and heat.

Lacey instinctively opened her mouth, allowing Jonas to

explore to his content. When he retreated, she followed, flicking her tongue over his and sampling his unique flavor as readily as a thirsty person might drink a glass of sweet iced tea. She'd missed this. Missed him.

He tunneled his hand under her sweatshirt, cupping her bare breasts.

She shivered at the sensation of his callused hands molding the tender tissue. Pleasure shot through her.

Frustrated with the material separating her from his warm skin, she tugged his shirt up and over his head. The second he lifted his arms to remove it completely, she explored his chest, never tiring of the feel of strong muscles snapping and flexing just under the surface.

"You next." He pulled her shirt off, leaving her bare except for her pair of borrowed boxers.

He gazed at her, leaned in, then found a nipple with his lips. He worried the peak with a couple of quick licks.

Lacey's need skyrocketed. She held his head to her and moved closer. Anything to enable him to tend to the fire he created in her.

He slid his hand between her thighs, dipped under the boxers, and pressed against her slit. Using two fingers, he petted her. "So wet for me." He slid a finger inside. "So fucking hot, tight and wet," he muttered against her breast before sucking on it.

Lacey cried out at the nearly overwhelming feeling of her body being played by an expert. She hung on, bowed her back, and offered herself for his taking.

Jonas lifted his head and stared at her with hooded eyes. "Take my pants off." The softly spoken order kicked her into gear.

Ever so carefully, she lifted the waistband over his thick erection, then paused to bend over and sample the bead of moisture emerging from the tip.

"Oh, damn." Jonas' hips jerked as he cupped the back of her head and guided her back to his cock.

She took the hint, opened wide, and received the

mushroom head into her mouth. After swirling her tongue all around, she added vacuum and a small groan to the mix.

"Lacey." His thigh muscles tightened under her hands.

She felt him tug at her boxers. Lifting, she assisted in removing them until they fell to her ankles, forming an impromptu pair of shackles. As soon as she curled up into a kneeling position next to him on the couch with her face buried in Jonas' groin, he trailed his hand over her back and down to squeeze her rear. He hesitated only a second before edging lower and finally touching her where she needed him the most. She pushed back into his touch as he slid two fingers inside.

He teased her for a few seconds before removing his hand altogether.

She whimpered in an urgent plea.

"Up you go." He placed his hand under her chin and pressed until his cock popped free and she sat up nearly straight.

The tension in his face mirrored what existed in her body. Hunger and stark lust radiated from his molten gaze. All for her.

"Condom." He gritted out the word, stood up, kicked off the sweats, then disappeared in his bedroom.

A couple of seconds later he returned with the rubber in place and his shaft bobbing enticingly with each and every step.

Lacey licked her lips in anticipation.

Jonas sat back down on the couch, spread his legs, and patted his thighs. "Come on, cowgirl. Mount up and ride your stud."

The words acted like gasoline on a raging wildfire.

With a small yip of excitement, she straddled his hips, stopping when he latched onto her with a fierce grip. Glancing up, she met his eyes.

"Easy. Nice and easy." He gripped his cock, slid the tip between her folds, found the spot he'd been searching for, then nudged inside.

Lacey bit her lip as the erotic play began. Her body welcomed him back with snugness and a fine trembling Lacey had no way to control. She lowered herself, eagerly taking more of him, before pausing to catch her breath.

Jonas' gaze flickered between her face and the place where they were connected. His jaw clenched as she grunted with the impact of full penetration.

"Okay?"

She nodded and wiggled, trying to accommodate his full size. "You're bigger this way."

"Probably looks that way too." He grinned wolfishly. "We fit together before just fine. You creamed all over me then and will do so again."

His risqué statements sent another ripple of arousal zinging through her. An ache between her legs prodded her to get with the program.

Lacey slid the rest of the way, closed her eyes, and threw her head back at the exquisite pleasure. Unable to sit still, she experimented with different motions, lifting then dropping for a few seconds, then circling her hips and finally grinding against him in a desperate plea for more.

While maintaining his grasp on her hips, Jonas used the other hand to once again slip between her folds. He tapped her clit, sending white-hot fire shooting through Lacey's veins.

She cried out and started to rock with jerky, clipped motions. Each movement rubbed his cock against all her hot spots. Except one. Her aching clit. His fingers took care of that.

"That's it, baby. Take me. All of me. Harder." He adjusted his angle.

The result had Lacey nearly going over the edge. She mewled and grunted, panted and held onto his shoulders as she went on the ride of her life. Staying in the saddle wasn't a problem. Refraining from screaming out was.

"I'm getting close, sweetheart. Come for me. Let me watch you come for me." A press of his fingers directly on her clit followed the gruff command.

He strummed. He circled. He plucked.

She exploded.

One second she sat at the very pinnacle, then next she took flight. Strong contractions milked his cock, lodged deep inside her body. She clung to him as one rapturous peak after another filled her with orgasmic bliss.

A hoarse shout followed. She absently realized Jonas had made the sound as he took flight after her.

Gradually, she returned to herself, struggled to catch her breath and had a chance to do inventory.

Jonas had thrown his head back, resting it on the couch. His eyes were closed, his face scrunched in obvious intense pleasure. His chest expanded with a deep breath before he whooshed out once again.

Inside, she felt him. Still large, full and potent. He'd come, which meant his erection would start to fade soon. Until then, she savored the moment and reflected on the event.

He'd been gentle. Caring. Easy with her. No matter how badly he'd wanted to pound away, he'd let her take the reins instead and showered her with pleasure so that she'd find her way to another brilliant orgasm. At the expense of his own. At least for a short amount of time. He'd held back his own pleasure in order to make sure she experienced hers first. Lacey knew not every man would be so generous. She knew that for a fact, just like she knew it would snow in the winter.

His actions touched her to her very soul. "I love you, Jonas."

He lifted his head from the back of the couch in order to peer straight into her eyes. "I love you, too." He gently wrapped his hand around her neck, drew her in, and kissed her with such passion and tenderness she nearly cried.

She gave everything back to him and then some. Her heart. Her love. Her life.

Chapter Twenty-Five

Two weeks later

Lacey edged Knight toward the entrance of the arena, keeping a firm hold on the reins. "Easy, boy. I know you don't want to do this, but you've got to try. For me."

His ears flicked back and forth as he danced in place. His antsy motions increased and sweat broke out on his neck.

Lacey blew out a breath and tried to remain calm and keep her wits about her despite her sinking confidence. She and Jonas had been at the small arena for the past couple of hours, first acquainting Knight with the setup, then trying to settle him down once the lights and loud speakers were in use. He'd flat-out balked over and over again, refusing to go near the entrance even with Mabel, his mule friend, already inside. After a time-consuming battle, Lacey had managed to coax him into entering the arena, but not enough to get him to try the cloverleaf pattern even once.

The music boomed through the speakers, setting Knight off. He reared, lashed out with his front legs, then came back down only to try to bolt in the opposite direction. She yanked hard on the left rein, keeping him moving in a circle instead of running flat out toward the road. The whole time, she spoke to him, trying to calm his rampant nerves.

Jonas called out to her.

She eased her grip on the reins, allowing Knight to trot in bigger circles, and glanced up to see Jonas' concerned expression written clearly on his face. "I'm not sure about this, Jonas. He's beside himself with anxiety."

Jonas reached out, caught Knight's bridle, and rubbed

his forehead. "It's all the noise. He seemed okay with the lights." He blew out a breath. "If we could only have a muted rodeo, it might work."

Lacey snorted. "Wishful thinking." In truth, the events were loud. Not just because of the announcer, but because of the sometimes thousands of people milling around — the talking, the cheering, the constant activity. "Maybe he's not cut out for this." She uttered the sad truth.

Jonas shook his head. "Don't give up so easily. This is our first time exposing him to all the noise. It'll just take time. Rome wasn't built in a day and neither were a horse's fears erased."

I wish I was as optimistic as he is. "He's starting to lather. I think we should call it a night." Lacey knew they'd pushed Knight hard. She hated to keep at it when he showed such distress despite knowing her dreams rode completely on his being able to adapt.

"Not before you run the barrels. He has to know that he's here to do that job, if nothing else. Letting him leave before it will set a precedent."

Knowing he spoke the truth, Lacey maneuvered Knight near the exit, holding him with a firm hand as he started to exit the arena of his own accord. "No way, boy. Let's do what we've come to do."

A bit of nudging with her heels and sawing on the reins got him back into line and facing the barrels.

She waited a heartbeat, then slammed her feet into his sides. "Go."

He balked.

She did it again and growled at him. "Go, dammit."

As if realizing she meant business, Knight took off. He bounded toward the first barrel, circled it with precision, scurried to the next, and finally the third. Lacey pulled him up by cantering around the ring after he crossed the make-believe finish line. "There you go." She patted his sweaty neck once again.

Jonas met them at the exit, holding Mabel's lead. "Nice

job. For a second I didn't think he'd do it."

"Me too. Guess when I started cussing he decided I was scarier than the noise." She grinned at the irony.

"Hey, whatever works."

She slid off and started walking Knight, needing to cool him out before loading him into the trailer. Never a good idea to put a hot horse up.

"We can try this again tomorrow if you want. Hank loaned me the keys to the gate and booth." Jonas stared at Knight for a long moment. "What will it take for you to settle down completely without Lacey resorting to the vocabulary of a pirate?"

Knight chewed the bit and pawed the ground, obviously discontented with standing still. Lacey kept Knight walking in order to cool him off. She peered over at Jonas and chewed her bottom lip. "What are our chances?"

Jonas didn't answer for a few ticks. "I think he'll pull through. We just have to acclimate him to everything."

Lacey bobbed her head and kept moving. She understood that Knight needed time, and lots of it. He'd come a long way thus far. Logic said, given a few more weeks, he'd finally adjust enough to actually run in a real race. Unfortunately, Lacey's luck hadn't held up lately. She didn't dare push him too hard. Yet she needed to get back on the circuit and fast if she was going to have a shot at making it back to the finals.

A quandary with no easy answer.

Jonas slowed his steps to mirror Lacey's. He looked over his shoulder at the two equines as they reunited. "At least he seems okay with the arena when she's around."

Lacey watched Knight dote on the old mule. "Which brings up another question. How are we going to get him to the gate if she's outside the arena?"

"I'm hoping with all the other horses around, he won't fuss about that."

"Possible, I guess." Her shoulders sank all the more.

"Hey." Jonas cupped her cheek and lifted until she met

his eyes. "Giving up isn't part of the Lacey that I know. You've been through hell and still keep pushing forward."

His vote of confidence bolstered her spirits marginally. "Thanks."

"We'll figure out a way to make this work." He lowered his lips toward hers, only to get shoved by an impatient Knight before he could make contact. "Jealous beast."

Lacey grinned and patted the gelding. "Guess he doesn't approve of any hanky-panky."

"Uh-huh. Glad he's not coming home with us then." Jonas smiled wickedly.

"There's that." Lacey started toward the trailer, leading her charge. "Although I'm not sure anything would keep me from stripping you down and climbing in your saddle once we get there." Never before had she been so bold with a man. Jonas gave her the ambition and confidence to be herself and flirt openly. The rewards he bestowed on her were well worth the effort to bypass shyness and head straight to wanton.

Jonas' intense gaze burned through her. "You sure know how to motivate a man."

Lacey loaded Knight, then Mabel, before stepping out of the trailer. Jonas closed the back gate and locked it securely.

She took a second to enjoy the view of his Wranglers painted over his perfect rear.

He turned, caught her staring, and arched an eyebrow.

She shrugged. "I told you. The best ass this side of the Mississippi."

"Uh-huh." Jonas closed his eyes then opened them once more. "Keep talking like that and we might have to make a short pit stop in the barn."

"Hmmm." Lacey pretended to consider the option. While not entirely out of the question, she preferred Jonas' extra-large, warm bed for those kinds of activities. Instead of teasing him further, she climbed into the passenger seat, shut the door, and strapped herself in. *A change of topic might be in order.* She waited for him to start the truck and pull out onto the road before speaking. "What can we do besides repetitive exposure to different arenas and loud noise to break Knight of his anxiety?"

Jonas watched the road for a long time. "This is all I know to do. Just desensitization."

"Too bad we can't turn down the volume in his head some."

"Maybe we could." Jonas' eyebrows furrowed for a second before he lifted one hand off the steering wheel and placed it on his leg.

"What are you thinking?" She could almost see the hamster wheel turning inside his head.

"Cotton."

"What?"

"Cotton." He glanced her direction for a second before focusing back on the road. "We can put cotton in his ears in order to mute the sound."

Lacey blinked at him. "How in the world did you come up with that idea?"

"Just came to me."

She shook her head in amazement. "You're incredible."

He grinned ruefully. "I'd rather you tell me that *after* I make love to you."

Lacey laughed. "If I still have a brain then, I'll remind you."

She watched him drive, the easy way he handled the wheel, the looseness to his body. A man in his element. With horses, machinery and in the oil business. A complex guy who knew who he was and wasn't afraid to get dirty or lay it on the line. He put all other men to shame in her opinion.

No wonder I fell for him.

Jonas' phone rang. He answered immediately. "What's the verdict, Jason? Uh-huh. Okay. What does Dad think about this?" A long pause followed. "I'll be in first thing tomorrow to meet with them. Yeah. Okay. Later."

Jonas' expression turned serious as he hung up.

Lacey couldn't have helped but eavesdrop on the one side of the conversation. Jonas' reaction set her warning bells off. "Everything all right?"

"I've got to meet with the others tomorrow. We've been preparing for a hit on the oil stocks. It looks to be coming sooner rather than later."

Lacey pulled up all she knew about the oil business and the stock market. All of the information could perhaps fill one page in a book. "What does that mean for you and the company?"

"We take losses." He turned toward her for a second. "The market is volatile at best. Oil prices are pretty much determined by the big guys. Locally, we're producing efficiently and have whittled out excess cost where we can. It's part of the business. That's why we're investing some of our capital into wind power. Spreading it out. Diversifying."

"Wind power is getting popular right now. I heard something on the news about it."

"Yep. We can put wind turbines in the same areas as the oil wells and drills. That will help offset the cost of pumping."

Her respect for him grew even more, if that was possible. "I never knew much about your other career. It's amazing you can keep up with what sounds like two full-time jobs."

He flashed her a wry grin before facing forward once more. "Full-time trainer. Part-time oil man. I grew up in the oil business. It's second nature. Yet being chained to a desk isn't for me. I'd rather be outside with the horses even though the pay is so much less."

"I understand that. There's more to life than money, especially when you're making a difference in the lives of needy animals. It's not a job, it's a calling, or so I've heard. I felt it too when I started working at the farm."

"Exactly. Which is why I gave most of my stocks to Jason when I started training horses. He works his ass off keeping the business going. I'm there, but in a more limited capacity. He deserves the lion's share of the profits for taking on the lion's share of the problems."

Lacey studied Jonas, noting the square jaw, the sharp, intelligent eyes. Everything she knew about this man impressed her. "You, Jonas, are a wonder."

He peered over at her and grinned mischievously. "I think the word you promised to use was 'incredible'."

She laughed. "That's right. I did, didn't I?"

"Uh-huh."

The look he gave her sent a sensual shiver all the way to her toes.

* * * *

Lacey lowered her body to the bed with a tired yet contented sigh. Jonas sat back on his heels and watched her stretch out before him. Her beautiful body trembled now and again even as her position allowed him a perfect view of her moist folds, still a bit swollen from his aggressive penetrations. He'd been unable to keep to a slow, methodical pace. The fire in his blood, along with his immense arousal, initiated much earlier, had stolen his control and lashed him to a hard, fast round. Thankfully, the moment he'd put Lacey on her hands and knees in front of him, she'd seemed to catch his urgency and fever. She'd met him with every thrust, begged for more, and cried out his name as she bolted into orgasm.

Sated and still tingly from a powerful orgasm, he took a second to collect his thoughts and allow the blood to return to his brain.

"You really are incredible." She turned her head to meet his eyes and grinned like a woman well satisfied with her man.

He chuckled. "I'm glad to know I pleased you."

"That and then some." She rolled to her side and pulled her legs up toward her chest while still maintaining eye contact.

The slight hint that she was getting cold spurred him into

motion. He climbed from the bed, removed the condom and tossed it into a nearby trashcan on the way to the bathroom. After cleaning up, he gathered up another cloth, added warm water, then returned to Lacey.

He sat down on the bed next to her. "You'll sleep better after a bit of washing."

She hesitated. "You don't have to."

The small bout of shyness amused him. "Open your legs, sweetheart. The longer you wait the colder that bath will be."

She settled on her back and splayed her legs.

Jonas wasted no time in gently cleansing the area.

She jerked as he ran the material over her clit, but otherwise accepted his attentions without complaint.

"Okay?" He searched her face, finding only sleepiness and satisfaction. His pride buoyed. Even with this wild brand of lovemaking, she seemed to ride the high tides with him.

"Uh-huh." She closed her legs as soon as he'd finished.

"Good." He returned the washcloth to the bathroom, tossed it into the hamper and returned to the bed.

Jonas tucked Lacey against his body and pulled the covers over them. She felt right in his bed. Not just because of the amazing sex they'd just shared, but because of something more.

"I love you, Lacey." He punctuated the words with a light kiss to her shoulder.

"I love you, too." She cuddled in for comfort, rested her head on the pillow and closed her eyes.

He smiled as her body relaxed against his and her breathing evened out as she drifted off to sleep. A protective streak a mile wide reminded him to hold on to what was his. Possessiveness soon followed.

He'd meant what he said about loving her. Never before had he uttered those words to a non-relative. Doubts that he'd ever say them to a woman at all had lingered in the back of his mind. Then Lacey had entered his life.

She'd arrived like a summer storm and washed away his

worries and insecurities. The analogy seemed to describe her perfectly. Strong. Cowgirl strong. Yet sweet and gentle at the same time. He couldn't recall the last time a woman had possessed all those qualities together. Hell, he couldn't recall the last woman he'd been with. Lacey had erased them all as she went.

The future appeared bright with her by his side. He'd just needed to overcome that last hurdle. Commitment. The greatest fear for many men. He'd been in that very boat as well not so long ago. Now the thought of tying his life to Lacey's resembled more a walk in a park on a sunny spring day.

She deserved respect and the long-term promise that only came with marriage. While getting hitched might not be the answer others expected, Jonas knew he and Lacey could make it work. Their love would make a solid base. The rest took effort, patience and flexibility.

He could and would do all that. For Lacey.

Which meant he needed to make a stop in the next few days. He mentally added it to his list and rested his chin on Lacey's crown.

I'm keeping you, baby. Forever and always.

With those words, he shut his eyes and headed toward sleep.

Chapter Twenty-Six

Three weeks later

"Whoa, Knight. We're almost there. Take it easy." Lacey clung to the saddle horn as he reared in the air.

Jonas pulled him back down with a sure grip on the bridle. "Are you sure you can handle him?" Worry coated Jonas' face as he stood next to a tied Mabel at the very end of the line of panels, well away from the other competitors, who passed them by with curious expressions.

Lacey would have waved or said something to the other girls, but was too busy trying to keep Knight from bolting or tossing her to the ground in a fit.

She nodded. "Yeah."

Jonas' frown didn't convey confidence.

The last couple of weeks they'd worked hard to get Knight ready for the small rodeo nearby. Jonas felt that they'd done enough with practice that they needed another way to judge his progress, namely getting to a real rodeo and seeing what he did. Lacey echoed his sentiment with a bit less solid conviction. Still, she understood they had to take that big step at some point. Might as well be now rather than six months from now.

Lacey patted Knight while keeping a firm hand on the reins. "No other way to find out if he can hold up under the pressure," she reminded herself and Jonas.

Knight sidestepped, knocking into Jonas, who took the hit in stride before stopping at the end of the line of other racers.

"It's okay, buddy. We're almost there. Just have to wait

our turn."

Knight's ears flicked back and forth as he shook his head. Still antsy, he trotted nearly in place. Probably would have headed back the way they'd come if not for Lacey's and Jonas' holds on him.

Slowly but surely the line moved forward, allowing Lacey to see the starting line clearly. She took a second to scan the arena, found nearly every seat full and sighed. The crowd would erupt at some point and Knight wouldn't be able to help but react. Her gut clenched at the very idea of him going off in the middle of the race.

"Settle down, big guy." So far, the cotton seemed to help. He wasn't nearly as panicked as before, although he remained far from calm.

Jonas led them through the partition that separated the horses coming in and the horses exiting the arena. Knight slammed into him again as the announcer called the previous racer's time.

Jonas grunted, but maintained his footing. Gradually, he let go of Knight and stepped to the side. "Just be careful out there."

"Will do." She lined Knight up, turned his head forward when he looked back at Mabel. "She'll be waiting for you. When we get back."

"Next is Lacey Bright. That's right. Our local girl who made it all the way to the finals. She's riding her new horse, Knight, for the first time tonight."

The attendant raised the green flag.

Lacey sat up straight before moving Knight forward with much encouragement with her legs before slackening the reins.

He reared once again. She held on, collected him, pointed him at the first barrel and bumped him with her heels. "Go."

For a second he seemed to stall, deciding to fight the bit rather than obey. Then, in the next instant, he took off like a shot.

Lacey barely had time to guide his turn before he slammed

into the barrel, knocking it over. He galloped for the second one, executed a nice turn, and darted for the next. Wide, but clear, Knight seized the bit and sped for the finish line and Mabel.

"Whoa." Lacey pulled back on the reins to no avail. Knight hit the dirt outside the arena, spun around, and bucked a couple of times before she could get him under control, nearly toppling her from her perch in the process. By the time she had all of his feet on the ground at the same time, Jonas was hurrying over with Mabel in tow.

"Not bad considering..."

Lacey wiped the sweat from her forehead. She knew his words for the truth. As much as she'd hated to knock over the first barrel and put herself out of the running, she realized the facts. Knight had managed to run the pattern in full view of hundreds of people. That in itself was a small miracle considering his anxiety issues. "I think the cotton helped."

Jonas nodded. "Probably so." He glanced over at Mabel, who appeared put out by the whole experience of being dragged here and there. "She's not thrilled with all the fuss."

Lacey noticed Mabel's ears pulled back and her teeth showing. Equine body language for 'I'm pissed'. She couldn't help but grin. "Seems like all the attention is fine as long as she doesn't have to do more than stand around."

"Well, she's a mule after all." Jonas smiled and patted the old girl's neck. "Stubborn and all that."

"Uh-huh." Lacey wheeled Knight around and started back toward the trailer. No sense in hanging around since she would be well out of the placings.

She spent several minutes walking him in a circle to cool him down. Probably not a necessity, but she didn't want to take any chances. "What are we going to do, Knight?" She patted his neck and kept up the sedate pace while Jonas loaded Mabel in the trailer. "You're my only hope for this season. I'll do whatever it takes to help you through this. If

I only knew what that might be."

Knight snorted and kept walking. His skin no longer rippled and the sweat had started to dry. Away from the limelight, he'd calmed considerably.

She reached up and removed the cotton from his ears.

His response didn't change in the least. Just a well-mannered pet following his owner around.

Stopping, she stood right in front of him, peering into his beautiful blue eyes. "What do you need me to do to help you get over this?"

He lifted his head and stared back.

"I know you can do this. You're smart. Really smart." She rubbed his forehead before bestowing a kiss to the area. "Trust me, big guy. We'll get through this together."

He nudged her in the chest.

She smiled, scratched under his bridle, then turned to find Jonas watching her with an intense look. "What?"

Jonas shrugged. "For a second there, I think he was actually listening."

I really hope so. She patted Knight's neck once more before leading him into the trailer next to Mabel.

She had a week until the next small rodeo. If Knight couldn't work through this hurdle, her dream of returning to the finals was finished long before it had really got started.

Patience. He'll adjust. I just have to have some patience.

* * * *

The phone rang, jarring Lacey from her light doze. She picked it up, checked the caller, and sighed before answering. "Hi, Mom."

"Lacey. How are you?"

She sat up in the bed and glanced at the clock. Nine p.m. Not quite bedtime, but late enough that she could have easily slept through the night. The last few days had left her fatigued and in need of some catch-up rest. "Okay."

"We missed you at Thanksgiving."

Tension rolled over her. She'd spoken to Tate and her mother well before the holiday, explained her reasons for not attending, and received their verbalized understanding. The last thing she wanted to do right now was rehash the past or receive a guilt trip for skipping the occasion. "You know why I wasn't there. Besides, I was busy at the farm."

"Oh, I know, dear. I just wanted to let you know that the others missed you as much as I did."

"As much as Dan did?" Sarcasm came through loud and clear.

Lacey couldn't quite go back to calling him 'dad'. That word signified a close bond and a loving relationship. Neither of those described their situation for now and probably for the future as well.

Her mother paused for a second. "I know we screwed up and you bore the brunt of it. I'm sorry. Really sorry. I just wish I could fix it."

"You can't, Mom. What's done is done." Lacey brushed her hair away from her face. "Like I said before, I have my own life now. Should have had it a long time ago, but better late than never in my book."

"I'm proud of you for standing up for yourself. Your father told me what you said."

"Tracking me down at work to try to strong-arm me into something doesn't earn him or anyone else any brownie points." Tired of the discussing the bane of her life, Lacey blew out a breath. *Not like it would change anything, anyway.* "Was there something else that you wanted?"

"Well, no. I just wanted to see how you were doing." Her mother's voice carried hesitation.

"I'm fine. Working hard. Nothing new. Living my own life and I'm happy about it." She didn't delve into details.

"That's good then." Another few beats of silence followed. "Lacey, I know you can't forgive your father and I respect that. But you are still part of this family. I've forgiven him for what happened during our separation years ago. We're trying to make it work. I want you to be part of that."

Lacey narrowed her eyes as a jagged wave of irritation ran through her. She tried to rein in her temper but failed. "I worked my ass off all my life for that farm, for you and for Dan. Did everything humanly possible to please that man. Nothing made him accept me. You didn't stand up to him or do anything about the way he talked to me. Anything to keep the peace, right? You can stop playing that role, Mom. I'm done. Just because I'm not halfway across the country doesn't mean I'm going to kiss and make up. I can't forget. I refuse to forgive. I might take your calls but count me out for any family events."

"But you're alone in the world. Everyone needs a family for support."

Lacey snorted. "I have some wonderful friends. And no, when a family can't find it in their egotistical heart to be supportive, then they aren't needed."

"Lacey. We've always been behind you. Supported you."

"No, Mom. That's not true. Maybe you did to some extent. Tate and Ransom too. Yet when you read the writing on the wall, it doesn't pan out. How many rodeos did you attend? How many, Mom? I can tell you. None. After I turned sixteen I never saw any family member at a single rodeo and there have been hundreds of them."

"We can't afford—"

"I'm not talking about the finals. I'm talking about the local ones. A fifteen-minute drive."

"Your brother and Ransom had football games in the fall."

"I'm well aware of that. Instead of dividing up the time spent with each of us, you and Dan put Tate's games ahead of me." Lacey's shoulders slumped. "I get it. Always have, always will. But you need to understand that I no longer care if you attend the rodeos or anything else. I don't need your approval or your presence. I'm living life on my own terms now."

"Lacey…"

"No, Mom. Look, I'm tired and have to work early tomorrow. Good night." Lacey clicked off the call and tossed the cell phone down on the bed.

Her mother had seemed to take her side lately. Until now. Trying to make her feel guilty for not forgiving her father and stepping right back into being the naïve devoted daughter. Pretty damn small of her.

Whatever her mother's agenda, it wouldn't work. Lacey had spent too many hours fretting and worrying about that family. Now she'd washed her hands of their problems, stepped into the light, and intended to shine brightly on her own.

Come hell or high water. Anxious barrel horse or not.

Her determination to turn Knight into a top-notch barrel horse strengthened all the more.

She just needed to fight through the rough patches and get to the spotlight once again.

Chapter Twenty-Seven

Lacey flicked the whip, encouraging Knight to pick up the pace of his trot as she held onto the long lunge line. She'd been granted permission to practice at the fairgrounds arena where the next rodeo would be held in a few days in order to work with her nervous horse some more. With the music blaring from the PA system and the bright lights on, she tried to mimic the situation of a real race, minus all the fans, of course.

By getting him used to this new place, she might have a chance.

Knight had planted his feet at first, not about to return to the ring. She'd insisted by bringing in the lunging equipment. Since then he'd been trotting in large circles, no longer fighting her wishes.

"Much better. See? There's nothing to be afraid of." She clucked to Knight and watched his effortless motion as he broke into a pretty lope.

A sudden loud bang had him slowing down and his head coming up.

"Go." She snapped the whip, keeping the lash well away from him, and kept rotating to counter his circles. She ignored the sound, knowing Knight would take his cues from her.

After the less than stellar performance of a couple of nights ago, she'd stepped up her training routine. Hard. In order for Knight to become the barrel racer she knew he could be, she had to take a tough stand, desensitize him to his fear of noise, and try to pry him away from Mabel for the runs. Buddy sour and high-strung did not a top-level performance horse make.

At the moment, she'd chosen to work on the arena issue first. Get past that and she'd start prying Knight away from Mabel for short periods of time for him to work. She didn't have any illusion that he'd need her for his down time, but hoped he could learn to be more independent for the short breaks needed to do his job.

As it was, Mabel waited at the entrance to the arena, tied to one of the bars separating the stands from the ring. Just getting Knight away from her had been an ordeal. Today seemed to be one of the especially needy ones. Lots of nickering, swinging around and refusing to leave her side. Lacey had managed to get him going into circles, then started moving him down the arena and away from his mule friend. Once he'd started working, he'd settled down and fallen into line.

Which told her many things. Namely, that once he began his job, he'd be fine. Great in theory, a bit more challenging considering his task lasted an average of fourteen seconds.

No matter. I'll make it happen.

Her career balanced on that fact. She refused to throw in the towel.

Too bad Jonas hadn't been able to join her. He'd promised to dedicate his day to the oil business he and his brother ran. While he spent most of his time as a trainer, he didn't let his other job slide. He'd been going to the office at least a couple of days per week lately due to the coming changes he spoke of now and again. Papers piled on his coffee table next to the laptop always reminded her how hard he worked. She knew lately he'd been in the midst of serious conversations about adding in wind turbines to the property as well as bracing for a hit in oil prices. He never complained about the challenge of juggling two jobs or the fatigue it caused. Just went about his way quietly and efficiently, from what she could determine. She only hoped his office day would prove routine and nothing worth stressing over. For his sake.

Both of them had been stretched too thin lately.

After checking her watch, she slowed Knight down, brought him to a stop, then walked up to him. "Such a good boy." She patted his head, noted the slightly elevated breathing from his exercise. "Ready to saddle up now?"

She led him to the side of the arena, placed the tack on him with practiced ease, and slid into the saddle. He danced under her, starting toward Mabel. "Nope. Other way."

She spun him around, clamped her heels to his sides, and moved him forward and away from his friend. He chewed the bit, but didn't fuss much more. "Much better. Now we'll do a couple of easy laps and some barrel work."

The sun had sunk well below the horizon before she'd finished with Knight. He'd done well with the new regimen. As long as she kept him focused and moving, he didn't seem to pay the noise much mind. Same with Mabel.

Hope welled up and established a firm foothold.

Three rounds of the cloverleaf pattern finished off the long workout. Lacey patted Knight's neck as she walked him back toward Mabel. Once there, she slid off then collected Knight's reins and Mabel's lead rope before leading them to the trailer. They loaded without incident.

She picked up her phone, called the control box in the arena, thanked the man, and told him she was done for the evening. He invited her back the next day. She agreed, knowing the more she exposed Knight to the noise and arena, the more he'd settle down when race time arrived.

* * * *

Lacey returned the last plate into the cabinet, wiped her hands on the kitchen towel, and turned back to Nila, who sat at the kitchen table doing the accounting books for the farm. With Jonas at a late meeting about his other job, Lacey had the night to herself and had decided to spend it with her boss.

She studied the middle-aged woman leaning over the

laptop, entering receipts into a software program. As kind and generous as Nila was, she should have men a-plenty knocking at her door. As long as Lacey had worked there, she'd never seen one or heard about Nila going out on a single date. She found the realization somewhat sad. "Why aren't you married, Nila?"

Nila lifted her head and blinked at Lacey, her mouth falling open at the out-of-the-blue question. "Wow. Warn a girl next time."

Lacey grinned then plopped down in the seat across from Nila. "You're pretty. Smart. Successful. Sweet. Why aren't you at least dating?"

Nila snorted. "Date whom? All the men around here want young, beautiful ladies. Even men my age. Old ladies with hot flashes and sagging boobs need not apply."

"Not all men are like that."

"True. There are some special ones out there. Like Jonas. He's a keeper."

Lacey nodded. "I'll agree wholeheartedly there. That still doesn't explain why you're not married."

"You of all people should know that marriage isn't always as blissful as everyone thinks and hopes." Nila rested her pen on a pile of receipts. "That's not to say it isn't either. I know my Henry was the world's best husband. He pampered me, doted on me."

Stunned, Lacey stared at Nila. "I didn't know you were married."

"For seven short years. Henry was killed in a car wreck. Broke my heart, but left me with some wonderful memories."

"I'm so sorry." Lacey couldn't imagine the pain of losing the love of your life, especially in that manner and after such a short period of time.

"Life happens. We take what we get sometimes." Nila removed her pen and started entering figures into the computer again.

"Have you thought of dating since?"

"Oh, I've dated off and on. Nothing serious and no one that could hold a candle to Henry."

That said a lot. Lacey thought of Jonas and knew she'd feel the same way. No other man would do. At least until she was able to have plenty of time to mourn and move forward with her life.

Her respect for Nila increased all the more. Lacey wracked her brain. "What about Dr. Thornton? He's here a lot. A widower, I think."

"Dr. Thornton?" Nila stared at the computer screen for a long moment.

"Yeah. You've both lost spouses. Around the same age. In the same profession. Sort of." The more Lacey thought about it, the better the match clicked. "Ask him out sometime."

Nila met Lacey's gaze then grinned. "I just might do that."

"Wonderful."

For a short time no one said anything. Lacey wiped down the countertops as Nila continued to work on the accounts.

Finished, Lacey spread the wet rag over the center of the sink to dry then turned back to Nila. "That black stud that came in with the other semi wreck horses. What's his adoption fee?"

Nila twisted in her seat. "You're interested in him for a barrel horse?"

"No." Lacey leaned back against the counter. "But Jonas is. For a roping horse, that is. I want to buy the stallion for him."

"Like he did Knight for you?"

"Yes." Lacey nodded. "He's still on the fence about trying the rodeo again. I thought gifting him the horse might help him decide to give it one more try."

Nila pursed her lips. "What if Jonas decides he's really retired for good?"

Lacey shrugged. "We'll cross that bridge when we come to it. Right now, I want to adopt that stallion and let Jonas take it from there."

"Okay then. He's yours." Nila spun back around and

started typing on the keyboard.

"How much?" Lacey stepped closer, needing to seal the deal for good.

Nila paused. "You've worked enough overtime that I think we can call it even."

"But..." Lacey knew Nila was offering up a beautiful gift. However, she'd never wanted anything for free. She'd always earned everything before.

Nila waved her hand. "His adoption fee right now would be only a couple hundred dollars. We don't know what his training background is and would need time to find that out. Training adds to the price. Since we don't have much invested, his fee is negligible. Thus, he's yours."

"You don't have to do that."

"You've earned it and more."

"Thank you!" Lacey hugged her. "I can't wait to tell Jonas."

Nila smiled. "I have a feeling when you do, I won't expect you to come home for the night."

Lacey chuckled even as her face heated. "Probably not."

"You're good for him. And he for you. You two make a great couple. I hope you know how rare that is."

"I do." Lacey worried her lip. "I love him with all my heart."

"Well, well. I hope you took my advice and told him."

"Yep. He told me that he loved me too." Lacey recalled that moment happily.

"I have a feeling that's just the start of a lifetime of loving," Nila said.

"I sure hope you're right." Lacey hugged Nila again then headed to change the laundry. Chores never stopped and she had a few days away to make up for around the house.

Chapter Twenty-Eight

Jonas made one more round with the tall sorrel gelding, then pulled him up. They'd had a great training session where the horse had responded well to each command. He was ready for adoption and pretty much any level of rider could handle the young horse.

As happy as he was for the gelding, Jonas couldn't push aside his sour mood. He'd been all over the place that day. From the hospital for his quarterly scan to the office where he'd been inundated with information on the pros and cons of dipping into wind power along with the concerning reality of falling oil prices on the stock market. They were already working on a bare-bones budget. As far as he, Jason, and their father could see, there were no other slashes that could be made in order to keep the business afloat. While not pressed financially at the moment, they needed to prepare for the future. That meant sinking money elsewhere with high potential rewards.

The start-up costs were a bit staggering, but after that, maintenance costs were much lower. They could use the wind power to their benefit and also sell to power companies once they were established. Not a bad deal. If they could check out all the ins and outs, come up with a foolproof plan, and proceed.

It'll get there.

Long brunette hair caught his eye. Jonas twisted enough to see Lacey coming toward him. Dressed in jeans, a sweatshirt and a heavy jacket, presently unzipped, she appeared as beautiful as ever.

His gut seized as he considered the fact that they'd just

discovered each other, announced their love, and that his time could be waning.

Stop being so morose.

Every time he thought of the future, he saw Lacey by his side. Unfortunately, he couldn't give her a worry-free life or even promise to be there long. Each doctor's visit took him one step further from his disease and closer to a cure, which gave him confidence that he really could be there down the road. Although he had to remind himself that no guarantees were given along the way.

He halted the gelding, climbed out of the saddle, removed the horse's gear and set it aside. After trading the bridle for an everyday halter, Jonas patted the horse's neck and sent him about his merry way in the large enclosure.

Jonas slung the bridle over his shoulder and collected the saddle and cloth in his hands, making his way toward the small gate.

Lacey beat him there and held it open for him to exit. She took a second to shut and latch it behind him before striding to catch up. "How was work? Getting the wind energy figured out and all set up?"

Her chattiness usually made him smile. Not today. Too much worry pushed his spirit down and crushed his mood. "Yeah." He kept walking, not slowing or bothering to look at her as she tried to engage him in conversation.

"Are you going to put the wind turbines on the same land as the oil drills? Or try to spread them over more places?"

While he appreciated her interest, the last thing he wanted to do was to talk about the same drivel he'd heard all day long. "We're checking into both options." He entered the tack room, placed the saddle on a holder, then hung the bridle up on a hook attached to the wall.

She stepped aside to let him past long enough to get a rag to wipe the bit off.

When he returned, he cleaned the bit then stuffed the rag into his pocket in order to toss it into the laundry bin later.

"You're tense. What is it?"

He met her gaze, sighed, and decided that she deserved an answer. The last thing he wanted was for her to start questioning his feelings for her and he knew she'd engage that particular idea soon enough if he didn't answer. Besides, he expected honesty from her so could do no less himself.

Striding outside, he paused at the enclosure containing the black stallion he'd had his eye on, rested his forearms on the railing and watched the horse for a few seconds. Lacey followed, standing next to him in silence, seemingly patiently waiting for him to open his mouth once again. He'd give her kudos for not pushing and nagging.

"My oncologist checkup is tomorrow. I had the CAT scan today before the meeting."

Lacey linked her fingers with his. "And you're worried about the results?"

He couldn't lie. Not to her. Not even to appear more of a man in her eyes. "Yes."

"Is there something new going on?" She scanned his face.

He shook his head. "No. I just can't help but think about those results. The what-ifs."

Lacey rubbed his back. "You'll make it through. I read that testicular cancer is nearly always curable."

"Yeah. That's what I'm banking on. Why I went ahead with the optional radiation therapy to increase my odds." He ran his hand through his hair, finding comfort in her presence and touch. "I've never asked this of another person, but will you go with me to the visit?"

"Of course." Lacey offered up a warm smile. "I'll be with you. Together we can get through this. Promise."

He'd bared his greatest fear, his largest weakness, and Lacey hadn't blinked. Instead, she'd offered up hope and encouragement with her steadfast promise. His heart buoyed all the more.

Jonas stared at the powerful black stallion as he trotted around the small ring. He'd calmed greatly since first arriving, allowing staff to groom him without much of a fuss. His concussion had prevented the vet from gelding him yet, but presumably that would take place sometime in the future. Afterward, Jonas would start working with the big guy, finding out what lessons he might have had in the past and teaching him more.

He watched the stallion's strong hindquarters bunch then snap as he spun on a dime only to stretch out in a flaring trot in the other direction. Grace and power. Speed and agility. And most of all, intelligence. Those qualities would make a great roping horse. He'd wager the black horse had them all.

"Have you decided what to name him?" Lacey asked as she leaned against the railing.

"Not for me to decide. Nila normally comes up with those."

Lacey nodded. "I think this one might be different. You should name him."

Jonas turned toward her, trying to read her face. Obviously, something was up. The evidence showed in her words and her eyes. She'd best never sit down to a poker table. Bluffing, she couldn't pull off. "What are you not telling me?"

She met his gaze with a tiny smile. "He's yours. I paid the adoption fee in order to give him to you."

His mouth fell open. Granted, he'd done the same for her, but that was different. She hadn't had the extra funds to buy Knight even though she'd desperately needed a barrel horse. He could have easily purchased this black stallion once he decided if he'd for sure give roping another try.

Lacey's lips turned down and she found the ground enthralling. "I know you see something in him. Now you have the ability to find out what his potential is." Her softly spoken words prodded him into responding.

"I can't believe you did that." He placed his finger under her chin and lifted until she looked directly at him. "That's the nicest thing anyone has ever done for me."

Relief briefly crossed her face. "I wanted to make you

happy."

"Sweetheart, just being with you makes me happy. This… this is remarkable." He praised her with a kiss. "You're full of surprises, love."

She offered up a crooked grin. "I bet I can find a couple more surprises for you."

He arched an eyebrow. "Such as?"

"That's for me to know and you to find out. *After* we're back at your place and you've stripped down to your birthday suit."

"I like the sound of that." He forgot his concerns in the face of Lacey's sensual teasing.

She beamed. "So, how long until you can slip away?"

"Right now." The sun still shone, but dusk would be arriving soon enough. He'd had a long day thus far and could stand to quit a bit early. Especially when Lacey wanted to take him home and shower him with love. No way would he turn that proposition down.

"Perfect. I've already taken care of Noggin and Candy for the evening, hoping that you'd be free. So I guess we're good to go."

He couldn't resist swooping down and brushing his lips over hers briefly. "You think of everything. Thank you."

She rested her hands on his shoulders and grinned saucily. "Here I was hoping you might help me out in the idea department."

"Hmm?" He wrapped his arms around her waist and waited for her answer.

"Well, you see, I've done some reading recently…"

His cock tightened at the way she coyly peeked up at him through her eyelashes. "About?"

"Oh, lots of things. Namely what men like in bed."

Her admission didn't quite shock him. Lacey might have been an innocent when she'd come to his bed, and still retain many of those qualities, yet she'd never really been shy or inhibited when it came to sex. That quality always stirred his libido and amused him at the same time. "I can pretty much attest to the fact that I like everything you do to me in bed."

Lacey smiled wide. "I'm glad to hear that. Because I have a craving to taste you again."

Jonas groaned, grabbed Lacey's hand, and led her toward his truck, eager to get in out of the cold, arrive at his house, and let her have her way with his body.

She laughed at his rush. "You sure you don't want to work with one more horse before calling it a day?"

He slowed his steps, snorted and shook his head. "Climbing into the saddle with a hard-on isn't comfortable or in my plans, either. I'd rather be lapping up your cream while you suck my dick." Normally he wasn't so graphic in his words, but Lacey unleashed all his faculties at times, especially his tongue.

"Mmm. Yeah, I think that does sound like more fun. How fast can you drive home?"

He dropped her hand in order to stride to the driver's side of his truck. After jumping in, he shoved the key in the ignition, waited for Lacey to fasten her belt, then started the engine. "Pretty damn fast." He drove down the driveway and made a beeline for his house, pushing the speed limit, but not outrageously so since he intended for them to arrive safely in one piece.

Several minutes later, he tapped the button on the wall to close the automatic garage door and led Lacey into his house.

The moment he stepped into the kitchen, he yanked her into his arms and sealed his lips over hers. Heat unfurled in his stomach as he thrust his tongue between her lips and explored with a hunger born of passion too long denied.

She met him with equal enthusiasm and want, accepting his plundering before mirroring his actions, giving as much as receiving.

Jonas parted long enough to push her coat over her shoulders and lift her shirt over her head. By the time both hit the kitchen floor, he had her bra unsnapped and discarded nearly as quickly. "I need you right now. This very second." He gritted out the words and went to work on her pants.

She gasped, ran her hands over his chest, and started pulling at his shirt with a near frantic quality.

Jonas paused a second to let her step out of the shackle of garments at her feet and strip down as well.

He ran his hands over her bare flesh, reacquainting himself with the softness of her skin, the hard muscles underneath, and the divine curves that set his blood on fire. As he brushed his thumbs over her already taut nipples, Lacey wrapped her hand around his hard cock and began to caress. Soft. Gentle. Reverent. She moved her hand over his entire length, leaving small bursts of pleasure sparkling in her wake.

A hard shiver pulled him to reality enough to take a pace back and catch his breath. Much more of her hand job and he'd be well on the way to stretching her out on the kitchen table and taking her hard and fast.

"What do you want?" He read her face, watched as she reached for him and whimpered when he stayed her hand. Her smoky eyes and parted lips told him she was just as desperate as he. "I can't last much longer if you keep touching me like that. I need to know what you want. Do you want me to get you off with my tongue or with my cock?" He hoped the words permeated her distracted brain enough to click. Before he went up in flames and made the decision without her input.

"I want you." Her gaze locked with his.

"How?"

She opened her mouth but no sound came out.

He growled, picked her up, and pressed her back down on the table. "Stay there and open those pretty legs, Lacey. I'm a thirsty man."

The moment she did, he dove in, bending over to press his mouth to the juicy pink folds revealed when she lifted her legs and wrapped them around his head. The awkward position didn't matter right now—although he knew he couldn't stay the course for too long without a backache interfering with his pleasure.

He gave her everything he had. Licking, sucking, running his tongue up, around and over. He thrust it inside her slit and found even more moisture waiting for him.

She cried out and bucked when he focused his attention on her clit. Her grip on him tightened as she began to writhe on the table.

His dick started throbbing with need. He ignored it for a bit longer, his only goal to bring Lacey to the very brink.

"Jonas…" She partially sat up and stared at him.

He held her gaze as he laved her clit with wild abandon.

Lacey's eyes hooded, her mouth fell open, and she began panting as if she'd run a full-out sprint.

Knowing she was getting close, he brushed his tongue over the nub twice more, felt the tension in her legs, then reluctantly eased back.

She whimpered and tried to hold him with her legs.

He raised them from his shoulders and lowered them back down. "Condom." Hurrying over, he found his jeans, pulled his wallet out and collected a condom. He opened the wrapper and immediately rolled it on.

Turning back, he paused at the erotic sight before him.

Lacey stretched out across the table. Her feet rested on the edge, giving him a glorious view of her assets. Her chest expanded in quick fashion, making her breasts jiggle slightly, drawing attention to their rosy peaks. Her narrowed eyes, the sultry look she aimed at him, all told him one thing—she wanted him more than her next breath.

He closed the distance quickly, placed the tip of his cock against her folds, and gazed down at Lacey. "Wrap your legs around me."

She did so, then pulled.

He sank into her depths, not stopping until he could go no farther. "So fucking hot and tight. I'll never get enough of you." He started moving, setting up a quick rhythm, knowing he'd never have enough control to take her with slow, gentle penetrations. Too revved, he could only thrust with power, speed and a primal drive that lashed him to greater heights and demands.

Lacey grunted then gasped as he set up such a frantic pace.

"Hurt?" Concerned, he slowed considerably.

"No. Jonas. Oh my God. Please. Harder. More." She rolled her head back and forth on the table and dug her heels into his lower back.

Reassured, he let loose the reins and went wild. The sounds of their bodies slapping together filled the kitchen along with heavy breathing and an occasional cry. He pounded into her, never getting deep enough or powerful enough to send them both flying over the edge. He tried harder, giving her everything he had and then some.

Tautness began to overtake her body. He saw and felt the difference just as easily as he became aware of the tightening of his ball and the tingling in his spine.

Jonas surged for home. "Come on, Lacey. Let go already." He reached down, tunneled high in her folds, found her clit and brazenly caressed the area.

A high-pitched mewl emerged from her throat.

Relentlessly, he strummed the area, knowing he stood on the pinnacle and was fighting a losing battle to hold that position.

The orgasm blasted through him, sending huge waves of rapture crashing through his body. He shouted, slammed deep and rode the crests to their fullest.

Just as he started down, Lacey's body clamped his cock so tight he saw stars once more. With a little yelp, she bucked against him. The clenching of her body drove him back up to the heavens, extending his climax to a level he'd never reached before.

By the time the tremors subsided, Jonas' ability to even stand up came into question. His legs shook with the strain of his position. Lacey's legs fell to his sides and hung off the table, providing a new angle to their joining. Too bad he didn't have the energy to explore its potential right now. *Later. Much later.*

He scanned Lacey, finding her still recovering with deep breaths and flashing eyes that told of contentment and the white-hot pleasure they had just shared. This round had been hard. Rough, even. He hadn't been able to help himself, though she'd seemed to revel in it. Still, he needed to make sure he hadn't hurt her in the course of such wild lovemaking. "You okay?"

She smiled softly and rested her hands on her stomach. "You are amazing. Incredible. A sex god."

He chuckled, wrapped his arms around her, and assisted her into a sitting position. "Maybe you're biased?" Happy that she'd loved their adventure as much as he had, he peppered kisses across her face.

"I never knew sex could be like this," she whispered against his ear. "But only with you."

He pulled her against his chest and rubbed her back. "Love makes it better."

"Good thing I love you, then. Much better and I might not survive."

The teasing in her tone put a smile on his face.

Just get through tomorrow. Find out the results. Then I'll take the next big step. He hoped that everything would be fine. After just finding Lacey, he wasn't ready to let her go. But he would have to if his greatest fears came to light.

He held her snug and sent up a small prayer.

Chapter Twenty-Nine

"Hello, Jonas. Good to see you again."

An older man, a little over Lacey's height, with dark hair graying at the temples, closed the door behind him then shook Jonas' hand. His white lab coat had his name stitched in red over the right pocket. Under that, he wore a dark brown, long-sleeved dressy shirt and black slacks—Dr. Graham's typical choice of wardrobe every time Jonas saw him.

"Dr. Graham." Jonas gestured toward her. "This is Lacey, my girlfriend."

Dr. Graham lit up, a wide smile creasing his face. "Well, well." He quickly appraised her before turning back to Jonas. "You did a good job."

Lacey smiled at the friendly doctor's compliment. "Thank you."

He shot her a grin and sat down on the small stool with wheels in front of a computer. "Now, Jonas." His attention focused back on his patient. "The standard questions. Have you noticed anything different? New lumps? Swelling? Soreness? Anything out of the ordinary?"

"No." Relieved he could answer in that way, Jonas rested his hand on his knee and waited.

"Good. Good." Dr. Graham pulled up to the computer and clicked the mouse a few times. "Still riding horses?"

"Every day." Jonas'd had the discussion with Dr. Graham ages ago about his profession. Some people in the field believed there was a link with bicycle riding or horseback riding and testicular cancer. From what the oncologist said, the studies didn't support that.

"I haven't seen anything new on that front in research. So, keep doing what you're doing." Dr. Graham clicked a few more times.

Jonas glimpsed Lacey sitting straight in her seat, silently watching and listening to the proceedings. He reached over, took her hand in his and squeezed.

She returned the favor.

"Your CAT scan is clear."

Jonas blew out the breath he'd been holding. "Thank goodness."

Dr. Graham swiveled on the rolling chair to face him. "The longer we can go with clear results, the closer to being cured."

"Five years." Jonas had that date marked on his computer calendar. He couldn't wait.

"Exactly." He stared at the screen for a few seconds. "All your labs are excellent. Your blood pressure. Everything is great." He spun back around, looked at Lacey, then back to Jonas. "Have you reconsidered having the implant done?"

Jonas shook his head. "I really don't want to take on those risks."

"You don't need it, Jonas. Not in my opinion." Lacey smiled at him reassuringly. "You're perfect in every way."

The rest of his worries dissipated into thin air.

He nearly welled up at her words. Instead, he drew in a deep breath, cupped her cheek and kissed her with all the love he felt in his heart. A chaste lingering kiss, but filled with his very soul.

Dr. Graham cleared his throat.

Jonas focused on him with a small grin. "Sorry."

"Oh, don't apologize." Dr. Graham waved his hand. "I wish all my other patients had a woman such as her at their side. Half the battle is in the attitude of the patient." He winked at Lacey. "I think this one will keep you on your toes and healthy as a horse for decades to come."

"I'll do my best," Lacey promised.

If possible, Jonas fell in love with her even more.

"Now, if you'll excuse me, we have the exam next."

Lacey's eyes widened. "Oh. That would be my cue to leave."

Jonas hesitated then offered to let her stay. "You don't have to. After all, you've seen it all before."

Lacey stood up and paused at the door. "True. But I'd rather give you some privacy for this part."

Dr. Graham gave a brief nod.

"I'll just go to the waiting room and hang out there." She slipped out of the door, shutting it softly behind her.

"Where did you find her?" Dr. Graham asked.

Jonas moved to sit on the exam table. "She found me."

"Some men have all the luck."

"Yeah." Jonas watched the doctor pull his stethoscope out of his pocket, his thoughts on how true Dr. Graham's statement was. A while back he'd considered his life possibly over. A broken leg. Cancer. A job riding a desk that he dreaded. The darkest day had soon turned to light, allowing him to see many things. Positive changes, but they lacked something. Something important.

Then Lacey had come along, taught him what love was about, and given him a reason to get up every morning.

He couldn't imagine life without her, for she held his heart in her keeping.

He did have all the luck. *Good luck, that is.*

* * * *

"What did he say after I left?" Lacey asked as they made their way back to Jonas' truck.

"That I'm one hell of a lucky man." Jonas grinned. "And that I'm good for the next three months. All clear."

"Thank goodness." She paused a beat before speaking again. "Does that mean we can celebrate?"

"Sure. What did you have in mind?"

"One of your special grilled cheese sandwiches."

"That's it? Nothing else?"

"Well..." She lowered her gaze to the ground. "Maybe we could do a private celebration afterward."

"Hmmm."

She raised her chin and glanced at him. "You know. A bit of mattress dancing?"

He couldn't contain the grin or the flare of amusement that accompanied a hot flash of arousal. "Mattress dancing?"

"Yep. Heard that in a song." She grinned wickedly at him. "So what do you say?"

"Count me in."

He unlocked their doors, settled into the driver's seat, clicked his seat belt, and closed the door. A second later he had the key in the ignition and the engine started. "You don't want to eat out?" His homemade sandwich paled considerably in comparison to some of the local restaurants.

"I'm easy. Whatever you want. But I do love your grilled cheese."

He ran some options through his head. "We can pick up something to take home."

"That works."

"How does pasta sound?

"Okay. Anything is fine. Really."

His phone rang, interrupting the conversation. He pulled it off his belt, checked the caller ID, and answered without stopping to talk on the phone. "Hello?"

"Hey, bro. I wanted to let you know that the merger went through without a hitch. We're now in the wind turbine business."

Relieved, Jonas smiled. "That's great news. With the spiraling oil prices, it's nice to know that something is on upward trend."

Jason hesitated. "Is there something else going on?" Concern filled his voice.

Jonas cussed himself, belatedly realizing how his wording came across. "Actually, we're leaving the doctor's office. I'm still clear. Lacey and I are going to celebrate."

Jason whooped. "Wonderful. Another visit under your

belt. Way to go." He paused a second. "You took Lacey with you?"

"Yep."

"Wow, bro. That's a serious step."

A few people had offered to go with Jonas to his quarterly visit and scans over the past year or so. He'd declined each and every one, needing to face his fears alone. If bad news came, he didn't want to break down in front of his family. Instead he would pull himself together, make a plan, and tell them down the road. He'd never had to do that yet and hoped the trend would continue.

Lacey was different, though. She provided comfort and hope. Just her presence alone had made his visit easier and more relaxed. If someone had asked him at his first visit if he'd bring along a girlfriend and offer to let her stay through his exam, he would have sent them straight to the funny farm. Today he couldn't imagine Lacey not being with him as he learned his latest results.

"Yeah, but it's the right one." Jonas peered over at Lacey, found her hand with his, and squeezed.

She looked at him with a quizzical grin.

"I'm going to be your best man at the wedding, right?"

"We'll see. Let me get back to you on that later."

"Okay. I'll try not to bother you tonight." Jason snickered.

"I'd appreciate it. Bye." Jonas disconnected the call.

"Everything okay?"

He stopped at a red light and twisted toward Lacey. "Just fine." The urge to kiss her battled with the reality of being unable to reach her as she sat on the other side of the truck. With their seat belts on, his mobility was too constricted to allow for such.

As soon as we get back home I'll make it up to her. And then some.

"The merger went through on the wind farm issue. The family is now vested in not only oil, but wind."

"That's what you wanted, right? To diversify?"

"Yep. Oil is volatile and will eventually be replaced with

renewable power. Better to get in on the early stages than be late to the party."

"I always knew you were a smart businessman."

"I do okay." He called in their order, swung by the restaurant on the way, and carried the food into his kitchen several minutes later, still piping hot.

"Smells delicious." Lacey started unloading the food.

Jonas produced plates and utensils before filling glasses with ice. He pulled a bottle of soda from the fridge and placed it on the table. After sitting down, he filled their glasses then started loading up his plate.

Lacey dug in, eating hungrily.

He watched the way she pulled the macaroni off her fork with her soft lips and had flashbacks of the way she'd sucked his dick. Greedily. Enthusiastically. So damn hot she'd nearly made him shoot his load way too early.

She peered over at him a second before her eyebrows furrowed in obvious puzzlement. "What?"

Oh, just thinking of you eating something else is all. His cock hardened to granite firmness and began to throb. He scooted in his seat in an effort to ease the pressure. All to no avail. "Just glad that you seem to like the food."

"I do. Thank you for buying it."

"Welcome."

She eyed him for a second before giving a small shrug as if discounting him as plain old odd.

Somewhere along the line I've turned into a randy stud during breeding season. He mentally shook his head, focused on his meal, and ignored his body's demands. For now.

"If you turn that black stallion into a roping horse, won't Jason need one as well?" She took a long drink of her beverage.

"Already ahead of you. I've kept my eye open around the farm. If nothing pans out, we'll look into buying one. No hurry, though. We have to make that commitment and get back up to speed. I, for one, have lots of rust to shake off and won't know if the bug has bitten me again until I get back in the saddle and rope something." He finished his meal, took a sip of his drink, and wiped his hands on a napkin.

"Sounds like you have a plan." She put her fork down and closed the box, obviously finished eating.

"I always have one of those." He tossed the away the trash and washed his hands.

Lacey followed suit.

The fresh scent of vanilla teased his senses, adding to his sensual hunger. He sniffed her hair and closed his eyes at the delicious aroma.

Lacey elbowed him and shot him a curious look. "What are you doing?"

"I can't get enough of you. From the smell of your shampoo, to your beautiful body, to your fiery spirit and sense of humor."

She peered up at him coyly. "Glad to know. However, right now, I have a craving for some dessert."

He arched an eyebrow. "Such as?"

Biting her lip, she slipped her hands down to his pants, undid the button and pushed the zipper down. "Oh, I don't know. Something big and tangy to lick on."

Jonas chuckled. "I just happen to have that very thing."

Her eyes flashed with abundant desire. "I was hoping you'd say that." She boldly cupped the bulge in his pants.

Arousal leaped tenfold, setting Jonas into a simmering burn. "Two can play at this game."

She tilted her head as he ran his hand between her legs and nudged her folds through her jeans.

The sound of her hitched breathing added more fuel to the fire burning in his blood. "Let's take this to the bedroom." He grabbed her hand and led her down the hall. Pausing next to the bed, he stripped down quickly then helped her do the same.

The instant she stood nude before him, he roamed her body, reacquainting himself with her curves, her tidbits, and hit every hot spot he could find in order to bring her need up to match his own. He sucked the peaks of her breasts into pebble hardness and dipped his fingers into her slit, finding her already wet and eager for his touch.

Lacey stroked his cock for a few beats before moving lower, to lightly caress his one remaining testicle. "You're gorgeous. Perfect. Just seeing you like this makes me wanton."

Her whispered words shoved past his tightly held control. "Damn, baby. You're driving me crazy." He scooped her up and placed her on the mattress. Task complete, he climbed in next to her and stretched out on his back. "Come here."

She eyed him quizzically for a second.

"Climb on top. I want to lick your sweetness while you give me head at the same time."

Understanding lit up her face. She flipped around, shimmied over to his side, then lifted to straddle his chest.

Jonas guided her movements with a strong grip on her hips. "Move back a bit. A little more. There you go." He lifted his head, pushed a pillow underneath, and licked along her slit.

Lacey hissed and jerked. He felt the shiver go through her body and knew he'd found the perfect way to bring out her wild side.

He didn't have long to savor her response as she wrapped her hand around his cock and commenced laving as if he were a favorite dessert treat threatening to melt if she didn't eat with gusto. Burning pleasure shot through his veins. His dick swelled even more and began to ache with need.

"Damn, vixen. You've got one hot tongue." He moaned at her next pass then again when she took him deep in her mouth.

Pulling his attention back to the task at hand, he pressed his tongue against her slit and into her juicy center. He lapped up the treat then tugged her backward just enough to be able to easily work her clit. He teased and lipped until bright stars danced before his eyes.

Lacey groaned and slurped. The combination sent him rocketing to the top and right on over.

"Oh, fuck." Jonas bucked upward, unable to stop himself from demanding more of her talented mouth. He wrapped his arms around her lower back and cried out as he hit the rafters with pulse after pulse of brilliant rapture. She drank down each spurt and tickled her tongue over his tip as if begging for more.

All too soon, he returned to earth, finding Lacey still spread out before him like a feast on a table.

He drew in great gulps of air and grinned. "My turn, baby. Turn around and sit on my face."

Lacey slid off only to sit on the bed beside him, her eyes wide as saucers.

Jonas arched an eyebrow in challenge. "Come on, sweetheart. You'll love it. Trust me."

"How will you breathe?"

Her nearly breathless question amused him. "I'll manage. Now come on. I need another taste of that cream."

She hesitated only a second more before assuming the position, straddling his head.

Jonas held her steady, found the correct angle, then explored with his tongue until he discovered her clit. He worried the small nub relentlessly.

Lacey writhed and made all sorts of sexy little sounds that only encouraged him to push her that much harder.

After slipping two fingers into her slit, he focused his attention on her clit, strumming, sucking and tapping it. Over and over he worked the area while using his tight grip to hold a squirming Lacey still.

"Oh. Yes. Yes." Lacey tried to bounce then lowered enough to press her folds hard against him.

A frantic jerk followed by a sudden increase in moisture told the story. She was close. So very close. He drank up the treat, making sure to thrash his tongue over her nub in the process.

Lacey's body tightened and stilled. Her breathing escalated. Finally, with a loud cry, she shuddered against him, followed by a series of spasms that clamped down solidly on his buried fingers.

Jonas stayed the course, only removing his touch when she flinched. He assisted her to sit back on the mattress, then lifted enough to wrap her in his arms, embracing her with all the passion he felt. "I love you, Lacey."

"I love you, too," she whispered back, resting her chin on his shoulder.

For the longest time, he soothed her, finding comfort in her response as well as the unconditional love she presented each and every day.

He hadn't been sure any woman could have accepted him after his surgery. Now he knew that he'd worried for nothing. Lacey didn't care if he had a single ball or one arm or even no legs. He knew that for a certainty. She saw him as a man. A whole one. From the inside out.

Nothing could mean more to him.

Chapter Thirty

Jonas attached his pen to the stapled pile of printouts and stretched. He, Jason and their parents had been working all morning on the ins and outs of their new venture along with checking on the futures in oil. Combined with going over their quarterly budget with a fine-toothed comb, the endless numbers and information had turned Jonas' mind to putty a while back.

"Damn. If I see another spreadsheet this week I'll get my gun and use it for target practice," Jonas' father, Garrett, grumbled as he collected his own allotment of papers.

"We knocked out a lot of office work today. That's saying something." Lola, his mother, pointed out the positive in the nearly five-hour-long marathon session.

Jason stood up, twisted, and cracked his back. "Much better. Those kitchen chairs leave a lot to be desired." He eyed his mother.

She rolled her eyes. "They do just fine for what they're meant for. Eating. Most meals don't last all morning, you know." After standing, she started picking up coffee mugs and depositing them in the sink.

"I still think we're on the right track. While the investment cost is pretty substantial, over time the turbines should pay for themselves and then some." Jonas nodded as he pushed back and straightened out his legs.

"We shouldn't ignore solar power," Jason cautioned.

Garrett rubbed at his face. "Keep that on the back burner, son. Right now, we've got more than enough on our plates with this merger. Let's see how this goes first. Research it if you want. Find out the start-up costs too. But right now we're spread thin enough. Taking on more just isn't an option."

Jason nodded. "True. I'll keep my ears to the ground. If we take one more project, I think we'll have to open another office and hire someone to manage the solar sector."

"You need a girlfriend, bro. Too much time on your hands to think about work. Makes you old and boring." Jonas regained his feet and smacked Jason on the back.

"Uh-huh." Jason cut him a slightly annoyed look. "This coming from the guy who recently jumped back into the dating game."

"Yep." Jonas grinned. "Speaking of, I probably should get to the farm and do some work. With all those extra horses that recently arrived, we're busting butt to keep up and lagging behind in the process. Lacey is doing her best, but she can't sit in a saddle twenty-four-seven."

Garrett glanced at his watch, then stood up. "It's lunchtime anyway. We might as well go out to lunch before going our separate ways."

Lola stepped next to Garrett. "We can go to the corner diner. And…the Humane Society farm is on the way." She grinned at Jonas.

He blinked at her. His tired brain took a couple of seconds for her unsaid suggestion to register. "Meaning we can pick up Lacey and take her with us?"

"Yep. About time we met that girl, don't you think?" Lola asked.

"You'll love her. Sweet and pretty. Smart, too. She can run circles around Jonas. He has to get his lasso out now and again in order to catch her." Jason chuckled.

Jonas rolled his eyes then sobered. "Speaking of roping… have you been practicing? If we're going to hit a couple of rodeos in the spring, you need to be shaking some of the rust off soon."

"Yeah, yeah." Jason grinned wickedly. "I bet I've been practicing more than you have. After all, I hear your nights are occupied."

And here we go. Jonas faced the three other people in the room and sighed. Judging by the expressions on their faces, they weren't about to let the topic drop. "Yes, Lacey is the one. Like that's a big secret anymore. We love one another and I intend to spend my life with her. No, we haven't talked about anything more than that, but I'll keep you updated when we do."

"Then it's past time we meet this girl," Garrett replied. "Seeing as she will be part of the family."

"Soon," Jason added.

Jonas opened his mouth but no words emerged. After all, he really couldn't argue with the truth. Now that he and Lacey were a solid couple, there wasn't a reason to delay discussing the next step. He just needed the right time and the perfect words. Oh, and a ring. That might help as well. Mentally, he added the task to his list. "She believes in me and doesn't give a fig about my surgery except that I stay on track to be declared cured." He quietly offered up the truth.

Jason squeezed his shoulder. "That's all that matters. You love her and she loves you just as much. A rare find these days."

Lola and Garrett shared a look.

"Rare and pretty damn special. Get a ring on that girl and fast. Before someone else snatches her up." Garrett wrapped his arm around Lola's waist.

"Don't worry, Dad. She's not the kind to stray. Besides, I have no intention of stepping out of line and giving her any cause to worry. If she's happy, then I'm happy."

"Then let's get rolling. I'm hungry and Lacey is waiting." Jason turned toward the door and led the way out.

Jonas brought up the rear, a grin firmly on his face. Lacey might not know what hit her today, but he knew she'd soak up the attention. After the fiasco of her own dysfunctional family meltdown, he knew that his family would prove steady and supportive, eagerly accepting her into the fold.

She might have started out with few friends and a

crumbling home life. Now, he vowed to provide her with everything he could and share his life and love along the way. They'd be there for her, he knew that fact without a single doubt. For in their eyes, she was already theirs.

I better get my butt in gear, then.

He picked up his packet, walked out the door, and shut it behind him.

Twenty minutes later, he pointed toward Lacey in the far pasture, riding a pretty bay mare. "There she is."

"Rides like a champion. I had no doubt." Lola lifted her hand to shield her eyes from the bright sunlight.

"You should see her barrel race. It's breathtaking." Jonas raised his hand and waved, catching Lacey's attention.

"Yeah, he's got it bad." Jason snickered, then moved to open a nearby gate when Lacey drew close.

She scanned them all with her gaze before focusing on Jonas. "You brought guests, I see."

"Lacey. These are my parents, Garrett and Lola. Jason you already know."

She reached down to shake their hands, holding the little mare steady at the same time. "Nice to meet you."

"Same here," Lola said.

"We just finished our business meeting. Heading out for lunch. Thought to bring you along." Garrett stared at her with a small smile.

Lacey's eyes widened. "You want to take me to lunch?"

"Yep," Jonas answered.

"I'd go if I were you. We're all set to tell good old blackmail stories about Jonas." Jason waggled his eyebrows.

Lacey giggled. "Since you put it that way…" She nudged the mare to sidestep around them. "Just give me a few minutes to take care of Constance and I'll be right with you. That is, if you don't mind me smelling like horse, leather and a bit of sweat."

"That's the cologne of nature, don't you know?" Jason shut the gate back and secured it.

"Okay then. Thank you." She stopped next to Jonas, bent

down in the saddle and brushed a kiss over his cheek. "Thank you for thinking to invite me."

He smiled. "Don't worry, you're not the forgettable kind."

She laughed and trotted off.

Jonas watched her go, his heart in his throat.

"You picked a good one, son." Garrett drew closer and stared as horse and rider went directly to the barn before disappearing from sight.

"I think so."

* * * *

"Your parents seem really nice. Funny, too," Lacey said as she approached the round pen.

"They adore you already." He offered up the truth, having heard enough compliments from not only his parents, but Jason as well. Not just today, either. Jason had been singing her praises for a while and his parents were sure to follow suit.

"I can see where you guys get your business sense and your looks. The acorn doesn't fall far from the tree."

"Don't tell me you were checking out my father."

She crossed her arms over her chest and snorted. "Jonas Marshall, you know me better than that. I wasn't 'checking out' your father. I just happened to notice that you resemble him. As does Jason."

He grinned. "There's no denying the paternity there." He saw her flinch and cringed. "I'm sorry, Lacey."

She waved her hand. "Nothing to be sorry for. It is what it is."

He hated that he'd inadvertently said something that reminded her of her own situation and the basis for a lifetime of poor treatment from her own father. Wracking his brain, he tried to come up with another topic that might put the smile back on her face.

Before he could come up with something, she started speaking. "I've been reading up on wind power, but I'm sure there's tons more stored in your head that would be easier to learn from than clicking links to Internet sites. Would you please teach me about it?"

Intrigued by the out of the blue comment, Jonas turned to face Lacey, earning a sharp nudge from Granite, the black stallion she'd gifted to him, who wanted another baby carrot. "You want to learn about the turbines?"

"Yep. All about it. And oil too. Both sound interesting. But changing the way the world uses power with wind is a huge thing. It's a neat concept and one that has great potential." She leaned against the railing of the paddock, her heavy jacket unzipped enough in the front for him to glimpse a sweatshirt underneath. Two lead ropes rested over her shoulder.

A stiff breeze sent a shiver through him. The chilly air reminded him that spring was still a few months away.

He heard sincerity and curiosity in her voice. In his past experiences, women didn't want to hear about his job. They enjoyed the profits made from it, but that was where it stopped. Lacey, on the other hand, truly wanted to educate herself about a part of his life.

The realization put a grin on his face. "I'm an open book."

"Thank you. I'll be sure to read closely and often." Her tone held a healthy dose of teasing mixed with sincerity — a combination all Lacey and one that he'd grown to crave.

He fed Granite the last carrot then held his hands up. "All gone."

Granite snorted and stared at him as if trying to determine if he was telling the truth or not.

Chuckling, Jonas rubbed the horse's forehead.

"When can you start working with him officially?"

"Another couple of weeks probably. The vets want to go real slow with him due to his concussion. The less stress the better for now. Another reason he's not been gelded. That particular surgery might be a long time coming."

"Not a problem for you. I have a feeling that as long as you have carrots, that stallion would follow you anywhere."

Jonas patted Granite once more then headed to the gate. He stepped through as Lacey met him. "He's a good horse. Not sure how much he knows, but he's been around people quite a bit. An attention hog, definitely."

"Sounds like the perfect roping horse for you." Lacey fell into step as they walked toward yet another pasture.

"I think so. Thanks to you." He caught her hand and brought it up to his lips.

Lacey grinned. "You gave me Knight and my future. It's the least I could do." She glanced up. "Speaking of, I need to groom him and Mabel before calling it a day."

"I'll help." He held out his hand and waited.

Lacey handed over one of the ropes. "You don't have to. I know you've had a more than your fair share working with some of the trailer wreck horses. Nila said there's a lot of interest in those and pressure to have them ready to go real soon."

He shrugged. "Yeah, but that's a good thing. Out of a tragedy some good things are happening. If people are too impatient, Nila is allowing them to line up their own trainers. So we're not holding any of them back."

"That helps."

Lacey had been working with the other horses, trying to keep them progressing in the program, giving Jonas ample opportunity to check out the trailer wreck cases. Some were in great shape, had prior riding experience and just needed a refresher course. Others were still recuperating and probably would never be able to carry a rider. Those would be adopted out as pasture pets only.

Her prior comments replayed through his mind. "You really want to learn about wind power?"

"Absolutely. It's intriguing enough by itself. But knowing that it's a huge part of your life makes me want to know all about it, too." She flashed him a grin, entered the area where Knight and Mabel dozed in the afternoon sun, then attached the rope to Knight's halter.

She's definitely a keeper.

Jonas did the same with Mabel, turned, and led the mule out of the paddock and into the nearby grooming shed, where they could be cleaned up away from the brisk wind.

He tied Mabel's lead to one of the rails and gathered two buckets of grooming tools, one for him and one for Lacey. By the time he set one down, she'd entered with Knight and secured him next to Mabel.

He got right to work, his mind never far from the woman who had entered his life not too long ago and turned it upside down. She'd shown him guts, resiliency and an unbreakable spirit filled with love and kindness. He'd never known anyone like her.

Jonas watched as Lacey ran the soft brush over Knight's already gleaming hide. Between his contrasting black and white spots, his intelligent deep blue eyes and his powerful build, the horse stood out. Yet as striking as Knight was, he didn't hold a candle to Lacey, at least not in Jonas' opinion.

Absently, Jonas brushed Mabel, his attention on the woman a few feet away, separated by both equines.

"He's as ready as I can get him, but it's still going to be a fight." Lacey sighed and pushed a stray strand of brunette hair behind her ear. "If only he was as laid-back as Candy. I didn't know how good I had it."

"With you on his back, he'll pull through." Jonas had watched her struggle with the gelding time and again. She always managed to get him back in line and focused on his job, despite the dozens of distractions presented to him thus far. That didn't mean Knight was calm, cool and collected. Just the opposite. Wired to the hilt described him much more accurately. Somehow, Lacey got through to him. So far. Only time would tell with the big rodeos. Namely the first one in a couple of days.

"I hope so. I'm banking on him." She bent over, nearly disappearing from sight as she cleaned Knight's hooves. "Oh, did you hear? Crackers has an adoption application. Nila told me this morning."

"That's great." Jonas grinned at the knowledge that at

least one more of their horses had potentially found a home. "She's going with that mare and colt. That should make quite the pretty pasture."

He'd heard about the interest in the pretty little colt who'd become quite spoiled since arriving at the farm. A few people had inquired about him, but Nila had proved relentless in finding him the right home. Hopefully, this one would be it. For all their sakes. After that semi wreck, those poor animals needed every good break they could get. "Were you thinking about him?" He knew she spent time every day playing with the youngster.

Lacey stood back up again and met Jonas' gaze over Knight's back. "Oh, I'd love to have them all. But that takes land, money and time that I don't have."

He heard the mild regret in her voice. "You'll have your own tyrant baby soon."

A small smile returned to her face. "There's that. I have a feeling Candy and Legacy's foal is going to be a handful. We won't be lucky enough for him to inherit Candy's laid-back personality. He'll wind up just like his hot-headed daddy."

Jonas nodded. "The same hot-headed daddy that took the finals by storm."

"Yep."

He took a minute to check Mabel's hooves, then placed his brush back into the bucket along with the rest of the grooming tools. He watched Lacey for a couple more minutes before vocalizing the question on the tip of his tongue. "Will you regret not taking a job at the thoroughbred farm and living near Trinity and Cody?"

Lacey blinked at him. "No."

The one-word answer didn't quell Jonas' concerns. "Are you sure? Kentucky is miles away from your troublesome family. You can start over there."

A frown played on Lacey's lips. She exchanged brush for comb and started working on Knight's tail. "Here's the way I see it. Oklahoma is my home. Yes, I have issues with my family that will never go away. My best friend is two states away. Neither are ideal. But I have some really great things here, too." She fanned out Knight's tail and ran the comb through the coarse hairs. "I have a job that I love. Both the training one and working for Dr. Moore. No, I'm not getting rich from either. However, I'm making a difference in the world. That's meaningful to me."

He read the sincerity on her face. The constriction in his gut eased a smidgen more. "Okay."

"I have Nila, who is like a surrogate mother to me. I couldn't ask for a better roommate or boss." Lacey dropped Knight's tail and stuck the comb in her back pocket. "But all those are minor reasons."

"Oh?"

She pinned Jonas' gaze. "Why would I want to move when the man I love is here?"

Hope flared brightly. Still, he had to make positively certain. "Are you sure?"

She approached him with a playful grin. "Sure that I love you? Definitely. Sure that I want to stay in Oklahoma with you? Yes. Sure that you're my future? Absolutely."

Relief rushed over Jonas. He smiled, met her halfway, and swept her up in his arms. She squealed as he twirled her around.

Chuckling, he set her down, stared into her face, and just knew the moment was right. He kneeled down on one knee, took her hand in his and peered up at her. "Lacey. I love you now and always. Will you be my wife?"

Her mouth fell open and her eyes widened. A split second later, she squeaked out, "Yes."

He stood up just in time to catch her as she threw herself into his arms.

The equines snorted and sidestepped, not as thrilled with the commotion as he and Lacey were.

Jonas carried Lacey well out of the precarious reach of hooves and placed her back on her feet near railing that separated the areas in the barn. He sought her lips, found her lifting toward him, and met her with all the enthusiasm and passion bursting inside him to get out. "I don't have a ring yet. Hadn't had time to look. Maybe we can do that together. Get the perfect one."

Lacey smiled and cupped his cheek. "You don't need a ring, Jonas. I'd marry you if you only had a piece of twine to wrap around my finger."

His heart warmed. "I think I can do better than twine, sweetheart." Leaning in, he kissed her once again, pouring his love into every second. "You're mine and I'm going to do my damnedest to keep you happy for the rest of your life."

She laughed. "Make that ditto for me."

Jonas meshed their lips, sealing the deal in a promise for decades to come.

Chapter Thirty-One

"Don't tell me that's your new barrel horse." Trinity blinked at Lacey, mischief flashing in her blue eyes.

Lacey recognized the voice, then swung around, saw her best friend, and chuckled. "What? You didn't know that mules are the latest trend in barrel racing?"

"Well, umm, no." Trinity laughed and peered into the next stall at Knight. "Don't tell me. She's his babysitter?"

"Yep. Think Seabiscuit."

"Well, it's always good to have a friend around."

"Isn't that the truth?" Lacey hugged Trinity, thrilled to see her again. "I'm so glad you're here. How's life? How's Cody? And Legacy?" Even though Lacey strove to call Trinity fairly regularly, she'd fallen behind lately with her efforts to get Knight ready for the next race. Not to mention Jonas distracted her more times than not.

"Everyone and everything is good. Legacy is enjoying his retirement with the ladies."

"You and Cody?" Lacey didn't really need to hear the answer, she saw it on Trinity's face.

"Wonderful. He's a dream come true." Trinity smiled warmly before suddenly grabbing Lacey's hand. "What's this? Did you forget to tell me something?"

Lacey laughed. "It just happened a couple of days ago. But yes, Jonas and I are engaged."

"That's fabulous." Trinity hugged her again. "I'm so happy for you. He's a keeper."

"Speaking of keepers, where's Cody?" Lacey glanced around. "Didn't he come with you?"

"Yeah. He stopped by to talk to the vet manning this

event. They worked together last year too."

"Ah. I guess he'll be along shortly. I can't imagine he leaves you by yourself too much these days." Lacey was thrilled for Trinity. After everything Trinity had been through she deserved happiness. Besides, she was one hell of a person and friend to boot.

Trinity reached out her hand and rubbed Knight's forehead. "He's a beauty just like you said. Big. Strong. His coloring is so eye-catching."

Lacey heard the admiration in Trinity's voice. "He's got the full package all right."

"Too bad you had to geld him. I imagine people will be watching him run and thinking of lining up a few babies out of him." Trinity patted the horse once more before turning back to Lacey.

"I know. But rules are rules. There's plenty of unwanted horses right now. To breed him would be like a slap in the face of everything the farm is trying to do." As much as Lacey would have loved a foal or three out of Knight, it just wasn't to be.

"How's things on your end? The family drama any better?" Trinity leaned back against the stall.

Lacey kicked her toe at the dirt floor. "I cut ties with my father completely. Told him what I thought. No sense in trying to please a man who would never be able to see me as anything other than another man's mistake." She glanced down at her hands before lifting her chin once again. "The others understand. I still talk with them."

"That's something." Trinity's lips thinned into a straight line. "I'm so sorry. I never knew the difficulties you faced at home. If so —"

Lacey waved her hand. "There's nothing anyone could do. It was up to me to decide to change my ways."

"Still…"

"You were there and still are. That's above and beyond in my book." Lacey smiled.

"I'll always be. Us girls have to stick together."

"That sounds ominous," a male voice answered.

Lacey peered down the aisle, finding Cody walking their way. She grinned mischievously at him. "Never took you for the type to get antsy when women got together."

He pulled up next to Trinity and kissed her temple. "Every man gets a mite bit nervous when women talk of teaming up. We're usually on the receiving end."

"Is that so bad?" Lacey asked.

Cody glanced down at Trinity with such love Lacey's heart skipped a beat. "Not at all."

"Smart answer." Trinity smiled up at him as she linked her hand with his.

"Barrel racers get ready. You ladies are up next." The announcement carried through the barn.

Lacey didn't hesitate. She grabbed Knight's bridle, entered his stall, and slipped it onto him.

Cody handed her the leather saddle and took a minute to appraise Knight. "He's built, I'll say that. I can see why you wanted him for a barrel horse so badly."

"Yep. He's a star. With a few issues."

"As evidenced by the mule." Cody chuckled. "I know everyone's jaw is falling open when they see her standing there. Not your usual barrel horse, that's for sure."

Lacey laughed, tightened the cinch, then double-checked it before tying the knot to hold it in place. She'd seen that very expression on more than one person's face as they ambled by. "True, but it works. For him."

"Which is all that matters." Trinity opened the stall door, allowing Lacey to lead Knight into the aisle. Since she'd chosen the very end stall on the open side of the barn, Knight hadn't freaked out at being inside. Arriving a day early had allowed for plenty of practice time and a chance for Knight to get used to the new arena. All a necessity with her gelding.

"I thought Jonas would be here." Trinity turned her head this way and that.

"He is," Lacey answered. "He went to meet a couple of

friends but said he'd be back soon."

Trinity shut the stall door behind Knight as Lacey walked him out onto the grass. Out of the corner of her eye, she caught sight of a familiar person. "Speak of the devil."

Trinity and Cody paused and turned.

"Jonas Marshall. I'd recognize you anywhere." Cody smiled and held out his hand.

Jonas responded in kind. "Cody. Been a long time."

"That it has. Heard you retired your roping saddle."

Jonas glanced over at Lacey. "Well, I thought so. I've been practicing again. Still a bit rusty, but might see if Jason will join me for a few rodeos next year."

"Great news." Cody inclined his head toward Lacey. "Also heard you found a cowgirl of your own."

Jonas met Lacey's gaze and grinned. "Oh, yeah. One that will have me."

"Oh, I'll have you all right." She gestured toward Trinity. "Trinity. Jonas. Jonas. Trinity."

Jonas shook her hand and inclined his head. "I've heard a lot of good things about you. And your horse."

Trinity grinned. "I've heard all kinds of things about you, too. No horse included."

Lacey chuckled. "I've got to get going. I'll catch you all after the race." She climbed into the saddle and pointed Knight to the warm-up arena. Unfortunately, she didn't have time to dawdle when she'd be racing within a few minutes. He hesitated only a second before moving forward despite the absence of Mabel.

All the lessons had started to pay off. Hours of arena time and hard work had finally given Knight the confidence to handle the chaos of the rodeo, the noise and being apart from his girlfriend for a short period of time. The sacrifice in time had been worth every minute, as Lacey could finally see her dream back on track once again.

This would be his biggest test yet. A major rodeo, an arena filled with thousands of fans and incredibly strong competition. If he could hold it together, he stood a chance.

She trotted him around the small ring a couple of times, then moved up the pace to a canter. He moved fluidly and effortlessly, testament to his conditioning and innate power.

In the distance, she heard the announcer's booming voice, the crowd's loud applause, and sent up a small prayer. The noise levels would be higher than Knight had experienced before. She could only hope all their desensitization training would help. Well, along with the cotton. Which Jonas would supply as he met her outside the arena when she took her place in line.

A couple more circles and Lacey pulled Knight up. She directed him out of the warm-up pen and slowly toward the east entrance to the building. Several of the other racers were already there, some already struggling with their excited horses.

Jonas stood by the panel separating the girls coming in and the racer exiting. He glanced up, caught her gaze and gave a brief nod.

She trotted Knight right up to him, noting the way Knight's ears flipped forward, he stood still, and lifted his head to check out his surroundings. A slight ripple ran through his body.

"How's he feeling?"

"Peppy. Pretty good so far. No panic attacks. *Yet.*" She bit her lip and kept a firm hold on the reins. They were at the back of the line, but the closer they'd get to the ring, the more he'd react.

They'd left Mabel back in the stable area, hoping that with all the other horseflesh surrounding Knight, he'd be okay for a few minutes without his best friend.

"Good." Jonas pulled the rolls of cotton out of his jacket pocket before grasping Knight's bridle, lowering the horse's head and placing it in both of his ears.

Knight snorted and shook his head, then seemed to settle into acceptance fairly quickly.

"Good boy. Just for a few minutes. Until we've had our turn." She stroked his mane, finding a light sheen of sweat already on his neck. He was going from warm to hot pretty fast.

She eyed the line and cringed. "We need to get this over with now. He's starting to get wired."

Jonas kept a firm hold on Knight's bridle, leading him forward as the line started to advance fairly quickly. "Settle down. We're almost there." Knight began to dance in place, bumping into Jonas a couple of times in the process.

Jonas stayed the course, absorbing the jostling without difficulty. He glanced up at Lacey. "Are you sure you can handle him?" Furrowed eyebrows broadcasted worry.

Lacey nodded, then raised her voice to be heard over the announcer. "Yeah."

The girl in front of her went.

Knight half reared, wanting to follow.

Jonas pulled him down while Lacey kept a death grip on the reins. "Not yet. Wait for it."

Knight shook his head and fought the tight holds on him. He sidestepped, crashing into Jonas once more.

Jonas pulled him around in a big circle before straightening him up once again.

"Next up is Lacey Bright. She's riding Knight, her gorgeous paint gelding. A nice story here. She adopted him from the local Humane Society and trained him herself to run barrels."

Applause erupted.

Knight screamed and reared up fully this time, nearly dragging Jonas with him.

"Back off, Jonas!" Lacey ordered. She pulled on the reins and brought Knight to his feet once again.

Jonas released his grasp immediately and stepped out of the way.

Lacey clung to the saddle, glimpsed the green flag out of the corner of her eye, then set her heels to Knight's sides. "Go!"

Knight shot off like a canon. He darted to the first barrel and turned. Lacey held on as they crossed the arena, and zipped around the second barrel, then encouraged him as they made their way to the last barrel. As soon as he completed the circle, she bumped him with her heels, leaned over his neck and hollered for him to run.

He ran. Like the hounds of hell were nipping at his heels. Long strides ate up the distance until they surged across the finish line and past.

Lacey started hauling back on the reins, trying to seize control of Knight once more. He didn't slow down until she sat back in the saddle and eased him into a large circle.

By the time Knight slowed to a trot, both Jonas and Cody bracketed Knight, each taking a firm hold on the bridle.

"Damn, Lacey. I thought he'd throw you before you even got started." Cody patted Knight's nose as he looked up at her.

"Believe it or not, that's actually an improvement." She breathed in deep in order to catch her breath.

"Not everyone can ride a horse like that." Cody shook his head.

"No one else could do it," Trinity said as she came closer and whispered to Knight, who nudged Cody aside to get to her. "That was one hell of a ride. Put up a blazing time, too."

Lacey had been too busy trying to keep Knight on the straight and narrow and her butt in the saddle to pay much attention to the stopwatch. "I didn't hear."

"It's no wonder, trying to get this big guy to chill after such a harrowing round." Trinity grinned up at her. "You like to live dangerously, huh?"

Lacey smiled for the first time since getting near the arena with Knight. "You could say that. Barrel racing isn't for the faint of heart, after all." She glanced over at Jonas. "I think we might need to leave the cotton in a bit longer."

Jonas smiled and shook his head as if amazed. "Yeah. You blistered that course. A victory lap might be a bit of a challenge, though."

Lacey chuckled and patted Knight. "As long as he stays

on all four feet, it'll be fine."

"Lacey. Time for your victory lap," a man hollered to her.

She nodded, gathered up her reins, and would have eased Knight forward, except the two guys didn't appear eager to let him go. "I've got him."

Jonas lengthened his strides as Knight began to trot. "We'll escort you to the entrance."

"Yep. Get you to that point in one piece at least," Cody replied.

They took her to the door before releasing their hold.

As soon as they stepped back, Knight began to dance once more. His head went up and a twitch ran across his neck. "Okay, boy. Nice and easy." She clucked to him, asked for a lope, and encouraged him to enter the arena once again.

His eyes whitened then he took the first couple of strides before picking up the pace to a full gallop.

Lacey didn't check him until he neared the exit. Only then did she pull him in, managing to slow him down to a walk several feet outside the building. He'd lathered, but held himself together enough to get through it all.

She'd never been more proud.

Jonas removed the cotton as she slid from the saddle. Taking the reins in hand, Lacey began to walk Knight, trying to cool him down before she put him back in his stall.

A small group of people approached. She paused as she recognized them. Her mother, Tate, Lizzie and Ransom all came her way. Each wore a smile. "I can't believe you're here." Not since she was sixteen had her family shown up at a single rodeo.

"We wanted to be here for you." Her mother stopped several feet from Knight.

The others did the same.

"He's a handful, isn't he?" Tate asked.

"I couldn't believe you stayed in the saddle, Lacey. I thought when he reared up you'd be dumped to the dirt and trampled," Ransom added.

"He's got some issues, but he's worth every bit of effort."

She rested one hand on Knight's cheek, relieved that he'd calmed after leaving the arena.

"She's one of the best riders on the circuit." Trinity came forward. "We're lucky to have her."

Lacey flashed a grin toward Trinity.

"She's also responsible for taking a stallion who'd run free for a while and turning him into one hell of a barrel horse." Jonas patted Knight's shoulder. "Do you want me to finish cooling him out for you?"

Lacey hated to ask, but didn't want this precious moment to end. "Do you mind?"

"Not in the least." Jonas snagged the reins from her hand and started walking Knight once again.

"Thank you." Lacey turned to find her family staring at her with curious grins. "Yes, Jonas and I are still an item." She slowly held up her hand.

Her mother covered her mouth with one hand and used the other to grasp Lacey's. "That's wonderful. Congratulations." She pored over the ring some more. "It's beautiful."

"I'm happy for you." Ransom grinned wide.

"Me too," Tate said. "I had no doubt he'd be the one to lasso you."

"Uh-huh." Lacey snorted at her brother.

"He's certainly built right." Lizzie watched Jonas for a second before Ransom tugged her against his side.

"You don't need to be checking out other men." His teasing tone belied the challenging words.

Lizzie grinned at him. "I can look. It's touching that's a no-no."

"Exactly." He nuzzled her cheek. "Wait until we get back home. Then you can touch all you want."

Lacey couldn't help but smile at the love and affection on display. At one point in time, she'd thought she'd make the perfect bride for Ransom. Now, in retrospect, she knew that wasn't to be. For several reasons, certainly. All the hurt had been worth it because Ransom had found the perfect woman and Lacey had moved on to find Jonas.

"I'm so proud of you, Lacey. Watching you ride is exhilarating." Helen stepped closer. "I know you've fallen through the cracks way too often. I promise that won't happen again. Especially now that there will be a wedding in the future."

Lacey nipped that in the bud. She and Jonas hadn't started planning yet. Besides, she didn't have a clue what she wanted to do. Considering the recent past, a small ceremony would be ideal. Maybe even eloping. "We haven't even set a date, Mom. Focus on Lizzie and Ransom instead."

"Just let me know." Helen grinned happily.

As sentimental a moment as this was, Lacey couldn't quite put all her faith in her mother's words. *Actions speak louder than words.*

Unsure what to say, Lacey simply hugged her mother. "Thank you for coming. It means the world."

"We want a list of all the rodeos you'll attend, especially the local ones. We'll try to get to as many as we can." Tate hugged her and stepped back.

"Okay."

Ransom and Lizzie also gave her a quick squeeze.

"We'd better get going. Besides, you have a prize check to pick up." Helen brushed a single tear from her cheek.

A lump lodged in Lacey's throat. "Thanks again, Mom."

She watched her family walk away with a feeling of hope and accomplishment. If they proved true to their promise, she'd be over the moon at having her family back.

"Everything okay?" Jonas stopped nearby with Knight still in tow.

"Yeah. It's wonderful." She stepped close, brushed her lips over Jonas', and smiled. "Thank you for giving me my new life."

He cupped her cheek and pressed his lips over hers, lingering a few seconds. "You did that all on your own. I just got the ball rolling with this big guy."

"And this might be our cue to leave." Trinity's voice broke

through Lacey's distraction.

She took a pace to the side and smiled happily at Trinity and Cody. "You drove all this way. The least you can do is hang out for a while and spend the night."

They glanced at each another.

"I've got a spare bedroom with your name written all over it," Jonas offered.

"I would like to see Candy again. And visit the farm to look over all those horses." Trinity gave Cody an imploring look.

The corners of Cody's lips curled up. "Searching for a new barrel horse?"

"Well…" Trinity shrugged.

Cody laughed, pulled her against his side and kissed her temple. "Whatever makes you happy, love."

"It looks like you're staying." Lacey's spirit soared. Not only had her family attended the event, but her best friends were going to hang out for a bit. She couldn't imagine a better ending to one fine day.

Knight whinnied.

Another equine from the stable area answered. The distinct cross between a bray and a whinny carried easily to them. Loud and unique. Lacey recognized the mule immediately — Mabel.

"I think Mabel is actually missing this big guy." Jonas smirked and started walking that direction.

"Love is where you least expect it sometimes." Trinity fell into line as she slipped her hand into Cody's.

Lacey did the same, lacing her fingers with Jonas'. "Wiser words have never been spoken."

She peered over at Jonas and knew her feelings shone through.

He squeezed her fingers lightly and grinned at her with such happiness and emotion, Lacey knew she'd never forget that moment as long as she lived.

Epilogue

Ten months later

Lacey watched as Candy's colt, affectionately called Toffee, bucked and jumped in the closest paddock. He snorted and made a quick dash around his mother and Noggin. His long legs assisted in speed while adding even more cuteness to his playful rambunctiousness. He slid to a halt, took a nip at Noggin's tail, then hurried off again.

To his credit, Noggin had become quite attached to Candy and her foal, protecting them and watching over them despite the mischievous foal proving obnoxious from time to time. Even Knight had been adopted into the small family. Mabel was included, although she tended to ignore the energetic baby. Granite, Jonas' roping horse, grazed contentedly in the next field, happily away from the little troublemaker. Caprice, Jason's buckskin roping mare, shared the space with him.

Horses, rodeo horses in particular, grazed across the land. *A beautiful sight, indeed.*

The sun peeked out from the clouds, warming her as well as brightening up the temperate October day. Lacey soaked in the scenery under the filtered light, knowing that soon enough snow would once again blanket the area.

Thankfully, they were ready.

Jonas had recently added to his original barn in order to compensate for the number of horses in their possession. He'd also purchased more land, ensuring ample pasture for the animals that had become an essential part of their lives. Her career choice, certainly, but Jonas' renewed hobby as well. He and Jason had returned to the rodeo and earned their fair share of winnings along the way. While the guys hadn't committed to their craft full-time, Lacey appreciated each and every rodeo they attended. The barrel racing girls were fun and sweet, but she couldn't help but miss the love of her life when he was away.

The creak of the front door caught her attention.

Speak of the devil…

Lacey sighed in happiness and grinned as Jonas joined her at the railing. "Just like his father. I knew it."

"Think of it this way. He'll have a mind of his own, a strong spirit and the want to please his mistress."

"Uh-huh." Lacey giggled as the baby tugged at Noggin's tail once more, earning a chastising glare from the gelding. "He'll have the size and build all right. It's the attitude that I worry about." Lately the little imp had taken up biting as a new hobby. She tried to discourage that every chance she got.

Jonas' parents and Jason had just left after having lunch with them. They still awed her with their easygoing ways and outright acceptance of her into their fold. No censure. No browbeating. Just happiness and love from all of them. Unlike her own family. While the others had turned over a new leaf in support of her, Lacey knew her father would never follow suit. Too set in his ways and too bitter, he'd always treat her like muck on the bottom of boots. No longer did she care, though. Instead, she avoided him like a sidewinder snake and focused on the things that really mattered in her life—Jonas, their horses, her friends and a bright future ahead.

The baby trotted over to Knight then lifted his head and nipped on the paint gelding's halter.

Knight snorted and shook his head, sending the foal flying back to his mother.

Jonas chuckled. "He's a handful. No question about it. Think he'll gray out like his daddy?"

Lacey shrugged. "Maybe. Fifty-fifty from what I've read.

Either way, he's going to be a looker."

"Definitely." Jonas edged closer and wrapped Lacey in his embrace. "No matter how cute he is, you'll always be the apple of my eye."

She grinned up at him, well pleased with her husband. They'd ended up having a very small, private ceremony where only a few people had been invited, a couple of months ago. It had suited them and sealed their commitment for a long time to come. *A lifetime, to be exact.*

"You sure you won't get tired of me?" She licked his chin.

He chuckled. "No way. You keep me on my toes and pretty damn happy. I never thought I'd find a woman who could love me after my surgery. Then you came along, shook up my world and showed me what love can be."

Lacey wrapped her arms around his neck. "You've been a rock for me. Kind and caring. I could never have found a man half as wonderful as you."

They'd been through some rough patches and managed to persevere. She had no doubt they could conquer anything as a team. Her unbreakable faith and confidence in Jonas told her so.

"You forgot sexy." His wicked grin proved contagious.

She rolled her eyes then ruined the effect by giggling. "Yes, you silly goose, you're the sexiest man alive. One look, a single touch, sets me to burning for you." She dropped her voice as she pressed her lips to his briefly. "I don't need much as long as I have your love."

"Always, Lacey. Forever and always." He kissed her with passion and feeling.

Lacey knew she'd found the gold at the end of the rainbow. And his name was Jonas.

Cowgirl Up

Excerpt

Chapter One

"We've found a foal for Star."

Trinity blinked at her mother. Star, her former champion barrel racing mare and Trinity's best friend, had given birth less than twenty-four hours before to a stillborn baby. Almost immediately Lora, Trinity's mother, had signed up Star as a nurse mare in an effort to help the obviously grieving horse and give a needy foal a wonderful mama.

"Where?"

"Golden Aspirations Farm in Gentry." Her mother collected her purse. "Let's get moving. The sooner we get Star there, the sooner she can dote on another baby and be happy again."

Which was all that truly mattered. To them all.

Their world revolved around the mare, once one of the best to take on the cloverleaf pattern at regional rodeos.

Probably would have made it to the big time if Lora hadn't had a quick fling with a bull rider named Buck, ended up pregnant, then traded in her saddle for diaper duty and a job as an elementary school teacher, determined to make it as a single mother and raise her daughter right.

Trinity knew love, caring and the giving nature of her mother. What she missed was knowing her father and getting the opportunity to follow in her mother's abandoned footsteps. She wanted to surge straight to the summit of barrel racing not just by being invited to the national finals, but by winning. Her best friend, Star, might have been the springboard for her mother, but with the mare's advancing age, Lora had opted for retirement for the beloved mare and breeding her in hopes of raising the next generation of a speedy and nimble barrel racing horse. That bubble burst yesterday.

Now Trinity's dreams lay as lifeless as Star's first foal. Considering they subsisted on a teacher's salary, a kitchen garden and the fee from breaking a horse now and again, the ability to pay a hefty stud fee remained well out of their grasps.

"What happened to the mother?" Trinity glanced out of the window of the old truck, her mind whirling at this latest development.

"Complications from delivery, I'm told. Perforated bowel from what they could determine. She's already been rushed off for emergency surgery."

Being raised around horses all her life, Trinity realized how dire the situation was for the unfortunate mare. Most people wouldn't bother with the effort, but this mare obviously had an exceptional owner who strove to do right by her animal.

Maybe not all wealthy people were heartless after all.

Couldn't prove it by her. Not since her father had made a career out of his sport, raked in the prize money and still stubbornly refused to offer up financial assistance to her mother. Since his name and signature were absent from her birth certificate and he refused a paternity test, legal pursuit remained way out of reach. Oddly enough, Lora had never blamed him or held animosity for the man who'd left her pregnant and alone. Instead, she brushed the harshness of life off her sleeve and moved on.

A skill Trinity wished she could learn.

Less than an hour later, they arrived at their destination, left Star in the trailer for the moment and walked into the first barn as they'd been directed. Three people stood waiting, all with thin lips and pensive expressions. Worry emanated from each one in abundance. One of the two men flanking the lady had to be either the farm's owner or perhaps a manager, leaving the middle-aged woman with silver hair to be, presumably, the owner's representative. Trinity doubted most top-of-the-line thoroughbred breeders and owners attended the birth of their latest foal.

"Thanks for coming so soon. I'm Jerry. I spoke with you on the phone. This is Mrs. Hunter, the mare's owner, and John, the broodmare foreman." He tilted his head toward the woman next to him, then once more toward the other man.

Mrs. Hunter. The name rang a huge bell. Not only did the woman own a few racehorses, she owned some of the best, including last year's winner of the Kentucky Derby and the Preakness. Another Victory Gallop had fallen short by a nose in the Belmont Stakes to pulling out the rare and nearly impossible Triple Crown.

Totally amazed and impressed, Trinity studied the woman closer, deciding she liked the lady who stood in the middle of a stable after dark, trying to help a motherless foal even as her mare underwent surgery at the university's vet hospital.

"Yes, of course." Lora held her hand out and shook his. "I'm Lora Crocket and this is my daughter, Trinity."

The others inclined their heads toward Trinity, but her mother held their attention.

"Let's get the details ironed out so we can unite the colt

with his new mother," the second man said.

"Mrs. Hunter' is generously offering a nurse mare rental fee of ten thousand, including the care of your mare while here, and the farm has a handful of studs at their disposal both here and at another location, including a couple of quarter horses, to breed her back to as is traditional in this situation."

The woman pursed her lips. "Thank you, John, but I can speak for myself." She pinned Lora with her gaze. "If that amount is agreeable to you..."

Lora opened her mouth, but Trinity broke in. "We want her bred to Another Victory Gallop."

All eyes stared at her.

Jerry blinked. "Do you know what his stud fee is right now?"

"One hundred thousand as of last Wednesday." Trinity lifted her chin and met their gazes steadily. "An amount we'll never see."

Mrs. Hunter studied her for a long moment. "You realize what you ask is way overboard?"

Trinity nodded. "Yes, I do. But I know this— Star was the best barrel racer of her time just like Another Victory Gallop was in his. I know it's almost unheard of to mate a top-level thoroughbred stallion to a quarter horse mare, but it will work out. Wonderfully so. I just know it." She poured her heart out, willing the older woman to agree. Her future hung in the balance.

"What do you intend to do with the resulting foal?"

"Ride him to victory at the barrel racing national championships," Trinity answered truthfully, then held her breath.

Silence reigned.

A ghost of a smile crept up on Mrs. Hunter's face. "I believe we have a deal."

Ten years later...

Trinity plopped down in the chair directly in front of Legacy's stall. The portable tent and stanchions emulated a barn fairly well, considering only the hit-and-miss breeze broke the stifling humidity of early summer. She much preferred to be in a pasture full of shade trees, but at least the thick material offered relief from the sun and the worst of the Oklahoma heat. Not much could be done for the mugginess except a cold cloth, a bath for her horse and the fans blowing constantly at nearly every electrical outlet.

Finally, after years of hard work, she'd arrived. Well, not to her peak destination, but to the first of the large rodeos on the docket for the year. Up to this point, she'd only attended the smaller ones close by—a single night and done. Made for a lot of driving in a short span of time, but she had no choice. Money and points earned punched her ticket to the big dance at the end of the year. Luckily this one filled an entire weekend, giving her a bit more downtime from the driver's seat of her truck, but it also forced her to camp out overnight. Just par for the course.

She opened the cooler next to her and pulled out a bottle of water, resting until time to groom and saddle Legacy for the first night of events. Even now she could hear the announcer in the large building, muted, but still mostly discernible despite the walls and three hundred yards separating them.

While not the most comfortable, the lawn chair and her cot suited her for the overnight rodeos. Since she refused to leave Legacy's side, she made do with a few provisions and dreamed of her own small but cozy room at home.

Legacy. He'd grown up stout. Big for a barrel horse, brave, determined and way too smart for his own good. He made up his own mind and followed through, no matter what. Most riders wouldn't tolerate such stubbornness, but Trinity didn't mind. They'd been best buddies from day one and he'd do things for her that not even her mother had been able to make happen. Others doubted a thoroughbred could ever make for a good barrel horse, even a cross. She knew better.

After digging a peanut butter sandwich out of her

makeshift fridge, Trinity took a bite, not particularly hungry, but knowing she needed something in her stomach before sliding into the saddle for a fast and furious sprint.

A tall, dark-haired man with piercing blue eyes walked up. Recognition clicked, but for the life of her she couldn't put her finger on why. Her heart sped at the prime specimen he presented, dressed in her favorite outfit—jeans and cowboy boots. "Been a while, Trinity."

That unforgettable voice from her past did the trick. Soft, sure and low, the baritone timbre still sent shivers down her spine. He could mesmerize the most frightened animal with such a vocal gift. Probably did so on a routine basis if he'd stayed true to his roots. "Cody? I haven't seen you in ages."

Cody Winters rodeoed, just like she did. Although he was a handful of years older than she, they still crossed paths. He originated from Oklahoma and she from Kentucky, but the circuit knew no boundaries in the Midwest area of the country. Those serious about such a career drove over several states from one event to another, thus running into the same people over and over again.

If you were one of the top names in the business, you could afford to skip the smaller rodeos and focus on the largest ones held all over the continental U.S. and into Canada. There a person could rack up points and prize money in a hurry, giving them the luxury of more time off, although they balanced the reward with extra time on the road, driving all over the place from one big event to the next. Unless you were the names in the business. Some of those owned a plane and simply flew from location to location.

How they got their animals to the rodeo, Trinity didn't know, but figured it involved a hired hand performing all the hard legwork.

He stepped back, met her gaze and grinned softly. Her belly somersaulted as a small dimple popped in his cheek. The tall frame contained more muscles than she recalled and he'd been built way back when. Now he resembled a sculpted, handsome tank — tall, powerful, meaty and unmoving unless he decided to cooperate. She'd bet her saddle he carried no fat. Not with the way his clothes fit. Not tight, but cut perfectly to give plenty of tempting glimpses with each easy movement of his physique. Combined with a chiseled face, a square jaw that reminded her of a seasoned warrior and twinkling blue eyes sparkling with intelligence and something more, he presented a hot tamale package. Yeah, she enjoyed the eye candy, but drew the line there.

Over the years on the circuit, she'd seen it all. Everything from drinking and drugs to sex. Oh, man was there sex. In the chutes behind the scenes, in horse trailers, in stalls. She'd even caught a couple going at it in the bathroom. Something about attending a rodeo sent people into full-fledged heat. With the exception of her. She knew personally what happened when a woman got careless and downright stupid. She'd lived it. Still heard the mean whispers concerning her parentage and conception today.

"Yep." His attention turned to Legacy, who at that time decided to stick his head over the stall door. "That's a beaut of a horse, if I ever saw one." Cody reached out.

"I wouldn't do that if I were you," she offered in warning.

Legacy snuffled him in open curiosity for a couple of seconds before making his displeasure known. Just as Legacy showed his teeth, pinned his ears and made to bite, Cody jerked his hand back.

"Damn." He stared at the big horse with a mixture of annoyance and awe. "Just like his father, from the dappled hide and stocky build to the aggressive temperament."

Trinity cocked her head. She hadn't seen Cody in forever, yet he seemed to know lots about her and her horse. She couldn't say the same since she rarely participated in gossip and had pretty much kept to herself at each stop so far. "You know his bloodlines?"

"Who doesn't?"

She shrugged. Ever since she'd first showed up on the

huge gray stallion with the four white stockings and a blaze, they'd received more than their fair share of attention. Since she didn't care for the spotlight, it had become a prickly thorn in her side. Not to mention Legacy didn't play well with others. He bit, he kicked. Basically, he judged a person by his present mood and most of the time they came up short.

His behavior had worsened lately. The blame rested on her shoulders. Since the funeral, she'd been on a roller coaster of emotions, mostly heartache and loneliness, and Legacy picked up on each and every one. As much as she lectured herself to pull it together, she couldn't quite shake the constant companion of sadness.

Time heals all wounds.

How many times had she heard that particular quote? As many times as her mother said *'if only'*.

"Damn lucky to get a baby out of Another Victory Gallop. I'd still love to hear that story."

So would a lot of others who barraged her with questions, both media and fellow competitors. Too bad she didn't feel like talking.

She took another bite and chewed slowly, refusing to give in to Cody's curiosity.

The click of horseshoes caught her attention. Turning her head, Trinity spotted Lacey leading her paint mare, Candy, down the aisle before opening the door and placing her in the stall next to Legacy. The stud immediately plastered his nose to the bars separating them and nickered. Candy ignored him, turned around and started pulling hay from the net tied in the corner.

Lacey might be a couple of years younger than Trinity, but they meshed well. Both were in the business for the long haul, but not at the expense of their mounts. Their horses came first, something that most riders believed, but not all. She'd been Legacy tested and approved at the first event, which said everything in Trinity's book. Add in the fact that Lacey didn't yap all the time, knew how to keep a secret and had a good heart—Trinity counted her as one of the few close friends she possessed.

Cody chuckled and nodded. "Spoken like a true stud."

Lacey stepped out of the stall and secured the door behind her. She glanced over at them, then gave a lopsided grin. "Legacy keeps trying, but Candy isn't the least interested." She chuckled and leaned back against the row of stalls. "Haven't seen you in a while, Cody. Whatcha been up to?"

"After I burned out steer wrestling in high school, I decided it was time to get serious. Went to vet school after a stint in the military first."

Trinity blinked. She hadn't heard that juicy tidbit before. Especially the military part. She eyed him in another light. He carried himself differently than she remembered. More fluid, confident and flowing. His gaze flicked here and there as if constantly checking out his surroundings. Definitely not what she remembered of his actions way back when. Oh sure, he'd always been cocky, but this spoke of something else. More self-assurance and ability than just conceit because the women flocked to him with his link to money and good looks. Pain flashed and departed in his eyes so quickly Trinity wasn't sure she even saw it. Still, she opted to avoid the whole topic of service. From what little she knew about war, none of it made for great memories.

"Good for you. I always thought you would go in partnership with your father," Trinity said.

Cody's family owned a large ranch where his father raised both bucking bulls and horses to provide for the many rodeos around the country each year. Cody had been born into the profession, although he'd made sure to enjoy himself along the way. More than once she'd caught him flirting with a woman, then sneaking off for some alone time after the events were finished for the night. A bona fide playboy, that's for sure.

Absently she wondered if the term still stuck.

Truth be told, she'd wished she were in the lucky woman's shoes each night, absorbing all of Cody's attention, as she'd had a crush on him almost from the first time she'd laid eyes on the strapping, good-looking steer wrestler. Not surprising since every other girl appeared to feel the same way. Only she'd steadfastly refused to act on her whims whereas others jumped in with both feet. Of course, she'd been fourteen at the time, so way too young for his attentions. That hadn't stopped her from daydreaming.

"I did. Still help out around the ranch, but spend most of my time on the road treating large animals in my practice." His focus shifted back to Legacy. "Just be careful with that one, Trin. He's the last horse I want to have to work on."

"You're the vet here?" Lacey asked.

"One of a handful, yeah. I signed up to be at all the events for the circuit this year." He smiled at Lacey, wide enough to show a hint of straight white teeth. "My luck, they'd assign me to that stud and laugh as he kicked the shit out of me. All part of being the new guy on the block."

"No worries. Legacy's an angel."

Cody snorted.

"With women," Trinity added with a wry grin.

"Like that helps me. A bit short in the estrogen department lately if you haven't noticed." Cody shook his head. "Lacey's been around for a while, but I haven't seen you, Trinity. When did you come back?"

She met his gaze steadily. "This year." For the life of her she really disliked this topic of conversation, which inevitably led to the question about her mother.

"Miss the sport?" He tilted his head and met her eyes as if trying to read between the lines.

She didn't give him the chance as she gestured toward Legacy. "Finally got a horse to get me back."

"We're lucky to have her," Lacey chimed in. "She reminds the rest of us about the good old days."

Trinity rolled her eyes. *Like I'm that much older than Lacey and the other younger riders.* At twenty-five, she was hardly ready to be put out to pasture.

"Yeah, those were the good times." The corners of Cody's

lips hitched up but the smile didn't reach his eyes.

"Yeah, they were," Trinity answered on a somewhat sad note. If only she could go back.

His cell phone rang. After plucking it from his belt, he answered the call, listened for a moment then held up his hand. "Got to go, ladies. See you around." He spun on his heel and strode out of the improvised barn.

"Holy crap. Did you see that ass?" Lacey whispered, still watching where Cody disappeared out into the sunlight.

"Unfortunately." Trinity sighed. She'd always been a sucker for a man with a great rump covered in Wrangler jeans. Cody possessed one of the finest. She drew in a breath and committed the sight to memory. Because that was' all it would ever be.

* * * *

Cody couldn't shake the image of Trinity out of his head as he strode back toward the arena. She had been a gawky girl the last time he'd seen her, just entering the high school circuit. Damn if she hadn't grown up, filled out and turned out pretty. More than that. Beautiful and downright sexy.

Long, dishwater blonde hair framed an oval face with big blue eyes, the windows to her soul, where he could easily lose himself. From what he could tell from her sitting position, jeans covered a nice curve to her hips while the Western shirt, though loose, hinted at modest yet perky breasts. The top of her head might tickle his chin, but good things came in small packages. Trinity did.

Odd, he hadn't thought much about her before, when as a freshman in high school she'd attended a handful of the same events as he. He'd noticed her, seen a child, and turned his attention elsewhere. In truth, he'd spoken perhaps a dozen sentences to her in the past, a fact he now regretted.

Now, it seemed fate deemed him worthy of another chance.

He'd been surprised to see her back in competition after such a long absence. He'd thought she'd exchanged her boots for chasing men, and had long since gotten married and popped out a couple of kids like most of the girls who barrel raced as kids. Not that he put them down. No way. Everyone deserved the chance to do what they thought best, even if the phase lasted a short time. Besides, he'd essentially followed a similar path. Well, the part about leaving the rodeo and moving on to other things, anyway. The marriage and kids part, no.

A trickle of longing meandered through his system. Absently, he shoved the morose thoughts aside. He'd come to terms with everything that had happened and moved on.

Yeah, right.

The mocking voice in his head refused to allow him to live in a fantasy. In all honesty it was a good thing, but now and again he wished things could be different.

If only…

Shaking the useless phrase aside, he turned his attention back to the unforeseen yet intriguing contestant by the name of Trinity. After noticing her name on the docket and double-checking, he'd decided he had to have a peek for himself. And was glad he had.

Their short conversation ran through his mind. He recalled her facial expressions, the surprise at his approach, and when he'd called her by name. Also the spark of interest in those baby blues before they'd clouded over with sadness once more.

Curiosity piqued. He'd wager his next paycheck she grappled with emotional turmoil and discomfort instead of anything physical. After all, she appeared healthy as a horse with her trim build and slight rose hue to her cheeks. For all intents and purposes, she looked to be in tip-top shape, which pointed him back to his original assumption. Something must be bothering her.

Racking his brain, he tried to remember any hint of rumor including her, to no avail. Not surprising since he'd been out of the loop for a while, first in the SEALs, then busy in vet school before graduating a few months back and struggling to establish his practice. Now that he'd been hired by the Rodeo Association to help oversee the health and care of the livestock through the long season, he'd no doubt hear a few tidbits. Always did. After all, with pretty much the same group each weekend and ample opportunity for trysts and gossip, word would get around soon enough. He'd just have to either be patient or ask a few subtle questions here and there to appease his inquisitiveness.

On the other hand, that gray stallion of hers proved a hot topic. Understandably so. Best damn horse he'd ever laid eyes on, and he'd seen a lot over the years, both on the rodeo circuit and on his father's ranch. Despite being only half quarter horse, he had been put together just right. Muscles to his ears and a conformation judges would drool over in the halter class at shows. That horse could get the job done whatever the task, from show jumping to racing to cross-country at the Olympics. While he had yet to see Legacy in action, he didn't doubt the stud could perform. Hell, Trinity wouldn't be at this event if he ranked in the mediocre range. No, Legacy had earned Trinity's place here and, if speculation held true, would carry her all the way to the finals.

Anticipation washed over him at the thought of watching their first run tonight. Odd, since not much had captured his interest and brought excitement to his life lately. Barring a few one-night stands over the past few months, he'd been too busy working and plodding along through daily life to feel any sort of rush. Compared to active duty with the SEALs, jet-setting all over the world, battling the worst of the worst, his life had tamed to a dull beige. He enjoyed his profession, reveled in the slower pace, but still knew his life lacked something important.

Something told him Trinity and Legacy might just change that. At least for now.

More books from
Cheyenne Meadows

Breaking barriers on the ice is just the start for a woman who craves so much more.

When a wounded man shows up, Lily agrees to nurse him back to health, not realizing she will fall for his scowling brother.

Partner two mated wolf shifters and one alpha lion shifter
to find a rogue and watch the sparks and fur fly.

When the heart longs for one more…

About the Author

Cheyenne Meadows

Growing up in the Midwest, I began reading romance novels in high school, immediately falling in love with the genre, to the point where I decided to write professionally for a career. However, that dream splattered against a brick wall, resulting in a quick death in my first writing class in college when my professor told me bluntly that I wasn't any good at it. I shifted gears quickly, and left my writing dreams behind, eventually settling on becoming a nurse.

A few years back, I stumbled across a fan-fiction writing site on a favorite author's webpage. I began to read stories others wrote, not only making some wonderful close friends from the experience, but also, really learning to write for the very first time. Here I was able to share short stories, practice my writing skills, and truly develop into a writer. More than that, the experience allowed me to revitalize my dream, as I rediscovered joy in writing. Now, I spend my days off with my alpha male characters, quick witted heroines, and see how much trouble everyone can get into.

When I'm not working or writing, I enjoy working in the garden, canning, and seeing my backyard as a living canvas for my whimsical landscaping, and, of course, reading romance novels.

Cheyenne Meadows loves to hear from readers. You can find contact information, website details and an author profile page at https://www.totallybound.com/

Home of Erotic Romance